P9-DBY-401

THE **CORN HUSK** EXPERIMENT

THE
CORN HUSK
EXPERIMENT

— A NOVEL —

ANDREA CALE

NEW YORK

LONDON • NASHVILLE • MELBOURNE • VANCOUVER

THE **CORN HUSK** EXPERIMENT
A NOVEL

© 2018 Andrea Cale

All rights reserved. No portion of this book may be reproduced, stored in a retrieval system, or transmitted in any form or by any means—electronic, mechanical, photocopy, recording, scanning, or other,—except for brief quotations in critical reviews or articles, without the prior written permission of the publisher.

This is a work of fiction. Names, characters, businesses, places, events, and incidents are either the products of the author's imagination or used in a fictitious manner. Any resemblance to actual persons, living or dead, or actual events is purely coincidental.

Published in New York, New York, by Morgan James Publishing. Morgan James is a trademark of Morgan James, LLC. www.MorganJamesPublishing.com

The Morgan James Speakers Group can bring authors to your live event. For more information or to book an event visit The Morgan James Speakers Group at www.TheMorganJamesSpeakersGroup.com.

ISBN 978-1-68350-659-1 paperback
ISBN 978-1-68350-660-7 eBook
Library of Congress Control Number: 2017910630

Cover Design by:
Rachel Lopez
www.r2cdesign.com

Interior Design by:
Bonnie Bushman
The Whole Caboodle Graphic Design

In an effort to support local communities, raise awareness and funds, Morgan James Publishing donates a percentage of all book sales for the life of each book to Habitat for Humanity Peninsula and Greater Williamsburg.

Get involved today! Visit
www.MorganJamesBuilds.com

For Dorothy, Melodie, Kelly, Barbara, and Charlotte

PART 1

CHAPTER 1

CAROLINE
THE TROUBLED ONE

L ittle Caroline stared at the ghostly fog through her bedroom window and hoped for her wild mother to appear in the dark of night. After forcing herself to take three deep breaths, the little girl spotted some hot- and cold-colored lights of a police cruiser in lieu of the woman who had a history of arriving home late and with a stagger. The lights of the cruiser flickered and swerved up, down, and around Caroline's young but tired-looking face.

The sight delivered a powerful shiver to the officer below, who had come bearing news.

In Caroline's small state of Rhode Island, residents had an ironic tendency for having a connection with seemingly any other. October of 1999—a time just a few years before this damp night, for example—had marked a period of mourning among Rhode Islanders for the loss of state native and US Senator John Chafee, a man who had died suddenly from congestive heart failure. Senator Chafee's son Lincoln succeeded him. After seven years of service in his late father's seat, Lincoln would lose his job to an opponent named Sheldon Whitehouse in a competitive, closely watched race. The elder Chafee and Sheldon's father had been college roommates at Yale.

The Ocean State weaved uncanny, intimate webs such as this. The Cranston police officer with a shiny new badge understood the phenomenon well as he prepared to knock on the apartment door of his former high-school sweetheart, whom he had once called "the loveliest Lindsay." He swallowed hard in acceptance that the home also belonged to Lindsay's husband now, as well as the little girl who was staring at him through some sheer, ghostly white curtains. The affable men hadn't cared for each other for several years despite one relationship with Lindsay being current and the other long over. Lindsay was the type of woman a suitor never got over. Both men were soberly aware of that fact.

Officer Rory tapped on his woolen police cap, which was the color of mourning, and nervously cleared his throat in anticipation of stepping into the cool rain and the even more chilling experience of telling a man that he had just lost his wife.

Losing someone was not the type of experience the officer wished on his worst enemy. Little did he know during his recent training that the closest person he had to an enemy would be the first man he'd need to console.

Rory's size thirteen officer boots created small waves and splashes atop the steps as he reluctantly inched toward duty. With another roll of life's dice, he thought, he could've been the man on the other side of the door.

It opened before Rory could knock and provided a surreal glimpse at what his life might have been. The place looked warm and humble with a picture of Lindsay laughing in sunshine on her wedding day, a trio of little Caroline's knotty-haired Barbie dolls on an otherwise tidy carpet, and a cream-colored pug puppy sleeping obliviously on a window seat. The sorrowfully sweet sights were topped only by the expiring scent of Lindsay's drugstore musk perfume that hit him at the door.

From the other side of the threshold, the confused eyes of a kind man named Kenny dropped to his own pair of size thirteen shoes, loafers Lindsay had purchased as a gift just before she went missing.

>>>>— <<<<

She had presented the shoes to her husband with pride on a hopeful morning as Kenny had nervously prepared to interview for a temp position in town at Harper Manufacturing. Neither the husband nor wife had expected the loafers to be Lindsay's final gift as they shared coffee and a cautious dream that his new assembly-line post would one day become permanent.

It had taken Lindsay seven exasperating tries at tying Kenny's plain navy tie, an unfamiliar accessory that irritated his neck on the nerve-filled autumn walk to his prospective employer. He had glanced often at a plain digital wristwatch that alerted him he was running five minutes early, but ten minutes later than he planned. He had dabbed at sweat easing slowly from a freshly shaved face with a worn burgundy handkerchief that served as his good-luck charm ever since the day he was introduced to Lindsay with it in his pocket. He had carefully folded and tucked the hankie away as though it were a promising fortune cookie slip before finally stepping inside Harper's front office. His tie looked sharp.

"When can you start?" asked a svelte Human Resources woman after only a few minutes of questions with zero curveballs. She wasn't lacking a backbone or lackadaisical; she just read people well. The Wellington Avenue company had a fine reputation in the community, and its work was steady. Kenny had been thrilled to land the job.

"I'll start now, if your need be, please."

With caffeine from Lindsay's coffee still buzzing in his system and new loafers on his feet, Kenny had found himself adjusting to the busy sounds of productivity on Harper's manufacturing floor even sooner than he had dreamed.

Whiz, drum, POP! Whiz, drum, POP! Whiz, drum, POP!

With every pluck of a fluorescent orange earplug manufactured by the company, he had resisted easing a couple into his already aching ears. Ever determined to make a good job work, he had distracted himself from the noise with quick glances at his new colleagues behind a pair of thick plastic goggles. There was a guy dropping zinc bars into a melting pot for the production of small auto parts. Another plopped freshly manufactured cufflinks into a bucket. A third separated cooled medical parts and chucked the odd leftovers into a pot to be melted and used again.

Finally, he had spotted on the floor's bustling center a busy man tending to the machines. The position looked most appealing to Kenny, who quickly promised himself to work up to that spot someday. He had once dreamed of becoming an engineer and blamed himself for letting application deadlines slip by for continuing his education. As he added to the growing mound of earplugs in his bucket, he had promised not to let his little Caroline make the same mistake.

Kenny had observed the man tending to the machines all day as he plucked. At three o'clock, after eight hours of work, it was quitting time. Kenny had walked the few blocks home feeling like a million bucks.

"How was work?" Lindsay had asked that promising fall evening as she shucked corn next to a humming pot of water.

Lindsay had a fiery charisma matched only by her red hair. She was not a natural in the kitchen or ambitious in keeping the home tidy. Their clothes were always lacking in the cleanliness department even though she worked at Cranston's Soap Opera Coin Laundry on Park Avenue, but those types of things didn't matter to Kenny because Lindsay was the type of young woman a guy would always wonder how he managed to catch. She made a room come alive. After only fifteen minutes of conversation, she would make new acquaintances feel as though they'd known her for fifteen years.

Kenny was a bit handsome, but, unlike his wife, he was far from a head-turner. He was horrible at expressing his feelings. He was subdued. He hadn't been a whiz in the classroom. He was a wallflower at a party. He did, however, have a kind, old soul that Lindsay adored.

Lindsay had always known deep in her heart that he was the better catch in their pair.

Kenny wrapped his arms around her and gave her a kiss hello.

"It went that well, huh? Must've been the shoes. Or the tie. And how 'bout my kick-butt 'good luck coffee?' I'm so proud of you, by the way. Shake your money may-kah! Shake your money may-kah!"

Lindsay had grabbed each of Kenny's giant paws in her own little freckled hands and shook them until a smile appeared on her husband's usually serious face. To make the moment even sweeter for him, a six-year-old miniature version of Lindsay came bouncing down the rickety stairs of their two-bedroom apartment.

"I'm a bunny! Daddy, you're back from work! Momma, can I drop in the corn? Can I set the time-ah too?"

"Well, I'm so glad you asked, Miss Caroline. Your fathah's too clumsy. When he drops the ears in the pot, the hot watah comes splashing out," Lindsay said. "I could use some sweet little hands."

"Mommy, you know Daddy will get better from all the manufattering practice. Hey, we're having ee-ahs for dinnah?"

The parents exchanged content looks and winks.

Kenny's life with Lindsay and Caroline felt perfect except for one big, seemingly unsolvable problem.

"Caroline, take my hands, little girl," Lindsay instructed. "Shake your money may-kah! Shake your money may-kah!"

The young mother and daughter twisted, sang, and danced in circles on the old black-and-white checkered linoleum floor of their tiny galley kitchen. They felt the cool floor under their bare feet, and the sensation snapped Lindsay back into her own harsh reality.

While Lindsay's loyalty to and love for her family was strong, she was a party girl at heart who also loved the drink. It was a quality Kenny had hoped would change with adulthood and then motherhood, but once their little girl was tucked in for the night, Lindsay still heard a bottle named Jack call her name.

She wouldn't keep anything in the house, so she would often sneak out to get her fix. Kenny would man the home whenever she was out and worry every minute until she returned. He had never fretted about her fidelity, but he had agonized regularly over the list of other things that could go wrong for a stunning young woman with an addicting—and addictive—personality.

On the especially late nights or early mornings, Kenny had questioned whether Lindsay was a woman who should've been caught. As much as he loved her, he knew in his bones that she was meant to be left wild. After hours of stress, his release for conflicted feelings over seeing a jovial wife stumbling safely through the family door was typically an argument.

Caroline almost always awoke from a deep, middle-of-the-night sleep during their confrontations. The fights were the only times Caroline heard her father swear.

"Jeez, Lindsay, what is wrong with you?" she'd hear him say to her mother.

"Ya need to loosen up, I'm not hurdin nobody," Lindsay would slur. "I'm not allowed to unwind after work n' half a lil' fun? What is wrong wid you?"

"You're not hurting anybody? If you don't care about hurting you and me, then what about the little girl sleeping upstairs? She'll soon uncover the painful truth about her very own mother."

These late-night scenes always went around and around and over and over without being resolved. As young as Caroline was, she understood her mother's drinking problem, but similar to when she found out the year before that there wasn't a Santa Claus and preceded to write the fictitious man a letter, she pretended life at home was the illusion. She didn't want to upset her parents further.

>>>>- <<<<

Caroline had awoken with a start on the spooky, rainy evening that lured her to her window. The girl initially assumed she had been roused by her father during one of her parents' fights. When she heard only a calming rain sprinkling outside and the heavy, familiar pacing of her dad downstairs, she rolled over and tried to drift back to sleep.

She couldn't.

Her father's pacing hadn't prevented her sleep. He often paced at night. It was the time on her cotton candy-colored alarm clock reading 1:13 a.m. that scared her. She was groggy and only six years old, but wasn't it significantly past the time that her mother typically came home?

Caroline found temporary comfort in the silky edges of a blanket Lindsay had made when she dreamed of having a baby girl. The young mother had a knack for sewing and turning her own bargain outfits from secondhand stores into more fashionable styles with only some scissors, needles, and threads. She didn't own a sewing machine or patterns. Instead, the pictures of glamorous movie stars in tabloid magazines had served as Lindsay's blueprints for recreating her own gear. She had paired each of her own outfits with a Celtic locket that sparkled brightly from seven diamonds in the shape of a flower. Lindsay wasn't educated in karats, nor did she care to be, but she knew the diamonds were more plentiful than any she'd seen her girlfriends wear. She had treasured the necklace third to only her daughter and husband. Lindsay kept tiny pictures of each of them locked tightly inside.

It wasn't the value of the little diamonds or even the pictures that made the piece so special. The necklace had produced some of Lindsay's favorite moments with Caroline, when the little girl would sit on her lap with a warm, puppy-like breath hitting Lindsay's neck. Caroline would clumsily open and close the locket and touch the tip of the piece to her nose. She'd pull it snug for a better look at the sparkly gems, then zig it to the right and zag it to the left on its chain. She'd release it with care, only to open and close it with keen concentration all over again. The steps would repeat in varying order with Caroline's soft breath continuing to brush her mother's skin. The moments had made Lindsay sleepy with a sense of fulfillment. They had made her forget about needing a drink. She'd close her eyes, tuck wisps of hair behind her freckled ears, and try to memorize every nuance of her daughter's milky, sleepy smell.

The locket had been passed down from Lindsay's great-grandmother to grandmother; from grandmother to mother; and from her mother to Lindsay. What none of the generations of family members predicted, except for Kenny in his worst thoughts, was that Lindsay's daughter would inherit the piece at the young age of six.

As Kenny and Caroline paced and cuddled on either end of the lonely feeling apartment, they grew increasingly worried with every minute that ticked past. Kenny looked at the wristwatch that helped him pick up his pace a couple weeks earlier during his walk to his interview at Harper Manufacturing. Caroline fixated on the fluorescent red numbers on her pink alarm clock.

And as their clocks struck 1:30 a.m., Caroline tiptoed from bed to open her door a crack, hoping for the first time in her young life to hear an argument. She retrieved her blanket, listened, and waited by the fog-filled panes before hearing her typically predictable father do something unusual.

"Hi Lou, it's Kenny, Lindsay's husband," he said to the manager of Fitzpatrick's Pub in Cranston before raising his voice to cut through the noise of the bar on the other end. "Fine, fine. Look, sorry to bother you, Lou, but I wondered if my lovely wife is there?"

As Kenny hung up without success, he remembered that Thursday night was DJ night at Aria Restaurant and Martini Bar, where martini specials cost five dollars. The thought delivered a quick, mean punch to his gut before sending some aftershocks to his limbs. His wife was accustomed to drinking Jack Daniels. She functioned a little too well on it. Vodka was a different, less predictable game.

"Becca? It's Kenny, Lindsay's husband. Fine, thanks. Is my wife there by any chance? I see. What time did they leave? I see."

As Caroline sensed fear for the first time in her father's strong voice, Kenny's mind buzzed. He felt another one of life's cruel punches land. Its delivery was harsher than the first, sending him straight to the kitchen sink in anticipation of vomiting. At the core of his queasiness, he instinctively understood this to be the night he had been dreading. He hung his oversized head over the drain and slid a pair of slippery palms along the cool countertops. The manager at the second club had confirmed Lindsay's appearance there. The manager also said she left one or two hours earlier with a new sidekick named Natasha, a friend whom Kenny knew only three things about: She drove a small off-road vehicle. She lived in Pawtucket. And she could not hold her liquor.

He remembered a recent weekend when his daughter had a long-awaited visit with her grandparents. While Kenny had envisioned a romantic, quiet dinner at home with a video rental and takeout sandwiches from Carmine's Sub Shop, his wife had plotted instead for them to party at her friend Natasha's house.

"Doesn't she live in Pawtucket?" Kenny had asked, thinking he had one up on his wife since they didn't own a car and a trip to Pawtucket included a five-mile trip on Rhode Island's I-95.

Kenny had lost the battle that night just as he did on nearly every other. Hostess Natasha had picked them up herself in her vehicle, got tipsy after two games of Beirut, and as a parting gift tossed Kenny and Lindsay her keys so they could get themselves home.

On this rainy evening, Kenny worried that Natasha once again drank too much to drive. Apparently, it didn't take much. He knew his wife well and could predict how she'd react to the situation. Her moves were as predictable and sobering to him as they were unpredictable and wild to everyone else.

"Linds, I don't feel so good," Natasha managed through hiccups.

Lindsay recalled an old high-school sweetheart named Rory who had inadvertently ended many of their evenings together from uncontrollable hiccups. Rory was a fine guy, but he wasn't Kenny. Lindsay wondered if Rory ever succeeded in getting his police officer badge. A smile spread across her stunning face as she thought about Kenny's new manufacturing work at Harper. Feeling proud of her successful husband, she took a final sip of her apple martini in lonesome celebration before offering to take Natasha's keys.

Lindsay would succeed, at least, in getting her friend home.

"Night babe," Lindsay whispered to the passenger, who stepped down from her own vehicle and skidded off the side of one of her black faux-leather high heels.

As the young lady left Lindsay to fend for herself, a deep feeling of regret became Lindsay's only passenger.

"What a mess," she announced to no one as she worked her way back onto I-95 to begin her drive home in the empty, unfamiliar vehicle.

The young mother rarely had an opportunity to drive, but when she did, she preferred doing it in silence. There were few sounds more peaceful to Lindsay than the steady humming of tires against the pavement and the clicking of an occasional blinker. On this rainy evening, the wipers joined the soft, sleepy chorus.

Lindsay grimaced at the wipers as her hands found the wiper switch especially complicated on this night.

The rain pounded faster. The wipers swished too slowly. The vehicle approached Pawtucket's well-known S-curve too quickly.

Lindsay fumbled with the switch.

Despite traveling on the interstate thousands of times as a native Rhode Islander, she failed to react precisely to the curves now. With the car speeding through them, Lindsay yanked the wheel too far left, forcing the loving mother and wife officially out of control. The vehicle sailed across the wet pavement as pictures of little Caroline and Kenny flashed through her fiery head.

The brutal impact of a concrete barrier drove the front half of the vehicle inward like the nose of her pug dog, leaving Lindsay's locket as one of the few items remaining intact on the front seat of the car.

Without a word, Kenny slowly motioned Officer Rory inside toward the family's modest living room.

The policeman felt frozen in discomfort as he peered inside at the couple's lives and remembered only one of his chief's recommendations. "Get to the point quick. Darn quick."

Rory swiftly removed his drenched police cap and coat and held them close to his body. He didn't look for a place to hang his prized new police garments as he numbly crossed the threshold. They didn't matter much to him now.

"Please have a seat, Ken," the officer said gently.

Upstairs, hugged by her favorite blanket, Caroline listened to each word about her mother's death. The night marked the first time she heard her father cry. He didn't just cry, she noted. His tears came and went in stormy eruptions.

The reality of what she overheard the cop explain to her father didn't sink in as quickly for her. She wasn't as prepared for this night as he had been. She wondered what to do. She heard the nice policeman offer to make her father a cup of tea from their kitchenette. She heard her father decline. She pictured what her mother would do whenever Caroline had a nightmare. With each heavy step of the police officer's boots toward the door, the girl tiptoed to the bathroom to fill a flowered paper cup with tap water.

Spilling a few drops along the hallway, she retrieved a pair of shiny black Sunday shoes from her modest closet. They might need to go somewhere or do something or see someone, she thought. She would be ready. Her father wouldn't have to instruct her. She felt a purpose, although she didn't fully comprehend that she was now the woman of the house.

Her little shoes clip-clopped down the flight of thirteen stairs as she joined her father, who sat slumped in pain in his armchair. The vision of the red-haired, miniature Lindsay with pink pajamas, black Sunday shoes, and an outstretched arm offering the tiny cup of water didn't soothe him. Caroline's innocence only made the unbearable night that much more so. As Kenny stretched an arm out to hold her, he swallowed his daughter's gift in an empty-feeling half gulp and crushed the paper madly with his giant fist.

The tender moment would mark only the beginning of their rocky road as a pair, and Kenny would never know just how treacherous Caroline's side of the road would get.

CHAPTER 2

DEVIN
The Gifted One

On the evening of Kenny and Caroline's loss of the greatest kind, a little figure neither of them knew sat in a backyard atop a barn-red wooden picnic table as the weight of grand expectations lay heavily on his small but growing chest.

The sun had begun its descent behind rows of matching, quiet homes in the Chantilly, Virginia, neighborhood. The stillness of the evening had the opposite effect on the boy as he fidgeted on the worn, splintered table. His knees poked out of a cross-legged position showing little bruises typical of a playful eleven-year-old.

Devin shared little else in common with the other boys his age. His play, already as a pre-teen, was beginning to feel more like work.

A United Airlines Airbus took flight from Dulles International Airport and zoomed loudly over Devin's home. The boy peered upward and recalled a day when he was six years old and his parents had taken him on his first flight to Disney with his sister Jane. Times undoubtedly felt more carefree then, when his biggest worry was how long they'd have to wait in the lines.

"When it comes to crowds and waiting for the rides, always stay left," his instructive father had ordered.

During the trip home from their family vacation, air had become trapped in Devin's inner ear, making his eardrums push outward. His head had felt as though it would explode from the change in pressure. The sensation was not so different from how he was feeling on this autumn evening.

"Devin, come on in and shower up, ya hear?" called his mother through the window. "You'll need to start preparing for bed. Big day for y'all tomorrow."

Devin noted the jarring, singsong tone of the voice and thought of the grackle birds he often heard in their yard. He wondered why the outdoors sounded so nervously quiet tonight. The boy defiantly kept his gaze on the darkening sky. Just like the worry-free days at Disney, the plane he had been tracking was long gone. He was moments from turning in, but that wasn't quick enough for his parents.

Informally, Devin's father had become his personal football coach the moment the boy had joined the local "ankle biter" football league a few years earlier. Football marked the end of Devin's endless Virginia summers, when days had been filled at the local public pool with twirling baby-blue slides, undertones of squealing laughter, and snacks of frozen candy bars during the lifeguards' breaks. There also used to be the muggy games of hide-and-seek throughout the horseshoe of backyards encompassing their cul-de-sac street until the sun began to fade as it did on this much heavier night. On rainy days, there had been Monopoly with school friends. Parents had treated Devin to sugary fruit punch and chocolate cookies with warm, proud smiles at a time when adults hadn't yet received the pressure or knowledge to buy wholesome, organic foods.

These days, Devin's dirt bike spokes collected spider webs in the garage, and play times were a rarity. His fondest childhood memories were simply that: memories that had been replaced by sprints, agility drills, arm work, and studying the much older high-school team's practices.

As friends enjoyed summer break, Devin's work was just beginning. He had grown to accept that fact.

Devin was the older of two children. He would learn from a therapist much later in life that the order in which he was born would feed into his perfectionism and willingness to please his parents through athletics. Devin would also learn that his tireless drive to succeed was largely due to his father's and grandfather's own failures to meet personal expectations on the football field. Like an heirloom diamond necklace, the family pressures had been handed down to Devin. It was up to him to change their football story now.

⋙ ⋘

Devin's father made it much farther than most in the sport, yet his falling short in the most crucial of games still haunted him.

During his own time on the field, he had earned the nickname of the Hustler for his speed and incomparable desire to win. The Hustler had played the wide receiver position well enough to be recruited by the collegiate Houston Cougars, a team that won nine out of twelve games during his senior year. The record was enough to earn them a date with Notre Dame at the Cotton Bowl.

On the particularly frigid New Year's morning of 1979, the Hustler had believed the bowl game was his final opportunity to bring glory to his family name.

The field was so bitter cold that morning that the chill shot straight up through the soles of his cleats. His skin felt as though it could've been beneath old ski socks and boots after a below-zero day on windy slopes. His feet felt like ice blocks. The Hustler had been determined not only to win this game though, but also make the play of the year—one that would go down in the bowl statistics books. He demanded of himself a performance worthy of erasing the nagging failure from which his own father, Devin's grandfather, still suffered.

But in perhaps the most undesirable weather conditions, matter can eventually win over the mind. The joints from his ankles to the tips of his toes felt frozen in place. His knees felt more like the Tin Man's than his own. The nagging chill made his acclaimed fast running much more rigid than usual. To compensate, he had stayed in constant motion, exercising and tuck-jumping on the sideline of each of the Cougars' defensive plays.

It would be the very thing that wore him down.

The Hustler held his own through the beginning of the fourth quarter, when his Cougars led the Fighting Irish 34-12. While he hadn't scored any touchdowns, he had succeeded at least in securing a handful of first downs in the first three quarters. His play was good, but not nearly the level of greatness he needed. He desperately jogged up and down the sidelines as his talented quarterback kept warm in a parka. True to his name, the Hustler's desire appeared greater than anyone else's on the frozen field.

Everything had changed in the fourth.

The Hustler broke away from his defensive man and managed to get open down the field. He raised a toned arm, turned, and locked eyes with his quarterback. As he pivoted to fly toward the end zone, his quarterback threw deep in a pitch-and-catch play the pair had practiced in their sleep. But unlike other practices or games, the Hustler's speed decelerated. The ball landed in the right place—his quarterback did his job—but the Hustler failed to reach his spot in time. The failed play ended the Cougars' offensive drive. The quarterback dropped his head in disappointment. The Hustler's own helmet froze upright in a statue of shock.

The weather at the prestigious bowl game had kept attendance down to 32,500 people, and a majority of the fans at the Dallas field rooted for the Hustler's Houston Cougars. Despite the Hustler's missed opportunity, there was still an air of confidence among fans who felt content with Houston's double-digit lead and the dwindling time on the game clock. There were no boos rolling down the stands toward the Hustler.

Instead, he would become his own worst heckler.

No one in the stands, on the sidelines, or watching from rabbit-eared TV sets at home could have predicted that morning, even into the fourth quarter, that the game would take an extreme turn that would make it one of the most talked-about events in college bowl history.

In addition to less-than-ideal football conditions, the opposing team's quarterback had been battling the flu. The Fighting Irish leader's temperature had dipped to only 96 degrees, and like the Hustler, he explored ways to overcome the weather, including eating some hot chicken soup on the sidelines. The unconventional move had helped him find new energy, and in the final minutes, he quickly led his team toward a shocking 35-34 win over Houston. In the end, the Hustler's failed catch could've been the difference.

The game had immediately became one for the ages and earned the name of "The Chicken Soup Comeback." The Fighting Irish quarterback, Joe Montana, had gone on to become a legend. The Hustler's relevance had seemed to disappear with the heat of leftover soup.

>>>— —<<<

On the eve of his eleven-year-old son's season opener, the Hustler was growing anxious on the other side of the screened slider door.

"Devin! Not a minute to spare now. You heard your mother. You need a good rest to beat the Generals. Let's start the season off with a win, boy! Let's go. Now!"

If his mother's voice resembled that of a grackle bird, then the deep tone of his father's sounded just like a Virginia black bear. The boy hadn't played the first game of the season, yet the Hustler's vocals were already scratchy from growling recommendations over the sidelines of practice.

Devin untangled his sleepy legs atop the picnic table and began removing his grassy cleats. Tying and untying the laces of his shoes had become so regular that he could probably tend to them with one hand while throwing a spiral with the other, he thought. His teammates recently nicknamed Devin's cleats his "magic shoes" because the eleven-year-old player scrambled better in the pocket than most high-school quarterbacks. Devin could sprint faster than his team's receivers. He naturally planted his pivot foot, the left one on the opposite side of his throwing arm, and pointed it perfectly toward his target.

Devin's natural gift didn't end with his feet. He also had, among other things, a strong arm, a precise throw, and a strategic approach to the game. Becoming a star quarterback appeared to be the boy's undeniable fate.

Devin stepped into a steamy shower and washed away the dirt from practice. He wished the water could burn away his chilly stress as he shampooed his blond hair. From the tips of his magic shoes to the curls on top of his head, he was the Hustler's golden child.

The heat from the shower, combined with an omnipresent pressure to win, made the boy's typically tan legs appear like pink pig's skin. He dried himself with a royal purple-and-white striped towel and stepped into some matching polyester shorts. Inside and out, the young athlete was a Chantilly football player.

Devin clicked off his bedroom light and began his nightly bedtime ritual. He tossed about beneath a thin sheet and a blanket of Virginia humidity as his mind raced through each of his plays.

Nearby in the hallway, the Hustler eavesdropped over his son's restlessness and recalled his own sleepless pre-game nights. He poked his head through the boy's doorway, where in the dark of his bedroom, Devin pictured the black bear again: always listening, always rough, always in charge.

"Still awake, huh?"

Devin wasn't sure if it was the rare hush in his father's voice or if he was just overtired, but he felt relieved by the unexpectedly kind tone. It was a fatherly tone. The image of the bear disappeared as a mental vision of his aged, soft-spoken grandfather popped up in its place.

"Dad, can you tell me the story of Grandpa's loss?"

Devin's beloved grandmother had passed away a year earlier, but he wasn't talking about her. He was referring to his grandfather's own failed game that haunted him for years.

The Hustler swallowed hard in the dark room before beginning the family story of 1942, a year when the world was in the throes of its second world war. Devin's grandfather had played the defensive line in Boston, a city that instantly became—and would continue to be for generations—the family favorite. The team had been undefeated, and to all fans, they appeared to be heading effortlessly to the Orange Bowl. The final obstacle between the team and the bowl spot was a match against fellow Massachusetts team and rival Holy Cross.

It had appeared to be a small hurdle. Boston's players boasted a 14-1 record. The Crusaders had a losing one, winning only four of their nine games that season. For followers of the game, Boston had its bowl game spot locked before the Holy Cross match ever began. The team's victory party was already planned. The location was already set. Friends and family were in the mood to celebrate. Girls, including the date of Devin's grandfather, were picking out their celebratory outfits from closets of plain, knee-length dresses to go along with a shade of "Victory Red" lipstick that was popular during the war.

In the end, Holy Cross delivered an unexpected and decisive 55-12 win against Boston. Either the team's defense failed or the Holy Cross offense prevailed. Sometimes it's hard to tell. Many times it's both. Most times it's the fault of the entire losing team, yet Devin's grandfather had placed the failure solely on his own broad shoulders.

"It was for the best," the Hustler concluded.

Devin shot up to a seated position on his bed.

"For the best? When is a loss ever for the best? Dad, it was for a spot in the Orange Bowl!"

The Hustler cleared his throat and thought for a second about the old man who taught him how to ride a bike, put on shoulder pads, and shave his first trace of a beard. He wiped away a single unexpected tear.

"I think you're old enough to know, boy, that something horrible happened after that game."

Devin leaned forward so he wouldn't miss a word. His bruised and scraped legs shifted atop the smooth comforter.

"Boston's victory party was supposed to take place in the city at a nightclub called the Coconut Grove. The place caught on fire. It went down in flames that night. Almost everybody in there died—491 people gone; 491. Poor, poor souls."

The heavy news made Devin's stress finally evaporate like the steam from a hot shower.

"Devin, Boston's loss of the game spared Grandpa's life as well as everyone else's on his team. With the loss of the game, there was no victory party that night."

The Hustler's storytelling would mark the only time the hard man gave his son some perspective about the game of football.

On this night, it was enough to help his boy drift off to sleep.

MAXINE
The Lonely One

As Devin sat atop the picnic table on the eve of his season opener and longed for his distant days at Disney, a young woman sat stiffly upright aboard the United Airlines Airbus flying over his family's home. Unlike the people seated around her, she wasn't reading a book or getting prepared for sleep or planning to ask an attendant for cheap headphones to watch *Runaway Bride*, the feature presentation that was being offered to the full flight of 138 passengers.

Instead, Maxine sat and thought. Those were two things she always did on flights, at the grocery store check-out, or in the waiting room of the dentist's office. She'd think and ponder and stew over a trio of torments.

She regularly tormented herself about some worry from the day. She would mentally replay whether she filed too many photo options to her editor for his page-one story. On another day, Maxine would worry about whether she gave him too few. She'd feel guilty for arriving late for work even if it had been from being caught in a traffic jam following someone else's car trouble. In a quiet moment later on, she'd revisit everyone's stares when she had finally sat down at her desk in the newsroom. Was it her, or had their faces looked annoyed by her tardiness?

Maxine would also torment herself with an anxiety for every tomorrow. The conversations in her head were packed with so much paranoia that they'd regularly send rushes of nervousness throughout her restless body.

"What if I can't get close enough to the congressman for a decent shot at tomorrow's press conference?"

"What if the noon sun casts too many shadows on kids' faces during tomorrow's Boys' and Girls' Club outdoor ribbon cutting?"

"Am I pressing too hard for caption information? Too little?"

She'd agonize over social relationships too. She'd conjure up all the negative things other people could possibly think about her. Did her colleague, Ed, the government beat reporter, find her annoying as she put in free overtime while he arrived late, left early, and enjoyed long lunches at the Speak Easy Tavern? Did the old, rough-around-the-edges librarian at the paper think Maxine had the strength of a sickly-sweet gummy worm because she always agreed to step up whenever one of the obituary staffers called in sick? Would her brothers think badly of her for sending a belated birthday card again this year?

Her worries were as steady as her breath, but the twenty-five-year-old's constant state of suspicion is what made the photographer at a large northern New York daily newspaper so successful. For almost any hurdle that popped up, Maxine's mind operated a couple paces ahead. Despite carrying more stress than the average person, she'd lock her thoughts inside a deceptively calm, tough shell of an exterior.

As a result, the newsroom counted on her for a range of duties. Editors gave her the lame assignments because they knew she wouldn't complain. They also gave her the most newsworthy ones because they trusted her to do the job. She was an anomaly on staff, but she'd never rested long enough to enjoy that reputation.

The great appreciation Maxine had received during just a few years of young adulthood contrasted starkly with the lack of attention she had received from elders during her school-age years. From kindergarten through her senior year of college, one pesky cliché had seemed to follow her through the most challenging years of her life. The youngsters who acted up usually got the attention. The ones who hung around after class to complain about the poor grades on their term papers usually got the raises. As the most easygoing of three children in her family, she'd get positioned in the middle seat for long road trips. The squeaky wheels always seemed to get the oil. Maxine disliked all clichés, but the usually forgiving girl secretly loathed that one.

As she sailed through the transition into adulthood, she had felt a welcome shift. The attention-getting students were now graduates bouncing around from job to job, creating friction wherever they went at her place of work and others, while she was the one left getting the raise despite being the only employee in her department who never asked for one. The higher-ups at the paper needed to keep her around. She was talented and hardworking without unnecessarily ruffling the newspapers on others' desks.

Maxine never had reason to worry about her social relationships either. Everyone appreciated her easy way. Her friends found Maxine enjoyable to be around. Colleagues at the paper, even Beatrice the librarian, found her polite but tough—a quiet lion.

As the plane reached its cruising altitude and relayed the pilot's permission to unfasten seat belts, Maxine continued to sit stiffly in the upright position to avoid disrupting the person behind her.

Her worry of the moment had come from a simple act that made even the strongest reporters in her newsroom cringe each morning: the act of checking voicemail.

In perhaps no other industry is it so clear that you can't make everyone— or sometimes anyone—happy. While Maxine's northern New York news team strived for accuracy, that was also the very thing that most often evoked emotion from readers.

If a dozen of the local high-school basketball players got caught in violation of a zero-tolerance-for-alcohol policy and their parents confronted the school board about the suspensions at a lively public meeting, the same parents would unleash their anger the following morning on the journalist who reported the facts in the paper. Knowing their friends, neighbors, and coworkers were reading and gossiping about the article that morning over scrambled eggs and sausage patties always added to the frantic tone of a reader's voice in a message.

"Why didn't you cover the carwash we did for fundraising or the fact that my kid went to Camp Neyaga Hoop Dreams over the summer? All you care about is the negative stuff. Why don't you go back to the dump, you worthless hack?" went a typical voicemail.

In reality, Maxine and her colleagues felt it was their responsibility to cover news that was relevant and interesting to their readers. While a carwash or a trip to summer camp might warrant a local brief on a slow news day, readers would undoubtedly want to know more about why their well-supported basketball team had to forfeit their next several games.

In the newsroom, a wide range of tough and conflicting personalities bonded over one common motivator: the truth. The news team took pride in its own local investigative pieces that influenced local change as well as the legendary ones by their professional heroes, including the great Bob Woodward and Carl Bernstein, or the journalism students of Northwestern University who had uncovered a few years earlier that more than a dozen innocent people were on death row. In extreme cases, journalists were saving lives and redirecting them in significant ways.

This not-so-simple task of delivering simply the truth to readers is what often made even the crankiest editors to tell a reporter to "just blame it on me" in preparation of the inevitable hate calls over an A1 story on a local politician's embezzlement or a company's local layoffs.

As a photographer, Maxine absorbed far fewer abusive voicemails than her counterparts in reporting, but her personality fed into a deep dread of checking messages just the same.

Prior to her flight's departure from Dulles, Maxine had picked up a greasy pay phone to check her voicemail. She had hoped for the robotic woman on the other end to say "No. New. Messages." This time, she was correct to brace for attack.

"Maxine. This is Elizabeth Washburn here. I don't have to tell you I am the wife of the Carthage Supervisor, and I am also responsible for managing the Carthage Play Town fundraising campaign. I also probably don't have to tell you how immensely distressed and disappointed I am over the unsatisfactory photo in today's rag."

Maxine had raised her eyebrows as she listened to the message. She had tried visualizing the details of her picture that had featured construction workers as they broke ground on the massive playground with delighted faces of children in the background. Her goal had been to make a somewhat boring story, if she was being honest with herself, as captivating as possible by showing the action of hard construction work juxtaposed with the warmth and excitement on the kids' faces. There were smiles. There was news. There was motion.

Pleasing the manager of the Carthage Play Town fundraising campaign hadn't been a task she set out to achieve—nor was it her job—but she thought the woman would've been thrilled with the photo choice nonetheless. The message continued.

"Well, it wasn't so much the photo—that was just, well, OK. It was the horrible writing you used under the picture. Absolutely horrendous. What were you thinking anyway?"

Maxine's eyebrows remained up, but her delicate chin dropped the slightest bit now. She felt a rare pride in her captions. While other photographers on staff jotted down names, ages, and titles of subjects in their photos—just enough to get the job done so they could head back to the office and finish their remaining assignments—Maxine often pressed further. Her approach was very different. She'd often stay out of the way of the reporter and listen. When the perfect moment arose, she'd follow up with a question or two to learn something extra. Maxine's captions weren't fancy, but they enhanced the story. Editors and reporters often complimented her on them. On occasion, a reader would do the same.

Not this time.

The message had continued.

"You put in there that our campaign is 95 percent complete! How could you do that? What were you thinking? Clearly, you were not thinking. Here I was, sharing that information with you because you asked and I thought I'd be nice, and then you go ahead and print it! No one is going to make a damn contribution because they already think we're successful. How could you do this to the children?"

"First. Saved. Message."

Not even Maxine could've predicted Washburn's blow, but she had little time to dwell on it now. She was two minutes late pay-phoning her editor for a scheduled check-in thanks to traveling with Ed, the government beat reporter who was more often found at the local tavern than in the newsroom.

"Max," their editor had shouted through the phone. "Another minute later and I was going to have you paged in the damn airport. He's on my damn back. What the hell did you get for a photo? I don't have to tell you that it better be good."

Maxine knew that whenever her editor said "he" without naming names, he was referring to their publisher. She was also well aware of the pressure riding on her to get the perfect shot during the trip.

When Maxine's editor had first pulled Ed and her into his office to assign them coverage of northern New York farmers' testimony for federal crop insurance reform in Washington, DC, he had made clear that Maxine's reward for being sent on the biggest trip of her career would be having her job hang delicately on the line.

"Max, Max, Max," he had said as Ed coolly doodled in his government beat notepad and Maxine sat eagerly on the hard, uncomfortable edge of the old wooden seat in their editor's office. Her concentration had broken only for a second as she observed that newsrooms are never as glamorous as they appear in movies.

"You know we always rely on the wire for out-of-state shots. We never send one of our own. That is until now."

The editor's pen cap began tapping the top of his desk with each new sentence.

"You are the lucky one. You get to cover this for us. I am the one who fought for you to go. Both of our necks are on the line if you don't capture more emotion on these farmers' faces than the local TV station—they're also sending a team. He will snatch both of our positions, our lives, away if you don't get this one right. Am I being dramatic enough?"

Maxine had understood the pressure all too well. The local television news team was her daily newspaper's only source of competition in a rural network of smaller, weekly newspapers. The publisher was obsessed, as any successful person would be, with doing the better job. Maxine's editor was too. The competition trickled down to everyone else on staff.

As a result, Maxine had felt panicked every night leading up to the trip. When it came to capturing emotion, her broadcast competitors had the edge. The station had the advantage of motion. It could also capture more than a single snapshot of time. It had the upper hand with sound too.

In advance of the trip, Maxine had phoned the Northern New York Agriculture Development Program to learn the names of the three northern New York farmers who were scheduled to give a voice to the forty-five hundred other farm owners in the region. On three separate mornings before the warmth of daylight, she had met each of them on their land with cups of coffee fixed just how they said they liked them. All three were requested black.

At each meeting's dawn, she had wrapped the cups in tinfoil to keep them hot throughout the bumpy rides in her used, small car. She dressed as she would for any high-profile press conference. She sat on prickly hay in her best work khakis, leaned against a chilly John Deere Harvester in navy suit pants, and squatted in a knee-length cotton skirt next to a cow being milked amidst a sharp smell that reminded Maxine of a summer's drive by a ripe farm. She had resisted laying a finger to her nostrils.

As hard as Maxine worked and as stressed as she was, she had quickly realized that her situation could not compare to the work or stress of a farmer.

She had been honest. She looked each man in the eye. She was respectful. She cared about understanding their positions. She was ethical, even explaining in advance of the meetings that she was happy to deliver the coffee, but she didn't want the farmers to mistake the small gifts as bribes for good shots during their upcoming trip. She had let them pay the 95 cents for each of their cups, returning five cents per dollar.

From every conversation, Maxine had pieced together that nearly as frustrating to the farmers as the lack of adequate insurance itself was planning a day or two away from their farms to travel to Washington and testify.

In three short meetings over cups of coffee that weren't even drunk, she had successfully built some relationships.

Maxine had woken long before the autumn sun could break over the nation's capital on the day of testimony. Her sleeplessness was reminiscent of her premature awakenings in more youthful times, whenever a day marked the first of a school year.

As the farmers had readied themselves in these wee hours for the biggest—and only—public speeches of their lives within a hotel suite the three men shared, one of them had proactively dialed Maxine and invited her to join them during their nervous preparations to take a few shots.

"I'll be there in five," she had answered immediately.

The advance informal meeting would ultimately allow Maxine to present her editor with an option that would surpass both his and her expectations.

The foreground of her best shot would bring to life one of the men clumsily tying his colleagues' ties as their more practical work dungarees hung lifeless, yet cared for, on the sill of a hotel window featuring a contrasting city life on the opposite side. The image would perfectly summarize the story of men forgoing a day of hard work to step into a life that didn't fit them, only to testify for insurance reform that probably should've taken place long ago. But it was the third man in the corner who had made the image special. He sat at a desk as an overworked thumb and forefinger of one hand held his speech notes while the callused fingers of his opposite one pinched the inner corners of his eyes and the bridge of his nose.

Later on, back at the newspaper, Maxine would draft the following caption:

At 5:23 a.m. on a harvesting day, James R. Shaw (left) would ordinarily be feeding the cattle on his dairy farm. Rick M. Dailey (center) would be fueling up his combine harvester for a long day of work. Bill C. Lantzy (right) would be cleaning the chicken coops with his wife Laura. Instead, the northern New York men got ready in a Washington, DC, Marriott Hotel room before successfully urging the U.S. House of Representatives to strengthen the country's crop insurance law.

Maxine had sprinted in dress shoes to hail a cab to the Capitol building, where she had met Ed, her sleepy reporter, to take more shots during the testimony as backup. She kept her eyes on her competitors. She noticed the station's cameraman focusing his lens on the politicians' speeches instead of the intent faces of the farmers. She felt confident about capturing the emotion her higher-ups wanted.

Through the grimy airport payphone, with a *New York Times* tucked neatly under her arm, Maxine had relayed to her editor the success of her private meeting with the farmers.

"Hey Max," he had said in a tone that sounded a bit like air coming out of a deflating, hot tire. "Listen, you're doing a great job. Sorry I don't say it darn near enough. You make me look smart for hiring you."

He normally would've considered that compliment more than enough. This time, he had continued.

"Everything all right? You don't sound as happy as you should under the circumstances."

"Oh, I'm OK, thanks."

"What is it, Max? Where's your robotic 'I'm great, thanks, how are you?'"

The rare concern in his voice had prompted an even more rare look into Maxine's overworked brain.

"Well, it's not really that big a deal. This is going to sound silly coming off the heels of political reform, but I just checked messages before I called you, and I got a voicemail from Elizabeth Washburn."

"Oh, dear loving God."

Despite their newspaper covering a northern New York area the size of the entire state of Connecticut, the region often felt like a much smaller community to its staff. Around the newsroom, Mrs. Washburn had a reputation for unrealistic expectations.

"She claims I ruined their playground fundraising campaign because my caption revealed that it's 95 percent complete," the young photographer said with a nervous laugh and a tear forming in the corner of her right eye.

"I take it the fact wasn't given to you off the record?"

"No, of course not."

"I want you to call Elizabeth Washburn back as soon as you touch down at the airport in Syracuse—get it over with before your hour drive north to the office. I want you to tell her that I asked you to include an update on their fundraising in the caption. Blame it on me. Now hurry up and get back so I can see the shot of Shaw, Dailey, and Lantzy in their skivvies."

"They were in suits."

"I know, Max. Listen, you've really got to loosen up. Just call me as soon as you have the pictures up in the photo department. You can remind me then about three new assignments we need to go over too. Enough of this sappy stuff. Hurry it up!"

His comments should've set her at ease, but she was always her harshest critic. As Maxine sat in her fully upright airplane seat and clung tightly to the camera bag containing the golden film, her ears popped her back into reality.

She was sitting in the familiar middle seat, wedged between a napping Ed and a thin adolescent boy whose elbow rested in her territory as he watched Julia Roberts ride away on a horse.

Maxine's eyes, too weary for her age, peered at her colleague as she questioned why she couldn't relax like him. Her eyes were perhaps the only hint of her living a stressed-out, lonely life.

The rest of her was pretty in a white-T-shirt-and-Levi's kind of way. She was natural without being frumpy. She didn't waste much time getting gussied up. She wore little makeup. Maxine wasn't like other young women in so many ways, yet she was usually more beautiful.

She stretched her thin photographer's fingers, ringless in a year when friends from college were getting engaged at seemingly every turn. She ran them through her short brown hair. Her features were so dainty that she pulled off the tomboy haircut like few other women could. The look summarized her inner makeup— fragile and tough tangled up in one strong being.

Maxine had boyfriends in college and into her twenties, but the relationships always seemed to sour. One ex jumped in the air and clicked his heels together on the drunken night of their first kiss. Another wet the bed on the night of his twenty-first birthday. A third professed on bended knee his desire to get married on their third date. The images of the moments remained as vivid in her memory as one of her photographs.

She was as particular in her love life as she was in her quality of work. She didn't intend to hurt anyone. She didn't want to be alone on Saturday night with a ripped childhood pillowcase, classic *Full House* reruns, wet hair, and frozen mozzarella sticks that left a depressing hangover in her stomach before she made it to bed. Even so, she wasn't willing to settle on anything less than perfect, she decided. Not a photo. Not a caption. Not a boyfriend.

Maxine's single status never made sense to a number of guys who secretly had crushes on her. It didn't add up to her family members and girlfriends either.

"When was the last time you went out on a date?" one of them would ask.

"Why don't you put yourself out there more and work a little less?" another would offer.

"Do you even want to get married?" someone else would question.

The plane hit a spot of turbulence before Maxine glanced curiously at Ed to see whether it had woken him up. The buck of the Airbus was abrupt enough to release a bit of drool that had been balancing on the corner of his gaping mouth.

The snoozing bear of a reporter was secretly Maxine's latest admirer after they had bonded over Legal Sea Foods' fresh lobsters on DC's 7th Street on the eve of the farmers' testimonies.

To Ed's surprise, he had shared more in common with the delicate flower of a girl than he expected. She was a fan of his favorite form of entertainment, *The Howard Stern Show*. He could barely contain his mouthful of cheap beer when the photographer had revealed the fact in the restaurant that night.

"You? No way," he had sputtered loudly.

"You think badly of me, don't you?"

"No, man, I love Howard too. But you're so…Little Miss Perfect, with all due respect. I never would've pegged you as a fan. What do you see in the animal?"

"OK, so there is the edgy stuff with the ladies that I tend to zone out on, but he's so misunderstood. I love his honesty. He is actually very sweet. I could argue that he is a better man than many of the ones we cover. He's better at what he does than anyone else in radio. He's a perfectionist. He's a misfit. He's an interesting person with interesting, decisive things to say. I admire his ability to do that because, well, I seriously can't. I could really go on and on about him."

"Absolutely. I just don't know many other young ladies who'd agree with you."

They had moved on to coffees—one decaf, one regular—in hopes of sobering up from the beer. Ed had stirred a melting ice cube into his with a spoon to prolong the evening. Maxine had taken a hard sip out of her own cup.

"What's your favorite thing to cover?" Ed had asked.

Maxine's tired eyes lit up.

"Oh, that's easy," she had answered with a smile. "Sports."

"Sports?"

The big man had slapped an open paw on the white tablecloth as he looked in disbelief at the petite young woman staring back.

Maxine had laughed.

"I love football," she said. "I love the action shots. I love the looks on players' faces—whether they're on the sidelines watching with hungry eyes or in the middle of a dangerous tackle or feeling pained after a loss. It's fun to cover."

"Man, I would love to have been on the sports beat," Ed said.

"Why can't you?"

The reporter had patted his belly in jest.

"There's no way I could hustle around quickly enough with this volleyball."

The colleagues had shared another round of stress-free laughter. Maxine knew the real reason. Ed had a reputation in the newsroom of having impeccable instinct. He zoomed in on the truth like no other. If centers of influence in their community had something to hide, they dreaded a phone call from Ed. He was made for the political beat because he cut through the politics. He was lazier than all others on staff only because he could afford to be. It took him minutes to string together a long-lasting story.

Maxine had sensed a hint of sadness in him though for not going after his dream. It made her want to share a secret.

"So, on weekends off, when I'm not attached to the police scanner listening for fires or other northern New York breaking news that may need a photo for our great paper, I drive an hour south and stand on the sidelines of one collegiate Division 1 game or another to take pictures. You have to keep that one under your hat, though. I don't need our editor filling up more of my weekends."

Maxine couldn't hold back a broadening smile, the kind a book nerd might make at a keg party.

"You do not do that," Ed had said with a look of surprise and admiration. "How do you get a press pass? What do you capture? No, forget all that. Why?"

Maxine had graduated from a competitive journalism school that had taught the likes of other sports fans, famous sportscasters, and journalists over the years. Despite graduating, she had managed to keep her media pass and work the sidelines of football, basketball, and lacrosse games, just as she had during her pre-graduate work at the college's respected student newspaper.

Over the last several years, she had passionately captured the successful synchronicity of quarterbacks and receivers who would eventually go on to the National Football League. She was there as young lacrosse stars successfully executed behind-the-back shots at the goal in a rare style reminiscent of the great Gaits brothers. Maxine had been there too when a small basketball forward led his team through the NCAA Sweet Sixteen, Elite Eight, and Final Four of the NCAA tournament. She had captured the parties in the streets on campus where students out of control with happiness had found strength to pull parking meters out of the ground.

As Maxine was working for the daily newspaper seventy miles north, collegiate athletes were having exceptional years in sports. She had taken full advantage of the times.

"I'm building up a portfolio," she explained. "I've got to do this someday. I've *got* to make it in sports. It's my dream."

Ed had studied her closely as he finally understood her reason for being single. She already had passion in her life and appeared fulfilled by that. He was intrigued by her lack of interest in love. He knew she wasn't like any other girl he'd ever met.

"OK, what's your idea of the perfect date?" he had dared to ask.

Maxine had observed the corners of her strong colleague's mouth quiver up to an unusual, nervous smile and quickly deemed the awkward moment a fine time to jest.

"Lobsters and coffee in our nation's capital."

Ed, a born realist, knew he wasn't in Maxine's league. The ever-dogged reporter had enough beers in him though to stick with the question.

"No, seriously."

"Fine. You really can be pushy, can't you? Anyway, this is actually an easy one. My perfect date would include a sunny Saturday afternoon Red Sox game in the bleachers with Fenway Franks, beers, and nowhere to go after."

Ed had closed his eyes, hung his head, and let air escape harshly from his nose. He was right, he had thought. She really was perfect, except for one thing.

"That sounds horrible," he had said.

Maxine's eyebrows shot up.

"I would choose Yankee Stadium."

The unlikely pair had let out a final round of laughter until a familiar shot of nerves bounced through Maxine and prompted her to announce a need to rest up for the upcoming testimony.

As they had retired respectively to their lonely hotel rooms, Maxine had drifted quickly off to sleep, warmed by her decaf coffee, while across the hall, Ed watched hours of SportsCenter and replayed the dinner in his head as though it were part of the ESPN loop.

On the flight back north, Maxine's mind rested as the plane soared smoothly through a patch of clear sky. And as she finally nodded off for some much-needed slumber, Ed, awake in the seat beside her, gently reclined her seat a notch.

CHAPTER 4

JP
The Destined One

Maxine's plane made its descent toward Syracuse Hancock International Airport over a middle-aged woman who was tracking it through teary eyes, oversized glasses that would not be stylish for another decade, and the rain-stained skylight of her campus office.

The professor adjusted the glasses with one hand as she brushed dust off a painful memory—a book she was holding—with the other. *Infertility: A Practical Guide for the Physician* teased her nose and brought one more tear to her eye.

The book had been purchased a decade ago when she and her husband had been unable to conceive after months of attempts that had turned slowly into years. She had understood that the intended audience included doctors with MDs attached to their names. The closest qualification she had was a PhD in political science with a concentration in international relations, but after countless trips to the fertility doctors with her husband, she had been desperate to decipher her body on her own.

She had buried the guide in the work shelves several years ago when a doctor's appointment finally revealed that the culprit for their difficulties was her "poor ovarian reserve." Those three words hit her far worse than an "F" on one of her students' exams. To her, she was experiencing the ultimate personal failure. She wanted a baby more than anything she could imagine.

"Sweetheart, this happens," her husband had said as he tried to console her. "We'll keep trying. We'll have our baby someday. We will."

"Keep trying? We've been trying for years," she snapped toward her husband during a ride to their Syracuse College offices. "I'm done with trying. Dunzo."

"Where is this negativity coming from? It's been a frustrating struggle, I know that, but this just isn't your style, my love. You're ready to surrender being a mum? I'm not eager to give up on being a Big Poppa."

Like his wife, the man was an SC professor. He was also terribly unstylish with pants that rode too high around the waist and ankles. Nevertheless, the professor of anthropology was more in tune with pop culture than any other member of the faculty and began belting out Notorious B.I.G. lyrics in an attempt to make her smile.

The corners of her mouth gave way.

"I'm just done trying the conventional way."

The couple had been discussing a variety of options.

"IVF? Donor oocyte? Traditional Chinese medicine? What? Just say it—say anything—and I'll be your grandest support," the man said.

"I've been thinking about adoption."

Her words were soft yet powerful. He loosened his necktie. She moved the heavy pile of books that had been riding on her lap to the backseat. They both felt a weight lift within the car.

"That's not all," she said.

"You want to have more than one?"

"No. Well, I don't know. I just want to make a go for whoever needs us first. I've been doing some research, and I'm ready for our baby now. We know we want this, and we've already waited so long; too long. US adoptions can happen within a few months if we're open to any race or gender. Let's do it now. Let's just see where fate takes us on this one. I'm surrendering to it."

The man had traded quick glances between the windshield and his wife as he continued driving them toward campus. He held her sandpaper hand in between his shifting of the gears. He slipped their old maroon Saab into its familiar spot at the college with an unfamiliar feeling of hope.

"Let's do it, darling," he had said gently yet seriously. "Let's allow nature to take its course."

Her mood had already begun soaring too high to become dragged back down by his ironic choice of words.

"Er, so to speak," he had added quickly. "Let's adopt whoever needs us; whoever comes to us first."

The professor habitually carried two bags with her to work each day—one for books and one filled with papers waiting to be corrected. They often weighed her down like the thought of a seemingly unachievable task. On this particular day, though, they felt like helpful wings. They had given her the momentum she needed to reach her office in record time to make the first call.

Once inside, she had tucked *Infertility: A Practical Guide for the Physician* into the bookshelf to deal with on another day, and exchanged it for the Onondaga County phone book. She had excitedly fingered through the Yellow Pages in search of a local adoption agency.

>>>- -<<<

As the professor gazed up through her office skylight now, she could barely make out the contrail where the plane had been. She thought of her son JP, now seven years old. She was a philosophical woman and believed in free will, but JP opened her mind just a little to the idea of predestination. He was too perfect. He belonged with her. He was truly part of their Hemmings family.

"Thank you," she whispered to no one in particular toward an angel-white sky before delivering one last grimace at the aged infertility book that had interrupted her office organizing.

In a move that went against her progressive recycling ethic, she gave it a quick toss into a metal wastebasket, an item that seemed to let out a disapproving *thwong*.

"I know, I know."

She grabbed a jack-o'-lantern-toothed photo of JP from her desk and smiled back at the image of her beautiful boy. Only a couple weeks into his second grade, she worried about how he was fitting in today.

"How do I get you to realize how perfect you are?" she asked the photo. "How can I help you be more confident in yourself?"

Always an optimist, she reflected on how far they'd come as a family in their seven years together.

>>>— -<<<

The professor's long wait for conception had been put to rest with a phone call from the adoption agency's placement specialist, a man who would set into a motion a rapid turn of events.

"We have a possible connection for you," the man had said.

"You do? You do! That's most excellent! Tell me more," the professor had replied as she removed her signature glasses and unknowingly stiffened her back. "Please! Tell me as much as you know. Spare no detail!"

The specialist began ticking off the list of notes as matter-of-factly as unfolding a newspaper, adding to the surreal nature of the moment for the woman whose emotions were bouncing all over this new page of her life.

"Well, we have a teenager carrying a baby boy. This is an African-American family. This particular biological mother has made a decision that was very difficult for her, but is what she thinks is in the best interest of her son. She is clear that she wants him to have opportunities that she can't offer at this moment in her life. She's reviewed your application and taken your occupations as professors as sure signs that you're meant to be the boy's parents. She just reached full term. It could be a few days, it could be a few more weeks, but, needless to say, the baby is coming. The baby is coming soon."

The professor had known she'd remember every syllable of the conversation, yet she had jotted down every word as quickly as she could. The pen helped ground her to the paper, which in turn helped ground her to the desk and then to the floor, resisting her body's desire to rocket through the office skylight with excitement.

The specialist had gone on to explain that while the situation was what they deemed a best-case scenario, there were no guarantees.

"Now, please understand and embrace the fact that we tell all of our prospective parents that until all the paperwork is signed and the baby is brought home, we need to be cautiously optimistic."

"But can you tell me before we hang up—before I have my heart set on this baby boy—are there any stipulations? Visitation requests? A catch? You name it; we'll handle whatever comes."

"There is one unusual thing," he had said.

"Please, just say it."

The professor could hear the specialist flipping through notes on the other end of the line.

"So, the girl said she has been communicating with the baby each night before she sleeps, desperate for him to one day understand and come to peace with her decision. She calls him JP. She suggested that if you didn't already have your heart set on a name, well, she hoped you might consider it for him."

"But…huh?" the professor had responded. She had wondered why that particular name mattered so much to the birth mother. "You don't think it's so she can more easily locate him if she changes her mind down the line?"

The monotone nature of the specialists' voice finally turned more compassionate.

"She relayed to me that even though she knows it's impossible for the baby to remember their time together, she wants their conversations to be part of him. You can imagine, she's heartbroken over giving him up. She is a fine young woman in an impossible situation. She hopes you'll pass on the information one day when he's able to understand. It's up to you really."

After very little deliberation, the professors had opted to keep JP's name. They had an intuition that only parents could have, and they knew he would be with them to stay. They did wonder though about the significance of his pair of letters.

"What do you think they stand for," the new father had asked his wife as they looked proudly over the sleeping newborn in their home. "John Paul? Jack Palance? Jelly and Peanut Butter?"

The new mother had shot her husband a familiar look of exasperation, but she was too content to put up much of a fuss over his distinct sense of humor.

"All I know is he's our son," she had said in a gentle voice directed toward their new baby. "That's who he is."

As soon as he was old enough to understand, the professors had explained to JP that he was adopted. They focused on love—their love for him as parents as well as the teenage birth mother's love to give him life.

JP felt all of it.

He could feel the love whenever his mother's extra-large glasses appeared to stare at him as he pretended to sleep under the covers. JP felt it whenever his father seemed to nearly pop out of his jeans with happiness over JP learning something new, from sharpening his first pencil to making his first pancake. The professors were his parents, and JP didn't want it any other way.

"The young woman who gave you to us loved—and loves—you so much that she talked to you every night when you were in her belly. She named you JP, you know. It's what she called you on each of those nights. You are our son. This family is meant to be together. You fulfill us. You make us most happy," the professors would say on every birthday, Christmas, and Valentine's Day.

JP believed that the anonymous teen who carried him had loved him too, but despite all the love, he would make his adoption serve as the most dominating part of his ego.

His own name was a constant reminder of being different. Its symbolism smacked him whenever his teacher called on him, whenever his father asked him to clear the condiments off the dinner table, and whenever his mom hollered gently upstairs for him to wake up and start getting ready for school.

There was also the color of his skin. Having dark skin didn't make him so different at his diverse school, but it did make him feel quite different in his own home. The gentle act of holding hands with his mother or father produced a vivid realization, forcing him to come to grips with the fact that everyone at school must know that his birth mother had given him away. In the classrooms, he wondered if the black kids saw him as white and if the white kids saw him as black. At family reunions and holiday gatherings with cousins, aunts, and uncles, he felt as though he didn't quite belong either.

His father understood from a background in anthropology that getting the boy involved in some kind of sport might help bridge the distance between his son and the other kids his age. With great fanfare and effort throughout the summer leading up to JP's second grade, the professor had introduced a variety of athletics. While the professor resembled a soccer ball more closely than a soccer player, he gave the sessions his all. He had lobbed air balls on the basketball court and whiffed away at golf balls in the park. And while the pair didn't share any genes, it appeared that the father had handed down his lack of athletic abilities to the boy, who lobbed and whiffed right alongside him.

During the last September afternoon of their summer break together, the father and son tossed a football in their backyard. The lush leaves on the trees were just beginning their crisping process in preparation of an inevitably frigid central New York winter. They shook and whispered in the wind as though they were gossiping to one another behind the Hemmings' backs, just as too many onlookers had done over the years.

Neither the throwing nor the catching went well, and for the first time all season, the professor had begun feeling frustrated over his son's lack of skills. As the man crouched and located the ball hidden under his big belly, he exhaled noisily. He grabbed the football with his sweaty palm and accepted the fact that their summer of athletic attempts was all for naught.

His son surprised him.

"I think I'm gonna pick this one," JP said.

"Excuse me, young sir?"

There was something about the pale, old-fashioned laces against the dark, smooth skin of the ball that felt comforting and familiar to the boy. He liked it.

"I think I'm gonna be a football player," JP said. "Maybe we should find out about some tryouts or somethin'?"

"Well, hooray!" the professor said as he tossed the football in the fall air with both hands in an act of celebration. The ball delivered a swift blow to the professor's head, startling the man enough to make him fall back on his bottom. A grass stain smeared across the seat of his pants. He felt so happy that he didn't give his aches on either end of his body much notice.

"And that is why I just tell people to call me Mr. Roly Poly," the professor of anthropology said as he rose to his feet and shuffled back toward their house. "I'm all about embracing all qualities, no matter how popular or unpopular they are with society. That's neither here nor there in this moment. Anyway, let's go tell your mother. Mum, oh Mum! Have we got a surprise for you-hoo! Without further ado, Madam, let me introduce to you…our son, our star, our football player extraordinaire—Mr. JP!"

Between the exercising and the yelling, the man had to take a moment to catch his breath in the grand September air.

CHAPTER 5

HENRY
The Shy One

On the warm September night of a boy named Henry's conception, the moon and some distant city lights dimly outlined the young man and woman who would unexpectedly become a father and mother in the longest and shortest nine months of their lives.

The two teens appeared every bit a close pair as they took in the fresh air on the bed of Chad's old used truck, but aside from their high-school popularity, Chad and Misty shared little else in common.

While Misty was clumsy, Chad served as the star wide receiver of the Brockton Technology Minutemen. And as the girl turned heads with bright blue eyes that appeared to glow as much in the daylight as a wild cat's at night, Chad's face showed a farm of acne, fertilized each football practice as sweat dripped under a dank, maroon helmet.

It was Misty's eyes that ultimately drew Chad to her during their summer counselor shifts at the popular Youth-Brockton branch of the Old Colony

YMCA, but her kindness was perhaps her most beautiful—and also most unappreciated—quality.

Her heart was as warm as Chad's was cold, and as a stray cricket chirped loudly near the wheel of the truck, that difference was the reason that this otherwise pleasant evening was supposed to mark Misty and Chad's last as a couple.

She had cringed one too many times in the senior hall as Chad released his frustration over things as benign as a demanding homework assignment or a challenging pop quiz. He loathed school as much as he treasured playing at the Minutemen's Vincent Palumbo Field. One was the cage that kept him away from the other.

The victims of his angry lashes tended to be underclassmen who got too close to his locker or students who looked homely like Chad himself but lacked the prestige of his football status.

"Nice donkey, real nice," he had shouted recently in the hallway while clapping sarcastically at fellow senior Boris Domkee. "The square root of 5,159 is blah, blah, blah, wah, wah, wah," Chad had mimicked in Boris's higher-than-normal voice following their second-period Algebra II class.

The teacher had returned pop quizzes at the end of period, and Chad had flunked.

"What do you want, an award, Sir King of Friggin' Hand-raising?" Chad had added. "Who gives a flying crap? Why don't you get out of my face for once and take those annoying hands along with you?"

Misty had stood next to Chad during the outburst and felt mortified. She had watched her boyfriend's teammates look away in passive disapproval as they pretended to keep busy with other things. Worsening the moment, Misty held onto a fondness for Boris since grade school, when she had caught him placing an anonymous Snoopy Valentine on her desk along with a plastic bag of candy conversation hearts—all baby green. Somehow he had known her favorite color.

As she watched Boris slink away from Chad's rant, she realized that Boris, with all his awkwardness, odd outfits, and incessant hand-raising, was a much better young man than the one who shared her locker. Even the littlest charm Chad first used to woo her during their stints as summer counselors had worn off until it was impossible for even Misty to see a redeeming quality.

>>>— —<<<

As the cricket chirped on, they lay still on the truck bed with only an itchy blanket to cushion them. Misty was supposed to have finished the relationship hours ago. She wanted to relay an excuse along the lines of "It's not you, it's me," without actually using those clichéd words. That explanation would've been a lie, but she believed, as many in her seat do, that it would go over much smoother than the truth.

Like a shark drawn to the scent of blood, the teenager with raging moods and hormones sensed his own prey in Misty.

"Be right back," he snapped as his sizable teeth lit up slightly in the moonlight. It suddenly occurred to Misty that they looked more like jaws.

An athlete on a mission, he swung his legs up and over the truck bed, positioned himself halfway into the cab, and gently turned the key one click to power the radio. The iconic Boston station WBCN had recently switched its format from alternative to modern rock. Everclear's hit "Father of Mine" joined the sounds of the cricket.

Unlike her boyfriend, Misty enjoyed her years at school, and as she gazed into the dark night, she pictured her third-grade classroom where she learned that only male crickets chirp. The one positioned next to the tire had her attention tonight.

For less pure reasons, Chad was determined to do the same. And as the cricket raised its front left wing about forty-five degrees and jabbed it against its right one to let out more chirps, Chad softly jabbed his elbow into Misty's forearm to engage her. She made out the bumpy landscape of his profile and his saccharine smile through a creepy darkness.

"You have the most beautiful eyes," he said.

Too easily, Misty surrendered to his advances. She felt as though she were on a T ride through Boston, afraid to ring the bell and annoy the grumpy driver.

"I'm an idiot," she mouthed silently to no one as she let the player make his moves.

Misty focused on the cricket and began counting the insect's yips for distraction. She recalled a class lesson on calculating the temperature by counting a cricket's chirp for fifteen seconds and adding forty. She estimated the temperature to be sixty-one degrees, despite it suddenly feeling unpleasantly hotter to her over Chad's body and Everclear's lyrics.

As she listened to the emotional words and imagined how horrible it would be for someone to actually feel that way, Henry was conceived.

PART 2

PART 2

CHAPTER 6

HENRY
The Shy One

Wearing his treasured University of Boston Falcons football sweatshirt, Henry resembled a walking contradiction on the playground of his elementary school in Brockton. While he shared a few similarities with the athletic father he didn't know, neither the swiftness of a falcon nor the skilled movement of a football player was among them.

Henry was generally a mix of his parents. He had Misty's inner intangible qualities—her clumsiness, big heart, and love for school—and Chad's outsides—his oversized teeth, broad shoulders, and skin that would one day show blemishes.

To Misty, he was everything.

To Henry's fellow sixth-graders at the start of the school year, he was different at a time when fitting in was most important.

Henry preferred reading and writing—and if he was being honest with himself, spending time with his quirky grandmother—over the most popular elementary-school games. Henry particularly hated punch ball, his classmates' current game of choice. It had the flow of baseball, but in lieu of a pitcher, offensive players took turns launching a red rubber ball as far as they could by serving it volleyball-style. If the defending team caught the ball, it was an out. If a runner was tagged or hit by the ball between bases, it was an out. The offense and defense switched sides after three. The innings came to a stop only when the morning bell told them to come inside.

Before each game, two captains took turns picking their teams, and no matter which kids held the posts, Henry and a bull-legged girl with the nickname of "Patsy, Patsy, Four-Eyed Fatsy" were almost always selected last.

"Easy out," yelled the opposing team's captain when it was Henry's turn at the plate.

The captain's defense obediently marched a few paces toward the shy boy and surrounded him more tightly, like intimidating little soldiers.

Henry whiffed the edge of the ball with his fist on his first attempt at a serve. He had tried so hard for a home run that his own arm delivered a punch to his forehead. The soldiers chuckled.

"Do-over—you get one do-over," quickly reminded a pudgy boy named Oscar, Henry's best and only friend.

Henry took in a deep breath of crisp autumn air. He made a point to keep his eye on the ball this time. He connected with it, but he didn't disappoint the opposing team's captain, whose only mistake was not ordering his followers to move in closer. The ball shot up high, but not far out, and the captain himself retrieved it and nailed Henry's pointy shoulder with it before he could reach first base. Henry's face gave way to defeat while loyal Oscar kicked the gravel with a too-tight tennis shoe in genuine disappointment.

Oscar and Henry were two boys who experienced the gravitational pull of friendship through their shared misfit-boy status. Fortunately for each of them, the alliance grew much deeper than that.

"Don't worry about it, Henry," Oscar whispered. "You'll get it next time. I'm so sure of it that if I get to be captain tomorrow, I'm gonna pick you first."

Henry gazed up toward the fall leaves on the trees in hopes that a tear wouldn't escape his eye. September was usually Henry's favorite time of the year. The month annually charged him with a nervous hope as the cool, New England breeze mixed with a warm promise of a fresh start. Each year at this time, he hoped to dig his way out of being a perpetual misfit at school. He also hoped that

Boston's Falcons would win their opening football game of the season along with every matchup thereafter.

For Henry, September would easily serve as a better time of year than the real New Year, when he would pretend not to notice his mother's dark sadness over being unable to provide him with the Christmas presents on his wish list or a father to help them take the tree lights down.

As the wind hit the playground and shifted Henry's Falcons jersey, the boy stepped on a red leaf, hiding its beautiful color just as he always did his words, and prepared himself for an all-too-familiar defensive battle against his very own classmates.

As Henry struggled with punch ball at school, his mother and grandmother shared their morning cups of inexpensive tea in the modest two-bedroom apartment the three generations shared.

The month marked twelve years since Henry's conception. Misty was much more tired and much less stylish these days, but her eyes still carried that pretty spark that would always make her in vogue.

Misty was a busy mom by day, getting Henry ready for school, carefully washing, delightfully smelling, and lovingly folding his clothes, and if she was especially on top of things, preparing some make-ahead casseroles. By late afternoon, the single mother waited tables at a large, fast-paced pizza chain within a lively triangle of Fenway Park, Landsdowne Street clubs, and Regal Cinema in Boston.

A typical September day at the restaurant involved a heavy, pre-game wave of playoff-hungry Red Sox fans followed by a second sloppier crew of tired and drunk ones. Appearing intermittently were the moviegoers who would inevitably announce their rush to make their showtime. And whenever Misty felt the evening's wild pace begin to weaken, she would contemplate giving her sore feet a respite to grab a kid-sized order of pasta with tomato and cream sauce for herself. Her plans would usually change as a hostess sat her a few late-night tables of low-bill, high-maintenance college students en route to Boston's Landsdowne Street clubs. They'd fuel themselves with endless refills of waters and only an appetizer or brownie sundae, a dessert servers like Misty were responsible for making. The two cherries on Misty's night were extensive side work to clean up a trashed, sticky restaurant and a twenty-mile commute home in the finicky 1996 sedan that Misty shared with her mother, as she did many things.

Misty would reach their apartment after 2 a.m., around the same time the club patrons found their own beds, but instead of having her wallet thinned out by overpriced cocktails and cover charges, her pockets would be filled with the hard-earned cash necessary to piece together life as the primary earner for her son and mother.

Before finally lying down to rest, she'd peek in on her sleeping boy and recognize that each service of deep-dish pizza had been worth it. Each visit to a customer who asked to be served more quickly than another to make a game or movie had been worth the stress.

On this September morning, Misty began working her bed-head of long chestnut hair into a better ponytail as her mother poured them each a cup of tea.

"You know what I don't get?" the elder woman asked.

Misty winced slightly and braced for one of her mother's signature observations of the world. She stirred two spoonfuls of sugar into her tea in an attempt at sweetening her own mood.

"What's that," Misty managed without a hint of annoyance.

"Take the mall, fah' instance. If I go in a shoe sto-ah, at least fo-ah different workers ask me if I'm needin' help. If I walk in a depahtment sto-ah, I can't browse through a rack of underway-ah without someone bahtherin' me and askin' me the size of my own rack. If I trot down the atrium, I can't pay the cell phone guy in the kiosk not to skay-ah me out of my wits and harass me into talkin' about cell phone plans. They don't believe me when I explain how we share a cell phone, by the way."

"But?"

"But if I'm in the mahket and I need to find out where the damn honey for my tea is hidin', I can't get some attention from a wakah there for the life of me. It's like tryin' to make eye contact with a pokah playah. They pretend to be stackin' a shelf or fixin' a fruit, but believe you me, they know I'm there and they ignoah me. Sometimes they start walkin' the other way even."

The elder woman steamed, took a sip of hot tea, and swallowed hard before continuing.

"So why is it, my dear daught-ah, that when I want to shop in peace, people are on me like a hot young chicky, yet when I need help, they treat me like a diseased old hag? It's uncanny."

"Mom, it happens to everyone," Misty answered. "It's the difference between a structure with commission and one without."

"Commission," the elder woman hissed. "Wayah I come from, you help someone who needs help. You let someone be if they don't want to be baa-thaad. People would get more business that way. You mahck my words."

The family's ironing board let out a screech as Henry's grandmother unfolded its legs in preparation for her cashier's shift at the Belmont Street gas station in Brockton. She tightened her shoulders at the sound. Mornings before work were her least favorite times of day. She wasn't thrilled with her job, her bosses, or the moody people who flowed in and out, but the gig was enough to get her home in time to take care of the grandson she loved so dearly. Henry very quietly loved her back.

Misty's mornings, on the other hand, were like most others' evenings. Aside from some household chores, mornings were times when she could enjoy a little peace. Once her mother left for work, she'd take a bath, read, or watch part of a movie. Her love of film was one hobby that hadn't vanished since becoming a mother.

Misty was generally most relaxed in the morning, but not today.

"Do you think something's wrong with my Henry?" she asked.

"Oh, he-ah we go again," said the elder woman, waving her iron-free hand in disapproval.

Misty felt like her relationship with Henry had begun to slip away.

"Mom, Henry doesn't even ask you to bring him to the restaurant to see me anymore."

Misty felt his painful shyness like only a mother could. And as mothers often do, she blamed herself. She regretted Henry's lack of a male influence, and on bad days she questioned whether she should've found a way to stick it out with Chad. Deep down, she knew Henry was better off without him, but Chad would've at least been able to teach Henry the trick to scoring a punch ball home run, she told herself.

Unbeknownst to Henry, Misty knew her son's embarrassment over the game well. As other parents drove away from the schoolyard without needing to look back at their kids running happily toward the playground, Misty often watched her boy drag his feet toward a sea of students without saying hello to anyone—except for Oscar.

"I swear if it weren't for his friendship with Oscar, I think I would look into hiring a psychiatrist to help us," she said.

"With what money? And better yet, what fo-ah?"

"Maybe he wouldn't be so withdrawn if he had a father."

"Oh, that angry bump on a log? The boy would surely need a shrink if that man were in the pictyah. So would you. And so would I. Henry will have a man in his life someday. You just need to get out on the mah-ket more, if that's what you really want."

"How? When? And I thought we were talking about Henry anyway."

A wide range of men hit on Misty at the restaurant, but she had been out on only a handful of dates since Chad. The brief relationships all ended the same way. None of the men she attracted could see past either the living arrangement with her mother or the fact that Misty was a mother herself.

The elder woman took a sudden pause from wrestling with her iron. A thought hit her nearly as heavy as one before she softened her tone.

"Have you evah been in love, my love?"

Misty knew that the feelings she had for her son compared to the feelings she had for all of her ex-boyfriends combined were as different as a grand slam and a foul ball.

"Who needs another love when I have Henry?"

Misty also knew that she wasn't being honest with her mother or herself. Even though the clearest window she had to true love was her two-hour peek into the lives of characters in classic romance films, they made her realize how greatly she wanted it for herself. With every viewing of *Casablanca*, *Moonstruck*, or *The Bridges of Madison County*, Misty wept for the characters' heartbreaking quests for love. Whenever a film ended happily, her mood would swing up for just a moment until real life set in again, making her face what she was missing.

Misty's mother sensed her own child's pain and immediately sought to fix it with a change in subject.

"What wuh we talkin' about?"

"Finding honey in a haystack," Misty said.

The elder woman wasn't sure if her wise daughter was referring literally to her hunt that morning in the supermarket or the missing love in Misty's life. She didn't want to take a chance in guessing incorrectly.

"Henry! We wuh talkin' about Henry," the elder woman said. "Listen, the boy is fine. He's shy, so what? There's nothin' wrong with being shy. I may not have attended the fanciest of schools, but one thing I know about—even mo-ah than you, my smaht cookie—is time. In time, Henry will come into his own. He'll be mo-ah and mo-ah confident in himself. He'll do it with ah support, with o-ah without a man in his life. You mahck my words."

Back at the playground of the elementary school in Brockton, the morning bell cut through sounds of play and turned them into a mix of groans. The signal to start the school day was actually a relief to Henry, but he kept that to himself. And as he turned to head into the sanctuary of the classroom, the fiery red leaf broke free from under his sole and took flight in the September air as though it were experiencing new life and dancing for the kids beneath it.

Henry had no idea, but this school year was going to be very different than the others.

CHAPTER 7

CAROLINE
The Troubled One

A dozen years after her mother's fatal car crash, eighteen-year-old Caroline tugged gently on her treasured locket and wished it still belonged around the neck of the woman who wore it before her.

As she sat in a room filled with overstuffed bags and moving boxes before the start of her new school year, Caroline was a flashback of her stunning late mother. The red hair was their most obvious similarity, but those who knew Lindsay found smaller details, including their similar cheekbones and freckle patterns, uncanny. Caroline's image brought her father great joy and memories on some days and depression and heartbreak on most others.

Even though Caroline on the surface was her mother right down to her locket, she was someone very different from the wild, free-spirited woman who created her.

Caroline stared nervously at her boxes and bags as she touched the necklace again. Zipping it to the right and zagging it to the left was Caroline's habit whenever she sought comfort from any strong emotion, including her most common one of troubled.

She was troubled, of course, as a young lady working her way through life without a mother. Caroline had sweet memories of her mom, and she longed for the warm, overwhelming feminine love that the woman once brought to her childhood.

Lindsay's death, as traumatic as it was, marked only the first link in a locket chain of more trouble for Caroline.

Several years earlier, on the one-year anniversary of her mother's passing, Caroline's father had been called into the front office at Harper Manufacturing. After a year on the job, he had developed a sort of immunity to the machine's loud noises, but the sound of his name being called off the floor was unfamiliar. It jolted him to a stop from otherwise rhythmic work.

Kenny had folded his plastic work goggles in the neck of his shirt and smoothed the sides of his hair with rough hands. He reached for a roll of mints and unraveled the sticky wrapper to free one up. He took a deep breath and hoped this wasn't the end of the line for him at Harper. It had been a long, painful year following his wife's passing, and he didn't know if he could survive adding another complication to it.

He was greeted in the front office with a phrase he hadn't heard since the night of his wife's death.

"Please have a seat, Ken," the woman from HR had said gently.

Kenny had recalled Officer Rory's same request in his living room exactly a year before. With a look of dread that he couldn't think to hide, he once again took a seat with great fear.

This time, the conversation wouldn't go as Kenny expected.

"We have an opening," the woman had said. "It would be a promotion for you."

For the first time in many hours—or possibly even days—Kenny smiled just the tiniest bit.

"We could use a new machine tenderer."

Her news was as refreshing and mood-changing for him as the dips he used to take in Rhode Island's Narragansett Bay with his wife. Not only could he be finished with sorting earplugs, cufflinks, and a variety of small medical parts that the machines thanklessly and monotonously spit out at him, he would be taking on the very position he admired and studied since his first day at Harper. Kenny didn't know whether the higher-ups at the good company noticed his desire for the position or just felt sorry for his loss a year ago to the day, but he didn't care. His little family could use a break, no matter how or why it came.

"Your quality assurance rankings are the best on the floor," the HR woman had continued. "Your attention to detail is flawless. Your attitude is great. You're dependable. These things haven't gone unnoticed, and they aren't taken lightly here. You deserve a shot at a position with more responsibilities."

Kenny had realized the timing of the offer might have been a coincidence after all. Maybe for once, someone wasn't just feeling sorry for him. Maybe he had earned the promotion through nothing but hard work, he thought.

At Harper, hard work was measured with flags. A yellow one meant a box of productivity was being reviewed. A green flag signaled a box passed inspection and was ready to be shipped. A red one meant someone's work was rejected. Even though the single father had perhaps the most valid reason of any man on the floor for being distracted from his job every once in a while, he was the only one who had never gotten a reject flag. Ironically, red was his favorite color. It was his late wife's color. It was his daughter's color too.

"There's a catch, I'm afraid," the woman had said.

"Yes, ma'am?"

"The opening is for the evening shift only."

Kenny had covered the evening shift a few times, when a worker called in sick and the company needed a second staffer on the floor for safety regulations. He knew the shift's hours were firmly set for 3 to 11 p.m. He hung his head at the thought and smiled, not out of happiness, but as though he'd just won the lottery and lost the ticket.

Caroline was only seven years old when the promotion had come her father's way. Kenny knew back then that if he accepted it, she'd be getting out of school as he was heading off to work. They would be like lonely individual cars weaving through Pawtucket's S-curve in opposing directions every afternoon, traveling to and from their complicated lives.

Kenny had thought of his extended family and wondered if there was anyone left to lean on. His parents, who would've at one time lobbied for the opportunity to take care of their granddaughter, were getting on in age and had migrated to Florida. Kenny had an older local cousin, but he worked evenings as a chef at the great Cassanto's Restaurant in Providence's Federal Hill neighborhood. As Kenny sat in the plastic chair of the HR office, he couldn't help but get distracted by the thought of his daughter's uncanny ability to eat one of his cousin's cannoli in less than a minute. The image of Caroline with various flavors of pastry cream on her freckles turned Kenny's bittersweet smile into a more genuine one.

"I'm sorry," he had replied. "Don't get me wrong, this is the job of my dreams, and I appreciate it, but I have to take care of my little girl in the afternoons. My seven-to-three shift has been perfect for that. Thanks for thinkin' of me."

"What about after-school programs? A nanny? A sitter? It's up to you, Ken, but if this is something that'd be good for you and your family, we'd like you to have the job over anyone else."

Kenny had known that even with the promotion, he would still be a single parent struggling to make ends meet. He couldn't afford additional childcare programs or a nanny. His body slid down the plastic chair as he thought. A babysitter could be an option. Kenny pictured his cousin's son Jeremy, a teen who always seemed to be looking for odd jobs for extra cash. If Kenny was able to make arrangements with his nephew, not only could he accept the machine tenderer position, he might have just enough to give Caroline the dance classes she had been so quietly and patiently wanting.

"Can I get back to you tomorrow with a definite answer? I may be able to work out somethin' for my daughter."

Kenny had arranged to pay a small fee each week for Jeremy to watch his little girl. The arrangement lasted until she was twelve, when Kenny felt she was old enough to take care of herself.

But even from the age of seven, she would've been better off faring alone. Similar to many relationships that turn toxic, Caroline and her second cousin's time together started off well. They played board games, read stories, or put on a Disney film. Caroline's favorite was *Cinderella*.

But in little time, Jeremy grew bored and annoyed with babysitting. He wasn't ready to quit though; he needed the extra cash for firecracker purchases during occasional weekend drives to New Hampshire, or for booze from the mysterious woman around the corner from Kenny and Caroline's apartment. Like too many troubled teens, Jeremy could've used a babysitter of his own. Being responsible for someone else was not a position for which he was ready.

Eventually, Caroline had begun noticing the creepy looks her young caretaker gave her. When Jeremy talked to her, she noticed a change. Sometimes he looked at her, but not in her eyes. She began retreating to her room after school.

"I've got lots of homework to do," she'd say before fleeing like a little bunny with light, quick feet up the steps, leaving her heavy school bag downstairs. "Lots."

She would often hear sounds of talk shows down below while she brushed her doll's hair or rearranged her room, which was her fortress. She'd take comfort up there and pretend it was her own Cinderella castle, knowing that just like on the night of her mother's death, it was possible to be in a separate world despite being in the same apartment with someone.

The arrangement with Jeremy had soon turned from tolerable to tragic. Every six months or so, perhaps when he had a particularly bad or good day, Jeremy would slowly slither up the steps like a snake in hunt of its rabbit.

The quiet sound of Jeremy's slow, shoeless feet on the stairs made Caroline's heart beat even faster than the signal of the cop's lights dancing on her curtains had on the night of her mother's death. Like a rabbit feigning its own end, she pretended to nap with her back to the door. On his first couple of intrusions upstairs, Jeremy had stayed in the room, lingering about for a minute or two before slithering back down to bad afternoon television. But as time progressed, he had become a little more hungry and a little more daring.

On a few of the worst occasions, he had put one hand on the girl's body and another on his own. He let out a disgusting hiss that made her stomach turn. While Caroline wouldn't comprehend what was happening until many years later, she knew in these moments that she hated whatever it was.

Each traumatizing encounter with Jeremy marked another link on a growing chain of seemingly endless trouble for the girl. Jeremy's abuse was even more devastating to her than the unbearable absence of her mother. At least she hadn't seen her mother's death coming. She hadn't tortured herself like her father had with anticipation over that. The years with Jeremy were a different ongoing state of dread. For five years, Caroline did not know what her afternoons were going to bring. She'd spend the rest of her life trying to forget them.

Just as Caroline kept secret her unraveling of the truths about Santa Claus and her mother's drinking problem, she kept this much darker one buried inside her. Caroline was too embarrassed to tell anyone about what Jeremy was doing to her. She wondered if she had done something wrong. She knew that if her good father found out about Jeremy's abuse, the information would completely destroy the man's already broken heart.

The single bright spot of Caroline's childhood began shortly after her father's promotion.

"Guess what?" Kenny had beamed as he locked up their apartment and walked with his little girl toward St. Matthew's for Sunday Mass.

"What?"

"Is there something you've been wanting to do after school these days?"

"Uh-huh," the little girl had said with exaggerated, increasing interest. Her eyes grew wider as though they enhanced her ability to listen. She unknowingly made her clip-clopping Sunday shoes less noisy.

"And what would that be, do you suppose?"

"Da-yance?"

"That's it. With my new job, I'm able to get you started with a class! I called a local studio. We'll start ya off in a couple weeks with a jazz class. How does that sound?"

Ken had the old soul of a man who loved jazz music. He hadn't a clue that modern jazz dance included a wide range of music and styles. Caroline didn't know a thing about either the music or the dance, but she thought that it all sounded wonderful.

As she knelt with her father that morning in the pews before Mass, she had thought about how he once told her to pray to God for anything she was troubled about. He had also said she could pray for anything she really needed. Caroline had always wondered why her prayers to bring her mother back went unanswered. She had wondered why her prayers to make Jeremy disappear never came to fruition. On this morning, she realized that jazz dance class was possibly a start.

The girl glanced at her praying father. Kenny had a relaxed look on his face as he always did—and only did—at church. Maybe he felt closest to his late wife on those mornings. Maybe he took just a little pride in the fact that he thought he was raising a little girl, by himself, in the best way he knew how. Maybe it was both.

And so began the bright spot of dance in Caroline's otherwise troubled life.

To the studio staff's surprise, the little girl was blessed with grace beyond her years on the dance floor. She got lost in the movement. She poured all of her pent-up feelings—her anger, hurt, frustration, resentment, sadness, depression, and trouble—into the moves that her dance teachers laid out for her. There were no unanswered questions whirling inside her head when she was twirling or sashaying on the dance floor. There was no confusion. Just as church brought comfort to her father, the studio served as Caroline's safe place of peace.

She had quickly begun advancing to older groups' jazz classes until one sunny fall afternoon when the studio's director had pulled her aside. Caroline had always admired the woman's impeccably smooth gray bun of hair from afar. Their meeting was magically intense.

"You have a natural gift, you know. Do you love to dance?"

"Oh yes, it is my most favorite thing in the whole entire universe!"

"I thought so," the director had said. "The instructors can see; I can see; that is the case. You should be taking ballet, you know."

Caroline wasn't sure how to digest the comment. Her silence prompted the director to continue. "Ballet is the foundation work for gifted and serious dancers just as the natural sciences are for, say—medical students."

Caroline had thought of the older ballet dancers in the studio who had recently graduated to pointe class. Earlier in the week, she had watched them excitedly put on wooden shoes that were shorter than the length of their own feet before class and just as excitedly compare blisters and bloody bandages after it.

She was beginning to realize that for young dancers, earning that first pair of pointe shoes was on par with a first leg shave, bra experience, or tampon purchase. Caroline had often closed her eyes and pictured herself drumming across the floor with the tips of her own fancy pair. She looked down at her dowdy black jazz shoes with worn white spots over her big toes.

"We'd also like to get you started in tap and modern, and maybe get you into some competitions," the director had added.

Knowing there wouldn't be enough money to pay for more classes, not to mention shoes or costumes for the shows, Caroline had smiled a pained smile, just as her father had when he learned he had gotten a promotion but for a position at night.

The director couldn't help but notice Caroline's discomfort. She looked her deeply in the eyes.

"What's wrong? Do these other styles not interest you?"

Caroline peered around the studio to make sure the others, especially the older girls with the fancier shoes, were out of earshot.

"It's just that my dad and I are on our own."

It was an expression Caroline had heard her father say when he declined Saturday poker over the phone with one of the guys from work. She had continued with another one of the phrases she overheard. "Money is tight. Maybe next year I can take ballet instead of jazz," Caroline had said in an attempt to appease the powerful woman with the perfect gray bun.

But the director couldn't let a year slip by. By the time Caroline had gotten home from the studio, there was a message waiting on the answering machine for Kenny containing a proposition. The director got straight to the point.

"Your daughter is perhaps the most raw, natural talent we've had walk through our doors. It would be our privilege to have her take more classes here. Your girl says she enjoys dance. If it's fine with you, let's give her more of a shot. I'd like to personally offer Caroline a scholarship to dance here."

Kenny had eventually agreed on a payment system in which he covered the price of one class for the sum of all of Caroline's dance studies. As the girl grew in her adolescent and teenage years, she had become better and better—turning her talent from raw to polished—winning competitions and the admiration of both the girls her age and boys who couldn't help but notice the fine shape and easy movement of her dancer's body.

The director had saved Caroline in more ways than the woman ever could've guessed, and Caroline felt forever in her debt. She had wondered how she would ever pay her back.

In Caroline's freshman year of high school, the answer had come in the form of a tap on the shoulder in the same fateful spot in the dance studio where the director had first pulled her aside years before. It was the director's daughter who needed a word this time, along with a favor.

"Excuse me, Caroline?"

"Me? Oh, um, sorry. Hi."

"My mom mentioned you attend Cranston High. Anyway, I coach cheerleading there, and I wondered if you might be interested in auditioning for the team? We could desperately use talent like yours this year."

Cheerleading was much more structured than dance. Caroline could appreciate the sport, but she wasn't as interested in it. She needed dance to let loose and forget about everything. But Caroline wasn't one to put herself first. She viewed auditioning for the director's daughter's team only as a step toward paying off a little piece of her father's debt at the studio.

She happily agreed to try out.

It was without much surprise that Caroline excelled at cheerleading as well, because she was naturally able to do the lifts, flips, and basket tosses. Her moves were both delicate and powerful. Her red hair came alive in the wind like fire on the sidelines. Just as her mother would have, Caroline stole the attention of the fans in the bleachers, including the adults who secretly picked a favorite cheerleader in between football plays as innocently as they would a favorite contestant in network television beauty pageants.

Caroline was everyone's favorite.

Even though her heart wasn't into cheerleading as it was dancing, it was the sport, not the art, that would deliver her great opportunity. In Caroline's senior year at Cranston High, as her friends had anxiously awaited notification letters from their out-of-state universities of choice, she had received a letter of acceptance from her own "reach" school, the University of Boston, to study psychology there. When the letter had arrived, she had run with it up the apartment stairs toward her bedroom with the quick, rabbit-like moves she hadn't used in years. As she sat in her room that held so many memories, she had read the words of acceptance over and over and studied the gorgeous campus pictures in the packet. It all seemed like an unaffordable dream. The images collectively served as an escape from the very place she sat, the very place she had grown to loathe.

Caroline knew she couldn't attend UB. The local Community College of Rhode Island would cost her father $40,000 less a year. She was nearly ready to mail out her own acceptance letter to CCRI when for the second time in her life, a family of women other than her own showed Caroline they believed in her.

As she had paged through the smiling faces of UB students one last time, she heard the phone shrill downstairs.

"I took the liberty of researchin' cheerleading tryouts at UB for you," announced her coach. "They're tomorrow. Can I drive you?"

"Um, well, huh."

Caroline had intended to once again explain that money was tight. She had wanted to explain that trying out for UB would be a waste of time. But she was finding difficulty in turning down this family, as well as the offer.

"Are you sure?" Caroline had asked. "I mean, it's not too much trouble to take me?"

"Let's do it. So you'll need your acceptance letter at tryouts. Put it in your gym bag tonight. Make sure you stretch extra minutes in the mornin'. They're gonna want to see a standing back handspring and full twist cradles. For attire, you'll want to wear white tennis shoes. Your shorts and top should both be black and tight. Collegiate cheerleaders wear their hair curly. You should tie half of it up in a bow. No tight buns like the kind my mother makes you wear in ballet class," the woman had said before finally taking a breath and smiling through the phone. "Got it?"

"I hope so," Caroline had said.

The girl's stomach suddenly felt like she was doing a round-off back handspring.

"Listen, Caroline, you've got this. Just, well, do what you do best. Smile. Light up the heavens just like ya always do."

And so she did. As a matter of fact, she had done it well enough to be the only cheerleader among 260 University of Boston student athletes to secure a McArthur Fund scholarship at the UB for the 2012-2013 school year.

>>> <<<

Caroline sat alone in her packed-up room with her father still at work on the eve of her first trip to attend the University of Boston as a freshman student athlete. As she tugged away at her necklace, she recognized the moment as yet another time in life when she could've desperately used her mother's advice.

A medley of questions swirled around her troubled mind. What if she didn't like her roommate? Or worse, what if Caroline's roommate didn't like her? What if her coach regretted giving the scholarship to Caroline instead of another girl? What if she couldn't pull off her sales-rack clothes in Boston as she attempted to do in her smaller town? Would she be able to take a shower or a nap in the dorm without worrying about someone barging in and touching her?

Unfortunately, based on Caroline's past experience, each worry seemed as probable as the next. She pondered calling the two women who had stepped in to guide her over the years, but keying others into her trouble hadn't exactly been Caroline's strong point.

She lugged the oversized boxes and bags downstairs with loud, resounding steps and lined them neatly by the front door. She didn't want her father to worsen an already bad back in the morning. The heavier sound of her feet made the delicate girl feel even more mature and in charge. She breathed in the smell of the new perfume that her coach had given her as a going-away gift. The scent from the star-shaped, $100 purple glass bottle made Caroline feel nothing short of luxurious. She tucked her locket beneath the neck of her pajamas and decided it was time to get excited about her new life.

CHAPTER 8

DEVIN
The Gifted One

D evin took a couple of long sips from a pint of Sam Adams brew before
showing off the cool, handsome smile of a popular Atlantic Coast Conference
starting quarterback.

He sat crouched on a stool in the center of a handful of underclassmen
teammates at a tavern off Commonwealth Avenue. Earlier in the day, Devin had
offered to show his new teammates Boston's Allston-Brighton neighborhood
nightlife. Always comfortable in the spotlight, he was flying high now from all
their attention and admiration—two sensations of which the twenty-two-year-old
senior star of the University of Boston never tired.

The rookies, collaboratively weighing well more than a ton, looked more
like adoring fans than down-and-dirty players responsible for crushing others
on the field. They leaned in to catch each of Devin's words over bar chatter and
classic rock. They laughed at all his jokes and awkwardly chuckled at comments
that weren't intended to be funny. They were happy to be with him and secretly

couldn't wait to call their fathers, uncles, and godfathers to pass along the golden boy's stories.

"Why'd you choose UB to play at instead of headin' to a school closer to your home in Virginia?" asked one of the new backup linebackers on the team.

Devin felt the spotlight grow hotter.

"Have you ever heard of a club called the Coconut Grove?"

The players from New England hometowns nodded while the ones who grew up outside of the region shook their heads. All of them sat on the edge of their stools just as Devin had done atop his youthful bed nearly a dozen years ago when his father revealed the story of his grandfather's worst game at Boston, a loss that ironically and literally saved the man's life.

Devin retold the story nearly word for word before adding his own ending.

"And so I grew up wanting to attend UB. I agreed to red-shirt here my freshman year and passed up opportunities at schools like Virginia Tech and Texas A&M, where I could've played straightaway. I wanted to fulfill my grandfather's dream of winning a major bowl game for this school. I still do. And this is the year to do it, boys," Devin shouted. "It's my last shot to do it."

The senior raised a glass with his teammates quickly following suit, clinking and chugging until they were all dry.

"Who's got next round?" Devin asked.

As one of Devin's new offensive linemen jumped up from his stool as though he were following his quarterback's play call, Devin let himself enjoy the buzz from the last beer for a moment before revving up his performance again. The bubbles evaporated down his throat and radiated through his body before he turned himself back on.

"How about the Chicken Soup Comeback? Has anyone heard of that one?"

Because Devin's audience included successful students of the game, each player was familiar with the legendary comeback and replied with comments including "Hells yeah," "Sure man," and "The great Joe Montana." They weren't aware of Devin's father's connection though. The Hustler would've preferred to keep it that way, but Devin retold the story of his father's failed acceleration with defiance. Despite his love for the game of football, Devin had grown distant from his father over the years. Perhaps the Hustler had pushed him too hard at practice or had sung his praises too little after triumphant games.

The roughness had pushed Devin to depend on outside sources for attention over the years. He found it in fans of his football team, rookie teammates, and young ladies who fell in love with him too easily either for his status or movie-star features, including his golden locks and disarming smile. The girls often told Devin he resembled any number of blond movie stars. He liked the comparisons but always thought he was even better looking.

"To freakin' chicken soup," the golden boy shouted as the guys laughed, clinked glasses, and happily guzzled another round.

The carbonation hit Devin funny this time. The bubbles evaporated along the rear sides of his tongue.

He slid his empty glass along the bar and fetched his cell from his jeans to see which girl had texted him to get lucky. The Boston campus wouldn't come fully alive for another couple of weeks, but there were a few admirers from the city who were always ready for after-hours with him. The young ladies failed to interest him these days as much as they once did, however, so Devin closed his eyes and, in eeny-meany-miney-mo fashion, let his finger land on the scrolling cell screen in selection of the night's winning number.

Devin and his teammates had arrived on campus in July, when fall football camp had kicked off. The quarterback had been annoyed by the camp's name, because the session really began in the summer. He still regretted giving up his break while others had their fun.

He took a deep breath and smelled a sour, overworked bar rag nearby. It was enough to make his mood turn. As he dialed the chosen number from his cell with a look of regret, he had an overwhelming desire to meet some new girls—maybe a freshman, maybe a cheerleader, maybe someone who was both a freshman and a cheerleader. The thought brought him to his last toast of the night.

"To freshmen cheerleaders," Devin shouted before the rookies whooped it up and completed their last down of the evening.

CHAPTER 9

MAXINE
The Lonely One

Maxine sat stiffly in the newsroom on a darkening Friday evening and passed quickly through her photography from the day's assignments. Even though digital imaging upped her already high level of productivity in the dozen years since her work at the newspaper, she wasn't spending any less time working.

She drummed her delicate fingers atop her desk with her left hand as she deleted and saved pictures on her camera with the other. The thirty-seven-year-old was still single, married only to taking pictures. She still turned heads. And she still pulled off her signature short haircut with a feminine grace.

"You heading out, Max?" asked an admiring coworker who secretly hoped she'd join him for a beer at the pub nearby to celebrate the end of the workweek.

Maxine ran her left fingers through her hair and looked up from her work with a smile.

"Nah, unfortunately I'm not done just yet."

Both Maxine's smile and her response made him fidget. Her lack of an engagement ring, though, gave him hope.

"I've been assigned a series of profiles on superstar high-school athletes in the region, and I'm so behind," she added. "And then there's a busy weekend of games ahead of me that I need to prepare for. You know how it goes. It never stops, does it?" She intended to tack on the admirer's name in an effort to warm up her decline, but she failed to come up with it.

Maxine's years of developing a portfolio of Syracuse sports shots during weekends off from the newspaper had paid off. The International Presswire had picked up a few of her pictures over the years—with Maxine's cranky editor's reluctant blessing—and the wire had eventually offered her a job as a senior sports photographer in its Syracuse bureau.

Maxine watched her admirer head toward the door with a messenger bag slung over his shoulder and a press pass dangling from it. Did the name on it read Ted? Fred?

She thought of Ed, the government beat reporter who had accompanied her a dozen years ago on assignment to Washington, DC. She hadn't forgotten his name. She hadn't forgotten their dinner together when he refreshingly and surprisingly brought her guard down. Maxine also remembered the bit of drool that had escaped the corner of Ed's mouth on their plane ride home. At the time, it had been enough to end a romantic pursuit of the man before it even began.

Age had not changed the fact that Maxine was still impossibly particular with love. She wondered on this lonely Friday evening in a near-empty workplace whether Ed was still running the political beat for her former newspaper only an hour's drive north. Maxine toyed for a moment with doing an electronic drive-by—searching Ed's name on the Internet or checking the online archives of her old paper to see if he was still there. Instead, she opted for one more pass through her work before making the lonely trek home.

Maxine always chose to walk to her home at Jefferson Clinton Condominiums. Not even the harshest of Syracuse's lake-effect snowstorms kept her from doing it. Her walks were always in the dark of night, even on a Friday, when most of her colleagues tended to cut out a bit early. With each step, Maxine succeeded in erasing just a little bit of her worries from the office, only to trade them for other uneasy thoughts. More than any other time in her life, Maxine felt nagged these days by being alone.

This night was no different as she dodged the singles along the sidewalks of Syracuse's Armory Square. They were dressed in their best seductive clothing, overpowering perfumes, and expressions of excited hope as she longed to get out of her work clothes and into her yoga pants, soccer flats, and long-sleeved T-shirt filled with the comforting smell of fabric softener.

Each day of the week seemed to bring out its own type of love on the streets. On Saturday night strolls home from covering games, Maxine weaved around small fences of couples on dates, drunk from love, booze, or both as they linked arms. Sunday evenings featured the low-key, loving married couples who had the Sunday blues and weren't quite ready for their weekends to end.

Mondays attracted college students in search of a good meal off campus on an evening that wouldn't make them miss a moment of important nightlife back at the M-Street college bars on the hill. These patrons appeared to include boyfriend-girlfriend prospects from the weekend, each hoping they liked the other sober as much as they had tipsy and under poor lighting. The days would replay themselves over and over again in front of Maxine as she made her way home alone each night.

Having her right hand free of the buttons and soothing clicks of her high-end camera made her feel especially out of place during the walks. She'd attempt to fill the void with a dated gray cell phone to dial up friends and family members who, against Maxine's better judgment, had collaboratively convinced her recently to turn to the world of online dating.

"Max, what have you got to lose? Is it any better to meet someone at a bar or at work?" her best friend had asked last Thursday, a night that marked ladies' night on the square.

As Maxine's ears had taken in the familiar, unsolicited dating advice, her eyes had observed the irony that ladies' night brought out just as many men, and these guys seemed by far the most aggressive of the prospects on any other night of the week. On Thursdays, Maxine felt relieved to be armored by a boxy sweater or a conservative, button-up work shirt under her jacket.

Her girlfriend's case for giving online dating a try was the same one made by Maxine's mother, her old college roommate, her cousin, and seemingly everyone else in America who she overheard discussing dating in the twenty-first century.

On this Friday evening, the photographer passed a finale of singles on their way out of the condos as she inched closer to hers. She stepped into the elevator on the heels of a handsome, salt-and-pepper-haired man she hadn't noticed before in the building. She grew impressed by his designer shoes that looked nice without being too flashy. As they pushed their respective floor buttons, she unconsciously ran her ringless fingers through her short hair for the second time that night.

"Have you ever wondered why this place isn't called Madison Bush," the salt-and-pepper man asked. He was searching hard for conversation within their Jefferson Clinton building, but Maxine found that endearing and paid him a warm smile. He gave one back, unveiling a bit of arugula in his teeth left over from dinner while the elevator let out a high-pitched, mocking ding as though it had noticed the green salad bit too.

"Or Monroe Obama. Have a wonderful weekend," Maxine said as she exited quickly onto her floor. Always polite, she knew she might as well have told him to have a nice life.

"Could there be more wrong with me?" she asked herself in the empty hallway as the elevator door snapped shut behind her.

There wasn't as much as a goldfish or even a plant to greet Maxine in her condo, but some of her best photographs hung on the walls, and the work made her feel right at home. She let her body relax just a bit, but her mind, as usual, was still in overdrive.

"Or Fitzgerald Kennedy," she said to herself, broadening the possibilities of the puzzle the anonymous man in the elevator had laid out for her.

She plopped onto a lightly used sofa, opened her laptop, and began editing her online dating profile. For just a moment, she was quite content—and a bit excited—to be alone in her place on a Friday night as she clicked away at the dating boxes that best captured her interests, exercise preferences, and income.

But the feelings were short-lived.

"How do you describe your physique," she read aloud.

The petite, stunning photographer reviewed some of the options for women, including "a few extra pounds" and "big and beautiful." Maxine winced. There, in black and white, were words that made her feel just how overly critical she had been when it came to dating. Maxine's dearest and most loyal friend was married. She had supported Maxine for years through her dating process. The woman was far from being able to squeeze in a sample-size dress, yet she was the most beautiful person Maxine had ever met. Maxine wondered how her best friend would fare in the world of online dating if she hadn't already met her match, a man who easily saw through any meaningless imperfections to get to the good stuff.

Maxine thought of Ed's bit of drool that she had been unable to shake so long ago. She thought of the salt-and-pepper-haired man's bit of dinner in his teeth on this night. No one was perfect, especially not herself, she thought. She wondered if she'd get to see either of the men again before closing her laptop roughly.

Further into her condo, she found the yoga pants and soccer flats that had been on her mind during the walk home. She smiled in annoyance at herself because she didn't do yoga and she didn't play soccer. She vowed to do a better job at remembering that appearances aren't as clear as they seem on the surface.

CHAPTER 10

JP
The Destined One

An exhausted nineteen-year-old entered his family's home, wiped sweat from his dark skin, and looked happily into the eager eyes of the professors who had adopted him nearly two decades ago.

To them, the teenager's humble entrance felt as grand as a visit from the president of the United States himself, a man whom the family regarded highly—not necessarily for his politics but rather for his belief that with hard work and passion for America, a child can rise above any challenge and become destined for greatness. For the five-foot, six-inch JP, his dream, against a number of odds, involved landing a spot on a Division 1 college football team.

The teenager brought into the laundry room the dirty clothes that saw him through a full day of tryouts. JP's father, as roly-poly as ever, followed his boy and chanted his name as proudly and excitedly as a game-day fan repeatedly shouting "De-fence!"

"J-P! J-P! J-P!"

JP's own name still evoked tremendous emotion within him. It still made him think about the unknown woman who had put the two letters together as she had talked to JP while he was inside her womb. Deep down, JP wondered if the woman, wherever she was, would be proud of him on this day. On the surface, he gave the only father he ever knew an appreciative smile for his tireless encouragement.

"I'm going to hit the shower, Pops," he said before exhaling for what seemed like the first time all day. "I'll be down in a few to tell you all about tryouts."

The other Syracuse College professor of the household overheard the father and son's brief conversation and took it as her cue to stop grading her students' papers and begin assembling the bowls of hearty chili she had prepared earlier in the day. The woman had hoped that JP's favorite meal would be the perfect sustenance for either a celebratory dinner or a comfort meal following heartache. It was an act symbolic of her raising JP all his life with great thought, love, and kindness.

By the time a freshened JP returned to the dining room, every utensil was in place. Even the anxious mother and father had found their respective seats at the round family dinner table. The professors had already poured themselves a couple glasses of Merlot. They held off, though, from taking their first sips. With a soft navy hoodie, sweats snuggled against his clean body, and the aroma of his mom's cooking in the air, JP wondered if the moment could be any richer.

"To our son, who every day makes me more proud as a mother than I could ever manage to put into words," said the professor.

The parents reached across the length of the table to clink glasses and take a celebratory sip of the wine even though they still weren't sure what they would be celebrating. The professors knew they were proud to have raised a son who went after a far-out dream, regardless of his chances for success or failure.

"Well, my boy, we just wanted to say how much we love you, no matter the outcome from your day," the anthropology professor added as he awkwardly stretched and clinked glasses with his wife a second time. "Have a seat and tell us everything—the highs, the lows—everything."

JP took in a deep breath to enjoy the feeling of holding the information his parents so lovingly wanted. Before taking his spot between them, though, he exhaled and reflected upon the challenges he had overcome to get to this very point.

>>>- -<<<

While JP never had an ideal football build, his talent for the sport had grown throughout his youth with the help of a trio of supporters who descended upon his life in the form of out-of-shape, sullen coaches.

In grade school, JP couldn't catch the football or throw it. He was too small to power through a defensive tackle or block offensively for his quarterback. Nevertheless, his first coach had been insistent on finding a spot for every player and had rotated positions for weeks. One afternoon, he pulled JP aside to share a discovery with him.

"You can run, little man," he had said with a dry laugh and a rough pat on JP's fragile chest. "You can run!"

"I can?"

"Yes, you can, and you're going to be my new secret weapon," he had said before lowering his voice to an intense whisper. "Now don't go signing up for track or cross-country on me now. You are a football player and a valuable one at that. Stick with me, kiddo. I see some touchdowns in your future."

"You think so?"

"Oh, I know so. Someday, when you become a rich and famous athlete, try not to forget me, eh?"

Both JP and the coach had believed that dream was a wild exaggeration—or so they thought at the time—but the words had made the boy feel like he belonged on the field nonetheless. It was a welcome feeling.

"I won't forget."

JP had kept at the position throughout elementary school and on to the more challenging middle-school years, when the pre-adolescent boy's body became even more gangling. He had grown a bit bigger in height, but it only made him appear smaller in width.

As JP graduated to middle-school play, he had met coach number two. Just as he unintentionally managed with the first, JP quickly became his middle-school coach's favorite player. The man had noticed JP practice as hard as anyone he'd ever seen at that age. He had watched JP work the track before school, and he even met him there on a lazy and unseasonably warm September morning.

"You work pretty hard, don't you, JP?"

"You think so?"

"Harder than anyone else on the team," the coach had said with eyes so focused on the boy that JP wondered if the man could see into his soul. "What drives you?"

"I just like to play 'cause it makes me feel pretty good."

"It makes you feel like you belong?"

It was impossible to ignore the fact that JP was different. The kind coach hadn't meant to get personal, but he held a position in which players and parents constantly lobbied him for playing time and better positions. JP had touched coach number two's heart without trying.

The young player nodded weakly as the good coach softened his stare and his tone.

"Well, you do belong. You're pretty quick. I believe you'll succeed. Now go ahead, get back to work. Don't let me bother you. You know what you're doing."

The scrawny boy had accepted his orders and gone back to working the empty track.

Despite the support, JP hadn't earned the starting running back position in the middle school years, when his competition got bigger and faster and harder to dodge on the field. JP hadn't quit the sport though. His middle-school coach had at least succeeded in making sure the boy continued playing in high school.

As JP entered Jamesville-DeWitt High, his body had finally begun filling out, and it slowly transformed from a skeletal pencil to a thin crayon. He had started supplementing his before-school running with post-practice playbook studies. By JP's junior year, he had become the starting running back for the Jamesville-DeWitt Lions. By the end of it, he was breaking central New York rushing records with the support of his third mentor, a coach with the nickname of Crash, a man who would need to fight even harder than the others before him to keep the small running back advancing to the next level of the sport.

Coach Crash had earned his nickname when he was a student himself at Jamesville-DeWitt, back when bell-bottoms were stylish and Elvis Presley tunes from Vegas shows seemed to play endlessly through radios of cars including Crash's candy-red Ford Mustang. He had been considered a natural at playing the defensive line. His talent alone for stopping the opposition should've made him the star. But Crash had shared every practice, every game, every celebratory supper in his home—and even the Mustang—with a twin brother who had played offense nearly as brilliantly as Crash did defense.

The twin on offense had stood out because he was the one scoring the touchdowns, even though Crash was more often responsible for quietly winning the games on defense. The offensive twin was appropriately nicknamed Flash and was more outgoing. He had pizzazz. In the high-school cafeteria so many years ago, the twins' classmates had subconsciously gravitated toward him over Crash, who had been more than happy to let his brother take the spotlight.

Now in their fifties, the twins had continued on paths that were both similar and different. While Crash was still the football coach at the high school from which he graduated, never leaving his hometown, Flash took one coaching promotion after another as though he were climbing up bleachers with great determination until he reached his top seat—as the head coach for the Division 1 Syracuse College Orange and Navy nearby.

"Congrats, man," Crash had said when his twin had told him of his promotion a few years ago.

The brothers had been competitive on the field, but they had never let those feelings affect their treatment of each other off it. They never missed the other's games unless both were coaching them at the same time.

"You deserve this position more than me, you know," Flash had said. "You've always had the most strategic mind of anyone in the sport, including the pros, I'd argue."

"Just give the Orange and Navy some wins, will you? It's been a while since this city has had a team to root for in a major bowl game. I'm happy holding down the field here at our high school alma mater."

Both twins had known that the humble one never gave himself enough credit. He belonged somewhere bigger, just like his brother.

In each of his three years in his collegiate post, Flash had looked to his brother whenever there was a spot on SC's team for a walk-on to serve as a practice dummy on his best day and a water boy on his worst one. He knew Crash had studied the high-school competition extensively and would have the best take on the player who the Division 1 college managers overlooked. None of the picks ever saw much—if any—playing time, but both brothers had felt good about giving the spots to kids who deserved them.

Crash knew that this year, his pick was especially deserving. He also sensed that his brother would need special convincing.

On the bleachers of the Jamesville-DeWitt field where the duo had once enjoyed so much success performing on the same team, the brothers met to discuss the latest crop of walk-on prospects. Time had turned their athletic frames into looser bodies with bellies that pushed ever so slightly over their belt lines. They both wore five-o'clock shadows, black sneakers, and gray sweatshirts without planning the coordination.

"I've got one late spot this year for an offensive walk-on. So where's your ingenious local pick going to come from this year? West Genesee? Baldwinsville? Liverpool?" Flash had asked his brother.

"You're looking at the place," Crash had said.

"Right here at Jamesville-DeWitt High? You think Travis Addison can hold his own, do you?"

Travis had earned the recognition of becoming Jamesville-DeWitt's star receiver, but he wasn't the player on Crash's mind.

"No, my recommendation is JP Hemmings. I believe he should walk on the SC team."

The collegiate coach had let out a roar of a laugh, the kind that erupts immediately when something is seriously funny.

Like a wise defensive lineman who always studies his opposition's moves, Crash had expected this reaction from his brother. He still failed to see the humor.

His twin instantly tried to make amends.

"Listen, man. I've got all the respect in the world for that little guy. I've watched your games. He had a great season. I'm as impressed as you are at what that little piece of dynamite is able to achieve, but let's face it, he's too small for high-school play, not to mention D1 college."

Flash may have held the more prestigious job, but the humble high-school coach was on his home bleachers now.

"If you've been to my games, right here on this field, then you've seen JP play as a freshman and you've watched him steadily improve game by game and year by year. He's not done climbing, either. He's the hardest worker. He's got the best attitude. He's not necessarily a natural talent, but he's a fighter. He plays each dang game as if his life depended on it for some reason. He's responsible for converting more third downs than any other player on the team this year. He's a solid player now, worthy of D1."

Crash had brought a book of JP's performance statistics even though he already knew them by heart. He displayed the stat book like a salesperson clinging to his electronic presentation to get the yes.

"All my assistant coaches at SC—no, the players themselves—are going to harass me for this decision," his twin had said. "I'll never hear the end of it."

Crash encouraged his brother to bring the stats home with him. "Maybe the book will give the team some inspiration," he said.

"OK, listen. Let's not get crazy, but let's give the kid a shot. He can come practice with us for a day. It'll be an informal tryout. If he holds his own—*really* holds his own—then he can walk on and become a more permanent fixture in practices. If he has as good of a work ethic as you're describing, maybe he'll be a good addition. I think there is a greater chance of Syracuse seeing no snow this winter, though, than this kid seeing some playing time."

Finally, it was the high-school coach's turn to chuckle.

As JP took his spot at the dinner table between his parents, his broad smile revealed the success of the tryout. While his mother's chili cooled before him, he realized he had savored in the moment as long as he could. He unzipped the warm sweatshirt and unveiled his very own Syracuse jersey beneath it.

JP's father jumped up and whooped in celebration. The man's belly bumped into the table, rocking plates, glasses, and a halved avocado that would soon catch the proud tears falling from the face of the other professor.

CHAPTER 11

CAROLINE
The Troubled One

Caroline dropped a fluorescent pink-and-green tube of pharmacy mascara into her makeup bag with a clink and smoothed a wrinkle from her black dress, a simple frock that she had purchased at a Warwick, Rhode Island, discount store before leaving the Ocean State for college. While the wrap-style dress managed to hug her stylishly, it failed to protect her from feeling like a misfit among the University of Boston's freshmen girls who were shimmying into their finest designer wear in preparation of the momentous day.

She overheard one of the primping girls explain within the lively bathroom of Wellfleet dormitory that the number-one rule of fashion is to always have on one fabulous thing. Caroline touched her mother's locket. While she would've traded that most prized possession for her mother to be alive again, she felt grateful for the first time in her life that the piece of jewelry contained several diamonds.

Caroline watched the girls prance around the bathroom without much clothing or worry. Fancy outfits aside, they were still different, she noted. A dozen years had not been able to wash away the fact that at a vulnerable age, with Caroline's father out working to pay for her dance classes, food, and roof over her head, she had been violated by the young person trusted to care for her. Even the scholarship to attend the prestigious UB as a cheerleader—a scholarship earned by her own hard work and talent—hadn't lessened her intense feelings of being troubled, bruised, and tarnished.

"You look pretty," Caroline's new roommate told her. "You ready?"

Caroline's nude pumps felt heavy as she forced one thin, long leg after the other toward the exit of the girls' beautiful brick dormitory and onto Laurel Lane to officially become part of the freshman class marching to their convocation, an event symbolizing the beginning of their academic and social journeys at University of Boston.

Caroline had been tasked with carrying one of the many maroon-and-gold-trimmed torches. As she leaned in to ignite her flame from that of a fellow classmate and torchbearer in the fall wind, her red hair took flight and caught the attention and admiration of all around her. She may have been from a small pond called Cranston, Rhode Island, among a sea of intimidating fish now, but she was by far the most captivating in these cool waters.

As the large group of freshmen stood quietly, a senior priest from UB's Center for Ignatian Spirituality proudly spoke the words of the Jesuit founder, Saint Ignatius of Loyola:

"Set the world aflame!"

Even the usually pensive Caroline couldn't help feeling rushes of excitement. She vowed in that moment to work her hardest in her own steady personal journey away from her past.

Behind a banner reading "Class of 2017," the students were told that they'd complete the same march in four years, at the time of their graduation. For Caroline, a girl with a history of swimming in a perpetually rough sea, those words sounded well-intentioned but unlikely. She didn't know what the next day would bring, never mind the next four years.

A few weeks into the school year, Caroline slipped off sneakers that had been provided to the cheerleaders through a team sponsorship.

"Perks of the job," the coach had said when they were distributed to the girls in a bag filled with complimentary warm-ups, T-shirts, and sweats.

Caroline treasured all the items, but she couldn't help feeling unworthy of them. She glanced at the shoes, now sweaty from practice, and placed them in her bag as though they were Cinderella's glass slippers. As she tugged at her necklace with one hand and shifted her seat on the turf with the other, she began doubting what she was giving back to the school. Would someone really decide to attend University of Boston after seeing her cheer on the sidelines? Was her football team really going to win a game because of her backflips? Would she have received her scholarship if others had known about her past?

Her unspoken questions would've continued rolling on if her coach hadn't broken the silence.

"Can we talk?"

Caroline swallowed hard as she followed the woman into the coaching office. She carefully unrolled a mint from its wrapper, just as her father had on the day Harper Manufacturing offered him a promotion.

"How is everything?" the woman asked.

Caroline reflexively launched into a rehearsed speech.

"I love it here; everything is going great," she said. "I feel like I'm starting to get into a stride, but I know I can do better. I'm going to add extra gymnastics practices to our regular workouts. I know I need to get more height on my flips."

The coach raised a delicate hand, lowered her voice, and slowed the conversation's pace.

"Your flips are fabulous, actually. Have confidence in them."

"Thanks?"

"I'll film your gymnastics runs if that helps. Anyway, you're in here because I want to make sure you're happy. I know it can be a big move for a freshman, and you have a lot of extra responsibilities on your shoulders—your work study, being the youngest member on our traveling team, and so on. So, how is everything really going?"

"Oh."

Caroline tucked a smooth strand of her red hair behind a lightly freckled, delicate ear and awkwardly tugged at her necklace. She hadn't prepared for this topic.

Knowing only half of the girl's tragic story, her coach broke the silence once more.

"Listen, I know you haven't always had it easy. I can't promise things will be exactly laid back here either. Your days are already busy, and they'll soon be filled with studying for midterms and writing ten-pagers. I want to make sure you'll manage it all here, not only because you're my best girl but also because the most important thing above all else—including this cheerleading team—is that you're happy. You know, if you ever need to talk to someone, a female figure perhaps, I'm here. I'm really here, Caroline."

The kind words would ring in Caroline's head later that evening as she sat on her work-study stool at UB's Wiley Hall during her service as a dining aide to make ends meet. Even though cheerleading covered her tuition and Caroline's hardworking father paid for her room and board, the cost of living in the city of Boston was beyond what she expected.

"You're not in Cranston anymore," she said aloud to herself as she crunched her new expenses with a dull pencil and a page from a trendy local magazine that had been left at her workstation.

Textbooks had eaten up her lifetime savings of $825. The $8.50 an hour she made as a meal card cashier would have to go toward her own meal card and occasional dinners out with teammates or friends from her dorm floor, she thought.

She hadn't been on campus a month, yet she was already feeling the economic pinch. She wondered where she would get the funds for "mad money," as her mother had excitedly referred to extra cash before the car crash that wrecked both of their lives. Caroline wondered how she'd pay for new makeup, razors, or even toothpaste. She tugged nervously on her locket and studied a polished girl removing a meal card from a fashionable bag. The student handed the card shyly to Caroline for a swipe through the machine.

Caroline watched the stylish girl disappear toward the trays and wondered where she would get money for updating her own wardrobe. A request for new outfits would seem frivolous to her practical father, but on a campus of girls dressed in gear that looked like it came from Newbury Street, the ability to look good here might as well have been the base of Maslow's hierarchy of needs. The chart happened to be peeking out from Caroline's "Introduction to Psychology" text, an item that had cost her $61.80.

She mentally revisited her coach's kind offer to discuss any troubles before wincing at the thought of mentioning money problems to the woman who handed Caroline the only scholarship she had.

As Caroline's eyes focused on the magazine, an advertisement caught her attention. It read:

Start Your Week at the Gentlemen's Club
Monday Night is Amateur Night
Stop in for a complimentary appetizer with your favorite entertainer and help
us pick which amateur goes home with $1,000.
Help us make your Monday night an amateur's night!

Caroline drew in a long breath and smelled a collision of cafeteria smells from the dining hall's hamburgers, hotdogs, steamed vegetables, and pasta with meat sauce. As her colleagues in the hall pondered their best options for dinner, Caroline found herself faced with a darker, more unexpected choice. She knew that stepping foot in the club would be wrong, but the typically conservative girl also knew it would be one Monday night contest, and if she had the opportunity to dance, it would literally be money in her bag. She told herself it wouldn't be right, yet she discreetly slipped the ad into her pleather purse.

Caroline focused on a group of students arriving for dinner. As she swiped each of their cards with her left hand, she tugged incessantly on her locket with the other.

CHAPTER 12

HENRY
The Shy One

For the shy little boy named Henry, sweet relief from a seemingly endless childhood of clumsy punch ball whiffs, schoolyard bullies, and looks of pity from his well-intentioned mother came during special opportunities to watch his beloved University of Boston Falcons play football at Chestnut Hill Stadium with his best friend Oscar at his side.

"Gum anyone?" offered Henry's pretty mom to the two boys and her own mother, a woman who accompanied her to games just as she did through almost all other important occasions in Misty's life.

Henry could smell the artificial grape flavor of his mother's gum as she delicately chewed it. Misty's hair was tied in an effortless ponytail. Her eyes still glowed. She was relaxed yet energized by the sounds of the marching band and the enthusiastic chatter among the fans. It all brought her back to more youthful and carefree days.

"Yes, please, Miss Misty," Henry's friend Oscar said, cupping his hands and fidgeting like an excited puppy about to get his treat.

Henry's best friend was having a hard time containing his delight, for Oscar was away from home, a place that frequently felt more like a war zone than a safe haven, because his mother lacked sound judgment when it came to finding a good man. Her boyfriends' resumes ranged from convicted domestic abusers to drug dealers. Oscar's verdict was still out on what could be wrong with this month's man. The boy overheard the guy talking on a cell phone earlier in search of ice. If it had been anyone but a boyfriend of his mother's, Oscar would've politely told him to help himself in the freezer, but Oscar didn't talk to these men. To gain an ounce of control and comfort in an uncontrollable life, Oscar soothed his pain with food.

The aromas of the stadium's hotdogs and sausages made Oscar's mouth water. He felt grateful for Henry's kind mom, even if her small gift of grape gum was already starting to lose its flavor.

Misty considered her ability to get tickets for her family—her son's friend Oscar included—a lucky break in a life that so far had more downs than ups. Her boss at the restaurant was a University of Boston alumnus who held season tickets to the games. The man had learned of Henry's love for the team when the boy had visited Misty at the restaurant with an eager smile, his signature UB sweatshirt, and a writing pad and pen to keep happily busy as his mom worked. The boss hadn't seen Henry around in a while, but these days, if the man couldn't make it to a home game with his own family, he'd proudly pass along the tickets to his most valuable employee so she could take her own.

Misty temporarily set to rest her worries about her son during these occasional Saturday afternoons. They reminded her of the baby lap-sit story hours at the local library when Henry was a late-to-walk toddler. At the stadium in dreamy Chestnut Hill, her unassuming and awkward boy was safely tucked away from the things that made him different. He was away from the schoolyard games. He was away from the kids who called him names. He was just a regular kid in the sixth grade, cheering on his favorite football team with his best friend. Still missing was a father, but this moment served as a temporary bandage even for that.

Misty's mother glanced at her beautiful daughter unfolding gum wrappers for the boys and saw a vision of who Misty once was—a happy young person enjoying a game. The elder woman closed her eyes with a pinch as she envisioned the face of the salty, football-playing boyfriend whom Misty once fed the same gum to under a helmet and acne. As she opened them, she felt grateful that Chad had stayed out of their lives.

If she had to choose one quality for Henry to inherit from the man, she would've gladly selected Chad's homely looks as long as the boy was able to acquire his mother's cheerful way. It didn't matter that he had missed absorbing any of Chad's athleticism. It didn't matter that Misty and Chad's level of popularity eluded him too. She was just happy the boy had inherited her daughter's kindness.

The overwhelming challenges of low-income life in an aging body snapped the woman back into its more usual grouchy way.

"You know what's my least favorite word in the entie-yah English language?" she asked.

Henry typically amused his grandmother with a reply, but on an early-season game day just before kickoff, he was trying to scan Boston's sideline for any injured players. He was squinting too to see how the arm of his favorite player, UB quarterback Devin Madison, was working in the warm-up.

"What's that, Ma?" Misty asked while debating within her head whether the upcoming rant would have to do with the grocery store, politics, or the woman's work as a cashier at their neighborhood gas station.

"Well, let me tell you something. Yestahday at work, I suggested to my manager that he wrap some hotdog buns in tinfoil and put them in the hotdog wah-muh so customers could have a nice, soft roll with their lunch."

Oscar licked his pudgy bottom lip and tried to put the tasty images out of his mind.

"Go on," said Misty.

"Do you know what he said?"

"Tell me."

"He said, 'That's actually a good idee-yer.'"

"Well, good," Misty said, sincerely congratulating her mother for a job well done.

"No, not good," the elder woman snapped in disgust.

"What? Why?"

"His word 'actually' is why. 'That is actually a good idee-yer?' I hate when people say that crap."

"Mom!"

"Sorry, I get all revved up. See that? It's almost as though he assumes my idee-yers are going to be dumb ones. That is actually a good idee-yer—heh! Well, let me tell you, that guy is actually a royal butthead."

"Mother!"

The elder woman didn't always have the most elegant choice of words, but her ability to change a mood was often beautiful.

"Speaking of hotdogs, who would like one? Theyah on me," she said.

"Yes, please!" both boys shouted.

"Oh, look who's listening all of a sudden. Fine, then. Hotdogs all around. Please come give me a hand, Oscah. I'd ask my adorable grandson, but he's glued to the edge of his seat watching Bevin's preparations."

"Devin, Grandma. The quarterback's name is Devin."

"So sorry, my de-ah boy. I will leave ya in peace so you can study your stats."

The woman knew her grandson well. Henry settled into his hard seat and opened his program to review the players' pictures, sizes, and positions. He knew UB had a promising team this year—perhaps even a big bowl-worthy team—and he felt confident that the day's game would be an easy win.

Misty broke the silence—as she always did—between them.

"You know, Henry, your grandma said the dogs were on her, but we're gonna have to pay for them."

Henry peeked over the edge of his program with slight interest.

"We're gonna hear another speech about the cost of four hotdogs here. That alone will be a price to pay," she explained with a wink.

Henry nodded in agreement before quickly and silently returning his gaze to the program. Misty looked at it too even though her mind was on other things.

Her mother and Oscar returned with lunch.

"Good thing I make a whopping $300 a week as a cashie-ah," the elder woman said. "What is it with this place? Are hotdogs the new fine dinin'? Would you believe it cost nearly $30 for fo-ah dogs with sodas?"

Prickly on the outside and tender within, Henry's grandmother often reminded the boy of a porcupine. To prevent her beloved grandson from feeling guilty, she quickly continued.

"Ya know, I may be crazy, but I'd do it again tomorrah. Theyah no othah people I'd rather have lunch with and no othah place I'd rathah be at. Thanks for includin' this old lady. Cheeyahs, you guys."

"Thanks for lunch, Ma."

"Thanks," echoed the appreciative boys.

As four hotdog buns dripping in ketchup and mustard united in celebration, the crowd and marching band came to life. The red-and-gold Falcons had taken the field.

The match didn't take off as Henry expected. The opposing team's defense was powerful and relentless at rushing the passer, and after three quarters, the teams' points were tied.

"Yo-ah stah co-ah-taback is takin' a beatin' my de-ah Henry, but he's a fightah," Henry's grandmother bellowed.

Henry nodded, but he wished the score wasn't so close.

In the game's final minutes, quarterback Devin Madison showed everyone in the stadium why he was Boston's golden boy. With the number four on his back, he showed off a quartet of skills in the fourth quarter—late-game adjusting, calm play-calling, elusive scrambling, and aggressive throwing. In the last 15 minutes, Devin attempted a dozen passes and completed all of them for 151 yards. He also threw two touchdown passes and zero interceptions in the final quarter. His defensive line held strong when it counted and in the final moments gave up only a field goal to the other side.

As the seconds ticked down on the scoreboard, Boston's home crowd gave off renewed energy as its team exited the field. Most were thrilled to have witnessed a close game with their Falcons gritting it out in the end.

"It's gonna be a special season, man. Number four has got what it takes, I think," Henry overheard a chipper man say behind him.

To his front, a younger group of guys drunkenly sang part of the school's fight song:

"O Falcons' nest, O Falcons' nest, hither opponents come!
Set forth your best, through every test, your glory shan't be unsung!"

Despite the team's thrilling win, Henry and the rest of his party were subdued. They remained still in the stands like the last moviegoers to leave a theater. They sat as though they were clinging to every last credit. None of them wanted the game to end. Leaving the stadium meant returning to one kind of harsh reality or another. It meant returning to a challenging school, home, or work situation.

Instead of ripping their bandages off quickly to shorten the pain, Misty had another idea.

"You know what, I hate battling the crowds," she said. "Let's let everyone go on first."

And so they sat, enjoying every last bit of the crisp September air until the smells of pretzels and hot chocolate faded and the rowdy crowd dispersed into a quiet dusk.

"Alrighty, troops," Misty finally declared with as much cheer as she could muster.

The four worked their way out of the stadium, through the grand New England campus, and into Misty's old sedan that noisily made its familiar route out of the city toward home. As they passed the restaurant where Misty served pizzas and other greasy entrées in Kenmore Square, Misty hoped she wasn't missing a good night of pay. Even with free tickets, a trip for four to the game wasn't cheap, she thought.

"Do you think we should all stop in and thank yo-ah boss?" asked her mother from the passenger side.

"Nah, Mom, I'll thank him on Monday," Misty said before turning to her with a whisper. "We've stalled long enough. Time to get back now."

"It was a fun day, wasn't it, boys?" asked the elder woman in a voice loud enough for them to hear if they were sitting in the back row of a bus, never mind the backseat of the car.

"It was great!" Oscar shouted back.

"The best," added Henry.

Henry looked over at his best friend, who was battling the restriction of his seatbelt, apparently searching through his coat pocket for a snack. Henry reached into his own and handed over a baggie filled with pretzels, a favorite for them both at school during their show-and-tell time on Friday afternoons. The sight of the snack made Henry wonder whether he should raise his hand for once during the next session to tell the class about the game. He could try to relay Devin's level of coolness in hopes that the students would think Henry was cool for having witnessed it. But raising his hand wasn't Henry's style. Instead, he would stay quiet and hope Oscar would do the bragging for them both.

Oscar munched through the last salty bit as Henry took in every last sight of the city through the car window. In less than an hour, he would be back in the quiet of his bedroom, where he would hide even from his grandmother the fact that he was writing what he thought to be embarrassing stories or dreading the next school day.

CHAPTER 13

JP
THE DESTINED ONE

ven though JP could've easily lived at home with the Syracuse College professors he called Mom and Dad, it was his parents who had insisted that he live on campus with the rest of his SC teammates and classmates.

"Living there is at least half of the college experience," said his mother.

"It could save a lot of dough, you know," JP countered politely yet half-heartedly. "It would make sense if I lived here with you and drove in. Campus is only like a minute from home. I could practically run it."

"Nope, we're booting you out, you big shot!"

"Honey!" the professor shouted toward her husband. "JP knows he's welcome here anytime. That's not the least bit funny."

"Yeah, it is, and I love ya both for it," JP said. "Fine, I'll get out of your hair, but I'm still coming to visit for the home cooking. Or is that off limits now too?"

"No casa, no queso," the anthropology professor said.

The warm smile of JP's mother gave the young man the true answer, one he already knew.

So on a bright morning near the school year's start, the professors packed up both of the family's cars and drove JP and his belongings the seven miles to East Campus, a corner of Syracuse College that the professors rarely saw, despite working at the college each weekday.

While the community suddenly resembled stacks of concrete shoeboxes to JP's mother, the rows upon rows of far-from-fancy apartments were loved by the majority of the university's athletes who—like JP—chose to call East Campus home because of its proximity to the athletes' locker rooms, practice spaces, weight rooms, and coaching offices. The opportunity to live among teammates who silently understood each other's pressures to perform in and out of the classroom was perhaps an even greater unspoken perk on "East."

As the Hemmings' matching Saabs pulled onto Winding Ridge, JP's mother turned her scrutinizing gaze toward a handful of athletic giants who had squeezed into lawn chairs to cheer on a pair of wrestling teammates. She was accustomed to SC football and basketball players' extraordinary size as they struggled to fit the writing tables over their laps in her classroom over the years. Inside her car, she nervously adjusted her big glasses and decided that the giants seemed much gentler on her turf. She questioned whether moving out and moving on were the right decisions for her baby boy after all. Even though he was far from the fragile infant she had adopted, he was still especially small, particularly among these young men. Not wanting JP to detect her growing fear, she quickly felt grateful that he was riding in their other car with her husband.

"My money's on the big guy," the anthropology professor said inside the other Saab, as father and son watched JP's new teammates tussle on the lawn. "Can't go wrong with that bet, can I, JP? It's like flipping a double-sided coin."

Both cars pulled closer to a row of apartments, and as they inched to a stop, so did the playful fighting in front of them. All eyes were on the professors and the young man, who didn't look anything like either of them.

"My dear boy, I do believe this is the first time I've ever seen you blush. Shall we exit the car? Oh, and don't worry about them. I've got this."

His father "having this" was exactly what JP feared most in such a crucial moment. While he loved the man, he also understood that students more often laughed at him than with him. JP suddenly wished he were riding with his mother. *She has the ability to ease any situation*, he thought.

Three car doors opened and three family members stepped into the hot autumn sunshine with a quiet crowd and the smell of dry grass surrounding them.

"My dear boys," JP's dad said to the guys as he tucked his shirt cleanly into his pants. "Or shall I say men? Let me start over. My dear gentlemen! I would like to introduce you to, drum roll please, the newest member of your team."

All of the players' eyes went to JP.

"I'm sorry, mister, but if you're looking for the gymnastics club's row on behalf of your…little friend there, you might want to try those apartments over there on Small Road," said one of them through growing snickers.

"Can it, Whistler," JP's mother whispered just loudly enough for all to hear. "I have you in my political science class again this semester, and I know you don't want to fail again."

"Ohhhhhhhhh," sang a chorus of teammates with wild exaggeration.

"Ouch," replied Whistler with a dramatic curtsy. "Yes, ma'am. I can start over. So who do we have here? One of your more scholarly students than myself?"

"We have here the running back who rushed for nearly 1,000 yards for his team last year, a running back who can sprint the 40-yard-dash in 4.5 seconds. We have here…my son."

The laughter stopped. All that remained was the quiet panting from the two wrestlers.

"Thanks for all the introductions, Mom and Dad, but I can talk for myself," JP said with a laugh that managed to contain only a hint of embarrassment before turning his attention to Whistler.

"Don't worry, man. I'm used to the small talk."

Thank heavens, his mother said to herself. Like mother, like son with the comebacks. *Please, may he do as well on the field.*

As the teammates picked up the first round of JP's boxes and bags and made their way toward his apartment, Whistler jogged up to JP and removed a suitcase from his new teammate's small but strong hands.

"So you're JP," Whistler said.

"Yeah, man, how'd you know?"

"You're my new roomie."

The pair laughed at life's irony.

"Coach Flash told us about you, you know. The stats sounded familiar. Some of the guys said they practiced once with you."

"Coach told you about me?"

"We heard all about the local walk-on who had the thousand-yard season, thanks in large part to a quote-unquote hard work ethic and positive attitude. He even had a book of your stats. I don't know who your agent was, so to speak, but he sure sold Flash. Everyone was pretty impressed. Coach failed to mention your size, though. He must've been trying to win us over before the rest of us laid eyes on ya."

The new roommates laughed a little harder than before and found themselves on the second floor at their modest apartment.

"Listen, man, I'm a wise pain in the butt," Whistler said. "I can't help it, but I think you'll find I'm not that bad of a guy. So you can see I took the bigger bedroom up here, but in return, I promise I've got your back—or your front really—when you're rushing."

"I'm the fourth-string running back," JP said, suddenly feeling a need to manage others' expectations. "Dude, I'm pretty much here to make your practices better. I'm not going to see any playing time. Appreciate it, though."

"What happened to Mr. Positivity? You never know, JP. In this game of ours, far crazier things have happened."

"Mom, could you please pass the corn on the cob?" JP asked during his first Sunday dinner home since moving to college.

Despite only a week passing, JP's time away felt much longer for all three of the Hemmings. His father missed the noise in the house. The home suddenly seemed too quiet without JP bounding down the stairs for breakfast at a speed that made him sound like he was falling. His mother missed her son's hugs. As a boy, JP was cuddly. It was a quality that had dulled a bit with age and acting cool, but even as a teenager, it had never disappeared completely. JP missed his family's round dinner table, a spot in the house that reminded him that he belonged somewhere.

The professor instinctively passed her son the butter and salt.

"So tell us how it feels to be a running back for the Orange and Navy."

"Fullback," the other professor corrected.

"Backup fullback," JP corrected them both, baiting his mother to fire out questions faster than a quarterback's snap.

"What? You're not running the ball anymore? They're changing the position you've held since grade school?"

"Whoa! Mom, fullbacks are in the same family as running backs, just like the halfback or tailback."

"So you're still running the ball?"

"No, Ma. The halfback runs. The fullback blocks for the quarterback on passin' plays, and I'll block for the halfback on running plays. Shifts happen when there are multiple backs. I still start each play behind the quarterback, so you'll be able to pick me out of the lineup just as easily. You'll have to come to a practice if you want to see me play, though."

"This is all so confusing. It just doesn't sound very strategic. Your skill is running fast and avoiding people, not blocking. No wonder you sat down so gingerly. And you're doing this all for practice only," she said incredulously.

"Are you insinuating my size is too small to block?" JP asked sarcastically, knowing that his small height—and weight—were the elephant that seemed to follow him onto every practice field, in every classroom, and across campus apartments these days.

"Maybe you should have your old high-school coach talk with this twin brother of his," she said.

"Yes," piped up JP's father with a deep chuckle he couldn't contain. "Let's have Tweedledee talk to Tweedledum. My heavens, their nicknames are too much. What are they now?"

As JP's dinner cooled before him, his passion was beginning to heat up.

"Pops, the old coach is Crash and the new one's Flash, his twin. They also happen to be two guys who stuck their necks out for me. Can we take it easy?"

"I still don't think it would be a bad thing to at least clue your old coach in to all of these changes," said the professor with the type of tireless persistence a mother sometimes manages to get away with, if not this time.

"Listen. Holding out for a Division 1 school was a gamble I knowingly took with the crazy dream that I could start at the bottom as I always have and work my way up. I have a plan. I'm practicing longer hours than the first string. I'm still running extra laps on the track even though I'm not in a running position right now. We all just have to believe that it's going to happen for me. In the meantime, it would help a lot if you could just be happy for me practicing on the team."

Both parents suddenly felt rushes of guilt. JP's mother wondered when her son's maturity caught up with her own, and she unknowingly dabbed at her aching heart with her dinner napkin in a fruitless attempt to soothe it.

"Well, hopefully I can pull some of my insider strings to get into a practice and see my baby's new blocking skills," she replied.

"That'd be great. Just promise me you won't call me 'baby' in front of the guys, Ma. I get razzed enough."

"How is Whistler?" both professors asked together.

JP's frustration faded.

"Rooming with him is probably the biggest break I've gotten there, believe it or not."

After a few hours of rare rest, dinner, and conversation with his parents, JP closed his family's front door and opened the one to the new campus apartment that contrasted starkly with the home where he grew up. Smells of home-cooked meals and pumpkin-scented candles were behind him now, making the artificial aroma of microwave dinners and the fabric spray used to keep the scent of two athletic young men at bay that much more pungent. JP had given up cozy blankets on oversized couches and Grandma Moses paintings for futon furniture and cold walls that were bare except for a team game schedule that hung on the kitchen wall with duct tape. JP knew it could be so much worse.

"What's up, man?" greeted Whistler warmly.

"My mom sent me with leftovers of her signature sausage and peppers. This container's got your name on it, literally. Do you want it in the fridge or are you ready for a second dinner, big man?"

"Whoa-oa-oa, saw-sage and peppahs," Whistler exclaimed in delight. "I knew it would pay off rooming with you. I thought maybe I'd get some extra credit in your ma's class, but this might be just as good. The dinner surprises the hell out of me, though."

"I know. She looks like she could be a strict vegetarian or something behind those wise-lookin' glasses."

"No, man, forget that, I'm surprised your mom even knows how to cook."

The jovial friends took seats on opposing benches at a rectangular table made of faux wood. It was far from the round table at home, but it would suffice.

"So, what's your story, JP? I mean, if you wanna tell it."

"I thought Flash took the liberty of tellin' you everything about me."

"No, man, you know what I mean. Your family story."

"You mean, the fact that I'm black and my parents are both white," said JP, knowing that this observation was the second elephant that seemed to follow him through life.

Whistler nodded gently, just once, wondering whether he had pushed the new player too far.

"I'm kinda glad you asked, really. Oftentimes, people stare and try to figure us out. It's not really a long or complicated story. The woman who gave birth to me was younger than we are now and supposedly wanted to give me a good life. The professors wanted a baby and they raised me from infancy. They're the only parents I know."

"I knew I liked that woman, as much as she dislikes me."

"I think she's coming around. I put in a good word," JP said, shifting his weight to ease a bruised tailbone.

"Dude, you're killing yourself out there," Whistler said, changing the subject and shrinking the elephant. "You gotta at least knock off the extra practices."

"The extra practices are steps on my only hopeful path toward my dream."

A week earlier on the sticky, coarse grass among teammates wrestling foolishly by his side, the comment would've earned great laughter from the team's star blocker. On this night, though, Whistler gave only a nod of respect to the fourth-string running back who he thought might just make it after all.

CHAPTER 14

HENRY
The Shy One

As his mismatched, socked feet touched down from his bed, Henry looked no farther than his closet to predict that it was going to be a bad Monday. Staring into the dark space, he realized that the thrill of having witnessed his favorite quarterback pull his University of Boston Falcons to victory just a couple days earlier was gone. Nerves powerfully replaced the excitement he had felt over the weekend. Earlier thoughts of raising his hand at the next show-and-tell at school now seemed ridiculous. Feeding his anxiety more, his mother closed the restaurant on Sunday nights and had run out of time to do the week's laundry.

Henry's live-in grandmother believed in wearing most of her clothes a good four times because, as she often lectured, hers "rarely got soiled and the costs of a wash and dry at the Laundromat were $2 and $1, respectively, peh load."

So, without a closet filled with clean clothes like some of the more popular kids in his sixth-grade class, Henry was left on this Monday morning with two options. He could pull a top out of the dirty laundry bin like his grandmother often did, or wear the only item left hanging in the locker-shaped space—a tight green button-

97

up with a collar that revealed it was made decades ago. It was the type of shirt he'd seen teenagers wear on Halloween with bell-bottoms and curly wigs. The top wasn't meant to be a costume for Henry, though. His grandmother had picked it out last December from Brockton's secondhand store on North Main Street. She had wrapped it up with great pride that Christmas Eve in preparation of giving it to her beloved grandson.

On this morning, Henry wondered about the boy who had owned the unstylish shirt before him. He wondered what the kid grew up to be like. He wondered where his own future could possibly be heading. He was afraid to know all the answers.

Henry dug through the basket containing a week's worth of dirty clothes for a solution, making a mess on a floor that was otherwise tidy thanks to his constantly working mother. All the clothes looked like crumpled pieces of paper. He would need help with an iron, he thought.

Despite his incessant attempts to muffle it, Henry had a persuasive and kind heart. He couldn't bring himself to wake up his mother to help him flatten out the wrinkles, so he let her sleep as he shifted his thoughts to the other woman in his life. He knew the act of ironing put his grandmother in a bad mood nearly as quickly as did the Laundromat, so with one eye closed, he reluctantly took the ugly green shirt from its lonely hanger in the closet. As Henry entered the kitchen for breakfast, the look of pleasure on his grandmother's face almost made the inevitable embarrassment he knew was about to ensue at school worth it.

"Well, looky here, ya handsome kid," she said. "The girls are going to be fightin' today, boy. I think you've been hidin' your boyish fig-yah in those big sweatshirts of yours. I do believe. I do so believe."

Henry watched the woman smile so grand that he could practically count each tooth in her dentures. It was an unfamiliar expression he didn't quite like, but he made a mental note to wear the shirt again sometime, perhaps on a weekend when no one would see him. He would pick a day when not even his best friend Oscar was coming over.

"Honey-flavahed 'ohs' with chocolate milk," his grandmother said, placing Henry's plastic bowl in front of him. The wise woman knew that in the day of a sixth-grade boy, even the littlest things can feel bigger than life—chocolate milk in your cereal, a smile to greet you first thing in the morning, a new shirt for school.

"Don't tell your mothuh about the chocolate pa-aht."

Henry downed the sugary breakfast especially quickly and found himself belted in the family sedan with his grandmother behind the wheel all too soon for his liking. The pair ventured off toward the boy's school, leaving Misty peacefully asleep in their little apartment.

His mouth tasted funny from the sweetness of his cold breakfast. He felt warmed, though, by the fact that his grandmother's sugar-packed meal, exaggerated smile, and gift of the unique shirt were all signs that the woman thought he was great. *She might even be the only person in the universe who believes I am perfect,* he thought. As he looked at the aging woman with appreciation, Henry could tell something was on her mind. He wondered how long it would take for her to begin one of her signature diatribes.

"You know what I couldn't help but notice last night at your mothuh's restaurant?" she fired off as soon as her hand was off the ignition key.

The pair had visited Misty's workplace the night before to enjoy a Latin-style pizza dinner together. The unusual pairing of Tex-Mex and a pie had become a favorite on the menu for Henry and his grandmother during days when they were regulars at the pizza chain. The elder woman had always been eager to use her daughter's employment there to receive a discount. These days, it was more difficult to get Henry to be her date, but the woman had succeeded in convincing him to go for the first time in months and personally thank Misty's boss for their tickets to see Devin Madison and the rest of the University of Boston Falcons play. The reason, while plausible, served as a front. In reality, she was much more determined to get Henry closer to the loving mother whom the boy had been strangely avoiding.

"What'd you notice, Gram?" Henry asked as he slid nervous fingers along the smooth, cool door of the sedan with one hand and scratched at his itchy synthetic shirt with the other. Today, he welcomed any of his grandmother's distractions, especially if they bought him more time before school.

"Well, don't tell your mothuh I said this," she said. "You know I don't often speak badly about anythin' to do with that angel, but anyway, have you evah noticed that when a restaurant—any restaurant—is busy, the waitah refills your watah glass frequently, checks to see if things are cooked properly, keeps an eye on the progress of the meal, drops the check promptly, and most importantly, doesn't leave you waitin' a quarter of an hour for ya change?"

"Grandma, you make it sound like we were at five-diamond dining."

"Five-diamond dining. What is that?"

"You know. The fanciest restaurants."

"Five-diamond dining. I've nevah heard of that."

"Grandma, yes, you have. The ratings."

"Oh, ho, ho. My de-ah grandson, you mean five-stah dining. Why yes, but whey-ah I come from, it doesn't mattah if you-ah eatin' on a fast-food table or one with a fancy, schmancy white tablecloth. Good service is good service. Service don't cost a dime. Besides, yo-ah mothuh's restaurant is supah fine to me. She even used to have to wayah a man's tie with her uniform before the managahs changed things up."

"I think it's a nice place too, Gram. But what were you saying again?"

"I was sayin' that on busy nights at restaurants, you get great service. Not that I dine out that often, but you know, in my long life I've found this statement to be true. People are on their toes. On slow nights, like last night, things take forevah. Shouldn't it be the other way around? For me, this is one of life's mysteries. I couldn't help but notice last night that of the very few full tables on that giant cascading floor of a restaurant, customahs were waitin' to place ordahs with menus folded neatly on the edges of the tables too long. People had their credit cahds peekin' out of the billfolds tryin' to pay so they could get home and digest. Maybe I should tell your mothuh this. Were you miffed at how long things took for how slow it was, or am I the crazy one? This is fah from the first time this has happened to me, you know, at a wide range of places."

"I guess I didn't notice all that. I was just glad it was slow enough for Ma to actually sit down and eat with us." For the second time in one morning, Henry saw his grandmother beam.

"You liked that, did you?"

"Yes and no," Henry muttered under his breath and the radar of his grandmother's aging ears.

The real answer that had been eluding his grandmother, Misty, and even Henry himself was that Henry loved and respected his mother so much that he didn't want her to find out he was being picked on. His distance, in turn, made Misty worry. Her looks of worry made Henry feel as though his own mother pitied him, making the cycle repeat more intensely.

Henry reached across his shirt to unbuckle his seatbelt. He wished it were colder outside so a coat could stall the grand unveiling of the garment at least until after the playground games. He looked through the passenger window and saw his schoolmates playing punch ball. He thought of his mother's words to his grandmother on their way home from the weekend's game, when she hadn't thought Henry could hear: "We've stalled long enough."

"See you, Gram," Henry said.

"See you, hot stuff."

In the playground, Henry's teacher had what the elementary school staff secretly called "snooty duty," keeping an eye on the kids as they squealed at, played with, and teased each other. While others on staff disliked the assignment, Henry's teacher enjoyed watching his kids' personalities come out away from their desks, where they tended to be on their best—and not necessarily their truest— behaviors. In return, Henry's classmates adoringly and respectfully nicknamed the man Teach.

Teach was twenty-nine years old. He was young for teaching standards, but mature compared to his best buddies, fellow graduates of University of Boston who weren't ready to let their twenties end. As Teach successfully influenced and developed young minds, his buddies still slept during the day and held onto their college positions at night. Many were still bartenders and sound-check guys, giving Teach places to spend his evenings.

The young man wouldn't be hitting any of his usual hangouts throughout Boston's neighborhoods of Allston and Brighton on this night, though. He had what he considered to be an exceptional date. It was such a special one that he was having a hard time focusing on snooty duty. An eruption of childish laughter snapped him out of it.

"Whoa, look out everybody, it's Henry, the Incredible Hulk," said one of Teach's students as the others' laughter cranked up a notch at the sight of the boy's tight green shirt. Teach studied Henry's face as both of them shared in that moment an identical thought: at least Incredible Hulk was a better nickname than Patsy, Patsy, Four-eyed Fatsy's handle.

It would be a short-lived relief for both of them.

"I think our class has a new student named Polly," said the same boy who created Patsy's nickname. The little bodies on the playground froze for the inevitable punch line. "Everyone meet Polly," the boy continued. "Polly Ester."

Teach watched Henry's face finally turn color as the boy could no longer contain his embarrassment. A cool October breeze ruffled Teach's hair. He wished Henry had thought to wear a coat.

"Pol-ly Est-er, Pol-ly Est-er," chanted a couple of the boys.

Acting up in the classroom led to disciplinary action, but Teach believed that recess should serve as a place where kids learn life lessons, street smarts, and harsh realities on their own. He considered interfering just this once, but he didn't want to embarrass Henry further. By the time Henry stepped up to the punch ball plate with his green shirt and bright cheeks glowing in the autumn sun, Teach had forgotten all about his upcoming date.

The boy locked eyes with Oscar for a moment and wished his best friend could teleport his ability to consistently punch the ball over the mean kids' heads. Oscar was wishing the same thing. Teach wished it too.

"Over here, Polly Ester," the first baseman shouted before Henry punched the ball straight to him for another easy out.

Teach gritted his teeth. While the young man intended to keep students on a level playing field within his own mind, one student had already told him this morning, "You're my best friend," while another had snapped, "You're not my father, so leave me alone." In reality, it was hard for the teacher not to pick favorites. As far as Teach was concerned, Henry and Oscar were secretly his all-stars.

Teach admired the way Oscar kept his chin up despite the incessant jokes about his size. Henry clearly didn't recover like Oscar did, but Teach found Henry's shyness to be endearing and sweet. He watched Oscar mutter something to Henry as the teams switched sides. It seemed to help Henry a bit.

As one of the cooler kids in Teach's class stepped up to the plate in a $59.95 official New England Patriots jersey and punched the ball into the backfield for a home run, the sunlight that had caused Henry's skin to fluoresce slowly faded behind a cloud. With the depressing situation seemingly under control, Teach let his mind drift back to his upcoming evening.

CHAPTER 15

CAROLINE
The Troubled One

With her mother's locket around her neck and the contest advertisement tucked inside her pleather purse, Caroline read her psychology text atop a fluffy white comforter on her University of Boston dorm bed. She wasn't as natural in the classroom as she was on the football field sidelines or in the dance studio, but she still worked hard at her studies and felt comforted by her Psych 101 reading. The textbook served as the closest resource she had to a therapist, helping her understand a variety of inner battles taking place within her and others. She felt that she was not alone after all.

"I don't know how to put makeup on," squeaked Caroline's roommate beneath impeccable application. "You sure you don't wanna come out?" The girl's black trench coat was nearly buckled with one cuffed, suede bootie near the door before Caroline had a chance to reply. It was Thursday night, a prime time to party on campus. Caroline didn't understand why these outings were so important, but she never judged her peers for it.

"Nah, I'm good here, thanks. Just geeking out with my homework." Caroline stretched her lean, toned limbs in opposite directions and yawned.

Her roommate wished she could look like her for even one night as she left Caroline alone on a dorm floor that carried a stale, long-lasting stench of microwave popcorn. A shrill of their landline telephone brought life to the room.

"Hello?"

"Hey girl," blared a voice that Caroline immediately struggled to place.

"Hey?"

"You don't know who this is, do you, bi-otch?"

The offensive remark revealed the caller, a teammate named Amie who pronounced her name Ah-ME. "Emphasis on the me," Caroline had often heard the girl explain in introductions. Amie was a talented cheerleader on Caroline's squad, but her personality was as overpowering as her high kick.

"What have you got goin' on tonight?" Amie asked.

"Studying."

If Caroline's roommate's tone resembled a little mouse, then Amie's belonged in the goose family.

"Oh no, you need to get yourself dressed. Do you know where we're going?" Amie's nasal honk was louder and more piercing than the telephone ring that had shaken Caroline from comfort.

"What?"

"There's a party with the football team off campus. I'm on my way to pick you up, so hurry."

Amie let club music blare through the phone like an exclamation point before hanging up.

Incidents such as this seemed to follow Caroline through life. The more forceful girls who tended to burn bridges as frequently as they showered often sank their fangs into her. Caroline stared at the dead phone and weighed calling back her persuasive teammate to decline the invitation. She also considered going to a co-ed party like seemingly everyone else in her dorm. Before she could give herself time to change her mind, the beautiful girl decisively earmarked her page, snapped the text shut, and began preparing for an unfamiliar event.

She had witnessed her roommate's going-out ritual a dozen times and started using it as a guide. The first step involved opening their mini fridge and clicking open a can of cheap beer, a beverage left in a case that had been smuggled into the underage dorm.

As Caroline slid the heavy wooden door of her clothes closet over, she took a few long sips. Drinking came a little too easily for her even though she rarely partook. The ability was apparently passed down from her mother, but Caroline had the strong determination of her father. She wouldn't let partying develop into a habit. She let the liquid slip down her throat before grimacing at the sight of her near-empty closet.

With minutes slipping by and nothing to wear, Caroline ventured to her roommate's side of the room. Caroline's bed was less than ten feet away, yet she instantly felt as though she were in a foreign land. It was a crossover she never would've made if she hadn't been invited on move-in day to "borrow any clothes anytime."

"If you ever want to wear anything, feel free," her roommate had said when the girls unpacked their things.

As Caroline looked into a closet nearly identical to her own, but with completely different contents, she gently fingered the tags that still hung on her roommate's stylish pants and piles of cashmere sweaters folded neatly on their shelves. She timidly helped herself to a couple of basics—a pair of designer jeans and a white top with a neckline Caroline thought would complement her beloved locket. She drew her fiery hair in a ponytail and sat at her desk to apply a modest amount of foundation, mascara, lip gloss, and rosewater spray, her late mother's bargain secret weapon for making her skin glow like mother-of-pearl. In little time, she looked gorgeous.

Caroline inspected herself through her roommate's full-length mirror and felt similar to the way her father had on the afternoon he walked home from his first day of work at Harper Manufacturing. The clothes were the least colorful picks from her roommate's closet, but the fit, the soft texture against her skin, and the smell of life from a closet filled with new garments made Caroline feel luxurious and important. She smiled, realizing she looked like her mother. It wasn't the clothes. It was the confidence.

As she tugged at her necklace with a rare feeling of excitement, Caroline's cell phone buzzed and danced across her desk. She pulled her calf-length boots over the jeans and hustled out of the dormitory without even checking to see whether it was indeed Amie's signal. She didn't get many calls or texts or

Facebook requests. To others, she seemed untouchable. To her, she was eternally tarnished and bruised.

"You're coming?!" Amie questioned dramatically as Caroline opened the passenger door of her teammate's car.

"You drive a mean bargain," said the old soul of a girl. "What's your major, anyway? I feel like we don't get enough opportunity to talk much in practice."

"Ah, I'm undecided," said Amie, a striking sophomore with glasses that perfectly matched the color of her dark hair. "I just want to live in the moment now, you know?"

As the unlikely pair traveled to the party, Caroline felt troubled over how they'd return. She had never ventured out before with Amie—or really anyone at Boston—yet she predicted the lively girl would be drinking. Caroline knew she wouldn't let herself make the same fateful mistake as her mother. She tugged at her necklace in an attempt to lessen her worries, while Amie lit a cigarette, turned up the radio, and screamed along to the popular Black Eyed Peas. Amie's energy was contagious. Caroline stifled a cough from the secondhand smoke and joined her in the chorus with a bobbing head and a smile.

The music helped Caroline loosen up a bit, but before she could feel completely ready, the girls found themselves entering a crowded apartment. Classic rock blared and chatter descended to whispers as Caroline intrigued all the partiers. The turning heads and lack of space began suffocating her. The football players appeared twice the size as they did on the field. And then there were the girls filling in the cracks around the athletes in matching furry boots, leggings, fleece jackets, and bra strap headbands. Caroline felt different. She wanted to be back at her dormitory, hidden under the comfort of her bed covers.

Amie, on the other hand, soaked in every second of their attention.

"The party can begin, everyone!" she shouted.

"Let's get a drink," both girls said to each other for different reasons.

For Caroline, one beer led to another and another and another, and before she knew it, Amie had gone to get them a fifth round, leaving Caroline alone to lean on her more effective crutch—dancing. As though on cue, Jane's Addiction's "Classic Girl" began to play. The girl with the classic name and the unwanted past closed her eyes in a way that only she could coolly pull off and got lost in the movement. Others' eyes once again fixed on her. She didn't notice them. She didn't notice the smell of spilled beer at her feet or the stickiness under her favorite boots. More than the alcohol, dancing helped her forget about her uncomfortable surroundings. It even made her forget her troubles. She heard only the guitar and the lyrics until Amie shook her out of her trance by digging a pair of fingernails into her forearm.

"Ouch. Um, Amie? Hi?"

"He's looking at you," Amie said without letting go.

Caroline laughed and resisted looking around. She was just starting to enjoy the party.

"Who?"

"Obviously, I could only be talking about one person."

"Who?"

"You're joking, right?"

Caroline shook her head.

"You're serious! You don't know?" Amie said before adjusting her glasses and moving her lips as little as possible. "It's Devin Madison. Devin's looking at you."

Caroline laughed again. Her new friend looked like a bad ventriloquist.

"What does he look like?"

"Oh, come on!" Amie said with growing exasperation. "You are telling me that a girl on the sidelines of every game so far this year doesn't know by now what the team's star quarterback looks like? Every human being in the city of Boston, no, Suffolk County, no, the Commonwealth of Massachusetts, knows what Devin Madison looks like. The whole country will know once we make it to a major bowl game. The guy will be in the running for the Heisman, for crying out loud."

The status of others wasn't something that intrigued Caroline, even though she was constantly wishing she could change her own identity.

"I'm not kidding," Caroline said with a grin. "If he had his jersey on with the big number four then I would know, but when do I ever see him off the field? Oh, come on, Amie. Let's. Just. Dance!"

"Fine, but before you decide to ignore the most gorgeous specimen on the planet, maybe you should at least see what you're missing. Check four o'clock."

Caroline finally looked, and sure enough, there was a guy—an extraordinarily handsome guy—staring at her. She let a smile escape her sweet face, not knowing that for the second time in one night, someone would attempt to sink fangs into her.

CHAPTER 16

DEVIN
The Gifted One

"So what all went down last night with the hottie?"

Devin and his go-to receiver had begun practicing five- and ten-yard out routes in case they found themselves in need of quick yardage and an opportunity to get out of bounds to stop the clock during either of their remaining games of a so-far perfect season.

"Which hottie?" the quarterback asked even though his smile revealed that he knew precisely which girl his teammate was referencing.

The receiver planted his foot to fake right before quickly running left and catching the ball easily. Instead of tossing it back to Devin to start the drill over, the receiver walked it in so he could have another word.

"Fine, I'll humor you, Dev. I'm talking about the freshman cheerleader who we all seem pretty dang invisible to—even you, man. Until last night."

In an effort to sidestep wrath from the offensive coordinator who was overseeing practice, the receiver quickly handed the ball back to the golden boy before positioning himself to start the play over again.

Devin, however, had a different idea.

"Coach," he called to the offensive coordinator. "Can we take just a five-minute water break to talk over our timing?"

The excuse made little sense, as their timing was nearly perfect, but Devin was able to get away with far more than anyone else on the team. Devin asking for five minutes in this particular stadium was like Bono asking the stage crew of U2 for permission to take a bathroom break. Devin Madison had single-handedly led the team to an undefeated season so far, with more than three thousand passing yards already behind him. With only two games left in the regular season against teams Devin already had a significant hand in beating, a trip to the Orange Bowl— Devin's family's dream bowl—was in his sights.

Taking a break from it all to talk about a girl during practice seemed irresponsible, but Caroline wasn't just any girl, and doing whatever Devin wanted whenever he wanted was a perk to which the quarterback had grown accustomed.

Devin took a seat on the sideline and used a fresh, plush towel to dab the sweat from his face. His teammates were familiar with his quirky and pompous ways. But when they took the field, there wasn't a Falcon on the University of Boston team who wanted another quarterback at the helm. When a play didn't work straightaway, Devin scrambled to make yardage out of nothing. He had the guts to run for the first down if no one was open. To his coaches' dismay, he ran with his shoulders driving forward instead of sliding safely to the ground. If his defense failed during an opposition's drive, he'd change the momentum quickly on offense. His passes were precise. He never threw them too high, keeping his receivers as safe as possible. Most importantly, Devin won games.

"What can I say, the girl found me irresistible," Devin said.

For the first time in his college career, a girl intrigued him. Thinking about her made him happy. Reliving the previous night's events made him feel uncomfortably sensitive and vulnerable.

Devin didn't realize that evening—or even on this day later—that it wasn't his football hero status that got her. It was his smile that had disarmed her. When he wanted to be, Devin was irresistibly charming. The quarterback found himself wanting to replay every moment they had together that evening.

⟫⟫⟫— ⟪⟪⟪

"Let me introduce you to my future girlfriend," Devin had said about Caroline to anyone in his vicinity at the party, even when it was only five minutes from the moment the pair had first locked eyes. It was a line that his teammates heard him say at every social event or bar outing to any beautiful girl, but his buddies always played along as though they were hearing it for the first time. They were his wingmen on and off the field.

"Gimme a break," Caroline had said a number of times in weak protest, but her rosy cheeks gave away her pleasure. The color had given Devin the green light he needed to press harder.

"So how does it feel to be suddenly dating the most popular guy on campus," he had teased above the party music and chatter.

"You haven't even told me your name and you are introducing yourself instead as the most popular guy on campus and now my boyfriend?" Caroline never went out of her way to be in a relationship. It was a quality that earned her the label of "player" on the campus despite others' lack of facts to substantiate that classification.

"Stop laughing," she had continued with a grin. "What? You don't believe me?"

"Huh?"

"Ask Amie," Caroline teased. "She told me you were here tonight, and I had to do a little research to find out which one you were."

"Huh?"

Devin had looked at her with serious eyes. He wasn't offended by the comment—he had barely even registered it. Caroline's perfect freckles were distracting him. Her skin was an unusual color he'd never seen. He'd never laid eyes on anyone like her, and he'd seen many girls. Without thinking, he had grabbed a strand of her hair with his soon-to-be million-dollar fingers and tucked it gently behind her ear.

"Are we going to get married?" he had asked.

"What?"

A drunken girl who longed to be part of a sorority, even though the University of Boston didn't offer Greek life, had approached in the midst of Devin and Caroline's conversation. Instead of Delta Delta Delta, Alpha Phi, or Kappa Kappa Gamma, the young lady belonged to a growing sisterhood of DMA, Devin Madison Admirers. It was an unofficial group whose members, as Caroline would soon find, infiltrated every classroom, dormitory, dining hall, off-campus party, and bar scene. Even Caroline's roommate was part of the contingent of young ladies, whose quiet crushes came to life after a few drinks, a Devin sighting on campus, or dining hall chatter.

The stranger, whose beer had given her courage, pressed her lips together to better spread her gloss. She shifted her silky chestnut hair so it hung over the front of one shoulder. She cut in front of Caroline and drunkenly clasped her hands around Devin's neck. Caroline had immediately touched the clasp of her own necklace and scanned the apartment for Amie in hopes of a swift exit.

"Don't leave me!" Devin had shouted over what felt like a sudden 120-pound addition to his body. He gently removed himself from the stranger as though the act were as everyday as brushing his golden hair, and pulled himself within a few inches of Caroline.

Over the course of the night, a few other girls had made their plays on the quarterback. Under normal circumstances, it would've been enough for Caroline to stay away, but despite her good sense and caution, she couldn't help flirting back. She wondered if this was what falling in love felt like. She knew she never felt anything like it before.

"You know, I would offer you, my new girlfriend, tickets to sit in the players' reserved section for family and friends at the next game," Devin had said.

"But, as a cheerleader and an athlete myself, I already have the best seat in the house," Caroline had countered. She was used to guys' lines. She was used to handling them too. She just wasn't used to falling for them.

"As I was saying," Devin had continued, "you pose a challenge for me. Instead of offering you tickets, I'm going to dedicate my next game to you. And with the bowl games approaching, this next one's a big one."

"You are such a weirdo," Caroline had said, yet she smiled more than ever.

"So where do you live?" he had asked. "Can we hang out tonight?"

"I'm not that kind of girl."

"I just want to watch a movie," Devin had argued. "It's 110 percent innocent."

Caroline winced. She had a longstanding personal commitment of not trusting people who claimed anything was more than 100 percent. The girl, whose past made her cautious, also tended to feel leery of people who used the phrase "to be honest with you."

"I've got class tomorrow," she had said. "I really should get going."

"I've got a class tomorrow too, to be honest with you," Devin had countered. "I haven't gone all semester, and look how I turned out. Look at all these people out and about on a school night. You're fine to stay out late just once. Especially on the night you meet the love of your life. Just one movie."

Caroline had laughed again. Devin's charisma challenged her conservative ways. She wanted the night so badly to continue with him, but she quickly and emphatically decided to hold true to her rule of never going home on a first encounter with an unfamiliar guy—golden boy or no golden boy.

She spotted Amie near the keg and knew the girl was in no condition to drive.

"I'm here with a friend, and we've got to get going anyway. Before the T stops."

Caroline never cared that her comments sounded unpopular. And even though she didn't intend for the sayings to work to her advantage, they made her stand out to Devin and the long line of guys who had made their own plays for her over the years. They revealed her sweetness.

Caroline motioned for rescue by Amie, who had been watching their conversations jealously all night.

In his final seconds alone with Caroline, Devin had decided to throw one last Hail Mary.

"So, are we going to get married?"

"What?" she had asked, even though for the second time that night, she heard his proposal perfectly.

"Nothing," he said, finally resolving to drop his status of being undefeated with girls. "Hey, can I call you?"

Amie had finally joined them after weaving through the crowd with impaired balance. She held out her hand to Devin.

"It's Amie, emphasis on the ME," she had said. "I'm a big fan."

"And I'm a big fan of your friend here. Any friend of hers is a best friend of mine."

Amie beamed.

Devin winked at Caroline.

He is too smooth, Caroline had thought. He's dangerous.

"C'mon, Amie," she had said. "We'll pick up your car tomorrow. If we get a move on, we can catch the last train."

"I'm going to walk you to the tracks," Devin had said, revealing even to himself just how special Caroline must be to him. He never made the effort to open car doors or walk girls safely to their destinations. Until now, he had never felt the need.

Amie belched, which both caught her by surprise and mortified her. Caroline couldn't contain her laughter.

"So sorry to laugh, Amie. That was impressive, that's all."

In a world where young ladies put their best foot forward around him with spray-on tans, fake eyelashes, and expensive perfumes, Devin had looked at Caroline with added appreciation over her ability to find humor in her friend's crass behavior.

This one really is different, he had thought. She's dangerous.

The trio, all with a few too many drinks in them, walked toward the T—one stumbling, one sauntering, and one walking just fine despite the booze.

"So are you going to give me your number?"

Caroline had waited for Devin to retrieve a cell phone from his pocket. But the thought of being spotted by passersby as he plugged numbers in his phone next to a girl was a move that suddenly felt too desperate for him.

"I'm good with numbers," he had said instead while tapping his temple with his index finger.

Caroline had wondered if the comment meant he was good with math or remembering girls' digits. She sensed it was probably the latter, but gave hers to him anyway. His smile was a little too disarming, she thought. As they reached the outdoor platform, the frigid air of early December sobered them all just a little. Their lungs felt frozen in place. Devin wondered if it had been this cold on the morning of his father's failed bowl game, the Chicken Soup Comeback. In a brief moment of sobriety, he wondered if he had what it took to pull his team to a better outcome.

Amie lowered herself unsteadily onto the bumpy, yellow painted line to fend off an impending wave of nausea. Belching in front of the star quarterback was enough, Amie thought to herself. She was determined not to get sick in front of him too. Her mouth watered. Devin's did too, but for an entirely different reason. Bundled in a belted heavy coat that still managed to show off her figure, Caroline seemed to glow against the snowy cityscape.

"Can I get a kiss goodnight?" her suitor had asked.

"I thought I told you," Caroline said. "I'm not that type of—"

"Just one kiss."

For the first time that evening, Caroline had opted to break one of her steadfast rules.

Devin had happily sauntered back toward the party and plugged Caroline's number into his cell phone. In his long list of contacts, Caroline's number became sandwiched between those of girls named Carissa and Catolina. Back at the gathering, the golden boy had grown eager to find another, more temporary girl to appease him for the night. Despite giving his attention to someone else all evening, he would have no trouble.

〉〉〉〉- 〈〈〈〈

Devin's receiver exchanged anxious glances between his watch and the offensive coordinator's whereabouts.

"That's a good story, man," the receiver said. "I was hoping you'd get lucky at first, but after hearing that, she sounds different. As hard as it'll be for you, player, you gotta treat this one like a lady, my man."

A giant defensive tackle overheard the receiver's comment and puckered his lips before mocking them in the matching, popular classic by the Temptations.

"Hey, singin' wannabe," a defensive coach finally called out. "How about playing a little football? If you like singing and dancing so much, you can do a few extra rounds of karaoke drills."

The defensive tackle hung his head before stepping on the field without further protest. The three-hundred-pound player began working his feet quickly in grapevine fashion. His upper body twisted right and left with each movement.

Devin and his receiver shared a laugh before heading back, unscathed, to their own work.

CHAPTER 17

JP
The Destined One

J P sat patiently and quietly inside the office of Syracuse College's head football coach.

"Damn, when it rains it friggin' pours," Coach Flash barked into his office phone to an obvious bearer of bad news.

Unable to help eavesdropping, JP glanced quickly at his coach with a look of surprise that the backup to a backup to a backup running back was unable to hide. Coach Flash's demeanor on most days was remarkably calm, especially for a man carrying the weight of players, assistant coaches, a chancellor, an athletic director, media, faculty, students, fans, and critics alike—all on some overworked shoulders.

Whenever JP observed other coaches lose control on the opposing sidelines or in SportsCenter highlights from post-game press conferences, he appreciated the strong line of leaders that had guided him to the unlikeliest of spots on a D1 team. Coach Flash was perhaps the one he respected most out of the esteemed group.

Something was off today.

"We were on a roll," Flash whispered through the phone with a bow of his head. "We were on one hell of a roll."

Flash had taken leadership of the team following a rare decade in SC football history when the Orange and Navy had faced disappointing defeat after disappointing defeat, losing more than twice as many games than the decade before it. There was a lot of pressure to turn things around. There were a lot of ideas on how to do it. When Flash had assumed leadership, there were a lot of complaints about having someone with a funny, unfamiliar name and without D1 coaching experience call the shots.

Flash had taken the rough first few years at the job with a clumsy grace, tiptoeing through fans following some inevitable losses. He had resisted boasting this season when, finally, the record had turned drastically around for the team. Even the harshest sports critics had been impressed by his effectiveness in piecing a competitive team together again in the campus arena. A few months into the season, Flash's Orange and Navy were undefeated in conference games and had lost only one match in overtime to the better-ranked West Virginia Mountaineers. The coach believed the team's success this season was due to a solid defense and offense behind two superstar players: a defensive end named Whistler who had the most sacks this season and a go-to running back inevitably heading to the NFL.

For the first time during his telephone conversation, Flash observed JP fidgeting in the office. The sight of the hardworking practice dummy lifted Flash's spirits just enough for the coach to resist another outburst.

JP's small size was less than ideal, but Flash had been pleasantly surprised during the first several weeks of practice over JP's speed. In addition to having one of the fastest sprints on the team, JP had successfully used his small frame to his advantage. When he wasn't practicing in the fullback spot, he revealed his true talent at the running back position—his natural position. When he stood in the spot that supported him through the difficult elementary-, middle- and high-school years, he lit up. JP was harder to catch on the run as he slid through the defensive cracks. During a practice last week, Coach Flash had made himself a promise: if JP weren't fourth in line for the running back position, he'd consider giving him playing time. In the game of football, a lot can change in a week.

Flash's tired eyes broke away from JP as he wrapped up his call.

"Man, this is exactly why I've always said that you can never have enough running backs. It's a damn good thing my brother is smarter than I am. I have to say he was looking out for me when we created this year's team."

JP's heart soared.

"OK, my friend, thanks for the lovely news, but I've got to hang up 'cause a very important meeting is about to take place in my office," Flash said. "Talk to ya."

The coach moved a leathery palm to a sweaty forehead. The air seemed to carry a nervous charge amidst the aroma of the coach's cologne.

"So," Flash blared in his confident coaching voice. "Sorry to keep you waiting, JP. Trust me, the last thing I want to do these days is keep you from your training."

JP laughed nervously, not knowing how to respond to the man whose hands held his dream.

"So I called you in here to share news that others on the team aren't aware of just yet," the coach said.

Flash went on to explain that the team's backup running back ran into some trouble over the weekend in the young man's hometown.

"He basically lost his mind for a moment, giving up his chance at an education here. He also gave up his chance to play here. Maybe these weren't thoughts running through his knucklehead at the time, but this is not something I take lightly. What we can all learn from this is that sometimes we think we are invincible, when we are far from it. Anyway, I originally called you in here to offer you the backup running back position. I was going to tell you that you'll see some playing time as the backup for our superstar running back."

"You said *was*," JP said with a warm, calm smile even though his stomach felt like a cold, nauseating sea of nerves.

"But that call I just got changes everything," Flash said.

The stressed-out coach went on to explain that in addition to losing the backup, the team's star running back was injured.

"He's tried to hide it but he's got a pair of injured shoulders. A surgeon worked on him for five hours today trying to get the sockets back together with an anthroscope, or arthroscope? Damn, I don't know, I'm far from a doctor. But I am a football coach and I need you, more than anyone, to step up. I need you to start against Tennessee on Saturday."

JP's weight felt heavy in the chair. His aches from extra practices suddenly felt more real. His dream of seeing some playing time as a running back instantly felt like a dream he may not have been ready for after all.

"Huh?" he said. "So you're picking me, the fourth-string, never-to-see-the-light-of-day guy over your third one who is not only available to play, but also has some experience—some game time—under his belt? And what about some of the more talented guys in other positions? Aren't they more qualified than I am?"

It was the same argument the players, assistant coaches, a chancellor, an athletic director, media, faculty, students, fans, and critics alike were all going to make when they learned of Coach Flash's decision, especially at a time when their final regular season game against Tennessee would clinch a spot in a top bowl. Their combined pressure, though, wouldn't make Coach Flash second-guess his decision as much as the fear he saw in JP's eyes. The coach had witnessed guys twice JP's size slam him in practice. He watched the players bully and tease him for being different. He had seen JP greet his mother on staff bravely at practice in front of those same bullies. He had observed JP through plenty of intimidating moments, but today marked the first time the coach saw fear on JP's face. It worried him.

"Listen, JP," Flash said. "I know you came to us under special circumstances. I know my brother recommended you as a walk-on so you could attend school and practice with a D1 team. I know you are easily a hundred pounds lighter than many guys out there. I know you probably haven't felt like you belong. I am here to tell you that you do. If I knew during the recruiting process what I know now—your learning curve especially—I would've had you come play for us in a heartbeat. So, do you think you can do it?"

JP tried to find the words to assure his coach that he had picked the right young man, but he wasn't convinced it was the truth. Always a team player, he ultimately wanted what was best for the Orange and Navy over what was best for himself.

"I don't know," JP said. "I mean, I know it's what I've always wanted, but the team has been doing so well. God, I just don't want you to lose a great bowl game spot because of me."

"In football and in life, it sometimes takes a challenge to show greatness. Look at Tom Brady—damn Patriots, I'll be a Bills fan 'til I die. Anyway, the lucky dude wasn't drafted until the sixth round of the NFL picks. He was a backup just like you. Maybe not the fourth backup, but he was on the sidelines just the same. That was until Drew Bledsoe got injured. Brady went on to be the youngest quarterback to win a Super Bowl. I don't care if you are the youngest, the smallest, the oldest, or the biggest. All you need is the guts and the drive to pull through."

"Well, I've definitely had the guts and the drive all along," JP said truthfully.

"It's settled then," Flash said. "Actually, there is one piece of business left."

Flash hit the speaker button on his office phone and began dialing. The person on the other end answered without so much as a "hello."

"Don't you have better things to do than call me, your measly high-school coach of a brother, at a time in your life when you are finally in the hunt for a major bowl game?" Crash joked.

Flash looked across his desk at JP, who wore a smile the size of the ones he showed off in the grade-school pictures that were still perched on his mother's desk.

"Go ahead, you tell him," Flash whispered.

"Hi, Coach," JP said in a voice loud enough to travel clearly through the speaker.

"Yes," the twins responded, one in jest.

"JP," Crash shouted back through the phone. "I hope my brother isn't beating you up too much over there. How the heck are ya?"

"Coach Crash, I'm starting on Saturday for Syracuse College."

Crash's tone became serious.

"Well, I'll be damned," he whispered.

"You were right, bro. It always kills me to say it, but you were right. We need this little guy."

"Well, I'll be damned," Crash said again, as though the comment were meant only for him.

"We heard that," Flash said. "Anyway, we've had to pull two running backs off our roster at virtually the same time, Crash. And why, JP, do I have a feeling you've had some greater power looking out for you your whole life?"

The words gave JP more nervous chills. The man knew only the football side of his life, yet his comment accurately summed up the rest of it too. JP wondered what the biological mother whom he had never met would think of him in this moment. He wondered too what the only mother he'd ever known would say. He felt grateful that the professor he called Mom was that greater power who had given him this life of good fortune.

"Well, Coach Flash, you definitely picked the right guy, then," JP said. "You're about to need all the luck you can get."

The twin coaches roared with nerve-filled laughter as all parties felt great truth in JP's joke.

In what should have been another momentous, celebratory dinner that evening at the round wooden table in their central New York home, JP and his parents sat quietly as they went through the motions of eating baked ziti with garlic bread. Even the roly-poly professor had an unusually difficult time getting one of his favorite meals to go down. The smell of the spicy gravy made them all a bit queasy on this particular night.

The news of Coach Flash's decision to have JP start against Tennessee had spread quickly through car radios, water-cooler talk outside campus offices, and student chatter in dining halls. Many called Coach Flash crazy. JP's teammates went from seeing him as an admirable member of the team who practiced with great heart to the one who was singlehandedly going to cost them an appearance in a prestigious bowl game. Even Whistler found himself a bit short-tempered toward his roommate as dreams of leading the defense with a star running back on offense fizzled.

Earlier in the day, the professors themselves had begun feeling unpopular. They had lived their lives in a sea of Syracuse College fans who all of a sudden seemed to know of their son. But the professors didn't care about their students' and colleagues' thoughts. They were worried, however, about what would happen to their son if he didn't play well. Despite being his biggest fans, they didn't think he had the experience or the size to pull it off.

As JP pushed the ziti around with his fork and let a cold gulp of ice-water settle in his uneasy stomach, the chill reminded him of a moment in his junior varsity high-school career when he had agreed to help manage the varsity team to learn as much as he could from the seniors. With the upperclassmen seated on a flight of steps within the school, their coach had gone over some start-of-the-season housekeeping items ranging from sizing up uniforms to doctors' slips for physicals. In addition, he had introduced a tiny JP on the steps as the team's manager. One of the seniors had immediately raised his hand.

"What, exactly, are the duties of the manager?"

The senior player had spoken as though JP weren't there on the steps with them. The coach had ignored the question. JP had not. He wished on those cold stairs that he hadn't accepted the extra responsibility. It was not so different than how he felt in this moment, a few years later.

JP forced the painful memory to the back of his mind and finally broke the silence at the family table.

"Well, Mom and Dad, I'm used to the role of underdog. I'm used to proving people wrong. Everything is going to work out, you'll see."

The professors looked at each other.

"Win or lose, you are absolutely perfect," JP's mother said, while managing to wink at her son.

In what would kick off another unexpected turn of events on this already eventful day, the phone rang.

CHAPTER 18

MAXINE
The Lonely One

It was a sleepy Wednesday, Maxine's day off before her weekend coverage of Syracuse College football games. Even though the photographer still disliked clichés, she classified this day as her calm before the storm. Maxine was just about as relaxed as she ever got. Her press pass was tucked away in the silk lining of a coat pocket. Her cameras and lenses were placed carefully in their cases. Her photo editing in her home office was paused. Her family and friends were carrying out their nine-to-five jobs, preventing them from pestering her about working less and dating more.

Maxine sat on a cozy window bench cushion, the warmest spot in her stark apartment. The sun made her signature short, dark hair sparkle. It also warmed her skin and released a lavender scent left over from a long, lazy bath that morning. The rays rested softly across the delicate features of her face and petite body. If she had company, someone would've wanted to take her picture.

With most other residents within her building at work, Maxine's apartment felt peaceful. There was a growing hum from a red Le Creuset teakettle in a kitchenette that saw little cooking.

From the comfort of her window bench, she was captivated by Sebastian Junger's *The Perfect Storm* and wishing the six fishermen of the *Andrea Gale* would miraculously make it out of a convergence of two storms and a hurricane despite having already read the ending exactly six times before.

The title of the famous book was also an expression often used in Maxine's newsroom to describe a far less traumatic—but still stressful—phenomenon as big news broke at once. In the newsroom, it was common for a calm afternoon to turn into one filled with chaos as notifications flowed in about five-alarm fires, city layoffs, police chases or many times all of the above, all at once. It didn't matter in the newsroom if it was a staffer's day off, someone's kid's first violin recital, or even Christmas morning. The news didn't wait.

Maxine's teakettle whistled like a siren of a fishing boat in trouble. Her heart beat more quickly until she placed herself at home on her day off. As she poured the steamy water into her favorite Syracuse College football mug, her cell phone came to life and her heart quickened its pace again. She cringed at the site of an incoming number revealing the caller as someone from her office at Syracuse's International Presswire Bureau.

"Hello, this is Maxine," she answered calmly, despite feeling as though she awoke to the realization that her alarm clock failed.

"Max, where are you? Why aren't you in the office?"

Maxine's heart thumped harder still within her chest as she recognized the panicked tone of her photo editor, a mother of three and a successful work-around-the-clock manager who was constantly busy and tardy.

"Oh, you told me to take a day off because there's a big weekend of coverage coming up. But that doesn't matter, what's happening?"

"You're going to need to come in straightaway."

Maxine already had her most comfortable pair of yoga pants stripped off. She searched for a pair of work pants and shoes in her closet as she worked at keeping her tone steady.

"What's up?"

"With SC football finally out of the toilet and in the running for a real bowl game, guess who they just lost on the roster?"

"No way, their running back," Maxine guessed correctly.

She was fully dressed now, smoothing her hair and making her way to the bathroom mirror. Maxine knew Syracuse's star running back was the only team member who would cause a fire drill in the newsroom. He was the star of the offense. Without him, Maxine believed the Orange and Navy were in trouble.

"His shoulders are gone, so he's out," the photo editor explained quickly. "Simultaneously, they lost their backup to drama. The sports writers are going nuts trying to make late deadlines for the dailies with multiple stories."

"Do we know who's going to start?" Maxine asked. She hoped that the replacement was someone who was represented well in her stock of photos. Maxine's mind still operated a few steps ahead of her colleagues, just as it had at her former newspaper an hour north.

"So that's the biggest angle we're working on right now," the photo editor said. "The starter is going to be some no-name little guy named JP. There's big buzz in the newsroom about it. What've you got on file for him?"

Maxine's heart pounded even quicker as she explained to her editor that the young man hadn't seen any game time.

"And practices have been closed, so unfortunately I have nothing," she added. "I'm going to try and reach him now and set something up immediately."

"Well, exactly, but before you get started, we've got to dial in with headquarters in New York City. They're all over this too. They predict our wire coverage has great potential to be picked up in key markets with universities across the country. They want to make sure it's handled just right."

Maxine rolled her eyes, a move she would've contained if she weren't blocks away from the office. She hated conference calls. She hated wasting time talking in circles as colleagues tried to one-up each other. She especially disliked them when time was so sparse.

"I can be there in fifteen minutes if I book it over. Would you like me to dial in?" Maxine offered, despite hoping she'd be able to skip the talk and get straight to work.

"Yes, I need you to, Max. I'm running five minutes or so late. I've already let New York know you'll cover me for the first few minutes. Dial in from my office so it's ready when I walk in. You'll need to get here quickly. The call's going to start in ten minutes. Just make sure to tell them your plan for getting photos."

Maxine's directors never worried about her accomplishing the impossible because she always managed to surpass their expectations. As she locked her apartment door, she left her hot tea untouched on the countertop, yoga pants in a warm heap on the floor, and thoughts of a relaxing day away from the newsroom far gone.

She ran. She didn't care about the strange looks she got from people spilling onto the sidewalks as she raced in her kitten-heeled work shoes. It was 5:15 p.m. and workers were filling the streets of Armory Square, which on Wednesdays attracted young work groups of singles with office crushes on each other. With her camera bag slung around her back, Maxine reached for her cell to dial 411 so she wouldn't have to break pace. A monotone recording that rarely worked for Maxine greeted her.

"What. City. And. State. Please."

"Syracuse, New York."

"Please. Say. The. Name. Of. The. Business. Or. Say. Residence."

"Residence."

"Please. Say. The. Name. Of. The. Listing. Again."

"Residence!"

"Transferring. To. An. Operator."

"City and State, please?"

"Syracuse, New York."

"Is this a business or residence?"

"Residence."

"What's the listing?"

"The last name is Hemmings. The first name is JP, so it may be under JP Hemmings. It may also be under a name whose initials are JP—like John Pete. Please give any 'J' name with Hemmings."

"Thank you. One moment, please."

Maxine glanced at her watch and hoped she'd catch a break.

"I'm not showing a listing in Syracuse with the last name Hemmings. I do see a Mr. and Mrs. Harvey and Regina Hemmings in Jamesville."

Maxine recalled an assignment before the first game of the season, when she had waited for the team's best defensive player, Whistler, to emerge from practice. She had been determined to get some shots of him to complement the wire's pre-game coverage of the team. She was beginning to realize just how closely the new coach was protecting his players from all distractions, especially the media. She respected Flash for it, even though it made her job that much more challenging. On that autumn morning, she had stood for fifty minutes in the sun over steaming pavement at the practice facility until finally, she saw exhausted players emerge from the building.

Whistler had been among the first to appear, but a woman in her fifties had stopped him quickly. She unfashionably stood out with skin that had appeared to see no sun over the summer and glasses that covered half of her face. The woman looked kind.

"Whistler," the woman had called.

"Lovely afternoon, professor."

"It depends," the professor had announced with a smile finally beginning to break its way through locked lips. "It depends on how well you're treating my boy these days. Hopefully better than his first introduction with you?" She warmly held out her arms for a hug, and Whistler quickly and awkwardly accepted it.

"I'm lucky to have him as my roomie, professor. You raised one hell—heck— of a boy. I've never met anyone like him. He's cool shi-."

"Cool stuff," the professor had interrupted. "Very well, then. You'd better go home to your studies. You didn't hear it from me, but we're having a pop quiz tomorrow on this week's notes."

"Seriously?"

"Do I look serious?" she had asked, with her face back to its coldest form.

With a camera around her neck, Maxine had listened patiently to every word of their conversation. When she had seen her opportunity to finally move in, she reminded herself that her most successful attempts at earning the trust of players and coaches were when she avoided coddling them like everyone else on campus seemed to do.

"Do you bring your mother to all your practices, Whistler?" Maxine had asked with a warm grin.

"Who, Professor Regina Hemmings? Believe it or not, she's that little guy's mom," he had said.

Whistler had pointed to the small but handsome boy with skin the color of Maxine's favorite tea. He looked like he could be in high school instead of college.

>>>- -<<<

At the other end of the season, on the streets of Armory Square, Maxine pieced it all together as she raced toward the office with the operator still on the line.

"Yes, please, I'll take that number."

Within seconds, Maxine found herself on the phone with Professor Regina Hemmings. She knew she'd have to get to the point quickly and string her sentences together before the woman had opportunity to cut her off in protection of her son.

"Good evening, professor. I'm so sorry if I'm interrupting you. My name is Maxine and I work for the International Presswire. First, let me congratulate you on JP's wonderful news. I can only imagine the calls that have been flooding into the household. I take the SC football sports shots for the wire. I know this is short notice, but I would like to come take some shots of JP, with his permission. Do you know how I might reach him?"

"Well, he's here, but I don't know that this is a good idea. It's been a long day."

Maxine took in a hopeful breath.

"I know. I can share with you that from my experience, it's usually more helpful to stay ahead of the story than chase behind and react to the coverage. I can also predict that you will have a flood of reporters and photographers wanting the same things I'm calling about. If you let me take some pictures, you can refer other outlets to my shots for the wire. They all subscribe to our service. I don't mean to pressure you on a stressful day, but in the nature of the news, time is of the essence to get images for tomorrow's papers. It's up to you guys really, but it's my job to at least ask."

"I appreciate your candor. You've certainly given me something to think about, and I will certainly pass it along to JP." The professor went on to explain that her son was eating dinner and that she would give him Maxine's number to call him back. "Either way he decided to go," she added.

"Thank you so much, professor. Congratulations again to your family, and I'm sorry to have interrupted your dinner."

Maxine gave the woman her contact information as she swiped her key card inside her office building and ran to her editor's office. She had exactly four minutes to start the call with New York City headquarters. As though it were an everyday routine, she placed her editor's phone on speaker, punched in the numbers, put the phone on mute, and made her way to the other side of the desk in anticipation of her editor's arrival. The call wouldn't start for another three minutes. She hoped she had at least one to catch her breath. Over the speaker, she heard three distinct beeps.

"Dang it," Maxine mouthed silently to herself. Three beeps signaling three people, including her, already on. *I never know when to speak up on these things,* she thought.

"Hello! Who's on, please?"

"Shoot," Maxine mouthed again as she reached over her boss's desk to punch off the mute button and announce her attendance. The voice bellowing through the speaker belonged to the sports editor at the International Presswire's headquarters in New York. Maxine rarely had opportunities to speak with him because she usually worked through his assistant, Rhoda.

"Sports writers are all on in Syracuse, sir."

Before Maxine had a chance to tell the sports editor she was on to represent the photography department, he shouted his reply.

"Good! Rhoda, are we having anyone else on?"

Maxine could hear Rhoda speaking more quietly to him within their room. Her tone sounded much sweeter than the one the woman used whenever Maxine called.

"Syracuse photo is also coming on, sir."

Rhoda went on to explain how their photo editor was on another commitment and dialing in a few minutes late. "So sports photographer Maxine is going to cover for her in the meantime."

"Just as well," he bellowed through the speaker. "Maxine will do a great job and relay whatever I need. Folks, I'm going to step away from my desk for just a second, and then we'll start the call. Hold tight."

Maxine sat a little straighter and felt as prepared as she could.

"OK, everyone," Rhoda said. "He's coming 'round the corner. Maxine, are you finally on?"

"I'm here, Rhoda," Maxine said, rolling her eyes rebelliously in her boss's office.

"OK, sir, all are here!"

"Fine. So I guess I don't have to stress how sexy this Cinderella story is to you folks. But I do want you to keep in mind as you write, that this story and its sidebars aren't limited to Syracuse. We have other markets—the big college football cities—that will be interested too. Play up this boy's small size, his lack of experience, and his drive that got him to where he is. Play up the unlikely turn of events that gave him the opportunity. Play up the fact that Syracuse was finally turning things around for a shot at a major bowl game, and then this. This poor young man is carrying the weight of a university, a city, and a region on his little shoulders. Have we gotten in touch with him, by the way?"

Maxine's colleagues from the reporting side of the office next door jumped in immediately.

"No, sir, but we're trying. Coach Flash's staff is really doing their best to keep him away from us. We have people contacting their sources on the team to find out where he lives on campus so we can send someone over and wait there until we have success."

"Jeesh," Maxine mouthed again. Making her colleagues look bad was the last thing she wanted. Fortunately for the photographer, they knew that about her.

"I trust you guys are interviewing experts to help put this in perspective in the meantime?"

"Yes, sir."

"Good, well, I don't have to tell you that we need to work harder at getting in touch with JP himself."

"OK, Maxine! Where are we with photos? Do we have stuff on file for this kid?"

"Sir, practices have been closed, and he hasn't played one second of a game. I just spoke with JP's mother, though. It turns out she's a professor at the school. He's having dinner right now at his family's home in Jamesville. She promised to have him call me once he's finished. I don't know yet if he's going to meet with me. His mother said it's been a long day. I did give her our line about the benefit of working with the wire versus a million newspaper, TV, and radio reporters." Maxine cringed and wondered if her colleagues in the next room had hit the mute button and begun cursing her name.

"Nice work, Maxine. But why in the heck aren't we coordinating with each other over there?"

"Sir, I hung up with his mother only seconds before I dialed in to our call. I have every intention of trying to hook him up with one of our reporters when he phones me back."

"Fine. Maxine, if you get a shot—and I know you will find a way to get a shot—I want you to get a still shot versus an action shot. I want to see this guy's face. I want to see the pressure. Better yet, why don't you take a few shots with the parents too? Readers are really going to be rooting for this guy. You need to pass this along to your boss. Is she on yet?"

"No, sir, but I expect her any second."

"Fine. I'm putting my faith in you, Maxine. Let's talk for a moment to the writers about the story angles we're working on."

Maxine pressed the mute button and let out a long breath of air. Her boss opened the door, as panicked as usual, with her boys in tow from daycare.

"Only a fee of fifteen extra dollars today for picking them up fifteen minutes late. Are we on mute?" she asked in a whisper.

"Yes."

"What'd I miss?"

"He's talking to the writers. He wanted me to pass along to you that he wants a still shot versus an action shot. I got in touch with JP's mother, and she's going to have him call me after their dinner."

"Boys," Maxine's director managed to shout in a whisper to her sons. "Not one word."

She pushed the mute button off.

"I'm on, sir," Maxine's photo director said. "Maxine got me up to speed."

"Fine. Then she told you what I want for a photo?"

"Yes, you want an action, not a still."

Maxine frantically tried motioning to her boss with both hands that it was the other way around.

"No," the voice bellowed. "Maxine must have misunderstood. I want a still, not an action. You all need to get to work. It sounds like you have a lot to accomplish in very little time. Time is ticking. Tick, tick, tick."

Maxine let her lower back, sore from her camera bag smacking her during the run from her apartment, slump in her chair.

Maxine hustled home through Armory Square nearly as quickly as she had on her way in. She forgot to bring a coat in her rush, and the lake-effect snow that began floating down was yet another kick in her pants during an exhausting, unpredictable, and stressful day. Buzzed officemates stumbled from bars and restaurants along the streets and reluctantly made their ways home to prepare for a new day. Maxine noted how most of them looked more sullen than they had a few hours earlier when they were just leaving their offices, but a few along her travels appeared to have found love—or at least lust—that night.

She reached for her apartment key and made her way into the lonely space. She immediately spotted the mug of tea on the counter and dumped it in the sink without a hint of frustration for the evening had been a success for the International Presswire. JP had called Maxine back, just as his mother promised he would.

⟫ ⟪

"Hello, this is Maxine," she had answered.

"Hi, Maxine. My mother said you called. She also passed along your congratulations—thank you."

"JP, this is a big day for you, and undoubtedly an emotional one at that. I can only imagine. I would like to take your picture—no football, no runs, just you in your parents' home, if that's convenient, with perhaps a couple shots with them too."

"My mom said you're with the wire, so you'll be able to get this to other publications, making it easier for me to decline their requests? I have a lot of other things I need to be concentrating on right now."

"That's right," Maxine had said, sensing a scared tone in his young voice. "You know, my bosses would absolutely kill me for even asking this, but have you spoken with your coach about the press? I know he's protective of you guys."

"I have, actually," JP said. "He's quick to take my calls these days."

The pair shared a laugh.

"I'm surprised you asked," he had continued. "I appreciate it. Coach Flash said it would make sense to do one thing with the wire if it meant less distraction for me later."

"That's wonderful," Maxine had said. "I have one more request. Can I bring one of our reporters with me? I can tell him we need to limit it to five minutes."

"I don't know if I'm ready for all that. I'm going to have to pass on a reporter."

"I understand. You know, sometimes people give a brief statement in times like this. If you gave one to us exclusively, I'm sure we'd be making my newsroom very happy, but it's up to you."

"You mean, I could just prepare a couple of sentences on your way over and that's that?" he had asked.

"That's right. People here would only be able to quote you on those words you prepare."

"I'd like to do that, actually," JP had said. "Huh. You've been very honest and helpful. I appreciate it. I *trust* you."

Maxine had hailed a cab to the professors' Jamesville home and phoned in her update. She let her boss share the good news with the sports writers, who would be happy on such a short deadline to get an exclusive comment. Maxine had also suggested that the woman pass along the progress to the bellowing New York City sports editor with a note that she'd get a good still shot.

"Can you wait here, mister?" Maxine had asked the cabbie in front of the Hemmings' home. "It'll be about twenty minutes, but I'm on deadline and need to head back to Syracuse shortly. Please keep your ticker running. I'll pay for you to stay."

Upon knocking on the Hemmings' homey evergreen door, Maxine was greeted by the professor whom she hadn't yet had the opportunity of meeting. He had opened his arms for a big hug regardless. Maxine had squeezed him back.

"You must be the proud father," Maxine said even though the man seemed to share no resemblance with JP.

"Why, yes," he answered. "Please come in."

Maxine saw in that moment that the Hemmings' three faces shared the same look. They were excited and scared at the same time.

"JP," Maxine said. "I don't think I've ever had the pleasure of speaking with you in person." She held out her hand, and the boy gave it a surprisingly hard shake. "Thanks for doing this," she said. "I really think you'll be happy with your decision."

In reply, JP had handed her a single, folded piece of paper.

"Ah, your statement," Maxine had said. "May I?"

"Please."

I'm excited to play, and I'm looking forward to a win on Saturday with my teammates.

Maxine had smiled. The brief statement said nothing and everything all at once. Its tone might have come across as overly confident if it had come from any other player. But from a little guy burdened with the doubt of thousands of people, the statement was perfect. It would fit well into any of her colleagues' articles on why picking him was a risky choice.

Maxine had peered into his eyes and had seen the hungry look of a very successful, special person.

"I believe you will win that game, JP," she had said truthfully. She had hoped she could capture the eyes in her shot. She glanced around the snug home to find the right place to take it.

"I have the perfect place," JP had said, reading her thoughts. "Come on up to my shrine. My parents haven't changed a thing in my room since I left."

"Let's check it out. Parents, I'm going to need you too."

The four of them made their way upstairs into JP's room, a space that was filled with trophies and recognitions—from "Most Improved Player" certificates to "Most Valuable Player" awards. There was also JP's favorite, The First Annual JP Hemmings Award for Best Attitude. To: JP Hemmings.

"That one was from Coach Flash's twin, who happens to be named Coach Crash," JP had explained with a laugh. "He gave it to me last year at Jamesville-DeWitt High. It'll be interesting to see who gets the recognition this year."

Maxine had looked around in awe. She realized she was in the presence of a young man who enjoyed much support and even more success. She wasn't expecting it. Her readers wouldn't either, she thought.

"This is indeed the perfect spot," she had said.

To her delight, his eyes still radiated a powerful, hungry desire to succeed. She had snapped shot after shot. She glanced at her watch and spotted her cab driver waiting obediently through the very window JP had used as a boy to gaze up at the stars whenever he questioned his little place on earth.

"OK, if I could," Maxine said, "I would like to take a few of all three of you."

She was touched to see the parents' eyes sharing the same spark.

"I'm going to ask a question on the record that you don't have to answer," Maxine said. "I assume you both adopted JP into your family?"

"He is adopted. He's been with us since his birth. He's also our son."

"Of course, Mrs. Hemmings," Maxine said softly. "I'd like to thank you all for your time. I wish you the best of luck on Saturday, JP. So, as a member of the media, I'm not supposed to be partial, but between you and me, you'll have at least one photographer on the sidelines rooting for you."

"I have a feeling I could use the support."

Maxine made her way toward her cab and placed a hand on the frigid, snowy handle.

"Maxine, hold up!" one of the professors yelled. "So, like any good mother, I did a little research on you too."

She had offered Maxine a second folded piece of paper.

"This one's just for you, not the sports writers whose butts you're covering by letting JP's statement fall right into their laps," she said. "This one's for your caption, in case you need it."

Maxine unfolded the note and smiled appreciatively as she read it.

"This will come in very handy," Maxine said. "Thank you, Professor Hemmings."

"Very well, then. You see, I learned from my research that even though your captions are terribly long, papers usually pick them up word for word," the professor said with a wink.

Back at her lonely apartment that evening, Maxine brewed herself a fresh cup of tea.

"Let's try this again," she said aloud to herself.

In the last few frenzied hours, family members had deposited a couple new personal messages on her cell phone and asked whether she was working too much.

"Have you been on any dates lately?" asked one.

Maxine obediently opened her laptop and checked her online dating profile. She saw a request for a date. The man in the picture looked a bit like George Clooney. He was youthful and handsome. He reported enjoying hikes, movies, and football. Maxine decided she'd give him a shot.

"This can wait though," she said.

She was relaxed now and was terribly hungry. In the chaos, she had forgotten to eat. Stress often covered up her hunger until deadlines passed. She set her oven to 425 degrees and removed a frozen pizza for one from the freezer. She clicked open the electronic photo of JP with his parents so she could review the evening's work. Even when time was too late to change as much as a comma, Maxine always looked over her photos and captions to see if there was something she could improve upon next time.

On this night, however, she would enjoy her dinner looking into the eyes of the Hemmings family and the familiar black-and-white type of her caption, which read:

JP Hemmings (center) is the smallest member of Syracuse College's football team and until Wednesday, one of the least publicized, yet he sits in the Jamesville room in which he grew up with walls covered in trophies, plaques and MVP awards. His adoptive parents, SC Professors Harvey (left) and Regina Hemmings (right), raised him from birth. On the day she discovered her son was expected to fill the shoes of the leading offensive player on the team, Regina Hemmings said, "I have never been prouder of my son. Fans can rest assured that he is the hardest-working person I know. He never gives up until he succeeds."

CHAPTER 19

CAROLINE
The Troubled One

C aroline forced her head out from the warmth of her comforter and was surprised to find that her clock showed 11:13 a.m. For the first time in her college career, she was going to miss a class without a coach's slip relaying her need to travel for a game.

As guilt hit and tightened her chest, she needed to look no further than the other side of the room to spot another skipper. Her roommate lay still asleep with a black mask strapped across her eyes. The bright light in the room instantly brought aches to Caroline's own.

"I can thank Devin for this," Caroline whispered, but not softly enough.

"Debin," her roommate mumbled in her sleep.

"Apparently, a man of many girls' dreams," Caroline quipped back, even though there was no one conscious to groan at her pun.

As Caroline sat up, the dehydration from the previous night's beer consumption delivered a sharp bolt of pain. Despite that, she grinned and thought of Devin's smile.

With two feet on the floor and her sleepy brain beginning to recall the night's events, Caroline gratefully remembered that she had the good sense to hit her dorm's laundry room after the football party. Despite buzzing from the booze and the encounter with Devin, Caroline had succeeded in washing, drying, and folding the outfit she had borrowed. The items were now back in the closet of her roommate, who was still dreaming of Caroline's new man.

"Debin," the girl said again.

Caroline shook her red bedhead and made her way to the girls' bathroom. She hoped the guilt from missing her psychology lecture would wash away as easily as removing her messy mascara.

Missing a class wasn't the only proof that Devin was already meddling with Caroline's typically wise head. When she had reached in her bag for coins during her midnight laundry session, she had come across the ad for the amateur night at the Gentlemen's Club downtown. The alcohol in her blood that evening had seemed to make everything seem so clear. If she landed some cash she wouldn't need to borrow her roommate's clothes, she had thought. She wouldn't have to take a pleather purse with her on a date with the most prestigious player in Bowl Championship Series football, if she ever had the chance. She might even be able to insist on paying her way.

She had sat atop a laundry folding table fingering the ad like she used to do with her pink childhood blanket made by her late mother and watched the clothes swirl around and around in the washing machine. The smell of dryer sheets brought her back to Rhode Island's Soap Opera Coin Laundry, the place where her mother had once worked in Cranston.

"Sometimes, when I'm really bored working in this place, I stare at the clothes flip-flopping about in the machines and dream about gettin' our family to a better spot," Caroline's mother had whispered to her girl a week before the woman's fatal car crash. "I think about winning the lottery and moving us all to California, where you and I could go to the beach every day—even the rainy ones—and Daddy could go to college. What I wouldn't do for a little more cash. I could get some help," Lindsay had continued, not realizing that her little red-haired daughter was old enough to understand the meaning of that.

A dozen years later, a more mature Caroline had smiled a pained smile in the dormitory's laundry room and spoke to the heavens while she looked down at her mother's locket clasped around her neck. The borrowed clothes went around and around in the machine.

"Excuse the poor choice of words, but things go full circle, huh, Mom?"

Caroline had made up her mind in that moment to check out the Gentlemen's Club after a good night's rest. As troubled as ever, she had searched for some sort of permission. Her mother was the one person in her life who couldn't protest. Caroline had also believed that her mother was someone—the only one—who watched all of her secrets unfold from above.

"I'm just going to go check it out," Caroline had said quietly. "I'll even go in daylight, Mom."

A sobering sleep later, Caroline now stood in front of her dorm's bathroom mirror, washing away the last spots of makeup and feeling less sure about the previous night's plan. She knew she would have to get moving if she were going to go through with the visit. She may be skipping her first class, but she refused to miss her cheerleading practice at 3:30 that afternoon.

"It's time," she said decisively, before sneaking out of the dorm and leaving a bit of innocence behind her.

It was technically still morning, yet the Gentlemen's Club in downtown Boston was dark. It reeked of a permanent party. The bulky front door was propped open to air out the combined stenches of sweat and booze.

Through the darkness, Caroline thought the venue could be worse. Always tough enough to search for the positive, she felt glad that the Commonwealth of Massachusetts had passed legislation to stop smoking in public places in 2004. She also tried convincing herself that the atmosphere would probably appear less dingy at night. Wrapped in an old comfy sweater and jeans with a few little rips from heavy wear, she tried to picture cash flying around the poorly lit room. She wondered if it would be worth the consequences.

Caroline glanced timidly about the club for an employee and rummaged in her purse for the ad. Tall, thin, and beautiful, she looked like a picture of all the other girls on nearby Newbury Street digging in their designer bags for their lipsticks or cell phones. She wondered if the paper listed hours when the place was open to the public. Seeing nothing and no one, Caroline began thinking this was the wrong decision after all. She stalled a few moments more, looking around to take in the stage and poles, foreign objects that she recognized only from the occasional R-rated movies.

She turned and headed for the door. Each high-heeled boot stuck to the floor, and with every sticky step, she whispered the words of a prayer. Making it only to "Our Father who art in heaven, hallowed be," she was interrupted by a large man dressed all in black with slick hair.

"I thought I heard someone," he said. "Can I help you, young lady?"

Despite his somewhat intimidating appearance, he had a warm voice and a kind smile. He held out his hand as if he were kicking off a job interview.

"Phil," he said as he offered her his hand.

She resisted offering her own name. He didn't press for it.

Caroline's boots squeaked on the grimy floor as she turned toward him. She shook his hand and forgot to finish her prayer. She was wrapped up in her own head, debating whether she should run for the door or tell the man she was interested in trying to win some much-needed money, just once, on amateur night.

Caroline's natural beauty immediately hit Phil, a man who worked among scores of what he called glamazons, complete with extended hair, fake nails, and surgically enhanced features. He had good instinct and even better street smarts. He knew a moneymaker when he saw one. Not waiting for the redhead to answer his question or let her get to the door, he made his move.

"We had a girl quit last week 'cause her new boyfriend didn't approve of the job," he offered. "She gave her notice right away. How old are you?" Phil was desperate to fill the spot. Things weren't going well financially at the club, leaving his family's financial future in crisis too.

"I'm eighteen," she answered.

"Well, the dancer we lost worked five nights a week, so we have some space to fill. Is that why you're here?"

"Oh, well, I'm a college student, and I also have to balance work-study, classes, homework, and cheerleading," Caroline said. "I need money badly, but I can't do five nights a week. I could probably do two. Two max."

The conservative girl couldn't believe the words were coming out of her own lips. She pressed them together and spread the inexpensive gloss that she had applied that morning. Caroline could easily have been a fresh-faced pharmacy chain spokesperson for using drugstore products to look gorgeous. A regular job at this kind of place had not even been an option until now. She had just heard herself offer the most private parts of herself and sadly thought of how disappointed her father would be. It was as if the daring, wild side of her that she had always managed to keep bottled up—her mother's side of her—could not be caged any longer. Caroline thought of her expenses. She thought of treating herself, for once, to something nice in a life of otherwise unbearable tragedy. She thought, too, of getting ready for dates with Devin.

Phil tried to hide his excitement over hearing the word "cheerleader."

A genuinely nice college cheerleader. This one really would attract more regulars, he thought to himself.

Phil scratched his head, as he often did whenever he felt torn between working a shady profession and being a good person. He had never imagined his life would take this turn during much sunnier days, when he had managed a Polynesian-style restaurant on California's Pacific Coast Highway in Malibu. He had surfed every morning and closed the restaurant each evening before bringing home filet mignon or mahi mahi to a loving wife who was inevitably up late feeding one of the three babies they had raised there. Life had been sweet for Phil, but he always had a feeling it wasn't going to last. Even then, he had good instinct. The place had closed in the 80s. With five mouths to feed, he had moved the family to his hometown of Medford, Massachusetts, where they had lived with his parents as he searched for a job. He had begun working at the Gentlemen's Club as a bouncer and gradually climbed his way up the management chain despite feeling more and more down.

With Caroline appearing almost from thin air today, interrupting some depressing number-crunching in his back office, Phil thought of his wife, who had stuck with him through all of his ups and downs. He would not let this establishment fail too. He stopped scratching.

"Two nights a week could work," Phil said. "Have you done this before?"

"No," Caroline admitted quietly. "But I've done about every other type of dance, and while I'm not exactly a person who likes to toot my own horn, I can assure you that dancing—any type of dancing—comes naturally to me."

Phil was certain now that this was not the typical girl who came in for auditions. He'd never heard one of the glamazons use the expression "toot my own horn" before.

"I have to ask," Phil said. "I'm not trying to discourage you, but you need to know that this is an emotional, tough, draining job, and no matter how good of a dancer you are, you have to deal with some, pardon me, crappy aspects. Many of our girls get around that by thinking of other things while they dance—their shopping lists, where they will take their kids on their days off, escaping this type of life, and so on. As a nice cheerleader student, you might have a more difficult time with turning yourself on and off to the emotions, with all due respect."

Caroline wanted to tell this big stranger, of all people, everything that she had kept inside for so long: the pain, the suffering, and the slew of traumatic events that she had managed to cope with on her own. Tearing away layers of herself seemed far better than a misguided second cousin doing it for her at an age when times were even more confusing. *I can do this*, she thought. She was a breath from letting someone finally understand her past, but quickly opted instead to give the kind man the abridged version of her story.

"I'm tougher than I look," she said.

Phil scratched his head again. He thought of another stunning girl a few months back whom he had hired on the spot without an audition. Her lack of coordination on stage had forced boos and drunken heckling from patrons on what had been her first and last night as an employee.

"OK, then," he said. "Well, I understand you're a cheerleader and must be a great performer and all, but I still have to ask you to audition. It's policy." His head was beginning to acquire white scratch marks against red, raw skin. "I'll sit back a few rows," he added. "Not that it will make you any more comfortable." Phil had a hard time looking Caroline in the eyes all of a sudden. "Can I get you anything?" he continued. "A glass of water? A shot to wash away the nerves?"

"Tequila, please," Caroline said with a calm, steady tone that surprised him.

Phil glanced at his watch.

"Aw hell, I think I need one too."

He walked behind the bar as the girl thought about what she had on beneath her street clothes—bike shorts and a sports bra. *More material than any of my bathing suits*, she thought to herself before leaving her dorm less than an hour before.

Caroline walked up to the bar to retrieve her shot, which was a healthy pour. She clinked Phil's glass, and the pair snapped their heads back in unison. Phil winced a bit. Caroline did not. For the second time in two days, a man found himself thinking that she was most definitely different from other girls.

"Fine, then," Phil said. "Any type of music in particular?"

"Some classic rock. Please."

Phil blared Eric Clapton's "Crossroads" loudly through the club's speakers in an attempt to make them both feel like they weren't alone in the club.

As the lyrics accurately summarized Caroline's feelings, the troubled one began losing herself in the dance just as she had learned to do so many years ago. And just as she was able to pull off her routines without having to think much about the choreography, she removed layers of herself without much thought or effort.

Phil, as he always did with auditions, kept his eyes on the dancer's eyes. He wanted to give the girls—and his wife at home—some kind of respect. He avoided letting his gaze stray to other parts of their bodies like his patrons inevitably would.

Caroline wasn't thinking about Phil's presence in the room. Her late mother's locket caught her eye as its diamonds matched a shiny pole that seemed to point toward the heavens. She moved closer to it with her right foot and placed her right hand on it. She intentionally fell forward and then pivoted back, finally linking the back of her other knee around it and spinning down backward. She thought of a fiery hell beneath the rickety floor. She lost more pieces of her innocence, little by little, until not much else was left but her mother's locket.

Phil had seen more than enough and stopped the music abruptly. Caroline snapped out of her zone, knowing she had done enough to get the job.

"OK, then," Phil said.

He scurried back to the bar to clean their shot glasses and find other ways to keep busy as she pieced herself back together.

"Well, you got the job," he said. "Any nights you'd like. I know you have a busy schedule."

The visit had been emotional yet much less painful than Caroline imagined it would be. Oddly enough, she found Phil to be a gentleman. She wondered what run of bad luck had led him to a place like this. And she wondered if the run had resembled any piece of her own.

"I'll need you to fill out some paperwork, and we'll have to talk about your first night and the policies here to protect you."

Caroline tugged at her locket. She wasn't sure what she was feeling. She wondered if it could be happiness and sadness tangled into one. As she filled out the forms, her hand shook. It was something that always happened to her after performances.

After shaking Phil's hand a final time, she walked out of the club's door and felt her phone buzzing in her bag. The caller belonged to a number she didn't recognize.

"Hello?"

"Miss Caroline," said a deep and confident voice. "It's Devin."

Caroline blushed at the thought of the place she was leaving.

"Oh, hey," she said. "What are you doing?" It was the type of cool, casual response she always heard her roommate say over the phone to guys she liked.

"Nothing, what are you doing?"

Caroline searched for anything to change the subject.

"So, anyway, no four-day rule?" she asked. She was used to guys trying to play games with her, including making her feel like she wasn't worthy of a call until days following a first encounter.

"Come on, Caroline, I don't know who you've been dating lately, but they clearly don't know how to treat a one-of-a-kind girl like you."

While other guys had to resort to the four-day rule to make them appear harder to get, the act always had the opposite effect on Caroline. Two suitors had tried it on her earlier in the semester, and neither got a first date for that reason alone. She had immediately chalked them up to being players. In reality, Devin was the most notorious of them all, but he never had to resort to any desperate measures to get a girl.

"So when can I pick you up?" he asked.

"Oh, here we go. For what?"

"Our first date. A momentous occasion. Our first of many."

"Oh, really! And which day will this be?"

"Tonight, of course. Let me try this again, Caroline. What time can I pick you up?"

Even when she was sober, there continued to be something about Devin that Caroline couldn't resist. He was persistent. She felt his smile grab her through the phone. Her stomach flopped and she felt sweat finally begin to ease from a face that had managed to remain cool even through her audition.

"I have cheerleading until five."

"Well, I have football practice until six. Look at us, Caroline. The all-American couple. And you are my classic girl," he teased, thinking of the moment he had first seen her dancing alone at the previous night's party.

If his tone were serious, it would've made her feel sick from the sweetness, but as many of his comments would be throughout the course of their relationship, she knew he was being sarcastic. In this rare instance, it worked for him.

"I'll pick you up for dinner at seven," he continued.

CHAPTER 20

HENRY
The Shy One

When Henry's grandmother picked him up from school, the boy didn't feel much like talking. He quietly settled into the family car and strapped the seatbelt across the unstylish green button-up shirt that had earned him the nickname of Polly Ester that morning.

"See ya, Polly," shouted a classmate who was waving wildly at Henry from the other side of his car window.

The glass muffled the noise enough to mute the words for the elder woman's aging ears. Henry felt grateful for that.

"What did that boy just say?" she asked.

"I don't know, Grandma. Can we please go home?"

"Of course."

When the pair made their way into their Brockton apartment, the air in the old building felt heavy and awkward. Henry went straight to his room without a word, as though he were being punished. For this eleven-year-old boy, punishment never came from his mother or grandmother, guardians who secretly dared to wish he would act up just once. His punishment didn't come from the father he didn't know. It always came from the kids at school.

Folded neatly on his bed were the clothes that had been much dirtier and more wrinkled that morning before school. They were washed, dried, and organized now with a note from his mother on top of Henry's favorite University of Boston sweatshirt.

> *H -*
> *I missed you today. Sorry I was late getting to our laundry. You should've woken me up to help you and Grandma this morning. I'll check in on you sleeping when I get back from the restaurant tonight. Looking forward to driving you to school tomorrow.*
> *xoxo,*
> *Mom*

Henry let the paper fall to the floor. He quickly unbuttoned his green shirt as though it were riddled with germs and tossed it into the empty laundry basket with a shiver in disgust.

"What's wrong, Henry?" his grandmother asked, peering through the doorway to his room.

"Nothing, Grandma. The tag was really bothering me or something."

"Or somethin'," she repeated quietly. "I'll give ya some privacy. I'm going to find a bit to munch on if you wanna join me. Maybe we could tell each othah about ah days. I know I had a doozy of a mornin' at the gas station. Can't wait to tell ya all about it."

Henry reached for his favorite sweatshirt and began covering up.

"Um, thanks. I might be out in a bit for a snack."

He sat down on his stiff bed. With his grandmother out of eyesight, he reached beneath his pillow for his secret writing pad and pen. Before unleashing the day's emotions on the paper and trying to make sense of them there instead of in the kitchen with his grandmother, the boy sat up to straighten his lucky shirt. He hoped it would still be presentable enough to wear again tomorrow, when he hoped to run into a bit of luck for once.

>>> ‹‹‹

Twenty miles north of Brockton, Henry's teacher was nearing the end of his daily commuter-to-green line trek home to Boston's Allston neighborhood. He looked around at the eclectic mix of young adults and students on the train and noticed that nearly every rider was texting, tweeting, or talking on cell phones. He had grown annoyed with the devices for their powerful abilities to lure people away from the present moment, make bullying easier, and decrease personal interactions. Teach's back smacked the seat as he resisted the urge to shout, "Wake up! Wake the heck up!"

As he sat silently and sourly in passive disapproval, his own phone buzzed within his front pocket. He felt as though it was mocking him, and worried that his highly anticipated date that night could be calling to cancel.

To Teach's relief, he quickly recognized the caller as one of his buddies, a guy who had recently landed a job as a student relations specialist at University of Boston thanks to Teach's connections at his alma mater.

"I'll find a way to repay you one of these days," his buddy had said on the day the job offer came in.

Teach couldn't help but wonder what kind of favor the guy needed now. He hoped his friend hadn't lost the job already. He pressed the talk button and joined the crew of distracted passengers.

"Hello!"

"Teach! I finally found a way to get you back, dude."

"You're a hammer."

"You're a hippie. Anyway, you know I'm a Michigan State diehard till I die."

"You're a *Michigan* diehard," razzed Teach. "Hmm. Well, good thing you are a new employee of UB then."

"Funny. Well, that's my whole point, really. Listen! I was told my prestigious position here is guaranteed a few bowl tickets out of the reserved ones for staff, students, and very select alumni as a bonus for the overtime and complete madness that's about to ensue when your University of Boston Falcons land a major game in the coming days."

"That's great for you," Teach said as he quietly hoped that his prediction over where the conversation might be heading was correct.

"You can have 'em."

"Get the heck out!"

"All three of 'em."

"You sure? I mean, you're a football fanatic too," Teach said.

"Yeah, man, but unless my Spartans miraculously earn a spot against these undefeated Boston Falcons of yours—which they won't—I'd prefer watching my employer's team from the comfort of my own apartment, complete with a plasma TV, high def, a reasonably priced case of Long Trail Double Bag, and a takeout meatball parm sub from Bob's Italian Foods in Medford. Medfahd. Medfahhhhd."

"Sounds like you have your mind made up, then."

"I do, dude. I really appreciate you landing me this job. Seriously, I've been trying to come up with a way to thank you. You've made my dear mother so happy. You've made me happy. She's not calling me every day to harass me. It's all right up my alley. It's great work. And of course it's nice hanging around the young lady students and all."

"You're getting too old for that talk," said Teach.

"Whatever. I'm still in the same age decade as them."

"Age decade? Maybe the seniors. And only for one more year until you hit thirty."

"Any more of this talk and I may rescind my offer and just put the tickets up for sale online when they come in."

"OK, OK, let's not do anything irrational," Teach said. "What can I say? You are a kind, generous man. And wise too, because I totally agree with your previous statement. Your Spartans have no chance of getting into the same caliber bowl game as Boston."

"Now I really may hang up on you. But speaking of ladies. What have you got going on? I haven't seen you with any kind of girlfriend in months, Teach. Who was that last one? That annoying girl with a face to match."

"Oh, stop it. You are so shallow."

"No way, dude. I know what I know, and you're in a serious drought, buddy."

"Actually, I have a date tonight," Teach said.

"Tonight? With who?"

"She's a blonde dental student at Tufts. She's smart."

"What's her name?"

"You don't know her."

"I'm going to plug the old girl into some social medias to see if you speakah-zee-truth."

Teach reluctantly provided the girl's name, even though he didn't quite feel like he had something to prove.

"Don't you have better things to do in that office of yours, anyway?" Teach asked.

"I've been cranking out A-quality work, my man. I'm allowed to take a five-minute break to talk with my friend. Hang on. Here she is. I've got her up. Whoa! Solid 9.5."

"Let's just hope she has the personality to match. Hey, man, thanks. Seriously, thank you for the tickets," Teach said.

"One more thing."

"What's that?" asked Teach.

"Medfahd. I just love saying the town of Medfahd."

"Later, weirdo."

"Bye!"

Teach pocketed his phone in grand spirits. The news of the bowl tickets overshadowed even the upcoming date that had been preoccupying him. In Allston, the trolley squawked around the bend of Commonwealth and Brighton avenues as though it were tired from a day's work. A descending December sun peered through a couple of brick apartment buildings and dimly illuminated Teach's face. If all went well with tonight's date, he might ask the girl to accompany him in a few weeks to a bowl game. The hottest tickets in town should impress her, he thought.

"Next. Stop. St. Paul Street."

As the side doors thumped open accordion-style, a trio of college students stepped aboard. They were dressed all in black, from their combat boots to their backpacks. Their hairstyles were greasy and colored unnaturally darker than midnight. They spoke to no one, not even each other. The only feature that bothered Teach was the apparent lack of happiness on their faces. The other passengers couldn't help but stare. Teach wondered about the kids' stories and thought of Henry's torture on the playground that morning for simply wearing an unfashionable shirt. He wondered where Henry's adolescence would take him and whether the boy would be happy. He wondered if he could use a mentor.

"Next. Stop. Harvard Ave."

Teach quickly stepped off the squeaky train car and into a mix of hustling panhandlers, college students, and taxi drivers. There was much to prepare before the date, but the site of Blanchard's Liquor Store on the corner made his unusually dry mouth thirsty for the Long Trail Double Bag his buddy had brought up during their sobering, promising conversation. With 7.2 percent alcohol by volume, Teach couldn't resist grabbing a six pack to calm his growing nerves. What he didn't know yet was how badly he was going to need it.

>>>>— <<<<

A few hours, one beer, a shave and shower later, a polished Teach walked up to his compact car on Linden Street. He wore thin wool pants typically reserved for his attendances at winter weddings, a gray cashmere sweater that he saved for Christmases, and his signature black wool coat that he wore for all occasions. He cleaned up well whenever he put in the effort.

A fluorescent orange parking ticket on the windshield waved a mocking hello.

"Snow parking ban?" Teach said before stuffing the ticket in his coat pocket. "Come on!"

He hoped the annoying slip wasn't a sign of how the rest of the evening would go. He unlocked the trunk and placed a rose there so his date could receive it toward the end of the evening instead of the beginning. Then he worried if leaving it in the cold car would kill it. Fumbling with it in the restaurant would surely destroy the flow of the date, he decided.

He slammed the trunk door with one hand and gave his car a gentle pat. The green vehicle was his first and only new car, purchased eight years ago in celebration of his University of Boston graduation and new teaching job. Back then, it might as well have been a Bentley. It had made him feel cool and accomplished to drive something new off the lot. On this day, though, with an exceptionally pretty girl expected soon in the passenger seat, he wondered if its practical look would be acceptable.

He was running early—too early. The wheels slowly creaked against the snow in the parking spot as he left Allston for Somerville by way of a long-cut through the Harvard University campus in Cambridge. Despite the self-imposed detour, Teach still arrived at his date's apartment too soon. He circled her block three times, hoping she wasn't watching from her window.

"Right on time," she said when he finally knocked on the door.

"Good to see you again."

She looked beautiful. She was the most beautiful date he'd ever had, he thought.

"You look really pretty, as you have both times I've seen you," he said. "As I'm sure you always do."

"Thanks."

Teach ended a long pause with small talk about the mutual friend who had set them up at a dinner party where they had been the only singles in attendance. He ended another quiet moment by asking her about school. He ended a third by bringing up the weather.

On this cold night, as he opened the door of his beloved car and noticed a new scratch from parking on the street, Teach thought he heard a disappointed exhale come from the blonde beauty. He was certain he saw evidence of it from the cloud of breath near her lips that slowly disappeared in the frigid air.

"So where are we going?" she asked.

"I made a reservation at the East Coast Grille," Teach said. "I noticed at the dinner party that you liked the seafood apps. I mean, not that you were eating a lot of them or anything. I was just paying attention to what you might like. Not that I was stalking you. Just do me a favor and please forget this whole rambling thing I'm doing here." He hoped she'd find his attention to detail endearing. He hoped for a laugh to help set him at ease.

"Oh, East Coast. How absolutely fabulous," she said. "Love it there. Love it."

The restaurant was a safe choice for a date. Situated in Cambridge's Inman Square, an up-and-coming neighborhood of hip restaurants featuring a variety of cuisines, East Coast Grille's atmosphere was fun and classy. It made guests feel as though they were on vacation even though most diners needed to head back to their respective offices in the morning. The only downside for Teach was that the meal would easily cut into his budget for nights out with his buddies for the next month and a half. When he had made the reservation, he was sure the girl would be worth it.

"So, you can order me a Cocktail Tranquilo when we get there," she said.

Teach laughed, thinking she was making an adorable joke. He felt happy she was so thrilled with the restaurant choice, until he looked at her fashionably smoky eyes and saw a very serious face to match.

"I could call ahead and have it waiting for us," Teach teased.

"They would do that for me?"

"No, I was just kidding. Sorry."

"Hmmm. We could try," she said with an instantly disarming smile and a soft tone.

"Um. Well. Huh. They'd probably want to see an ID and all—instead of trusting a guy like me over the phone—especially with my boyish voice and charm."

Still nothing. The girl must be book smart versus street smart, Teach decided. He thought he could still work with that. He knew she'd look great on his arm at a bowl game in a Falcons football jersey.

"Do you like football?" he asked.

"I'm more of a tennis kind of girl. Yuck, football? Anyway, why?"

Teach suddenly felt her chances of earning what he thought was the ticket of the year fade fast. He answered her by lightly shading the truth.

"Well, there is a very small chance that I might get some tickets to whatever bowl game the University of Boston ends up in. It's such a small chance that I probably shouldn't even be mentioning it."

Teach crossed his fingers over the steering wheel as he drove, knowing that acquiring the game tickets was certain. His buddies had their undeniable quirks, but when any one of them gave him his word, Teach could count on it.

"The Falcons! They are hot right now. I don't know anyone in this city who has mentioned a ticket to their, what is it called, Super Bowl?"

"Bowl game."

"Close! I was close. Anyway, if you get the ticket, I would love it. Love it," she exclaimed. She touched his arm as she spoke the words. Her odds creeped back up.

>>> - <<<

Minutes later inside the restaurant, over grilled bread, mussels with ginger sauce, and a round of Cocktail Tranquilos, neither the conversation nor the chemistry progressed. It occurred to Teach that she hadn't asked him a single question about his life. He questioned whether she had paid attention to any of his best stories. He had no idea whether she was having a good time. Her beauty, though, was hard to resist.

As the date wound down over key lime pies, the thought of offering a bowl game ticket felt as serious and confusing to Teach as an engagement proposal. He looked at her with puzzlement. For once, she filled the silence.

"O! M! G! Did you see that?" she whispered incredulously.

"See what?" Teach whispered back.

"That woman who just left. She had a picture of a cabbage on the T-shirt beneath her coat. A cabbage! What are these people thinking sometimes with their senses of style? Look, there! There she goes, Mrs. Cabbage Patch Kid."

Teach winced and thought of the morning's events with poor Henry and the boy's own ugly shirt.

He suddenly knew what he would do with the tickets.

"Shall we?" Teach asked, before driving his date home and accidentally forgetting about the flower left frozen in his trunk.

CHAPTER 21

JP
THE DESTINED ONE

T he December wind-chill on the hill in Syracuse dipped below zero. Knee-deep, lake-effect snow made the Marshall Street sidewalks and streets feel especially crowded. The sound of ice scrapers could be heard on nearly every city block. The frigid temperatures, however, did not deter boisterous tailgating in parking lots on and around M Street. It didn't tone down the pre-game beers inside Faegan's Pub, where fans dressed mostly in bright orange stood warmly shoulder-to-shoulder. It didn't weaken the one-way movement of crowds toward the college stadium either.

Syracuse College football fans felt overdue for a win that would land their team in a premier bowl game for the first time in years. National news on Coach Flash's unexpected selection of the five-foot, six-inch JP to replace their injured star running back further amplified the buzz and anticipation before the game.

Two especially nervous fans walked among the masses toward the stadium.

"Wouldn't you say this is the last opportunity to open up to me and fill me in on how you're feeling about this matchup?" the SC professor of anthropology asked his wife. "You've barely made a peep all day."

"Oh, honestly, what do you think I'm feeling?" she said.

The two parents stepped out of the heavy current of foot traffic. Fans continued streaming by, unaware that the couple they were passing had raised the player whom many of them were talking about.

"It's just too much for his little shoulders," she said.

"Oh, come on, Mum. This is not a time for puns."

She swatted him.

"What?" he asked. "Seriously, now. You spoke with the boy this morning. I did not. What did he say?"

She cried, and her own shoulders shook gently, but not from the outdoor chill.

"That bad, huh?" asked the anthropology professor. "He's wigged out, as the kids call it?"

"No. He was trying to calm me. He said not to worry. He told me that no matter what happens, he'll never regret going for it on this exact day. No matter what I may overhear people say, he is more than tough enough to handle whatever comes. Or so he claims."

"Well, you and I both know all of this to be true. He wasn't just saying those things, you see? That's really him. Did he mention anything else?"

"He said he is going to help get them the win," she said.

"Well, then. What are we waiting for? Let's get to our lucky seats."

Long before JP had become a member of the team, his parents had taken turns bringing the little boy to SC games. Neither of the parents had cared much for football back then, despite working for the college. Their boy had loved the sport, and that was all that mattered.

Gripping each other's hands, the professors reentered the flow of an electric crowd. They walked silently toward the stadium's revolving doors that made their ears pop upon entry. They walked past the booth that kept the premium tickets safe for athletes' friends and family members whose names were featured on a special master list. Instead, like everyone else, they waited in line to hand over their season tickets and walk through the turnstiles. They made their way up flights of exhausting stairs to the pair of seats the professors had alternated sharing with JP for years.

They settled themselves in the familiar pair of seats, unfamiliarly next to each other.

"This is weird. I'm used to sitting here with JP as a father-son duo. Now I'm going to watch him take this field. Well, I'll be damned. The boy actually got his dream. He's somethin' isn't he?"

"It's just hitting you now, huh?" JP's mother snapped.

The sound of the marching band, the sight of the massive number of seats inside the country's largest on-campus facility, and the cameras lining the sidelines frayed the woman's nerves even more.

JP's father had decided much earlier in the day that he would be giving his wife's mood swings a pass.

"I think I need a refreshment," he said. "Care to share some nachos and pseudo cheese with me, Mum? Maybe a nice hot pretzel with humungous pieces of salt and some fluorescent mustard?"

"Sounds appetizing. I can't eat, but I'll take a draft."

"A beer?"

"Yes. Please."

"Do you think that's a good idea, Mum? You haven't had barely a bite to eat all day. Not to mention the fact that you don't drink brew-ha-ha."

"Beer, please," she insisted with a hint of frustration.

"Are you going to fare OK by yourself for a minute?"

"Of course, but hurry back."

JP's mother sat alone as the Orange and Navy took the field with the most fanfare and support from the crowd she ever remembered hearing. From a few dozen rows up, like only a mother could, she scanned her son's body language to see how he was handling the pressure. To her, and only her, he looked like he felt a bit out of place. He looked like the energy in the stadium was beyond what he had imagined. He looked the same as he had on his first day of elementary school, when the mother and son of two contrasting colors had held hands with all eyes of parents and kids alike on them.

There were more eyes on JP on this day than anyone else on the field, and they were all taking in his size for the first time.

"Snap out of it," his mother whispered to him as if he could hear. "You've got this."

After a few more minutes of stressful observations, her husband returned with a pair of beers and his favorite stadium snacks.

"I missed seeing them take the field," he said. "How'd our boy look?"

"He looked scared. He looked as though he feels he's over his head."

"Oh, Mum. There you go again with the puns. Look at those big bruisers. They're all over his head."

The glare the professor received from his wife made him quickly change the subject.

"Hey look, there's that roomie of his."

"Whistler?"

"Heading toward the ref at the center S."

With the team's star running back off the active roster, Whistler was left as the most experienced captain to represent Syracuse College for the coin toss. He won the flip, but deferred the choice of receiving the ball in the first quarter to Tennessee.

Coach Flash knew it was going to be a close game. No one had to remind him that it was going to be an important one. He had instructed Whistler an hour earlier that if he won the toss, he should pass up the chance to have the ball in first quarter. They would take a risk and open the game with SC's solid defense to buy the Orange and Navy's newly shaken offense some much-needed confidence. They'd choose starting off the second half instead.

The opposing team's quarterback began the game with one incomplete pass followed by a second. The Syracuse crowd was wild and hungry for a third. Most of them fetched keys from their pockets and began shaking them, a signature move in the stadium whenever an opposition's third—and hopefully final—down was about to fail. This year's defensive players were so successful at stopping their opponent on third down attempts that the fans and Syracuse media fondly referred to the Orange and Navy defense as The Keys. They also called Whistler the Master.

At the start of the third down, the deafening noise within the stadium made it difficult for the visiting quarterback to communicate his play to his offense. He caught the snap and scanned the field for an open man. The quarterback spotted one, but it was SC's Whistler who plowed him over for a sack. The sea of fans dressed in orange looked and sounded as though they were on fire.

JP's parents joined the crowd in celebration, exchanged high-fives, and screamed Whistler's name. JP's mother relaxed just a little, just for a moment. Coach Flash, Whistler, and the entire defensive line had done their opening work for the Orange and Navy. It was now her son's turn.

The stadium quieted to dull chatter and sporadic cheers when JP took the field with the rest of the Orange and Navy offense. Coach Flash and the offensive coordinators still planned to buy JP some time and get him comfortable on a field where he had experienced zero game-time minutes. They called two passing plays in a row, and the offense successfully moved its way close to a first down. The refs brought out the chains to measure whether they achieved it, and the Orange crowd ignited again, as though their support would make the difference.

It didn't. The head ref signaled the down as third and inches. Coach Flash and just about everyone else in the stadium knew that the ball would finally have to go to JP. JP's mother had watched enough football games to know it too.

"Here we go," she whispered, clasping her hands and closing her eyes for a moment to wish her favorite boy in the world well.

As the Orange and Navy broke from the huddle and lined up for the snap, the ball shot from the quarterback to JP. The hype around the small running back made the opposition especially hungry to stop him. JP's blockers were trapped. There was nowhere to run. JP fell on the ball to prevent a fumble. It was a wise play, even though it made him look bad.

"Oh, what the hell," yelled a man sitting directly behind JP's mother. "C'mon, coach. He had his shot now, let's pull the pipsqueak out!"

"Hold it together, Mum," JP's father warned his wife. "You'll have the last laugh. You know you will. Just ignore them. Remember what JP told you this morning."

The heckler's views represented a majority of the fans' wishes throughout the stadium, but following another three-and-out led by an unstoppable Whistler and the Orange and Navy's tireless defense, it was quickly time for JP to take the field again.

Coach Flash and the offensive coordinator opted to give JP an opportunity to run the ball immediately on this drive. They thought it might help get the nerves out with a play that didn't carry quite so much pressure.

JP's quarterback caught the snap. He quickly and accurately tossed it to the small running back. JP was used to running against players twice his size, but he wasn't feeling himself on the field. He felt just as he did in the classroom whenever a teacher called on him and he replied with, "Can you please repeat the question?" Instead of listening to the question again and thinking about a solution, he often found himself outside of his body, thinking instead about how he was being perceived. He wondered what people were thinking now. He wondered if he was fitting in.

On the field, the break in concentration made JP miss a defensive end coming at his rear, right side. This time, the failed drive would be his fault. As the defender drove JP to the ground, the ball popped out from under his small, chiseled chin. A Tennessee Volunteer landed on top of it for a fumble.

Syracuse fans had seen enough. Many joined a growing chorus of boos.

"I just can't take this," said JP's mother. "I'm out of here. I'm going to walk to my office. Call me when it's over."

"You're leaving?"

"Of course I'm leaving. It is unbearable to just sit here and watch."

JP's father found it hard to argue with that.

"What about me? I can't battle this entire stadium on my own. I'm not as spry as I once was."

"Oh, please," she said angrily. *You always treat the ones you love the worst,* she acknowledged to herself. Today, she was definitely taking things out on her husband.

He tried to come up with another reason—a better reason—for her to stay.

"But what about JP? Don't you think he needs you here?"

"Our seats are so far up my nose is practically hemorrhaging. JP will never know the difference. Call me when this is over."

Down on the field, JP absorbed the heckling, which came at him from every angle. He knew he deserved it. He had looked up at the exact seats in which he had sat during his youth. Back then, he was on the same side as the crowd, cheering when the Orange and Navy made a good play and running his exasperated little fingers through his hair when things didn't go the team's way.

As he made his way off the field on this very different day, he squinted upward to find his mother rise from her seat. He couldn't see her expression or read her body language from so far away, but he knew her frame. He'd spent his whole life beside it as her sidekick. The sight of her reminded him that there were bigger things in life than fumbling a ball. In this game and throughout his life, she unknowingly managed to mute the hecklers for him. Without her, life would've taken a much different and unknown turn. He was lucky. If he couldn't make his dream work this time for himself, he would do it for her. She would become his inspiration to turn things around. She would always serve as his calming force.

After working her way down flights upon flights of stairs of ticked-off fans, the professor pushed open a big, non-revolving door of the stadium. The air pressure seemed to kick her out like a big wind gust, like a big kick in the rear. She instantly wanted to go back and support her son. Had it really been too much to bear? She couldn't help him or hold him, she thought. She knew the position was a responsibility he had to take care of on his own. She decided during her familiar campus schlep to her office that she'd at least turn on the radio and force herself to listen to JP's every step. For better or worse, she knew the radio broadcasters would be covering him closely.

With all of her students' term papers graded and final exams corrected, the professor glanced nervously about her workspace for anything to keep her busy. She peered into the eyes of the youthful picture of JP that was still propped up on her desk. She looked up through her skylight at the heavenly view that saw her through good days and bad. Her foot tapped the trashcan that once caught the *Infertility: A Practical Guide for the Physician* book. Her fingers ran across the greasy black phone that had once facilitated the call from the adoption agent who so many years ago had said he might be able to give her a son.

The professor finally turned on an old clock radio and moved the dial along a blaring medley of fuzz and music stations until she finally found a young voice talking about the game. She was desperate for a score. Lucky for her, she chose a station operated by SC's communications school, where faculty taught budding sports broadcasters to give the score often, because that was really what the audience wanted most.

"Well, we're already at the half of a heavily defensive game, but the Orange and Navy have managed to put seven on the board to the Tennessee Volunteers' zero. And those points came from the unlikeliest of players. For those of you just tuning in, my colleague Derek here has the story."

The professor instinctively grasped the photo of her son in the office and clung to it like a lucky charm.

"Thanks, Matt. It's been a climactic half to stay the least. JP Hemmings is the unlikeliest of scorers indeed, especially following a horrendous start in the first quarter. Incidentally, how many times have you heard boos toward an Orange and Navy in their own stadium before today, Matt?"

"I think that was a first for me, Derek. We're here talking about Syracuse College's 7-0 lead against Tennessee at the half. Back to you, Derek, for the summary so far."

"Yes. JP indeed had a rough start. The pressure seemed to get to the five-foot, six-inch player, who laid down on the ball on his first carry and, even worse, fumbled it on his second."

"There was a lot riding on this little guy. We should add that those weren't just his first carries of the game—this game is the first he's played all season. And with the Orange and Navy's star running back out with an injured shoulder, JP took the starting position."

"That's right, Matt. You can literally feel the emotion here in the stadium. The walls have been rocking. We're talking about the Orange and Navy's 7-0 lead at the half. Those seven points came, despite enormous pressure, from JP Hemmings in an impressive 24-yard run in which he dodged three sizable Tennessee Volunteers to break free for the end zone and give SC the only points of the game so far."

JP's mother raised the boy's picture and shook it silently in celebration.

"I think there were a few fans in the stands left eating their words after that play. Talk about elusive. Talk about quick feet. Talk about going from nothing to something."

"That's right, Matt. Seven-to-zero at the half, with a touchdown by an unfamiliar backup to a backup to a backup running back named JP Hemmings. As you know, Matt, this is a big televised game with big consequences. The Orange and Navy's dream of a cream-of-the-crop bowl game hinges on whether they can pull out a win here today. When asked at the half how he managed to snap out of his funk and turn things around, JP told a major network's on-field correspondent that he saw his mother, of all people, rise in the stands and he collected himself for her. He said she's sitting with his father in the nosebleeds, the very pair of seats the parents took turns bringing JP to as a boy. Before hustling off the field, he added that back then, his parents didn't even like football."

"Well, I bet they do now, Derek. Especially today and …"

The radio voices seemed to trail off as the professor snapped out from the heavy blanket of stress. She still clung to the picture of her son that she had displayed proudly in her office so long before he had become just a little bit famous on campus and throughout the region.

"What am I doing here?" she asked herself aloud in disgust.

She gathered her winter clothes and hustled toward the building's exit, hugging the coat, mittens, and hat still in her arms. She didn't put them on until after she located her ticket stub in her mess of a purse. Her feet moved much more quickly during this trek to the stadium. By the time she finally climbed her way back up to her seat next to her husband, she was out of breath.

"I guess I'm not going to win Mother of the Year this go 'round."

"You came back," he replied, even though his eyes remained fixated on the field. "She came back!"

He looked sweaty from cheering. Four stacked, empty beer cups tipped over onto the couples' toes as a fan seated behind them handed him a full one. She thought her husband never looked more handsome.

"JP scored both the touchdowns that are on the board," he said with eyes still fixed on the game. "You just missed one. We're winning, Mum. We're winning!"

"I was wrong to leave!" she screamed toward her husband's ear. "It's easy to admit that now that the fans are cheering for my son instead of against him. Win or lose, I should be here." She kissed his sweaty cheek.

"Go JP!" the man screamed. "That is my boy! That is my boy getting the first down!"

It was the type of comment that the loving father had apparently yelled a few times already, as he began slapping fives with the fans below, beside, and above him in a choreographed, clockwise motion.

"And this is his mother!" he shouted, raising his wife's arm jubilantly.

The woman looked around the massive stadium and felt a few gentle pats brush across her shoulders as though she were suddenly a celebrity. She calmly watched JP run in his third touchdown. She smiled, feeling ashamed that she got to witness only one.

With the game clinched, she watched her son's body language finally loosen. She saw his teammates slam into him a little too hard before lifting him up like a ragdoll.

Down on the sidelines, another woman was watching him too and attempting to come up with words that could possibly capture the unlikely turn of events for a photo caption. The delicate International Presswire photographer got jostled a bit as she reached for a notepad in her breast pocket next to a press pass labeled "Maxine." As her competitors snapped away, Maxine hustled to ask Coach Flash a question before jotting down the words *magical* and *hat trick*.

CHAPTER 22

DEVIN
The Gifted One

A couple of weeks and University of Boston football wins after her first date with Devin, Caroline sat on an old, pilled plaid couch in his apartment with her cheerleading uniform folded neatly in a duffle at her feet. She nervously peered around a suit and a small row of immaculate jerseys with the number four on the backs hanging neatly from a horizontal brass bar of a floor lamp. She attempted to find out which students were bounding their way up her boyfriend's stairs now. Devin's apartment entrance was a revolving door of guys and girls who wanted to feel like they belonged with the most sought-after guy on campus—maybe even the most popular guy in the city of Boston. The Falcons' star quarterback had an ever-changing entourage.

This particular group of student bachelors spoke—as guys in Devin's apartment often did—about their latest female conquests.

"You had to see her, Dev," boasted one. "Smokin' hot."

Caroline's hair matched an orange stripe in the outdated sofa. The couch was perhaps the only place in the world where she seemed invisible.

"Hi," she said to the guys despite knowing they would not end up answering her back.

Devin looked at her and gave her a wink. He thought it would be just enough to keep her from walking out. He watched her pick up her locket from her chest.

"So I've got a group of friends ready to see me , Dev, who you gotta meet," said someone.

Devin cautiously wanted to hear more.

"Oh yeah? What are their names?"

"Andrea, uh, Andre, Stephanio, and Emilio."

Devin winced at his friend's inability to realize that Caroline was smarter than all the others who had sat in that seat before her. He watched her drop the locket onto her chest and gather the winter coat he had forgotten to help her hang up. The room fell silent and the air felt tense.

"Well then, what am I doing here?" Caroline finally asked.

The guys exchanged looks that would've said "Crap" if they had spoken out loud, while Devin leaped to her side and walked her to the door.

"Let me drive my princess home."

"I can manage," Caroline said without breaking step. "I'm pretty resourceful, actually. I'm pretty happy getting by on my own."

Devin couldn't help but laugh. In dating, on the football field, and even in life, Caroline was his only challenge. He grabbed her arm and gave her his golden boy smile. She didn't return one this time. She still looked more beautiful than any girl he'd seen.

"Oh c'mon, Caroline," he whispered. "You know those guys are bumbling idiots. Do you seriously believe I'd listen to them? You wouldn't break up with me on a day that I've been waiting for, like, only my whole life. You know what my itinerary is for today? Your man just so happens to have a date with the National Sports Network through a live feed at our stadium. Which bowl game announcement do you think it's going to be? Orange Bowl? FedEx BCS National Championship?"

"I think either'd be an honor," Caroline said in a tone that was somehow kind and cold at the same time.

Devin smiled.

"Do you want to meet my family, Caroline?"

"What?"

"When they come for the bowl game, do you want to meet them? I'd like them to meet you."

"Um, I guess."

"You guess?"

Caroline finally let a smile break through.

"Of course I would," she said.

"Fine. And are you going to watch my interview on the network tonight? It'll help my performance knowing that you are out there, somewhere, with me."

Caroline nodded much more weakly. She knew that after the upcoming bowl game announcement rally on campus, she'd have to hustle off to her secret job at the Gentlemen's Club, where she was bound to miss seeing Devin's interview unless it was being played repeatedly on one of the club's plasmas. As a backup, she would quietly ask her roommate to record the interview, she thought. Caroline knew the girl would probably be doing it anyway. She still had a crush on Caroline's boyfriend, just like everyone else seemed to.

"See you at the rally," Caroline said. "And then on TV."

"See you at the rally, Caroline. You sure you don't want to ride with me there?"

"I'm going to walk, thanks. I'm used to the cold."

Devin leaned in for a quick kiss before running back up his apartment stairs, skipping every other step.

"So tell me about this Andrea, Stephanie, and Emily," he said once he reached the top.

The guys erupted in laughter so loud that Devin wondered if Caroline could hear it from the other side of his front door. He hoped she wouldn't think the joke was on her. He knew she was smart enough to figure it out.

"Keep it down, morons," Devin snapped.

Devin slipped out of an ecstatic rally crowd of teammates and University of Boston Falcons fans into a black truck that was waiting to whisk him from the bowl announcement to the university's public relations office. His mood didn't match everyone else's outside of the vehicle. He sulkily tipped his head back and tried to catch a three-minute nap before reaching the media training he was already dreading. Before his body could fully rest, the driver was already rousing him.

"Excuse me, young sir. We are here."

"Great," Devin replied sarcastically.

He gazed through the window to see a gray suit with a matching coat; in it was a man presumably there to hold Devin's hand through the day's media process. The man opened the quarterback's door as though the quarterback were Prince Charles.

"Devin, I'm James O'Leary, the new director of public relations at the university," the man said. "Congrats on your spot in the Orange Bowl. I guess it would be an understatement to say how excited and proud we all are."

The man had a friendly face and a sincere tone. He was instantly likable and was obviously smart without being arrogant. None of that mattered to Devin. He would make this guy earn his money today, he thought.

"Fine," said James. "Well, let's get inside and get straight to work. You're a busy man."

Their walk inside the office building included no conversation. James knew not to force it another direction.

"Please have a seat," the man said once they reached his press office. "Can I get you something to drink—coffee, water, a celebratory bottle of champagne?"

"Champagne."

"That one was just a joke," James said.

"I know."

"OK, then, let's just get started. We're here to make today's media interview run as smoothly as possible for you. I want to make sure that in the end, you feel like there were no curveballs thrown at you. I want to make sure you aren't left thinking, 'I wish I said this or that.' We need to come up with one crisp message. Would some role-playing be helpful to you?"

"Whatever, man," Devin said. "Let's just get through this."

"OK. So let's pretend I'm NSN's Roger So-And-So or one of the station's esteemed college football experts on tonight's panel."

"You mean one of their has-been players?"

"NSN hasn't let us know which member of their team will be interviewing you yet from their studio. So here we go. Let's role-play. Congrats, Devin Madison, to you and the University of Boston Falcons for securing a trip to the Orange Bowl. How did it feel when you heard the news today?"

"Just ducky."

"Interesting choice of words, Devin. Let's continue with a little more seriousness if you can. How about this tougher one? The Orange Bowl is prestigious, but do you think the polls got it right? I mean, your team is undefeated while Texas A&M and Miami are going to the FedEx National Championship Game with a loss each. This is a happy day for the Falcons, but is it bittersweet in any way, to come up just short of a trip to the FedEx?"

Devin's cheeks flushed a little.

James realized he had stumbled upon the source of Devin's sour mood.

"Listen, Devin. You're going to be asked this question. Things could've gone either way. Let's just plan to make sure your answer gives credit to just how successful your team has been—how successful you have been—without coming across the least bit bitter."

"I think I'll say that the polls are jokes."

"Devin. I'm clear on the fact that there are other places you would like to be than my office. This may be one of my first days on the job at the college, but it's far from my first press interview. I've probably done a thousand. I know that you know better. I've done my research and watched some very successful interviews with you. I know you are playing with me, but I'm just tryin' to do my job. Listen, when you are asked this question, you can answer that your selection as the ACC Champion is a great recognition of your team's hard work and success this season, and that you are looking forward to the Orange Bowl, where two of the top teams in the nation are scheduled to face off. Something along those lines. Make sense?"

"Anything else?" Devin asked.

"Yes, actually. We need to go over what you're going to say about your opponent. So by now you know that you're matched up against Syracuse College's Orange and Navy, and you've had just a little time to think about how you're going to play against them. What will be your strategy on handling SC's defense, a unit that is called The Keys for their fans' support during their relentless third-down stops? In particular, how are you going to manage Craig Whistler?"

"I'm going to carry a padlock in my pocket and bonk anyone who comes near me over the head with it."

"Devin! Listen, the key to answering this question is to sound confident without giving away any of your strategy secrets. How about keeping it simple? Just give a non-answer. Say you are looking forward to a good matchup, but you also look forward to pulling it out in the end."

"I like my sound bite better."

"And I'm sure you do. Look, Devin. We don't have time to play around. We've got to get you over to the stadium where NSN already has a crew waiting to go live shortly with a feed. I know you're going to do better than this. Forget about doing anything for me. The chancellor, your coach, and your team are all counting on you. The entire student body is thrilled to cheer you on. Let's do this. I don't have to tell you that your team is the better team, but in just about any city outside of Boston, Syracuse College will be the sentimental favorite on game day, especially with that little JP Hemmings on the field. It's just a fact. It's not going to benefit the school if you come across the least bit—pardon my choice of words—cocky."

"Oh, Jim."

"It's James."

"Don't you worry about the sentimental favorite. I think I'll give JP a run for his money in that department. Watch my interview and see for yourself."

"I can honestly say that I am going to be anxiously awaiting this one. The truck is waiting. Let's go."

»»»- -«««

"We're here, folks, with the man of the hour, Devin Madison, who joins us from University of Boston's home field. Devin has led his Falcons to an undefeated season. He's in the running for the Heisman, throwing for three thousand yards already this year as quarterback, and he just landed his team a spot in the prestigious Orange Bowl. Welcome to the show, Devin. Congrats."

"Thanks. It's great to be with you."

The university's new PR director relaxed his shoulders just a little from behind the camera.

"So, look, the Orange Bowl is the Orange Bowl. It's not exactly easy getting into that. Do you feel the least bit slighted, though, that as the only undefeated team in the BCS, you didn't earn the spot in the FedEx BCS Championship Game? Do you think the polls were basically saying that your ACC Division was not as challenging as some others?"

"The polls have a very tough job," Devin said. "There are so many teams, and unless we all played each and every one, it's hard to predict who would've been on top over who. I personally believe we could've come out on top against any team this year with the group of guys we have. They have a lot of heart, but all of that aside, the Orange Bowl has great history in the sport and for my family too. I was personally hoping for the Orange Bowl."

The PR director instantly wished he had done even more research to uncover this fact himself before the interview. Devin's reason for testing his abilities was no longer a wonder, he thought. The staffers in NSN's studio were wishing they had been more prepared too. Luckily, one of the panelists vaguely knew about Devin's father.

"Yes, now your father was a great college football player. Didn't he play in that frigid game against Joe Mont—"

"Yes, he was called the Hustler and played for Houston," Devin interrupted. "But my grandfather played as well, and he's who I was referencing. He played in Boston and was about to lead his team to none other than the Orange Bowl until they lost their last game of the season very unexpectedly to a much less accomplished team. But the loss saved his life—literally. A celebration had been planned at the Coconut Grove nightclub in Boston after the game. The establishment burned to the ground that night, killing scores of people inside. Luckily for my grandfather, the loss of the game sent him home instead of out to the ill-fated club. His life was saved, but he never got to go to the Orange Bowl."

Devin looked into the camera with a somber face.

"This trip to the Orange Bowl is for you, Pops," he said.

Devin hoped viewers across the country were tearing up just a little. He wanted to wink at James from the other side of the camera, as if to ask, "Who is the sentimental favorite now?" Instead, he kept himself poised.

"Wow! And you've been playing in Boston, the same city as your grandfather. So it's safe to say, then, that both the Orange Bowl and the city carry very special meaning for your family."

"I think this particular game is meant to be."

"It's fascinating, Devin. Perfectly fascinating. Now what about those Syracuse Orange and Navy? How do you plan to take them on in such an important game— clearly important now for so many reasons? What will your strategy be against the pesky Orange defense, a unit everyone calls The Keys?"

"I think I'll lock The Keys up in their locker room before the game," Devin said, flashing his best smile at the camera.

The NSN panelists erupted in genuine laughter.

"OK. Right. Well, thanks again, Devin Madison. Good luck to you and the Falcons in your quest for an Orange Bowl win. Good luck to you in your Heisman run. Terrific interview. Just terrific!"

"This was my pleasure," Devin said. "There is no place I'd rather be."

The quarterback couldn't resist giving a sassy wink to James, whose body was framed by the bright lights around the camera. The man had no choice but to smile back.

CHAPTER 23

CAROLINE
The Troubled One

Caroline sat on her little stool in the Gentlemen's Club dressing room and carefully rolled a sheer white nylon over one of her thin, muscular legs. Outside the room, a few of the dancers' colleagues took the stage as 50 Cent's "In the Club" blared inside their own.

The bass made the dressing room walls and Caroline's nerves vibrate just the tiniest bit. The room of young ladies smelled, as it always did, like the saccharine mixture of cheap aerosol hairspray and vanilla air freshener. Caroline squinted at the mirror and took stock at who she'd become. As others chatted excitedly about their babies, boyfriends, and bills in matching white anti-sweat socks that would eventually get stuffed inside tall, lace-up boots, Caroline experienced the same unsettled feelings that stirred inside her within her dormitory shower room on campus. The club's dressing area was yet another place where she never quite felt like she belonged.

She sat somberly and silently as she positioned her blonde bob of a wig upon her head. The routine had become natural, even though it appeared far from that. Caroline let her red hair hang down before pulling the fake locks tightly on top. She'd twist pieces of her long, fiery strands and hide them neatly beneath the blonde ones with the help of sharp, punishing bobby pins that scraped against her scalp. Before long, not even she would recognize the girl staring back at her in the mirror.

Putting on the wig was a ritual that had begun a week earlier, when she had spotted her favorite psychology professor in one of the guest seats. She had stood frozen momentarily behind him before sneaking into the dressing room for cover. She had felt thankful there that she hadn't needed to transition their last conversation about the A- on her paper on multiple personality disorder—a topic she was relating to while living a secret double life—into something that began with, "What are you doing here, professor?" Or, "What are you doing here, Caroline?" Feeling confused, angry, and disappointed at the sighting, Caroline had immediately tugged at her locket. She already held an automatic disliking of the patrons of the club and had wondered if her professor had an unknowing partner sleeping at home in that moment. *Were there any men out there who could be trusted?* On that night, she had also wondered how she would be able to carry out her new gig on stage knowing her professor was in the audience.

Always a professional at suppressing her emotions, Caroline had managed to carry on. She had looked at one of the club's regular dancers and spotted the woman's wigs resting lifelessly on a short row of foam heads in the dressing room.

"Um, so I don't know if this is way too personal of a question," Caroline said.

"Shoot," the dancer had replied. She paused her application of midnight blue eyeliner and looked at Caroline with half-done, fully attentive eyes.

Caroline wasn't someone who tended to ask for help, and the woman had seemed to sense that.

"Well, would it be all right if I borrowed a wig tonight? Just until I can pick up my own?"

"See someone you know out there tonight, hun?"

"You've been doing this a while," Caroline had admitted. "You're good."

"Pick your pleasure," the woman had said. "Who do you want to be tonight? A short-haired and stylish blonde? A classy brunette with sharp bangs? That one seems to be a moneymaker."

"Thanks," Caroline had said as she selected the blonde one and immediately put it on.

"It looks good on you. Keep it, Caroline. I've got plenty more at home, sadly enough."

The disguise had worked that night and brought Caroline the added comfort of making herself feel a little more removed from her work.

Several performances had passed now with the wig as her security while Caroline popped in and out of the Gentlemen's Club, whenever there was time left after her studies, cheerleading, cafeteria card swiping, and dating the most sought-after guy on campus. The dancer had already brought home from the club more than $1,000 in cash. She wondered if it was already enough to get her through the rest of the school year.

As 50 Cent's song came to a close, Caroline slowly pulled the second white nylon up her other leg while the young ladies around her squeezed their long limbs into knee-length boots. As time brought them all closer to taking the stage, their moods matched Caroline's now. One of the dancers approached her and broke the growing silence.

"So, do you like football or something?"

The question made Caroline freeze in her preparations. Thoughts whirled inside her head faster than she could calculate a reply. Until now, she had managed to keep her other life a secret from the dancers in hopes that her controversial work at the club wouldn't intersect with her scholarship at University of Boston, a school she had grown to love. Her studies meant so much more than having the cash necessary for new outfits for dates with Devin or a dinner off campus every once in a while with the girls from school. Had Caroline's coworker spotted her on the sidelines of a Falcons game recently? Had Phil, the club manager, slipped on his promise to keep Caroline's background confidential?

Despite her confusion and worry, Caroline managed to reply in a sweet tone that carried not a hint of abrasiveness.

"Um, I like football, I guess. Why do you ask?"

"I just saw you watching sports on one of the club TVs before hitting the dressing room. Big bowl game announcement today. I'm a fan myself."

"Oh, wow, yeah. I'm excited for a local team to be going to the Orange Bowl," said Caroline as her mood lifted, even if only for a moment.

"I know. And that blondie quarterback you were watching in that interview on the news is beyond handsome."

Caroline couldn't deny that. The other dancer continued.

"You know, a couple of my girlfriends who work here say he's coming in tonight to celebrate. He may already be here. I'm Andrea, by the way."

Caroline's mood came crashing down.

"Um, I'm Caroline," the perpetually troubled girl offered, even though her mind was already somewhere else and her right hand had already found its way to her locket. "Have a good night."

Caroline had known deep beneath her locket that Devin, as charismatic and disarming as he was, could not be trusted. Still wanting to make excuses for him, she reached inside her backpack for her cell. She felt her heart pound harder as she spotted a freshly missed call from him. She plugged her outer ear with a painted index finger so as not to miss a word.

"Caroline, my princess, how are you, my true love?"

He had begun singing the lyrics to Debby Boone's "You Light Up My Life."

The golden boy managed to bring a smile to Caroline's face before the message continued.

"Hey, listen, did you see me on TV? I was thinking about you, you know, and hoping you were watching. Anyway, I'm beat from it all. Beyond beat. I'm going to head off to sleep now, so call me in the morning, will you? I will be dreaming of you tonight."

He belted out the first line of Selena's "Dreaming of You" in jest.

Caroline's face did not reveal a smile with his second serenade. His lie made sure of that. The message played on.

"Hey, did I ever tell you that you are the most beautiful girl I have ever met? Seriously now, I'm so happy we're together. I already love you."

Caroline let her phone fall into a new designer bag in disgust. She was disgusted at herself. She suddenly questioned her judgment, which until recently had guided her well through a life of challenge. *How could I be such a fool? How could I ignore all the signs time after time after time? Why am I even working here?* She thought about running from the club—white nylons and all—but something made her want to stay and see him. More than anything, something also made Caroline want him to see her.

A knock on the dressing room door prompted most of the girls to answer mechanically, "All clear."

Phil walked in, closest to Caroline's stool.

"Hey, Caroline," the manager whispered kindly.

Wherever she went, she was everyone's favorite. The manager's voice deepened so all could hear.

"Time for the shift change. Hope you ladies make a lot of cash tonight."

"Amen," shouted Andrea.

Caroline looked the girl over more closely now from wig to boot. Jealousy wasn't usually an emotion that brought Caroline's hand to her locket, but it did on this night. She quickly applied one last layer of lipstick, sadly straightened her plaid mini skirt, and led the way from the dressing room.

Phil always put Caroline on the main stage first in her shift. He knew she was the one the regulars were hoping to see. He knew she would set the right mood for new patrons too. On this night, though, he was oblivious that his selection would ensure a very bad night for one important new guest who had just taken a seat.

Caroline scanned the tables and chairs from backstage and spotted Devin's smile first. He still wore his suit from the day's interviews. An entourage of teammates and friends surrounded him. They were all drinking, laughing, and pointing out which dancer was their new favorite. Little did they know that someone with even more beauty, talent, and innocent seductiveness was about to take center stage.

From behind the curtains, Caroline couldn't help but feel both angry and guilty at the same time. Ironically, she had told Devin that morning that she also would be heading in early for study and sleep. She questioned whose lie was worse.

As Caroline watched one of her coworkers begin to loosen Devin's necktie from across the room, the troubled girl emphatically decided that Devin's double life was far worse than her own. Anger ripped through her and fully overtook her guilt now. Her ears felt hot under the blonde wig. Caroline thought about ripping it off, pins and all, but on came AC/DC's "Hell's Bells," her cue to take the stage.

She didn't let herself get lost immediately in the music, as she had on stage every other time. She wanted to see if Devin had truly cared about being with her. As she spun and danced, she watched Devin's friends whoop like idiots, hitting each other on the shoulders. None of them recognized Caroline in her wig. She could tell Devin hadn't either, although she knew it was only a matter of time for him.

She stepped inward to do the signature backward twirl that had landed her a job during her audition with Phil. As Caroline's locket took air around her neck, its sparkle caught Devin's eye. She watched everything else begin to look familiar to him too—her bare thighs, her slender arms, the nape of her neck that he had already kissed on many drunken nights only to get more of whatever he really wanted, and finally, when Caroline stopped spinning downward, he saw her face.

She made eye contact and absorbed Devin's own look of shock and confusion. Maybe he was angry with her and ashamed at himself, all at once. Maybe he was just angry. Finally, she let herself get lost in the music. Always able to use her emotions to her advantage in her dance, Caroline gave perhaps the performance of a lifetime, even if it was on center stage of a Gentlemen's Club.

From behind the club's bar, Phil noted the power and emotion behind Caroline's dance and, with mixed feelings, had a hunch it might be her grand finale at his establishment.

CHAPTER 24

DEVIN
The Gifted One

Devin awoke alone in his bed to the piercing beep of his alarm clock and the melancholy patter of freezing raindrops outside his apartment window. The evening of celebrating his University of Boston Falcons' upcoming trip to the Orange Bowl now left him with cravings for a tall glass of water and a pair of fast-food sausage, egg, and cheese biscuits with greasy hash browns on the side to help set the hangover straight.

Those weren't his only pangs. Devin was also starting his day with the kind of ache that was much more foreign to him. It was the type of sting he had easily doled out to others many times. A girl—as badly as he knew he deserved it—had just broken his heart.

The pain was something his pride had managed to keep hidden from his buddies as the night at the Gentlemen's Club unfolded. The guys had been too preoccupied with Caroline's captivating performance on stage to notice Devin's peculiar, frozen stare. They hadn't recognized Caroline beneath the blonde wig like Devin had. They hadn't noticed Devin's long trip to the men's room immediately following her dance either, where the quarterback had removed his cell phone from a pocket of dollar bills and quietly listened to Caroline's voice message from earlier that day, when the world had appeared so differently to him.

"I just wanted to say how great you were on TV today," she had said. "I had no clue of your family's connection with this game. Made me feel even more thrilled and honored to meet 'em. Anyway, I know you're busy, and I've got a lot of studying and sleep to catch up on, so I'm gonna turn in early tonight. I'll just say congrats again. Talk with you soon, I hope. Bye."

A sobering sleep later, Devin reached for his cell again to listen to her sweet voice from his bed.

Talk with you soon, I hope. Bye.

Her voice didn't sound so sweet to him anymore. Anger had begun to replace the shock. He grew tense in a bed that had seen many girls come and go, even during his short time with Caroline. She had been the only one who really mattered, though. She was the only one who had ever truly excited him. She was the only one who had the potential to straighten out his immature and selfish ways, he thought.

The alarm clock sounded again, reminding Devin that life was going on with or without him, and that nine minutes had passed since he was supposed to start preparing for practice.

Caroline's voice entered his head again and joined the alarm clock. He felt like everything was mocking him.

I'm. BEEP. Going. BEEP. To. BEEP. Turn. BEEP. In. BEEP. Now.

Devin's stomach felt less hungry as the prospect of life without her as his girl became more real with each sober second that he was awake. His mouth was especially bitter from either the taste of sleep, past beers, or the sight of Caroline nearly naked on stage as dozens of men watched her with eyes that pretended to undress the rest of her.

His strong fingers hit the snooze button as he decided to skip breakfast and instead use another nine minutes to plot the harshest revenge—one that would rip away from Caroline the thing she needed most if Devin were successful.

Caroline's cheerleading coach sat on the sidelines of University of Boston's practice field reviewing a fresh clipboard of information packets following a meeting with university staff regarding the Orange Bowl Festival's calendar of events. The staffers were gone now, leaving her with only the sound of UB's starting kicker, who booted away at the ball with field goal attempts he'd probably practiced a million times before. She looked up at the player and sensed the pressure riding on him to be successful at any moment, whenever his team needed him most. She had watched enough football games to know that he was often the young man needed in the last moments of any close game.

A chill ran through her body as she fought to control her own feelings of anxiousness. She thumbed through the details of the Orange Bowl Coaches' Luncheon, the Orange Bowl FANfest, and the Orange Bowl Tailgate Party— all events her team was expected to attend on top of participating in the big event. Her small staff was already helping her coordinate travel and lodging logistics for her team. Her assistant coach was busy selecting the latest music and finalizing new routines that were special for the bowl. She wished she had access to an intern who could serve as a liaison for all the cheerleaders, making sure each got to and from the various functions together and on time. She considered the cheerleading captain as someone she could lean on, but the coach was realistic and instantly dismissed the idea. The captain was in her senior year and wouldn't want to be playing secretary during her last hurrah at the Orange Bowl, she thought.

She watched the kicker successfully boot another one through the uprights, and a smile crossed her face. The coach thought of Caroline. The freshman had seemed burdened by the fact that she had received the coach's only scholarship. Caroline appeared to feel like she needed to work harder to deserve it. The rest of the team admired her. They would listen to her. She was the perfect choice for taking on extra duties for the bowl game. Caroline would happily embrace the favor, her coach thought.

"Um, hi there. I need to ask you a favor."

The woman's brainstorming was interrupted as she looked up and saw Devin Madison standing over her. He had seemed to appear out of nowhere.

"Oh, I startled you. Sorry. Your assistant coach at your office just said I might find you here," he said smoothly.

The coach immediately recognized the quarterback.

"Devin, hi," the coach had said with a laugh. "I don't think I've ever had the pleasure. Listen, congratulations on the bowl game announcement. What could I ever do for you?"

"I hoped to have a quick word with you confidentially."

Something about his artificial smile made the coach feel uncomfortable.

"What is it?" she whispered.

"Well, I'll cut right to it. I know this great college, my football team, and even your squad live up to the highest moral standards."

The coach wondered if she heard him correctly over his use of the word *even*.

"We *all* have high standards and expectations," she agreed in a tone meant to remind him that she was the grownup and he was still a student. "I wonder what you could be getting at, Devin?"

"Well, I'll just drop the bomb. I've heard that one of your girls works at a men's club. I don't know if this is in violation of the rules or code of ethics to be on your team, but as the quarterback for this school—a college with a great reputation that I obviously care greatly about—I thought I should pass this information along to you in case things need to be...fixed."

The coach sat in stunned silence for a moment as she watched the kicker slam the football into the uprights in a failed attempt from only thirty yards away.

"What the hell is wrong with you, Tommy!" Devin yelled toward the field.

The cheerleading coach instantly questioned the motives of the young man who had just preached to her about morality. She mentally scanned her roster of girls and couldn't come up with a single one who she thought could pull off living some kind of hidden life.

"Who?" she asked boldly.

"I'll tell you, but you didn't hear it from me."

"Why?" she asked even more boldly.

Devin's temper ignited. He wasn't used to being questioned by a coach, not to mention a cheerleading coach. In fact, he wasn't used to being questioned by anyone except his father. Less than twenty-four hours ago, the world seemed to revolve around him. That thought made him even angrier.

"Listen, let's not worry about why," Devin said. "Don't you have things you need to do—like teach some extra rah, rah, rahs or make some more signs with my name on it? Or how about this one, expose a girl who's been exposing herself?"

"I don't like your tone."

"And I don't like yours."

"Devin, you're asking me to pull someone off my team with allegations that are so far unfounded."

"So you would pull someone from the team for something like this?"

"Listen, I've never come across anything like this. I guess what I'm getting at is that I need more information first."

"Fine, but you didn't hear it from me. I've got enough on my plate. I don't need drama off the field."

The kicker booted a ball just short of the field goal from thirty-five yards away.

"Oh, what the hell, Tommy? Am I making you nervous? How do you think you're gonna feel when the entire nation is watch—"

The cheerleading coach cut him off before he had the chance to berate his teammate more.

"Fine," she said. "We have an agreement. Your hands are clean of this if that's what you really want. Who is it?"

"I heard it's Caroline."

The coach suddenly realized Caroline was somehow the unlikeliest and likeliest of her girls to pull off something like this.

"Where?"

"From what I hear, it's the Gentlemen's Club. That's one of the ones on LaGrange Street in Boston, so I'm told."

"I'll look into it."

"You do that."

Without a goodbye, Devin jogged onto the field to have a word with the kicker. He ran off as quickly as he appeared, but his visit left the coach feeling rattled on the sidelines as though she'd been sacked by one of the defensive tackles. As she watched the quarterback and kicker talk, she instantly had a newfound dislike for the beloved hero and a deep respect for the unsung kicker.

Within the hour, the coach was drumming her fingers on her office desk and searching for some phone numbers.

"There is way too much to do right now to be playing detective," she said aloud to herself as she dialed the number to the club and felt as though she were having an out-of-body experience. "This is the last place I thought I'd be calling when I woke up this morning," she added over several rings.

"Hello, this is Phil," said an out-of-breath man on the other end.

"Phil, hi. I don't know where to begin, really, but can I speak with the manager?"

"I'm the GM," Phil said cautiously. "How can I help?" *A conversation starting this way typically doesn't end well,* he thought.

"This may sound strange, or maybe not. I don't know. Anyway, I'm a cheerleading coach at a local D1 college, and I have a girl on scholarship here. I've heard that she may, um, dance at your establishment. Since this could be a potential conflict of interest for the team or her scholarship, I guess I'm asking whether you could confirm the information for me."

"No, no, no," said Phil. "She doesn't work here."

"I haven't even given you a name yet," the coach said, already sensing truth to the quarterback's accusation.

Phil scratched his head in the familiar spot and quickly began backtracking.

"I mean, yes," he said. "I can confirm a girl's employment, but I was just saying no because I know the girl you're talking about, and the last thing I would want is any trouble for her. Caroline's a good kid—a great talent—but an even better kid."

"I know," the coach agreed.

"There's a but," Phil said. "You would be pleased to know that she quit last night. She didn't give a reason, although I always sensed she was troubled over working here. Who isn't? Myself included. A bunch of the girls said that some prominent members of the football team from your school—Caroline's school—were here last night. Sometimes girls get spooked when they run into people they know."

"Was the star quarterback among them, by any chance?" the cheerleading coach asked.

Phil's long pause gave away the answer the woman already suspected.

"I really can't comment further on the patrons," he said. "But anyway, she's no longer employed here. I see no conflict of interest anymore. She's a good kid, that one."

"Thanks. All I wanted to know is whether she is working there. I got my answer."

Sensing they were on the same page with the girl's best interest in both of their hearts, Phil dared to extend the conversation.

"Do you mean to tell me, though, that there are people out there who would ruin a girl's future because of her line of work? Would you really drop her?"

Caroline's coach went on to explain that she wasn't yet aware of the rules for scholarship athletes in that type of scenario.

"I wanted to look into the situation myself without causing a big splash," she said. "But, yes, sadly, there are people out there who apparently care more about bringing someone down than focusing on their own greatness and achievements."

Armed with firsthand information, the coach hustled back to the practice field in an attempt to end the drama over Caroline before it fully took off. She positioned herself on a sideline bench and kept busy flipping through the pages in her clipboard of Orange Bowl events and appearances. She correctly anticipated Devin's second effort to seek her out. The coach soon felt an unsettling series of taps on her shoulder blade.

"You have a knack for sneaking up on people."

"Being elusive is my job here," Devin said. "I've got two minutes. Let's take a quick walk?"

The coach wasn't sure whether the quarterback was posing a question or making a demand, but the conversation—the closure—was something she wanted nonetheless.

"So, did you look into it?" he asked as they walked.

The coach decided to stick to the most basic facts.

"Yes."

Devin couldn't hold back a smug smile.

"I took your information very seriously and personally called the manager of the club this morning," she said. "Good news. He said he doesn't employ Caroline there. Good thing, because she is one of my best. It sounds like a bad rumor. Unless you have proof otherwise, I consider this case resolved."

She watched Devin's smile disappear with a twitch. She stopped walking and looked at him with disappointed eyes that dared him to say he had seen Caroline dancing at the club. She took a gamble that he wouldn't.

"That is good news," Devin said weakly. "I wouldn't want someone like that representing our team."

"Yes. This is a time to focus on positive things and positive people. Karma is not something any of us want to be messing with right before a major bowl."

The cheerleading coach had no idea just how superstitious Devin was—right down to refusing to drink the same favorite sports drink of his competitors. Maybe it was his family's history of failed attempts. Maybe it was his father's obsessive ways being passed down to the golden boy. Ever since the bowl game announcement,

Devin had been drinking orange juice even though he knew the act made no sense. He gave a nervous laugh.

"So you really believe bad things happen for each act of negativity, do you?" he asked.

"Um, I guess. Who am I to say for sure? It never hurts to stay positive, though. This I know."

"Whatever. I've got to get back to practice."

"Good luck, Devin," the coach said genuinely.

The player didn't know if she was wishing him well in play or life. He pretended not to care.

She watched him jog back to the field as the team's kicker attempted a fifty-yard field goal.

CHAPTER 25

JP
THE DESTINED ONE

The stairs of the home in which JP grew up made squeaks and creaks that sounded exactly how the small running back's sore joints and aching muscles felt. As he slowly crept upstairs to his childhood bedroom, he longed for a few moments of rest in the familiar old bed with the same faded, gold-striped sheets that had comforted him through years of overcoming small obstacles. JP noticed a newly framed article celebrating him overcoming a major one.

The unfamiliar piece contained a trio of news photos capturing each of the key breakaways that had led to JP's three touchdowns in a game that had secured a trip to the Orange Bowl for his fellow Syracuse Orange and Navy. He drew the frame in toward his tight, small chest to read the caption.

After a fall and a fumble that started off the biggest game of his life, Syracuse College's new running back, JP Hemmings, recovered and took control of the matchup against Tennessee to give his team the only points of the game. SC Head Coach John "Flash" Robbins, a man who gave the running back

186

*starting time amidst heavy criticism, called the player's "magical hat trick of
touchdowns the truest examples of grit, talent and inspiration" he'd ever seen.*

JP's smile showed off a rare pride that he attempted to contain, for even in the
lonesome stillness of his old room where no one was watching, he was still humble.
He never wanted to take a winning performance for granted. He didn't want to
get too confident. And he didn't want to work any less hard toward an even more
important game to come. Maxine's caption made him feel comforted nonetheless.
It hadn't even mentioned his size, he noted. JP felt relief, too, over Coach Flash's
credit—in print—for sticking up for him during unpopular times.

JP carefully hung the frame in its new place, straightened it with precision against
the old plaid wallpaper that served as a leveling tool for many framed certificates
and articles over the years, and removed his heavy sweatshirt in preparation for
overdue rest. His dark skin felt as comfortable as ever against the soft sheets, but
he tossed and turned in failed attempts at sleep. He was coming off the excitement
of winning a critical game for his team and exceeding even the harshest critics'
expectations. Then there were all the endless press interview requests, more intense
practices, and attention from newfound fans wherever he went.

In the kitchen downstairs, the professors spoke excitedly in hushed tones and
supported their overwhelmed son the best way they knew through the loving act of
family cooking. The well-fed professor rolled his signature garlic meatballs in clean
palms as his wife stirred some homemade gravy. A chattering lid alerted them that
another pot's boiling water was ready for the lasagna noodles.

In marriage, parenthood, and life, the couple was regularly able to communicate
with each other in shorthand.

"Can you put them in, Mum?" asked the professor. "My hands."

"Got it," she sang as she opened a box of lasagna noodles.

"You're chipper right now."

"Right now," she admitted. "It's because I feel like I'm being productive. I feel
like I'm actually doing something that can help my son."

"You make it sound as though the boy is headed for Doomsday. The boy is
instead a superhero right now."

"He is a superhero and I'm happy for him and proud of him, but wouldn't you
say that the fans and media set unrealistic expectations for superheroes? I fear this
is all too much for him. It's happening too quickly."

"Too quickly?" asked the anthropology professor in disbelief. "Too quickly? He's been working for this his whole life. You need to just go with the flow, as they say. Whatever comes, comes. We may not be religious types, but I think you and I would agree that ever since his time in the womb, his life has appeared predestined. Let's just enjoy this time, Mum. There's always been some greater power—whether it has come through an adoption agent or a coach—to help him find his way. We've taught him all we can to have the strongest backbone possible in a life where he feels different. We have no control at this point. Just focus on getting a handle on those sticky, floppy lasagna noodles you'll be wrestling with momentarily. That's more than enough of a challenge."

"You're right," the woman said as she opened a bottle of the couple's favorite Wildhorse Merlot and filled two glasses.

"Here's to JP running like a racehorse in the bowl game," she said.

"Yes, and here's to us just letting go, letting him run wild," countered her husband. "It's time for him to run a little more freely from us."

An hour and a couple of calming glasses of wine later, a polite knock on the door let the family know that their dinner guest had arrived.

The anthropology professor opened the door with a whistle.

"Never heard that one before, sir," Whistler joked. The defensive lineman's appearance was grand in many ways. He easily filled the width and height of the doorframe. He showed off a warm smile.

"Come on in, Whistler, it's freezing," JP's mother called. "Now how did we manage to luck out and have two star players at our family dinner table tonight?"

All their lives, the professors had been self-declared nerds, and proud of it. They suddenly found themselves in unfamiliar territory. They felt as though the most popular kid at school had chosen to sit with them at the misfit lunch table. And if they were being honest with themselves, they liked this feeling.

"Well, professor, I'd have to fly all the way to Alabama if I wanted to enjoy my family's dinner tonight," said Whistler. "Thanks for inviting me to yours. I smell something tasty."

"So that's where you're from," she said. "Poor thing, having to deal with this lake-effect wind and snow. Come here by the fire where it's nice and toasty. Let me take your coat."

"Um, we've come a long way, haven't we professor?" Whistler asked.

"How do you mean?"

Quick footsteps down the stairs interrupted the conversation.

"Whistler means, Mom, that you two have come a long way since the morning you first dropped me off on campus and called his grades out in front of the guys."

"How was your rest?" she asked her boy with instant concern.

"The best, Mom. Hey, man."

"Hey."

"It's not enough that I have to listen to your snores resound through our apartment on East Campus? Now you are horning in on my home-cooked meals," JP razzed.

"I just can't get enough of the man of the hour," Whistler said. "Can you sign my jersey later?"

"Yes, I can. I think I'll put, 'Dear Whistler, please try those nose patches I laid out so I can get some shut-eye before the big game. You have a very fitting name since you whistle through your nose. Your name would be even more appropriate, though, if it were called NGUH PUH, NGUH PUH, NGUH PUH—since that more closely resembles the sounds you make in the middle of the night. Signed: Your Friend, the Man of the Hour.'"

The anthropology professor clasped his hands over his mouth with chuckles that sent aftershocks to his shoulders. His wife's smile was as wide as either of her family members remembered seeing it.

"OK, Whistler, you're right," she said. "Let's just say that every once in a while a student teaches the professor a lesson about life. I admit that I may have pegged you wrongly in the beginning. But it wouldn't have changed those initial poor grades."

"I guess winning you over will have to be enough," Whistler said. "The achievement will be right up there with passing your class on the second try and, oh, winning the Orange Bowl."

"I'm so glad you kept just a pinch of your sarcasm," the woman said. "Let's eat!"

As the players settled into their seats around the table, the professors handed out fresh salads, warm rolls with honey butter, and the balsamic dressing they'd prepared from scratch. They found themselves quickly offering the young men seconds.

"So tell us, Whistler, about your upcoming competition," the anthropology professor said.

"Well, he means—if you want to talk about it," added his wife.

"Yes, my lovely partner is someone who can finish my sentences and subtly let me know if I'm being too intrusive."

"I don't mind talking about it," Whistler said. "It is what it is, basically. I never fully understood that overused saying until this moment. The University of Boston's Falcons are the favored team—the best in the BCS, in my personal opinion. The quarterback is headed straight for the NFL if you ask me. Beyond his natural abilities, Devin Madison has the uncanny ability to win games. They've won all of their games this season. We're lucky the Falcons are no longer in our Big East division. I'm not so sure we'd be heading to the Orange Bowl with them in our regular schedule. Too bad the guy's a putz."

"How do you mean?" JP asked.

"You know, dude, players have connections with other players, and you of all people know they talk. I've always heard that the guy changes girlfriends as often as he does athletic heat rub applications. He's rude to his coaches. He screams at his teammates. He's quirky too. Like many successful athletes, he has his odd superstitions and routines. People tend to just step back and let him do his thing since it's all working."

"He hasn't met The Keys," JP said. "Especially the Master."

"He hasn't met our new weapon, either," Whistler said with an appreciative nod toward the running back.

JP's mother could feel the stress entering the dining room.

"And how are you feeling about everything, JP?" she asked her son.

The homemade lasagna and gravy with meatballs at a family dinner table that had facilitated nearly every moment of JP opening up over the years made the running back want to spill it all in this moment too. If his mother had asked him a second time whether he had a good rest upstairs, he probably would've given her a more truthful answer now.

"I wish I could say dealing with the pressure is easy, but it's just not," JP admitted. "I don't know what's worse—having all the fans and media expect you to fail or having them expect you to shine. There's more pressure now, that's for sure. I don't want to fail them. I'm scared of failing them."

JP's parents looked at him with worried eyes and wished they could take away his fears. His roommate, an All-American athlete and team captain who could teach a course on dealing with great expectations, looked at JP with his own eyes, ones that contained anything but pity. His approach would leave more of an impact.

"JP, whatever, dude," said Whistler. "I don't believe for a second that you'd rather be watching from the sidelines now that the impossible has happened with Coach Flash giving you a shot at the unlikeliest of times. At its core, football is a game with inevitable wins and losses, triumphs and mistakes. It can make fans celebrate and it can make them have a worse day for like an hour or two. You need to forget about all these distractions and focus on what you love to do—you can run."

JP's parents looked at each other from across the table and understood that they were sharing a similar thought. They realized that on this night, Whistler was the greater power needed to pick up the relay stick that had guided JP through his seemingly destined life. It was a role they had each played themselves on many previous occasions.

JP thought about his very first football coach who had told him he could run as a little boy. He remembered too how the man had instructed him not to forget about him when JP became famous. It was a joke back then, albeit a kind-hearted one. He wondered if that coach from so long ago would remember his name now. Would his biological mother remember the name she had chosen for him? He thought of his long road of small successes and suddenly believed he would accomplish more.

"You know, I think it's our time, Whistler," JP said. "I think we're going to do it."

CHAPTER 26

HENRY
THE SHY ONE

Henry opened his eyes to a dark, eastern Massachusetts morning well before his mother had an opportunity to tell him it was time to get ready for school. The writing pad containing his secret hurt over the new nickname created by his sixth-grade classmates rested under his thin, lumpy pillow. His favorite University of Boston Falcons sweatshirt hung at the ready, like armor that he hoped would protect him from another day of being called "Polly Ester." The insides of his backpack were already neatly organized beside his bed and ready to go. A frigid wind rattled his bedroom window and reminded him that his toes were cold. The feeling didn't bother him nearly as much as the layers of anxiety filling up his insides.

The minutes turned into half an hour as finally a knock on the door and his mother's kind voice signaled his time was up.

"Henry, babe, it's about time to get ready for school. Do you need an extra little snooze first?"

"Sure."

Henry lay awake in bed, knowing that before long he'd have to get up and join the two women in his life over cereal downstairs.

"Good morning, Henry," said his grandmother.

"Hi."

"I never did get to tell you about my day yesterday. Do you still want to he-ah 'bout it?"

Misty exchanged glances with them both before reaching for boxes of cereal and raisins to fix her son a bowl.

"Sure."

"So, I was havin' a private con-vah-sation with a custuhmah at the station—maybe you know 'em—our neighbah a few apartments over named Mr. Delancey? Well, that pah-aht doesn't mattah. Anyway, he was the only custuhmah in the shop and we were talkin' quietly about the need to fix the railing posts in our apahtment building, and out of nowhere, my managah was ovah my shoulder, buttin' in."

"What did he say?" Misty asked.

"Well, he agreed with us and said it sounded dangerous to have fragile rails, and he suggested talkin' with our supah."

Misty tilted her head and moved it back into place as if to subtly say, "That's not so bad, is it?"

"It's not what he said," the elder woman quickly added. "It's the fact that he said anythin' at all. I was having a private con-vah-sation. There's nothin' worse than when you think you are talkin' with one person, and anothah makes an appearance and comments out of left field, makin' you realize he's been listenin' all the while. It's creepy. It's rude."

Misty remained silent with polite indifference.

"I was tellin' this story to my grandson, anyway," the elder woman said. "What do you think about it, Henry?"

"I don't know," said the boy. "I guess I kinda see how that could annoy you."

"You see that, Misty?" the elder woman asked. "We raised a smaht boy."

Henry's grandmother knew her story wasn't the most insightful addition to her signature collection of observations, but she correctly guessed that something had happened to Henry at school the day before, and she was anxious for him to open up. She kept this knowledge hidden from Misty, who worried enough about the boy.

Both women watched Henry silently force spoonfuls of breakfast into his mouth in a robotic motion. He stared only into the eyes of his cereal's Os. Henry was accustomed to his mother's stares, but both women's watchfulness felt too intense. The boy picked up his bowl, carried it to the sink, and jogged to his room to fetch his backpack. He checked beneath his pillow to make sure each corner of his writing journal was hidden from both women. He had no idea that a topic of one of his upcoming entries would feature his own observation: the worst days tend to come when you aren't expecting them, and the best ones hit you after starting them off with great worry. Against all of his household's expectations, Henry, the shy one, was about to have an exceptional school day.

>>>> <<<<

Throughout the morning commute from Boston's Allston neighborhood to the Kennedy School in Brockton via foot, T, commuter rail, and foot again, Teach frequently touched the rectangular envelope in his wool coat pocket to make sure its contents were safe.

"Morning, Miss Sally," Teach said to the school secretary, whose desk by the entrance showed off a new vase of red roses.

The woman, in her seventies, offered a rare smile.

"Hi, Teach."

"Secret admirer, I see?"

"Oh, Teach. Do you really think I could pull off a secret admirer? They're from my sister. It's my birthday, if I may say so myself."

"Well, happy birthday, Miss Sally. The flowers are seriously beautiful, just like their recipient."

As Teach hustled up the sparkly concrete stairs toward his classroom he finally remembered the rose left frozen and dead in his trunk. The flower had been intended for the beautiful Tufts dental student he had taken out the evening before. A night of sleep had made Teach certain he had made the right decision over who would get his extra bowl game tickets. Instead of being flanked in the stadium by a beautiful, albeit difficult, girl on one side and one of his best buddies on the other, Teach had opted to hold an academic contest and award the tickets to the winning student and his or her chaperone. It was the type of decision that summed up the young man's character.

Teach jotted down secretary Sally's birth date on his desk calendar. He removed the envelope from his coat pocket containing the details of the game and placed it in a terribly messy drawer. As the bell rang signaling the start of the school day, he surveyed the punch ball field and believed he knew which student's contest it was to lose.

The kids burst noisily into Teach's classroom. They hung up their winter coats, tossed their hats and gloves into personalized bins, and slipped their cool feet out of snow boots and into sneakers and loafers. They were chatting all the while, except for one. Henry was so preoccupied with staying under the radar today that not even his best friend Oscar heard so much as a whisper from him.

"OK, OK, my favorite kiddos," Teach said. "Let's quiet down now. Time to start filling your developing minds with fun facts and ferocious figures. We've got a lot to cover today. Please get your Current Events notes out of your desks and we'll update them with the latest news in preparation for Friday's quiz. Who watched the news last night?"

A handful of Teach's most ambitious students raised their hands to report a mining accident, Commonwealth legislation passage, and the passing of a US senator.

"These are all very relevant and important," Teach said. "At least a few of you did your homework last night. How about the category of sports? Did something happen yesterday that was sports related?"

Many more hands reached for the ceiling now. Henry knew the answer, but, as he usually did, he avoided making eye contact with his teacher despite him being Henry's favorite instructor so far.

"Patsy!"

A few kids sniggered in their seats as the girl nicknamed "Patsy, Patsy, Four-Eyed Fatsy" prepared her answer.

"Go ahead, Patsy. You've got this," Teach encouraged.

"Um, well, last night? I overheard my dad talking about this? Um, he said that University of Boston made it into a great football game. I think its name is Orange and Navy?"

"You are correct! That's exactly right, Patsy. UB, the college I happened to attend by the way, is going to the Orange Bowl next month to play against a team in Syracuse. It's a great win for Boston, and I think you'll hear people talking about it more and more. People may even wish they were going to the game."

Teach reached into his messy desk to remove his precious envelope.

"This brings me to tonight's homework assignment. It's a special one. I think you are going to like it," Teach said.

The same kids who chuckled at Patsy's name grumbled mildly in their seats. They were used to Teach's playful, sarcastic jokes and thought this was another one of those.

"I'm serious," said Teach. "This is going to be an assignment I think you are going to love, because—Oscar, do you mind giving me a drum roll, please?"

Henry's best friend happily pounded his big palms on his desk.

"The assignment comes with a—uh, thank you, Oscar, that will be all—a very special prize for the student who submits the best poem as decided by a small panel of independent judges who I will tap from our fine faculty. The prize is a pair of tickets to Boston's bowl game for the winner and his or her guardian. Your seats will be next to mine, so hopefully that won't put a damper on the bounty."

The shrieks and hollers that erupted within Teach's classroom revealed that sitting next to the coolest teacher at the grandest game they could imagine would be far from an issue for any of them. Even Henry showed the man a rare grin. The room's toughest bully bounced up and down in his seat like a kindergartener on Christmas morning.

"Jeesh," Teach said. "OK, no one has won anything yet. You guys are going to get me fired. Quiet down, now. So tonight's one and only homework assignment is to write a poem. It can be about anything that matters to you. It can be any length. It must, however, be written in couplets. What, you may ask, are couplets? Let's put away your Current Events notes and open up to page forty-four in your English texts. Henry, could you do us the honor of reading this example?"

As the kids quietly flipped through the pages, Henry located the poem and cleared his throat.

"'An Autumn Greeting' is written by an anonymous poet," Henry said.

He silently scanned the short prose before reading it aloud to the class of his harshest critics. Henry read the piece with perfect rhythm and diction, just as Teach knew he would. The man couldn't help but wonder whether Henry's red-and-gold Falcons sweatshirt was life's funny prediction at the winner while Henry, a boy his grandmother lovingly called the best autumn news she ever received, wondered if the poem's title was a sign.

"Anyway, easy question, but who can tell me what a couplet means?" Teach asked.

Teach's voice trailed off in Henry's head as the boy knew he was safe from being called on again for a while. His mind immediately searched for a topic that mattered to him. It was a dilemma that would preoccupy him for the rest of the school day, helping to silence the kids yelling "Polly Ester" later that afternoon in the same singsong rhythm as "Yankees Su-uck," a phrase one of the bullies heard his father chant during many Red Sox-Yankees games. Not even his best and only friend could easily break Henry's focus.

"Hey, Henry, wait up. Are you OK?"

"Polly Es-ter."

"Hey, Oscar. Yeah, what's up?"

"Polly Es-ter."

"Um, nothing, Henry. Hey, do you want to hang out this afternoon?"

"Well, I can't today. Maybe tomorrow? I have to, uh, help my grandmother with something. There's her car. Gotta run. See you tomorrow, Oscar."

Inside the apartment, Henry barely had his winter coat off before fetching his journal from beneath his pillow and bringing the composition book into the living room to get straight to work. His grandmother was happily humming an Irving Berlin tune in the kitchen. It made the boy think about how older people's singing sounded like an old-fashioned movie. Her voice was shaky and polished at the same time.

Within the modest kitchenette, his grandmother often made dinner the moment they got back from the school, insisting the boy must be hungry from a day of work and play. On this special afternoon, she was cooking Henry's favorite: spaghetti with meatballs from a can and toasted white bread and margarine with Parmesan cheese sprinkled on top. "Grandma's Specialty," as the family called it, was not a dish of which Misty approved as there was nothing green in it, but the elder woman worried only about the genesis of the boy's mood on the previous day, and sought to bring him some comfort.

As Henry busily worked in his notebook, jotting down a variety of ideas for topics, his grandmother was already feeling less worried in the kitchen.

"I like when you work out he-ah instead of bein' holed up in that room of yours," she said. "I get to see ya handsome face. Is my singin' botherin' ya schoolwork?"

"No," Henry said.

She walked into the living room to cover him with the crocheted multicolored blanket that she had made years ago. It was a piece well worn in an apartment that was kept at 65 degrees during the frigid months, when the average cost of gas heat for their two-bedroom apartment totaled $220 a month.

Between his grandmother's humming, the smell of her simple comfort food, the warmth of her blanket, and the hope of getting to witness his dream, Henry was in grand spirits.

His grandmother clinked ice cubes into a fizzing glass as she poured Henry's favorite orange soda, purchased earlier that day. She gave Henry a big grin. He gave one back, realizing that the perfect subject of his poem had been in front of him all along. The subject wouldn't be cool or popular with his classmates, but it might just win him the tickets to the best game of his life.

CHAPTER 27

MAXINE
The Lonely One

For only the second time in her professional career, Maxine found herself on an airplane ride to an assignment. The photographer watched with envy as the other business passengers on the small plane fell asleep before their brief seventy-minute ride from Syracuse to New York City began. Working in the financially strapped industry of print and wire media made her ride feel much more intense. Worry filled her tired head instead of dreams, just as it had a decade ago on her first traveling assignment to Washington, DC.

On this particular trip, the photographer felt stressed over a call that had come in when news of Syracuse College's trip to the Orange Bowl came out.

"Maxine, I need you to get into my office right away," her photo editor had called out a day ago within the newsroom of International Presswire's Syracuse bureau. "The sports editor at New York headquarters is on my line for you and me. I take it you are well aware by now that Syracuse College is heading to the Orange Bowl? Just a reminder that these are the types of things I need to be kept aware of. Immediately. We are in the news business, after all."

199

Maxine had walked with quick steps behind her boss's even quicker high heels. She had nodded in agreement, even though the news had been released only seconds before and she had intended to provide a prompt bowl game update all along. Maxine had taken a seat in the woman's office, a sunny space filled with happy faces of children in holiday cards, family vacations, and school pictures. The images had made Maxine wonder how the woman managed to juggle a high-powered job, a relationship, and multiple children. The photographer couldn't help but feel lonely as she pictured her more barren desk.

"Sir, I have Maxine on," the woman had said with her eyes fixed on the phone. "Sorry to keep you waiting. She is aware, of course, of her team's trip to the Orange Bowl. What a coup, by the way."

"Is the city going crazy?" the bellowing voice asked.

Maxine had watched her boss peer between the office blinds toward an empty street to come up with anything but an empty answer.

"People are ecstatic," she said while shifting her gaze to Maxine for help.

"Exactly, sir," Maxine added. "The city has been waiting a long time for the team to get back to the caliber they had grown accustomed to over the years. I think fans can thank Coach Flash and JP Hemmings for this wonderful gift."

Her boss had given her a silent nod in the office as they both waited for the man's reply. Maxine had always served as a calm voice of reason even though she was battling so much professional worry—and personal loneliness—in her own head.

"Well, that's why I'm calling, Maxine. Everyone in sports is talking about your underdog team. All eyes will be on them this holiday season in viewers' living rooms next to aging Christmas trees and leftover New Year's bean dip. I've been fairly pleased with your insider-like coverage of the team, and I trust you'll be able to do the same for Boston's Falcons, even though they haven't played Syracuse yet this year. Anyway, I'm telling you that I'm putting trust in you to be our lead photographer when the two teams meet at the Orange Bowl."

Maxine had felt cautiously excited as the news from headquarters made a personal dream of hers feel instantly in reach. She had looked at her boss, who beamed with pride. Maxine knew that in her hardworking life, there was often a catch.

"You should know that I'm giving this assignment to you over a veteran in our New York City office who has covered the Orange Bowl for the last dozen or so years," the voice announced.

Maxine's face had fallen while her boss had looked even more proud over the competitiveness of it all—especially with their Syracuse office coming out on top.

"I want you to fly here for a day and come meet him," he said.

Not even Maxine's boss's face could hide the difficulty of that type of awkward encounter.

"He knows the ins and outs of Sun Life stadium, the city of Miami Gardens, the press passes for events," the voice had continued over the phone. "Absorbing his insider knowledge will complement your own connections with your team. I want your meeting with our veteran to be in person because I'd like the chance to meet you too, Maxine. I need to finally see the talent behind these hard-to-get shots."

"Thank you, sir, for the opportunity and the honor of coming to the wire's headquarters," Maxine had managed.

She had sounded confident and appreciative despite feeling similar to how she did on a day when her boss had told her she could upgrade to a desk with a window view, but it would have to come at the expense of a colleague whose work had been lacking. Maxine had a difficult time making eye contact with that coworker ever since, even though she had pleaded with her boss to keep their seats where they were.

>>> <<<

As the plane cruised along now, Maxine kept her seat upright, reminiscent of her work flight a decade ago. She worried this time over whether the veteran photographer would be bitter at the sports editor's selection. She wondered what she would say when they met in mere moments. She fretted over how she would assure the sports editor he made the right choice. The photographer had some ideas, but none of them felt quite good enough. She questioned whether she was the right choice after all.

Maxine looked across the aisle to notice a family of three sitting together with a pregnant mother and wife in the middle. Her husband poured a bit of water onto a cloth so she could wipe her head. He held a paper bag for her in anticipation of sickness. The woman's toddler attempted comforting the woman on her other side with an innocently sweet voice.

"Is baby makin' you sick, Muh-muh?"

The woman looked pale green, shaky, and beyond uncomfortable. Maxine wished she could change places with her in a second. The ailing woman locked eyes with Maxine, who, in contrast, looked put together in her best photographer's suit, healthy and solo, carrying no dependents. The woman's pained eyes in that moment seemed to be sharing Maxine's wish.

The plane landed uneventfully, and Maxine gathered her single bag. She guiltily accepted the family members' offer to let her zip down the aisle first. Her pangs for a husband and children of her own stayed with her until she reached Manhattan, where the sounds of automobile horns and a collision of scents from street vendor offerings, perfumes, and pollution snapped Maxine back into her reality: her career. As her cab approached West 33rd Street, Maxine eyed the grand, box-shaped International Newswire headquarters. Intimidation gripped her now as she thought about the successful people who must be inside and wondered which one was scheduled to meet with her first.

A salt-and-pepper-haired man with an unsteady voice and handshake greeted her outside a bay of elevators and provided the answer. She knew in an instant that he wasn't the sports editor with the bellowing voice.

OK, she thought to herself. Gear up for the veteran you're being forced to replace.

Maxine mentally scanned the conversation ideas she had come up with during her plane ride. None of them felt good enough.

"Follow me," the man whispered. "We can talk in my office."

The man's colleagues eyed Maxine as the pair walked. The staff had clearly heard about her arrival, she thought. She could feel their stares crawl up and down her suit, but she still smiled as politely and humbly as she could manage. The veteran walked quickly, almost too quickly for her to keep up, and weaved between cubicles on the way to his corner office.

He was embarrassed, Maxine thought. It was the very thing she didn't want. The veteran immediately closed his office door and checked his pride enough to pull out her seat. Maxine wished he hadn't taken that last step. He was not only embarrassed, he was a gentleman too, she observed.

She took in the veteran's shots of tennis greats, basketball legends, and Super Bowl players—all captured in motion, yet hanging beautifully still on his walls. They were images that had graced the A1 pages of the country's most prominent dailies. Maxine recognized a couple shots that had appeared in the textbooks for her sports journalism courses during her communications studies.

"Look at the motion. The champion isn't just holding the trophy, he's tossing it in the air. This is a memorable shot," one of Maxine's professors had said so many years ago. "See how the player is perfectly framed? Never cut off a subject at the joints. It makes viewers uncomfortable, even though they might not be able to consciously figure out why."

The office was still and silent as her eyes enjoyed a quick, inspirational journey around the four walls.

"Wow, I recognize so many of these pictures," Maxine finally said. "You've covered every championship."

"The Orange Bowl has been my favorite of them all, you know. It's pretty special. Those are kids just playing their hearts out for their fans, their friends, their families, their school, themselves. Most of them obviously don't go on to the NFL. For the seniors, it's their last game. You can feel the desire on the sidelines of that field."

There was no friendly smile or excitement on the man's face. There was only sadness. He continued.

"So I was told I'd have to meet with the whipper-snapper who succeeded in going after my spot."

At thirty-seven years old, Maxine hadn't thought of herself as a whipper-snapper, but the look on the veteran's face told her it wouldn't be wise to disagree with that characterization. She would take issue with his other point, though.

"Going after your spot was the very last thing I intended to do," she said. "I was just focusing on my job up in Syracuse. I won't deny that being called in here is an honor, but you clearly deserve to cover the bowl more than I do. I'll take your lead on the assignment if it's what you and the sports editor really want."

The man forced a chuckle.

Maxine relayed her seriousness. She asked if she was scheduled to meet with the sports editor next.

"Do you want to see if he is available now?" she continued. "Why don't we propose both covering the bowl? This assignment is a dream for me and I'd honestly do it for free. You can take the lead on the play-by-play shots, and I'll back you up whenever I can assist with the relationships I've built with the Orange and Navy. Let's propose this idea. Together."

The veteran looked at her and finally calmed himself down enough to see a woman who was unshaken, genuine, and giving. The aging man wasn't used to her kindness inside a building of go-getters who seemed to vie for his position more vigorously with each new appearance of his white hairs.

Maxine watched one of the man's colleagues stroll slowly by the veteran's office window to see how the less-senior photographer was faring.

"Should I signal to that guy that I'm still in one piece or feign I've been attacked?" she asked.

The veteran finally gave Maxine a smile. It felt nice on him, even though he had been struggling for days with the fact that the higher-ups at headquarters clearly wanted him off the bowl game he most loved. Other coveted assignments would be going next, he thought.

"My agility on the sidelines is not what it used to be," he admitted.

"Oh, I don't know," Maxine said. "You moved pretty quickly through your peers to get me tucked into this nice corner office a moment ago."

As she winked at him, the veteran decided that if anyone deserved to take his place on this assignment, it was Maxine. To his own surprise, he thought he might even help her succeed.

"I saw your insider coverage of JP's game," he said.

"Sometimes after being behind the quiet of a lens, you put your work out there and you don't realize just how far-reaching it is," Maxine said.

"I was impressed."

"Well, that makes my career, coming from you."

"Listen. The Orange Bowl is your assignment—and yours alone—to screw up," he said. "Congratulations. I can't believe I'm saying this, but you have my blessing to take over. I'm going to help you succeed as much as I can."

Maxine had always wanted a mentor, but until now she relied solely on her tireless work ethic to guide her through the most challenging assignments from the most demanding directors. She hoped today's visit marked an unexpected change.

"I just want to listen to whatever you have to offer," she said. "I can't tell you how much I value your time."

"OK, let's get back to the listening part then, little whipper-snapper," he said. "How much do you weigh, anyhow? Oh, never mind that. Between my age and your appearance—which lends itself more to covering gymnastics than football—

we are a couple of misfits in this industry who have proven we can make it. Don't let me down now."

Maxine's notepad and pen were made ready.

"Now, Syracuse College and the University of Boston are two teams who've been to the Orange Bowl before, but not nearly often enough to make this trip old hat for either of them. Syracuse has had three dates there to Boston's one. Neither team won any of these games. History will change this year when one of them finally succeeds. Will it be the team with the flawless record or the one with the heart? I'm not sure the answer is as clear as everyone is expecting."

Maxine found herself wishing she knew her journalism colleagues' shorthand techniques as she tried to put to paper the man's thoughts on the bowl's past, present, and future. She knew his insights would bring texture to her coverage and captions, and for that she was beyond grateful. The veteran spoke without interruption for nearly an hour. When he finally stopped, Maxine was left with only one question.

"What about this angle of Boston's golden quarterback wanting to win this thing for his own unique family history? Is this as big of a deal as everyone else is making it out to be?" she asked. "If you turn on the cable sports channels, it's all you hear."

"That is an obvious angle and one that I omitted on purpose," the veteran explained. "Being in this business so long makes you hear rumors you don't want to hear and believe things you wished you didn't believe. You know how the best political beat reporters don't vote in government elections because they don't want their participation to influence their news coverage? When it comes to buying Devin Madison and his stories—and believe me, he has many great ones—I try to keep my vote out on that. I don't want it to influence my own angles. You'll meet the obsessive young man when you accompany an assigned journalist on pre-game press opportunities. Keep in mind that on the field, a superstar's impressive play is more important than his words. I'll leave it at that."

Maxine stopped writing and attempted to absorb his meaning with a squint of her eyes.

The veteran glanced quickly at his watch.

"You'll see what I mean. Anyway, I've got to walk you over to meet our beloved sports editor. I believe you two are going to lunch. Don't let him get to you, huh?"

Armed with the veteran's support and in-depth knowledge, Maxine felt unusually confident stepping into her second big meeting of the day. But by the time she buckled herself in for her flight back to Syracuse a couple hours later, that confidence was gone. Over outrageously priced salads and a couple glasses of fancy white wine—one of which Maxine didn't touch and the sports editor was happy to finish—the man with the bellowing voice had made clear to Maxine his Orange Bowl coverage expectations.

"Think of me as Coach Flash and you as JP before Syracuse's last game," the man had said. "I'm not exactly taking the sure bet in sending you to cover the Orange Bowl. I need to look like the genius and I need you to pull off the impossible, just like JP did. What do you think would've happened to JP's playing time if he hadn't pulled off the unimaginable in the last game?"

Maxine had quickly lost her appetite.

"Um, well, I guess he would've been benched," she had said.

"Benched or cut from the team. Don't make us both regret me taking a chance on you."

On the flight home, Maxine's stomach was just as tied up as it had been on the way down. She tried calming herself by replaying the veteran's kind wisdom inside her head.

You know how the best political beat reporters don't vote in government elections because they don't want their participation to influence their news coverage?

The observation made Maxine think of Ed, the government reporter who had accompanied her on her only other work flight a decade ago. She wondered if all these years later, he still refrained from voting. She recalled the moment he shared that fact with her during their memorable dinner in Washington over fresh lobsters and conversation. Their working date a decade ago was far better than any she'd been on for pleasure since. Ed and Maxine had shared each other's dreams and supported them. Their working dinner wasn't even comparable to the working lunch she had just experienced. As challenging as it was proving to be, not even Maxine could humbly deny that she was living her professional dream now. She wondered if Ed had managed to accomplish the same and if he was experiencing the added stress that had come with it too.

Maxine closed her eyes and rested her head against the plane's cushioned seat. She tried imagining what Ed might look like all these years later. She couldn't picture him now or then and moved on to visualizing her upcoming date, a man with whom she had become acquainted through her online dating service, to the delight of her family and friends. Maxine was cautiously excited over meeting the man, who had listed hikes, movies, and football among his interests. He was much easier to picture than Ed, because his profile picture had resembled a headshot of George Clooney. She kept her eyes closed as she hoped the date would serve as a welcome distraction from the stress and pressure of her upcoming assignment.

A bit of turbulence shook her, and she opened her restless eyes. She finally recalled a vision of Ed a decade ago when a bump on their airplane ride had knocked a little drool out of the corner of his mouth. She felt a fluttering feeling in her stomach, and it wasn't from the turbulence.

CHAPTER 28
HENRY
The Shy One

Henry tightly grasped his poem, written in his best handwriting on college-ruled paper, as his mother drove him the familiar route to school in the family sedan.

The young mom and waitress had closed the restaurant the night before. Henry glanced at her sitting behind the wheel and believed that despite being one of the most overworked parents around, she was by far the most beautiful mother of anyone at school. Like most of his thoughts, this was an observation that would be left unspoken. Henry had no idea what his father looked like, yet the quick glance at his mother on this morning made him realize that he must've gotten his unpopular looks from the man he didn't know. He returned his gaze to his poem and read it over for the seventh time that day.

"What's that you've got there?" Misty asked.

"Homework."

"Oh yeah? Anything good?"

"Um, I don't know. Could we please turn the radio to WEEI?"

Misty flipped her silky dark hair and moved the dial to Boston's Sports Radio Network. The voices speaking in fast tempos assured Henry that she had found the right one.

"And that is exactly why New England fans say In Belichick We Trust," shouted a raspy voice through the car's aging speakers.

"That was a play call from the Pats' coach that will go down in history," countered an equally coarse one. "Anyway, let's change gears for a moment from bickering about our beloved New England Patriots and focus on the team people across the region are talking about around their water coolers this morning. I'm moving on to collegiate play now. How about those University of Boston Falcons, Danny?"

"How about 'em? Listen, Ron, you know I'll be rooting for the local team as hard as anyone come game day, but I think it's clear they have their hands full. Devin Madison has to face that mean offensive lineman called Whistler, who has the most sacks in the BCS. On top of it all, there is the X factor. The Orange and Navy's star running back is out with injury, which could turn out to be a good or bad thing for our Falcons. The replacement, the five-foot, six-inch JP Hemmings, is coming off one hell of a great game. A lot of people don't think he can repeat it. I wouldn't sell him so short, though. That little guy is fast."

"Yeah, Danny, but who has the drive to win? Don't forget that Boston's star quarterback's grandfather, a defensive star himself back in the day, never made it to play in the Orange Bowl following an unexpected loss and a lucky decision not to go to the Coconut Grove after-party before the place burned to the ground. Devin Madison is hungry to give his family—and our local team—a win."

"I've heard the story, Ron. I just don't think it's going to be as easy of a win for the University of Boston as everyone is predicting."

"I'd check your tires before you go for your donut run to Dunk's later."

"Oh, stop it. Well, it will be an exciting game to watch nonetheless. I know a lot of people scrambling to find tickets for this one. Let's get back to the Pats now and give you the latest injury report, brought to you by New England Plumbing."

Henry excitedly switched off the car radio and placed his poem in the safety of his backpack.

"You know, I would give anything to bring you to that game," Misty said. "I wish my boss's season tickets covered bowls too. I had the courage to ask him about it last night, you know. But I didn't get the answer I was hoping for."

"That's OK, Mom. We'll get to see the game one way or another."

Misty pictured their boxy, outdated television set collecting dust at their apartment and nodded. At the very least, she hoped she'd get the day off to watch Henry's favorite team on it with him.

>>>> <<<<

As Misty drove her boy to school, Teach secured two friends on staff to step in as judges and decided to look to the top to fill the third spot.

"You can go in now," the school secretary said. "I think the principal is off the phone."

"Thanks, Miss Sally," Teach said. "Your birthday flowers are still hanging in nicely, I see."

The woman stood to adjust the floral arrangement as she motioned for Teach to move more quickly inside.

"Well, if it isn't the Teach," said a tall man in his fifties with a tidy but modest suit and a drive to make Brockton's elementary school the best public school in Massachusetts. "What mess have you gotten yourself into now?"

"I need a favor."

"Please, have a seat."

Teach explained how he had given his students the assignment of writing a couplet poem.

"And?"

"And I have a little contest going and wondered if you'd stop in this morning to help judge. I need an independent panel because there is a prize involved."

"I'm afraid to ask," the principal said. "What's the prize?"

Teach hadn't thought until now that giving away a pair of tickets to a major game on the southern end of the coast could pose a problem for the school. He felt instantly sick over the possibility of getting his kids' hopes up.

"It's very special, and the kids are already very excited," Teach admitted. "A pair of tickets goes to the winning student and his or her parent to watch our local University of Boston Falcons play in the Orange Bowl."

Fortunately for Teach, the principal was a man who cared more about kids' learning than red tape.

"You know, I would've submitted a poem myself if it meant a chance at getting my wife and me into that game."

The pair shared a laugh. Teach's was filled with relief.

"So you're OK with this? You'll judge?"

"It'll be my pleasure. I look forward to seeing the works of art that are about to come out of the woodwork for a prize like this. Just make sure you meet the winner's parent in person before handing out the tickets. Otherwise, I think it's great. You have my blessing. You're a kind man, Teach."

"Perfect. Thank you, sir. See you in my room in an hour then. I never thought I'd be encouraging you to come in and witness my teaching shenanigans. I'm usually dreading your popping in unannounced to observe."

The principal had a soft spot for teachers who went the extra step for their students. His voice turned more serious in tone.

"You know, I like to learn from the best every once in a while."

Teach nodded with appreciation and embarrassment before making his way up to his classroom to set the stage for the morning's poetry readings.

When the morning bell tolled throughout the punch ball field, Henry and his classmates hustled inside their school building especially quickly. The upcoming contest created an air in Teach's classroom that was similar to the kind that hung around whenever antsy kids waited to board buses on a field trip day. Even the kids' parents were anxious to hear the results back at their homes, appointments, and offices.

Henry removed his practical brown snow boots and replaced them with a pair of stylish Converse sneakers that his mother had bought him recently on a shopping trip to the local department store, a place that attracted the waitress whenever she had an especially great week of tips. The kicks, as Misty called them, were what Henry considered his coolest pair of shoes. He hoped they would help erase his recent wardrobe blunder. He was nearly certain they wouldn't. He wondered if the topic of his poem on this morning would earn him a new nickname, one even more embarrassing than "Polly Ester." He was nearly certain it would. He would've settled for getting one of two predictions wrong.

"Let's get started, everyone," Teach called from the front of the room. "You probably noticed already that we have a couple of esteemed judges visiting us for the readings. Did everyone bid our art teacher, Miss Cummings, and our school nurse, Mr. Haynes, a good morning?"

"Good more-ning," sang a handful of Teach's most obedient students.

"Very good. Let's not keep them waiting. Everyone in your seats now. We are expecting one last judge and a very prestigious one at that. Here he comes now. We have the pleasure of hosting Principal McMullen this morning. Thanks for coming in, sir. Please have a seat."

Many of the students, including the ones who were frequent patrons of the principal's office, looked uneasy upon the arrival of the tall man whose personality was an effective ratio of kind and tough.

"Before we get started, I should explain to our esteemed judges that there were only two expectations for this poetry assignment. The students were asked to write about something that mattered to them. They were also asked to write in couplets. Do we have any volunteers to present first?"

Henry loved his poem. He was confident in the work. Out of habit, though, he avoided raising his hand. He avoided making eye contact with the panel too.

"Patsy, thank you," said Teach. "Please, do us the honor of kicking off our poetry readings."

The principal's attendance bottled up some of the kids' sniggers on this morning. The room felt nervously still.

"OK, so my poem is about my cat. The title is 'My Cat.'"

"Very well, Patsy. Go on, please."

"My favorite pet is not a rat;
My favorite pet is a cat.
She likes to sit on the window;
I did not name her Glen-dow.
The end.'"

"Ah-ha. That is a couplet, indeed. Thank you, Patsy. And may I ask? What is your cat's name? You left me intrigued."

"Her name is Kitty."

"Of course. Thank you, Patsy. Who's next?"

Henry watched the best punch ball player in the school raise his hand.

"Taylor! You're up!"

"My poem is about my Nintendo DS."

"Off you go."

"The Nintendo DS is something I like to play;
It's something I could do all day.
The new Mario games are really cool.
They make my little brother want to drool."

"He's not allowed to play yet," Taylor quickly added.

"I see. Well, you are a lucky boy then, aren't you?"

Teach continued calling on the students one by one, until both the kids and judges began growing anxious for the readings to finish, and only Oscar and Henry were left to read theirs.

"Oscar. Without further ado, would you please read us your poem?"

The boy wiggled in his seat and brought smiles to the judges' faces. Oscar's looks may not have been popular among any of the classmates except Henry, but his adorable cheeks that plumped up when he smiled seemed to touch the hearts of the entire school's staff.

Oscar held up his piece of paper with oversized cursive handwriting and began to read.

"My favorite dinner is chicken parm;
It doesn't have to come from the farm.
I could eat it every night
Let's go Falcons, fight, fight, fight!"

As the novelty of the principal's presence began wearing off, a few kids forgot to stifle their guffaws.

Henry winced at his best friend's choice of food for a topic. Oscar's last line, though, about the University of Boston Falcons football team made Henry wish he had thought to write about the sport for his own poem. It would've been a clever topic and a less embarrassing subject than the one he was about to be asked to read about in front of his harshest critics, he thought.

"Your piece had nice rhythm, Oscar. Thank you."

As the trio of judges grew leery over how they would pick a winner from the pieces of sixth-grade work that were similar in quality, Teach smiled and realized that he had unknowingly saved the student with the most potential for last.

"Henry."

The shy boy looked at each of the judges and felt in that moment as though time froze. He wondered if the staff would feel sorry for him if the cool kids laughed him out of the room. He wondered if there was still time to bail. He contemplated telling a white lie and claiming he hadn't had time to finish the assignment.

"Henry. Off you go, please."

The obedient boy took a long breath and obeyed.

He read each word loudly, clearly, and from the heart. When he finished, he looked at the faces of the judges. He couldn't interpret their matching looks, but they displayed anything but pity. Henry met eyes briefly with his teacher, whose grin revealed that the boy made him proud.

Teach expected great things, but even he was speechless. Oscar smiled and immediately stood up in appreciation. The two prettiest girls in the class joined Oscar in a standing ovation. The boy who had given Henry the nickname of "Polly Ester" didn't stand, but he managed to clap quietly at his desk with many others. The boy felt sheepish toward Henry in that moment, even though he didn't quite comprehend why.

For the first time all school year, the unthinkable happened for the shy boy; he felt like he fit in. He achieved what he had failed to accomplish every school morning on the punch ball field. He had just hit a home run.

Henry beamed for a few minutes, but just like an unproductive football player who had an unexpected play of the game, the boy's glory faded throughout the day as, very gradually, his newfound fans' ways turned back to normal. By afternoon recess, Henry was picked last for punch ball as several kids screamed "Easy out." The shy boy punched the ball straight to the third baseman, who was singing "Polly Ester."

The morning's events, however, did not fade as quickly on Teach. As the final school bell rang and the kids gathered their things, he called Henry over to talk as the others hustled out of the room to their afternoon play dates, sports practices, and video games.

"So, where did you learn to write like that?"

Henry looked down at his new sneakers and shrugged his already slouched shoulders.

"I dunno," said the boy quietly. "I guess it just comes from inside."

Teach couldn't help but notice that the boy touched the area of his heart as he offered his simple explanation.

"Huh, well, I thought your poem was very cool, and I look forward to the judges' selection tomorrow," said Teach. "Good luck!"

"Thanks," Henry said, before running off to meet the elderly woman in his life who had unknowingly served as the topic of his poem.

Upon entering the family car, Henry nearly had the courage to tell his grandmother about his exceptional day, but her rough coughing fit paused his words. By the time she recovered, he lost the guts.

"So wait until I tell you about my day," the woman said once she caught her breath. "I have an observation on life that will knock your sneakers off."

Henry looked down at his feet and realized that in all the excitement, he had forgotten to change out of his favorite shoes before hitting the snow.

CHAPTER 29

CAROLINE
The Troubled One

I t was a crisp Sunday morning of stillness, reflection, and hope for Caroline as she quietly stepped from bed. Her roommate was only a few hours into slumber following her Saturday night out at Judy Lou's, a cash-only dive bar in Boston's Brighton neighborhood that attracted college students for its $1.75 Busch Light drafts and hookup opportunities. Caroline glanced at her roommate's bed and winced at the sight of an unknown second figure under the comforter. She politely tiptoed about the room even though a dorm fire alarm probably wouldn't have roused the sleeping pair.

The sticky situation was yet another reminder of Caroline's struggle to get accustomed to single life on campus. She had woken several consecutive mornings wondering whether the odd turn of events on her final night at the Gentlemen's Club had been part of a dream. Only a week had passed following her final steps on stage with her unsuspecting boyfriend in the front row, yet she knew her relationship with Devin was over. Questions replaced the anger she had felt over Devin's own lies that night. What would he do now with her employment information? Would he tell his teammates? Would she become the joke of campus? Would her cheerleading coach, a mentor who had given Caroline the only scholarship she had, find out? She asked herself how she could have risked everything.

Despite her frustration, Caroline decided to look forward. She would start with an overdue trip to church. She searched her closet for her best Sunday shoes and her soul, just as she had done every Sunday morning growing up in Cranston, Rhode Island, where she had walked to Mass four seasons out of the year holding hands awkwardly, yet lovingly, with her father. She moved the stiletto heels and knee-high boots to the back of the closet and pulled her most conservative ones toward the front. The cleanup marked a small, symbolic step toward reorganizing her life.

Caroline silently slipped out of the dorm room as she had on the morning of her Gentlemen's Club audition and dialed her father during the brisk walk across the University of Boston campus to Chestnut Hill's beautiful parish of St. Ignatius of Loyola. She stared at her shoes as she anticipated her father's answer. The black flats looked larger than, but similar to, the ones she wore to meet him on the night of her mother's fatal car crash more than a decade ago.

"Hello?"

Caroline smiled at the sound of the kind, deep voice on the other end. In another part of New England, Kenny was walking to St. Matthew's Church in Cranston. The father and daughter's love for each other was strong, even though a trio of deep struggles—the loss of Kenny's wife and Caroline's mother, the father and daughter's separation as Kenny worked long hours at Harper, and Caroline's secret abuse—often made the pair feel a world apart.

"Dad?"

"Caroline! How are you?"

"I'm fine, Dad. How are things with you?"

"Fine, thanks."

Their sporadic conversations always opened similarly—short and generic—even though the pair had endless deep topics they could discuss.

On this hopeful winter morning, Caroline dared to change up their phone routine.

"I was just thinking about you on my way to church. I miss going to church with you, Dad. I miss you."

"Well, anytime you want to come on home for a visit, come down."

"I know. I miss home too. It's just been so busy with the games and practice and everything."

There was an awkward pause as the pair separately walked to places they both hoped would bring them peace. The daughter continued.

"Speaking of games, Dad, we cheerleaders have been given a whopping one complimentary ticket each to the Orange Bowl for a friend or family member. You wanna go?"

Caroline knew money would be scarce for her father's airfare and lodging, but she had a feeling that the trip might serve as the highlight of his year. Aside from Kenny's occasional card games at coworkers' homes, he didn't visit many places other than St. Matthew's and Harper Manufacturing. Caroline realized in that moment that she'd rather be in her painful shoes than in her father's punishing pair. Hers offered more opportunity.

"You sure you don't have a boyfriend or someone who you'd rather have go?" Kenny asked.

The man was unaware of Caroline's dates with the very quarterback he read about in *The Providence Journal*. Their conversations never took that turn.

"No, no boyfriend, Dad. I should tell you, though. The game is in Florida."

"Oh, I know. Everyone in this town has been following the team. We're all so proud of you."

The comment, as everyday as it might seem for a father to a daughter, was the most spontaneous and loving gesture Caroline had felt from the man since the bone-chilling, rainy night of her mother's death when Kenny had clung so tightly to his little girl, his new lifeline. Caroline tugged at her locket now, feeling surprised and content at once.

"Then you'll come, Dad?"

"I think I will."

Sensing a new beginning on a couple of fronts, Caroline warmly said goodbye to her father and, more permanently, her Gentlemen's Club life as she stepped inside St. Ignatius Parish. She dipped a pair of fingers in the holy water and made the sign of the cross.

≫— ≪

"Bless me, Father, for I have sinned. It has been almost a year since my last confession."

Caroline felt at peace following the moving Sunday Mass at St. Ignatius. The grand archways made her feel as though she were ready to start yet another important journey away from a troubled past. The brightness of the church made her feel more upbeat. The strong columns made her feel as though she could continue being strong and brave.

The parishioners were filing out of the service, but Caroline made her way to the confessional booth to talk with someone for the first time about her problems. If she had the courage to stay that course, the conversation would take a while, she thought. She hung around the back pews until she was sure to be the last person to step inside the booth.

On the other side of the screen sat as good of a man as Caroline could've hoped for in a diocese that was still reeling from its own journey of trouble. Hearing confessions was Father Santori, a man in his seventies who had spent nearly all of his free time at St. Elizabeth's Hospital visiting ailing parishioners or the local Star Market to buy grocery items for anyone in his path who had hit a rough spot in life.

"Go on, my child."

Caroline could immediately tell by the sound of his calm voice that the priest was old and gentle. She felt grateful for his ability to overlook the long time she had reported passing since her last confession. She was skeptical of all men these days and always. But she loved her faith, and she hoped she was stepping into a safe place.

"Father, you'll have to excuse me as this could take a while. Do you have time?"

"I have as much as you need."

"Well, I've been carrying a burden since my mother's death, and I need a new start. I'm a good person, I know that, but I've recently made some bad choices."

Caroline felt annoyed with herself for sugarcoating the situation.

"Make that horrible choices," she continued. "Sinful choices. I take full accountability. I knew they were wrong. I did 'em anyway."

"Is there anything specific you'd like to talk with me about?"

"Where do I start? As a young girl, after my mother died, a distant cousin watched over me and did awful things as I pretended to sleep."

The quiet booth encouraged Caroline to continue.

"I've lived with this trouble all my life without telling anyone. I recently took up…" Caroline paused to search for the right words. Different options ran through her head.

"Well…a certain type of dancing. I'm not using my past as an excuse for making this mistake—it was actually more about greed for the money—but I did justify my job by turning to my past. I convinced myself that taking my clothes off on my own was much less wrong than having others do it for me, against my will."

Father Santori waited quietly for Caroline to continue even as her tears fell and her words stopped. She waited for the priest to scold her or assign her five, ten, fifteen, or fifty Hail Marys and Our Fathers in an attempt to magically erase her sins. He did not. He gave her instead what she needed most.

"OK, my child. Life includes mistakes. It's what you do after a mistake that reveals goodness. There is a passage in Romans 5 which states that 'We also rejoice in our sufferings, because we know that suffering produces perseverance; perseverance, character; and character, hope. And hope does not disappoint us, because God has poured out His love into our hearts.'"

The aging priest's voice broke. Caroline wondered if the strain came from a morning filled with service and confessions or his compassion for her own story. She heard him take a sip of water before continuing.

"Perseverance. Character. Hope," he said. "You have persevered. While no one can erase your tragic past, still no one can take away the perseverance you achieved. You demonstrated great character this morning. There is no question that you made a sinful choice recently, but you have shown to me great honesty, remorse, and a will to make things right. I know the seat you are in is not a comfortable one. So many lose the courage to confess as soon as they step inside the booth. You have not been dealt an easy hand at life, but with your perseverance and character, you should take away tremendous hope for your future. Perseverance. Character. Hope. Bless you, my child."

Caroline knew she needed to let her past be her past. It would no longer shape her future, other than having made her stronger. She was left with one major question. *But how am I going to start?*

She attempted a summary of her self-image problems to the priest.

"The troubles of my childhood were out of my control. I still feel like I carry a scarlet letter of sorts that people can see. The decision to try this type of work, though, was one I made on my own. I feel like I will always carry a letter for that too, but it's a different kind of burden. It's filled with more guilt. When I walk down the street, I feel like everyone looks at me and sees. With every man in a convenience store, bar, or even here at church, I wonder, Does he recognize me?

Was he a regular of performances? When I hear a woman complain on the T about her fiancé's bachelor party at the club, I wonder if she somehow knows who I am and hates me. How do I keep the past troubles in my past?"

"I have one thing to say about that," Father Santori said. "Growing up as a boy, I vacationed at my aunt's house every summer in Maryland's Chesapeake Bay. We would buy corn fresh from the on-your-honor farm stands that lined the country roads, and to this day, they were the sweetest I ever had. We also husked there some of the worst I've ever seen—bruised or worm-ridden. Whenever my aunt pulled out her coin purse to pick out a dozen ears, there was no telling how many good ones we'd end up with. By looking at the husks alone, there was no way to know whether she was buying a sweet one or a bruised one. When we got to her cottage and took the time to work with them in the humid summer air—shucking them piece by piece, layer by layer—we would get to really see. Most were good. A fraction were bruised. An even smaller fraction were rotten at the core, even though they looked perfectly alluring from the outside. As human beings, we are all made with the capacity to be good. We rarely get to see what causes another person's bruises. Everyone has a story. We are all changing. We can all do better."

Caroline hadn't fully absorbed what corn had to do with her story, but it made her recall the day as a young girl when she had helped her mother drop a few ears in a boiling pot before they sang and danced in circles on the old linoleum kitchen floor of the humble apartment in which her widowed father still lived. Back then, he was just finding out about his job offer at Harper Manufacturing. Life felt grand. Times were undoubtedly different.

The priest took another loud sip of his water and continued.

"Whether it's in regard to an appearance or an occupation or whatever outer quality people may use to judge others, hold dearly the knowledge that things are rarely as straightforward as they appear on the outside. The shyest boy in a room is rarely the one who has the least to say, as the loudest person in that same room isn't necessarily the one with the most knowledge to share. The most gifted young man isn't necessarily the hardest working, while the hardest working makes his own destiny in spite of people viewing him only as lucky. A single woman who appears alone isn't necessarily lonely, just as one with an abusive partner may feel very much so."

The booth was still as Caroline began to understand Father Santori's message.

"And with you," the priest said. "The one with the troubled and checkered past doesn't necessarily have a shameful soul, just as the one with the more respectful job doesn't necessarily have an innocent past."

He took a final sip.

"Some of your…" began the priest before a long pause. It was his turn now to choose his words carefully.

"Some of your…former coworkers…probably showed you greater character than some of the more celebrated people you know in your other social circles."

Caroline thought of a dancer named Allenny, the woman who had kindly given her the wig the night Caroline spotted her professor in the club. Allenny was a mother of four girls, dancing because the father of her children had left unannounced without setting up child support. After weeks of searching for work and only a few fruitless interviews, Allenny had struggled with her qualifications to find a legal job that could feed her girls, not to mention clothe them, house them, and give them little treats that meant the world, including new back-to-school backpacks, pads, and pencils in the fall. Allenny had regretfully settled on dancing as her girls slept—a job that carried big burdens in society.

Caroline shifted her thoughts to her semi-famous ex-boyfriend. The golden boy quarterback was undoubtedly talented and far more celebrated by the masses, but he carried with him far less character and decidedly fewer values than a woman like Allenny did, she thought. Caroline lifted her chin, letting tears trickle quickly down her cheeks. For the first time, she felt proud to have more in common with someone like Allenny.

The kind priest continued.

"To this day, whenever corn is in season, I buy it in bulk as a special treat for the local soup kitchen's service to the homeless. It's such an inexpensive luxury for them. Anyway, as I husk the corn with the volunteers, I think of my youth. The corn from the market here—while less sweet and starchier than the kind I remember from the Chesapeake Bay farm stands—is much more reliable, yet we still get a bruised ear from time to time. All these years later, I still can't predict what I'm going to get just by looking at the outside. It all takes time. The next time you have the chance to buy some corn, try the corn husk experiment. I think it will make you feel better. There is no magical way to tell a person's goodness just by looking at them from the outside. You are certainly not alone in having past troubles, and you are a good person, indeed."

Caroline smiled and tugged at her mother's locket. She repeated Father Santori's wisdom within her head. Things are rarely as straightforward as they appear on the outside. Try the corn husk experiment. You are certainly not alone. You are a good person.

"Anything else, my child?"

"No, that's enough from me," Caroline said with an awkward chuckle.

It had been more than enough. For the first time since her tragedies, she felt proud to be herself. She was proud to succeed at simply getting herself out of bed every morning, not to mention attending a prestigious school and working hard at her studies and her natural talent at her sport.

"Go in peace, my child."

Caroline still expected the priest to assign her at least a dozen Hail Marys and Our Fathers before leaving the church. While she received no such instruction as she stepped from the booth, she knelt down anyway inside the church to finish the prayer she had started on the day of her audition in the club. Her subconscious was always working overtime. She remembered just where she had left off when Phil had first surprised her by coming out of his office.

"'…be thy name, thy kingdom come, thy will be done on earth as it is in heaven. Give us this day our daily bread and forgive us our trespasses as we forgive those who trespass against us. And lead us not into temptation but deliver us from evil.'"

CHAPTER 30

MAXINE
The Lonely One

Only three days separated Maxine from her game-day coverage of the Orange Bowl in Miami Gardens, but the seventy-two-degree weather in January combined with the calming waterfront views helped keep her jitters under control in the lobby of Fort Lauderdale's Marriott Harbor Beach Hotel, the designated lodging for a steady in-and-out flow of Orange Bowl media.

"Maxine? Maxine, I'm Joy Jones, the lead sports writer from the wire's headquarters in New York. I hear we'll be working together quite closely over the next few days. It's a pleasure to meet you. You're early for our first introduction."

"We're both early," Maxine said with a smile and a strong handshake.

She felt refreshed to be paired with a woman in a profession that was dominated by men. She predicted that, like herself, Joy probably had to work harder to get trusted. Surely they had the same passion for sports. They clearly shared a respect for the value of other people's time too. *It's more than a good start,* Maxine thought.

"Our veteran sports photographer back at headquarters spoke highly of you," Joy said. "That says a lot coming from that guy, you know. He has the highest expectations."

"How's he doing?"

"You know, I think he's a little sad to be watching this year's Orange Bowl from home instead of covering it, but he's handling it better than everyone thought for some reason."

The women climbed into Joy's economical rental and checked their growing adrenaline by buckling their seatbelts. After a few minutes of nervous silence on both the driver and passenger sides, the reporter opened up to the photographer.

"It's my kid's birthday today," Joy said. "Don't let me forget to call her immediately following this interview. I want to catch her before she goes into her birthday party."

"How old is she?" Maxine asked.

"She's turning five. It's so hard not to be there. Do you have kids?"

"No."

"A husband?"

"No."

"A significant other?"

Maxine realized that she might not have so much in common with her new colleague after all. She wondered which way of life was more challenging: balancing motherhood and work or being married to a job with little more than a lonely apartment and some nagging voicemails to return home to every night. Her vote was on the latter.

"I've actually given up on dating for a while," Maxine said with a slight shudder. "It's a new decision after an especially horrible Internet date." The date with the George Clooney lookalike may have carried great expectations by Maxine, her friends, and family members, but it had been disastrous.

"So, your profile said you like football," Maxine had said as the man drove them to what would be their first and last date together.

"Yup."

"I'm leaving in a few days to cover the Orange Bowl."

"Yeah, I'm not a big fan of bowl games."

"Oh really?" Maxine had asked with sincere interest. "May I ask why? Are you an NFL fan over collegiate play?"

"I just don't like them. Hey, do you mind staying quiet a moment?"

The air in the man's spotless, plush luxury car shifted from awkward to uncomfortable. Maxine sensed George's temper rising, although she had no idea why. She gently folded her snowy knit hat in her lap so it wouldn't dampen his headrest nor his already poor mood.

"Damn butthole!" George shouted toward the driver in front of him who hadn't immediately noticed the stoplight turn green. He laid on the horn.

"Anyway," he snapped.

"Anyway," Maxine repeated more gently. "So where are we off to? You mentioned dinner, but I don't think you mentioned where."

"I didn't mention where," George said.

"And," Maxine said with a forced smile.

"We're going to the Dinosaur BBQ," George said. "Please tell me you eat meat."

"I do," Maxine said, exhaling slightly. The place was a favorite hangout of hers, along with the rest of her colleagues at Syracuse's International Presswire Bureau. The atmosphere was relaxed, fun, and intentionally not fancy there. It would be a much-needed change from the environment inside the stress-filled car.

But Maxine's relief had been short-lived. As she opened the door to the restaurant, George had plowed down the corridor like one of the big machines on the snowy roads that night. He had charged straight toward the hostess desk, knocking into a leather-jacketed man's shoulder in the process.

"Two," George barked.

"Your name please?"

"Why?" he demanded.

"We have a fifteen-minute wait," the hostess had coolly replied. She would undoubtedly be cursing George's name to one of the servers as soon as he was out of earshot, Maxine thought. "You're welcome to get a drink at the bar; I'll call you momentarily."

"I called five minutes ago and the person said there was no wait," George snapped. Maxine looked around in hopes that none of her press colleagues were about. She returned her gaze to the hostess, who appeared shaken by George's abrasive tone.

"You know," Maxine said to her date quietly. "I've found that the wait goes especially quickly here. The place also fills up on a dime. I'm sure there was no wait just five minutes ago. Let's just go to the bar and enjoy a drink."

"No," George said to her through clenched teeth. "We're leaving."

As the pair walked numbly outside, the frigid Syracuse air helped cool George's temper.

"How about the Blue Tusk instead?" he asked.

There was no place Maxine thought she would rather be in that instant than the comfort of her lonely apartment with a frozen dinner and bad Saturday night TV. She felt as though she might vomit from the discomfort of being around George.

"You know, I'm not feeling so well," Maxine said truthfully. "I was really looking forward to our date, but I think it would be best if I got some fresh air and walked myself home."

George had glared at her silently.

"It's not too far, really," Maxine offered, even though she knew that her safety was probably the least of her date's concerns. "Goodbye."

Maxine had pivoted toward her apartment and begun walking quickly without looking back. She found herself hoping she wouldn't be sideswiped by a beautiful luxury car with perfect side mirrors until she felt a tap on her shoulder and reluctantly turned around. To her relief, it was the patron with the leather jacket.

"You all right, miss?" he asked. He was missing a tooth and he looked concerned.

"Yeah, thanks for checking," Maxine had said with a purposefully dramatic roll of her eyes in reference to her date's scene at the restaurant. "I'm actually not that far from where I'm going. I really appreciate your concern. Have a good night. Eat some ribs for me, will you?"

Maxine safely reached her peaceful apartment, which already contained five blinking messages on her answering machine from loved ones wondering how the night went. All of them begged for an update that night, no matter how late.

The typically calm photographer angrily opened her laptop and closed the page that featured George's suddenly scary profile. She had fired off a reply to all five messages.

"This is it," Maxine had typed. "I'm not doing this anymore. I'm done with the bad dates and the crazies. I'm better off alone, and I mean it. Please, please, please just let me be happy plugging away at the job I love."

At long last, Maxine's friends and family members would get the hint.

During the car ride toward her first pre-game Orange Bowl interview, Maxine had clearly intrigued her new journalism colleague.

"And what happened on that Internet date to make you sign off on love for a while?" Joy asked.

"Let's just say the man was no George Clooney."

"Been there, done that," Joy said. "You know, everyone says that when you're not looking, that's when you finally meet someone. Maybe this is your time."

Maxine could've finished the woman's sentence herself. She knew people meant well, but if she heard someone tell her one more time that things happen for a reason, she thought she might self-destruct.

"So have you covered the Orange Bowl before?" Maxine asked, desperate to change the subject.

"This is my third year," Joy said. "I covered the first couple under the veteran's wing. I hope he would have equally kind words to say about me as he does about you. The first year, I was completely green as I battled competitors along the sidelines. The mass media at the head coach press conferences was pretty overwhelming. I did my best, though, and it was good enough to buy me another assignment here, followed by another. The key is obviously getting one-on-one time with the big players for some meaningful pre-game stories."

Joy's persistence had secured them their pending interview with Devin Madison, while Maxine, through her own hard work and relationship building, had succeeded in scheduling them the only pre-game interview with the highly sought-after underdog, JP Hemmings.

The two women soon found themselves waiting for Devin in a stuffy meeting room within the golden boy's hotel. Their small talk waned to silence as each of them mentally calculated the steps needed to get the best interview or take the best shot.

They ended up having more than enough time to think.

As the meeting room clock's second hand made nearly fifteen hundred quiet ticks, Maxine watched Joy attempt to hide her worry over missing her daughter by phone before the girl left for her birthday party.

Their silent wait finally ended with a barge through the meeting-room door. Both women shared the same thought: Devin Madison was even more handsome in person. That was until his words unraveled his image.

"Ladies, I think you're in the wrong place," the young man said. "I'm here to do some press interviews."

Maxine looked down at her bulky camera, peered at Joy's journalism pad, pen, and recorder, and wondered whether Devin was making a joke. A red-faced man who appeared out of nowhere was a signal that the quarterback had not. The man spoke in humble, fast tones. He was on his game, at least.

"You must be Joy and Maxine from the prestigious International Presswire," he said. "I'm James O'Leary, University of Boston Public Relations, and I know you're anticipating our boy Devin here, and you know all about him already. Devin, this is Joy and Maxine, the wire's lead writer and photographer for the Orange Bowl. I will step back now and let you all do your thing. Please let me know if I can be of further assistance to you after the interview."

"Well, I've never been one to complain about being alone in a room with two women," Devin said.

"Our quarterback has a unique taste for humor, and I'm sure you'll get a taste of it today," James said. "I think you'll find he has a wonderful story to tell about his family history and his drive to win this thing for the University of Boston."

"I thought you said you were going to let us do our thing," Devin said.

James bowed as comically as he could while attempting to hide his mortification. Maxine and Joy knew it was there, even though James did a fine job of rolling with it. For the first time in their careers, both women cared for the PR person more than the subject of their interview.

As the second hand ticked now with near-matching clicks from Maxine's camera, Devin relayed to Joy the aging story of his grandfather's failed attempt at making it into the Orange Bowl. Joy grew desperate for a fresh angle.

Devin was as close-lipped as they came, though, revealing little about his pre-game emotions or game-day strategies. After thirty minutes of going around in circles, Joy gave up.

Sensing the end of the interview, Maxine quietly asked Joy for permission to fire off one last question for her caption.

"Of course," the reporter whispered back.

Maxine thought of the veteran's brief notes on Devin during her valuable meeting with him at the wire's headquarters. The veteran had held back from saying much about the confident quarterback, but Maxine had quickly recalled his description of Devin being an obsessive young man.

"One last question, Devin, and then we'll have you on your way," Maxine jumped in.

"I was beginning to think you were mute," Devin joked.

"Well, my lens does most of the talking for me," Maxine pushed back. "Anyway, this is an odd question, but do you have any pre-Orange Bowl routines?"

"Orange juice," Devin said.

"You can take over if you want," Maxine whispered to the reporter, knowing that Devin hadn't given Joy much, if anything, for her story.

"Orange juice?" Joy asked with a thankful wink at her new photographer friend. "No Gatorade, no SmartWater, no milk? Just orange juice?"

"This is the Orange Bowl," Devin said. "There is orange in my blood now. There is orange in my hungry eyes, and yes, there is even orange in my diet. After the win, the color is going to be right up there as a favorite around our campus back home—it will soon be regarded as highly as maroon and gold. Just wait and see."

James sensed the journalists' abilities to zone in on the quarterback's quirkiness.

"I've got to get this guy to his next interview, but here's my card with the contact information of everyone on my PR team. My press colleagues and I are happy to assist if there is anything else you need."

Devin's emotional quote about orange juice would end up toward the lead of Joy's pre-game story. The colorful comment, paired with the exclusive pre-game comments that would flow in next from JP Hemmings, would make Joy's story a well-used reference by major newspapers across the country as well as sports broadcasters on television and radio.

While Joy should've felt relieved, Maxine could tell that her new friend's heart ached over missing the birthday message to her daughter, thanks to Devin's tardiness.

"Let's catch her immediately after her party so you can be the first she tells every detail to," Maxine offered. "I'm sure we'll get you back in time for that. I'm almost certain that our next interview will run on time."

"You think?" Joy asked, her teary eyes filled now with new hope.

"Oh, I'd bet on it," Maxine said as she visualized the humble young man who had once welcomed Maxine into the home of the loving professors he called Mom and Dad. "I know I'm not supposed to be biased, but let's just say the next one's parents raised him beautifully."

"OK, since you started it," Joy teased with a laugh. "I had to hold myself back from pointing out to that Devin character that orange is not only the color of his upcoming bowl game, it's also the color of his competition. Duh."

The women laughed together genuinely.

"I was thinking the same thing," Maxine said. "I think that poor PR guy was too."

CHAPTER 31

HENRY
The Shy One

By a unanimous vote and without any surprise to Teach, the trio of judges selected Henry's poem as the clear winner and wanted to learn more about the author.

"He's painfully shy," Teach explained. "He doesn't understand his talents. Kids' cruel comments seem to stifle his words, but when everyone matures, I'm sure Henry will find his groove."

As the kids filed into the classroom with great anticipation for the verdict, Teach glanced quickly at each of their faces and took attendance. All of them wore their usual expressions except for Henry, whose face looked like it belonged to a quarterback under a tackle who had just thrown a Hail Mary, risking everything to win the game. Teach decided to give the results right away.

"So you all did a nice job on the poetry assignment," he said. "I was pleased with everyone's effort. Our judges all selected the same winner. I think, by your standing ovations and applause, that you will agree on the winner too."

Henry felt like he had been holding his breath underwater and was finally coming up for air.

"The tickets go to Henry. Nice job, Henry. We'll have some papers and logistics to go over, but I will see you at the game."

"You've got to come in to meet my teacher," Henry said from outside the family car window when his mother arrived to pick him up that afternoon.

"What? What happened?"

"I found out today that I won us both tickets to watch University of Boston at the bowl game."

"What? How?"

"I wrote a poem and it won a contest," Henry said. "You need to come talk with my teacher about it." The boy swallowed hard. "Can we go?"

"My head is spinning, Henry."

Misty was already dressed in her uniform for her evening shift. She glanced at her watch in fear of being late to start side work before the dinner rush at the restaurant. There were endless ramekins to fill, salad fixings to prepare, and utensils to roll, or she would be in the weeds all night.

"Henry, we really need to talk more," was all Misty managed as she reached for her cell phone so she could inform her boss that for the first time in her career, she might arrive fifteen or so minutes late.

As the mother and son entered the classroom, Teach was sitting at his sloppy desk grading spelling tests. Papers with red checks and "X" marks surrounded him. The young man didn't believe in using flowery colors to grade papers. He believed the color red had an impact and kids were too coddled these days.

Forgetting he was expecting guests, Teach wore headphones that blared AC/DC's "Back in Black." He couldn't help singing enthusiastically—and badly—along.

Misty stood in the doorway of Henry's classroom and looked at her son in disbelief.

"This is your teacher?" she asked.

Henry nodded.

She knocked on the open door without success as Henry walked to Teach's desk and tapped the singing man on the shoulder. Teach jumped. With one look at Misty, his cheeks became the color of Henry's on the morning the boy was first called "Polly Ester." The woman was the definition of stunning, he thought.

"Holy smokes," Teach said aloud.

"We startled you," Misty said.

"Sorry about that. A little Brian Johnson makes grading the spelling word *larynx* a whopping twenty-six times in a row go by a little faster. Please, have a seat."

Misty understood the AC/DC reference.

"Wasn't Bon Scott still the lead singer for 'Back in Black?'" she asked. "That album had some of the band's best songs."

Teach felt immediately impressed that any parent of his students would know even that much about his favorite rock band, even if she was wrong about the timing of the lead singers.

"Oh, nooooooo no no," Teach said as he made an "X" mark in the air with his red pen. "Mrs. um…"

"Misty," the woman said, finally reaching out her hand for a more proper introduction.

"Ah-ha," said Teach. "Mrs. Misty. It's a pleasure to meet you."

"Miss," she corrected him.

"Mrs. Misty Miss?" Teach asked with pure confusion.

He was used to having kids and their parents carry different names, but this one was a tongue twister, he thought.

"No, Miss Misty," the woman corrected. "And you can just call me by my first name. It's Misty, if you haven't caught that."

"OK! Miss Misty, with all due respect, 'Back in Black' was released in July of 1980, five months after the death of Bon Scott. It was Brian Johnson's first album."

Now it was Misty's turn to feel a little flushed in the cheeks as she normally prided herself on her rock knowledge.

Henry felt embarrassed for both of them. He wondered why they were both acting a bit foolish.

Teach looked at the boy and reminded himself that he was still behind a desk in his classroom, not at a pickup bar.

"I see you're on your way to work," Teach said more professionally. "I hope this isn't an inconvenience?"

"No, it's fine," Misty said. "My son tells me he won a contest?"

"Yes, you have quite a talented little guy here. Did you read the poem?"

"No," Misty said, looking at her son with guilt even though the boy had been the one responsible for keeping it that way.

Teach pulled the winning poem from his desk drawer and handed it to her. As she read, tears streamed down her cheeks. Henry looked even more deeply embarrassed. Teach swiveled his chair around to retrieve the box of tissues that he always kept on hand for Patsy whenever the girl had a good cry. He offered Misty the box. She nodded gratefully and tried to compose herself, but it was as though all her stress and worries about Henry were set free by the poem.

"I'm sorry," Teach said. "I should've anticipated this. I should've warned you. It's a moving piece of work for sure."

Teach attempted to downplay the awkward moment and provided Henry with a thumbs-up, a gesture that was intended to relay, "Way to go—you even moved your mother to tears."

"Well, I for one was very proud of Henry when he read this poem aloud to the class," Teach said. "His schoolmates were very impressed, as were the judges. In fact, the principal himself would like the honor of meeting you sometime, Henry."

Misty's crying transformed into mild sniffles.

She is very cute, Teach thought to himself. *She is one of those girls who looks cute even when she cries.* He pictured his last serious relationship, a girl who had looked more like a pink walrus whenever she became upset during one of their many pointless arguments.

"On to the grand prize," Teach said. "I have three tickets to the University of Boston game. Two are reserved for the winner—one for Henry and one for his chaperone. I know from my grand serenade that you might already think I'm a bit crazy. I know this is not your ordinary field trip, but…"

"But you are not your ordinary teacher," Misty said.

"Well, thank you, I think," Teach said. "Anyway, I was going to say that this is an unusual trip, but the principal is fine with a signed slip. And here it is."

"Well, wow." Misty took a moment to process everything she had just learned—from the poem to the prize. "This is an amazing opportunity, and I don't know if you know this, but University of Boston is a team that Henry adores," she continued. "His father was a great football player. Maybe he still is, we don't know. I'm rambling."

"Then you'll come?" Teach asked.

Misty looked at Henry, who showed off the most hope in his eyes that she ever remembered seeing.

"We'll find a way to go," she assured her boy.

"That's completely stellar," Teach said. "There will be the expense of airfare and a night's hotel for you and Henry, but the game tickets and a dinner out before the game are my treat."

The man looked at Misty and realized he would be taking a beautiful girl on his arm after all. He felt as though he were crossing the teacher-parent line.

"Uh, the dinner part was already established in the criteria," Teach added.

Between Henry's beautiful and sweet mother, the woman's AC/DC knowledge, and Henry's love of football, Teach held a newfound respect for the boy who was already one of his favorites in class.

"One last test before we go," Teach said to Henry. "Finish this fight song: 'O Falcons' nest, O Falcons' nest, hither opponents come! Set forth your best, through every test…'"

Teach outstretched his arm for Henry to finish while the boy recalled the drunken fans sitting in front of him during the University of Boston's season opener with his mother, grandmother, and best friend at his side. The perfect day was still clearly etched in his memory.

"'Your glory shan't be unsung!'"

"Well, there you go," Teach said. "I'm excited. It looks like we have a Boston fan here after all. Sometimes you can't script life any better."

"Thank you, um," Misty said as she tried to come up with her son's teacher's name.

"The kids call me Teach, but you can call me Brian. Not Mr. Brian. Just Brian."

"Thank you, Brian," Misty said. "You are about to make one family's Christmas especially special. Can we take this?"

Misty held up the winning poem.

"Of course."

She folded the paper and put it inside her purse next to a utility bill so it wouldn't wrinkle. The mother and son left Teach to his grading. The man plugged his white earphones back in his ears and searched for the third song on the *Back in Black* album, "What Do You Do for Money Honey?"

Even though Misty's boss told her not to go to the trouble, she ended up staying late at the restaurant to help with that evening's side work. The poem was left untouched in her purse until the next morning, when she asked Henry if she could show it to his grandmother. Henry felt embarrassed all over again.

"She already knows how much you love her," Misty said. "But showing her that she was the topic of such a wonderful poem would be the highlight of her life."

"I'll show her sometime," Henry said. "But not now."

⤜⤜⤜ ⤛⤛⤛

The modest Brockton, Massachusetts, apartment was electric on the eve of Henry and Misty's trip to the Orange Bowl as their imperfect Christmas tree glowed with lights that were especially disorganized toward the top. A vintage, shimmering snowman stood proudly in the living room, plugged in each evening by the elderly woman of the house. Bing Crosby's version of "Walking in a Winter Wonderland" played happily on the radio. A mother, son, and grandmother buzzed about as they got two out of three of them ready for the first flight of their lives.

Writing the winning poem had turned out to be the least of the family's hurdles in getting to the game, as Misty had stressed over how to get the time off and the money needed to fly during the pricey holiday season, stay in a hotel, and eat. But the single mother had discovered that when once-in-a-lifetime opportunities come around, especially during the holidays, acquaintances rally joyfully in support. Misty's boss had not only granted her the days off, but also had secretly collected a holiday bonus from management staff for the restaurant's kindest employee. Misty's mother had brought several years' worth of change to the coin counting machine in the local supermarket. When the elder woman had brought home more cash than any of them predicted combined, she still deposited her two cents of complaint.

"Do you know I lost 9.8 cents on every dollah by goin' to that machine?"

"Thanks for doing that, Mom, but I guess it is a small servicing cost for all the time you saved by going there instead of counting all those nickels and dimes yourself," Misty had offered in an attempt to make the woman feel better. "It would've taken you until next Christmas to roll all that. Where were you keeping all that change anyway?"

"A woman nevah reveals her secret hidin' spot—whether it's ah place for the Christmas presents or ah spot for mad money to buy the Christmas presents."

Given the unusual circumstances, the family of three had decided to skip exchanging holiday gifts in order to afford the trip.

"But you deserve some presents, Grandma," Henry had argued when the woman first brought up the idea. "You aren't even going to the bowl."

"Seeing my grandson attend the game of his dreams with his mothah is the best gift I could've evah dreamed up myself," the woman had said truthfully. "I'll be watchin' from home and lookin' for ya both in the stands. Bring me home a soovenee-yah. That will be ya present to me this year. I'll treasah it too."

As the radio played the song's last couple of verses, Misty pulled from her bedroom closet the family's only suitcase—an outdated and underused piece of luggage with a floral pattern that looked like it belonged in the 1970s. She pulled her shiny brown hair into a ponytail and began plotting which pieces to pack. Her face carried the weight of a challenge.

"Even in ya sweatpants, ya look stunning," Misty's mother said. "You do know that about yahself by now, don't you?"

Misty rolled her eyes in humble disagreement.

"Don't forget to bring your winter gear too," Misty shouted to her son, who was excitedly pulling his favorite clothes out of his own room. "It's Florida, but it won't necessarily be that warm."

"Mom, won't we be wearing our hats and mittens to the airport anyway?" the boy shouted back happily.

Misty smiled at the comment that made Henry sound like a world traveler even though he had never been to the airport that was only twenty-six miles from his home. She fingered the tags on her latest discount store purchases and held up her favorite new sweater and jeans. Henry's teacher had mentioned treating them to a dinner, she recalled. She tossed her most stylish wrap dress in the case. She got out the faux leather calf-length boots she had splurged on recently at PayLess. She wondered if the outfit would be dressy enough for dinner and then immediately worried if it would be too dressy. She wondered if she was trying too hard to impress.

The radio station queued up "Let It Snow," Misty's favorite holiday tune because of the romantic lyrics. She stepped into her son's room to help him finish his own preparations and spotted his bare back. Without thinking, she kissed the nook between his shoulder blades. It was a spot she had nuzzled many times before—when he had scraped his knee at the beach parking lot, had a fever from the flu, or needed a towel after a bath. So much space had grown between his shoulders since the last time she had kissed him there. Instead of pulling away, the boy turned to his mother and gave her an overdue, tight hug around the neck.

CHAPTER 32

JP
The Destined One

After a dozen self-imposed cutting and exploding drills, Syracuse's new starting running back got called to the sidelines of the team's designated practice field at Fort Lauderdale's Nova Southeastern University.

"JP, I know you're used to practicin' like a madman, but let's not get ourselves worn out for the big game," Coach Flash instructed. "It is tonight, you know."

The pair exchanged uneasy smiles, subtly acknowledging the fact that the overwhelming pressure to win was weighing especially heavily on the running back's small shoulders. In only his second game of his college career against a number of odds, JP was expected to deliver another exceptional performance to fans, coaching staff, teammates, ticket holders, and television viewers.

His exclusive one-on-one pre-game interview in Florida with the International Presswire had helped keep the seemingly endless line of reporters at bay, but it hadn't stopped the most ambitious ones from firing questions at him in what had felt like the longest week of his life. Throughout the week, whenever the warm sun

240

shined on JP's face and tempted him to let his guard down, those media inquiries had seemed to work their way into his head instead.

"Do you think it's possible to pull off another miracle game?"

"How do you think your size will play out against University of Boston's larger defense?"

"With such little playing time under your belt, how are you mentally managing all the hoopla that comes along with being in the Orange Bowl?"

At Syracuse College offense press conference, Coach Flash and the offensive coordinators had taken turns defending JP.

"He's fast, he's elusive, and he's one of the hardest workers in the BCS," they had said more than once from memorized scripts.

There had also been the SC coaches' luncheon, where ticket holders sought out JP's autograph more aggressively than any other player on the team while comparing their own sizes to his. That evening had brought a team dinner outing to Miami's Fogo de Chao restaurant, where teammates had avoided JP like a major league pitcher on a bullpen break during a hot streak. Whistler had bravely sat next to his roommate for the meal, but even he had kept his signature sarcasm and razzing to a minimum. The pair had silently flashed restaurant cards whenever they were ready for more or less of the popular Brazilian-style service of meat. While Whistler had been happy to keep himself busy flashing his green feed card for more of the delicious meal, JP's uneasy stomach had kept his own card mostly showing red.

There had also been the team's visit to Joe DiMaggio Children's Hospital, where JP felt more drained than he had at any of the week's events as he attempted to put into perspective the value of winning life versus a game. And, finally, following a week's worth of practices held in between the public events, there was the team's family beach outing at Miami Beach's luxurious Fountainebleau Beachfront, where the professors had cautiously pulled their boy aside.

"Would it be fine with you if we took a family walk down this beautiful beach?" JP's father had asked.

As the family of three walked, the parents felt the rough sand beneath their feet and waited patiently for their son to open up to them.

The smell of saltwater combined with the push of a strong wave seemed to bring JP to life at long last.

"You remember our family dinner back at home that Whistler so graciously crashed?" he asked.

"Well, we invited him," his father corrected with a little laugh. "With his enormous elbows on our beloved round dinner table, I did fear that giant was going to end up smashing up the place, but yes, go on."

"With his advice—and of course your support—I really thought I'd not only come here without nerves, but also win this big game," JP said. "But after a week's worth of doubts from the media, the pressure is all I can think about. On top of that, fans seem to be doubling by the hour around here."

The parents had flanked their boy, subconsciously feeling the need to protect him as they finished their walk in silence.

In the hours before the bowl game, Coach Flash studied JP's face to see how he was faring from the week of physical and emotional challenges. The coach had fielded more inquiries about JP than any other player, and he had grown seriously concerned over whether the pressure could make them all lose the game. The good man had secretly called on someone who he thought could help the Syracuse Orange and Navy on game day, and out of the corner of his eye, Flash saw his special guest arrive. With a signal from his whistle, he motioned everyone in. A dozen Syracuse College coaching staff members and 125 eager players quickly circled their leader.

"You've all worked *so* hard to get here," Coach Flash said. "The moment is finally upon us. It is with great attitude, training, and heart that you turned this football team around for our school. You've made me proud. You've made the university proud. You've made football fans across the country who didn't know *anything* about you until a few weeks ago inspired. It is no secret that our team is considered the underdog. I'm here to tell you that we are *exactly* where we want to be."

Flash swallowed hard and continued.

"I just highlighted your positive attitude, training, and heart. Those are the characteristics everyone's been talking about. The one the pundits always forget to mention, though, is talent. We have the most solid defense in the BCS, led by the best middle linebacker with Whistler. We have an unsung quarterback. We have a new running back, JP, whose full abilities have yet to even be seen. I can go on and on, naming each and every one of you. We not only can win, we will win. More than anything, I need you to believe in yourselves. Do you?"

The ring of powerful bodies let out boisterous hollers as they slapped their hands atop each other's helmets.

"It's good, but not convincing enough," Coach Flash said. "I've brought in a special gift today for us all. I've invited a man who has the most strategic football mind I know. He just so happens to believe we will defeat Boston's Falcons. I'm sure he has a few wise observations to share with us on how to go about it too. He's a much better football coach than I am. And I may be biased, but I would say the guy is pretty damn good-looking on top of it all."

The circle of heads turned to see Coach Flash's identical twin brother approaching. JP locked eyes with his old high-school coach while Crash gave the young man a nod.

"I thought I was supposed to be the humble one," Crash whispered to his twin with a rough handshake. "You don't give yourself enough credit when it comes to your own coaching talent. Jeez, look where you are."

The guest cleared his throat before unleashing his coaching voice.

"Listen, I don't believe I'm anywhere close to being one of the most strategic football minds on this field even, but for what it's worth, I do believe you will win. I believe Devin Madison and his undefeated University of Boston Falcons are excellent, but they aren't flawless. They make some key mistakes, and you can take advantage of 'em. I believe your strengths are underrated. I believe all of this puts you in a great position to win."

Crash went on to reveal how the opposing team's golden boy tended to twitch his right shoulder in the huddle when he was about to throw deep. The coach also warned that the Falcons' center on the offensive line often drew an opposing team offside for a penalty by snapping the football quickly whenever a competitor tried to put in subs. Crash spoke for a few minutes without pause, unveiling more observations, weaknesses, and strategies. From the front row, Whistler absorbed every word of the unexpected knowledge and wondered how he hadn't noticed these seemingly obvious observations before.

When his twin brother finished, the head coach took back the stage.

"I told you he was the better coach," Flash joked. "Orange and Navy, I know you will win. This talented football fanatic brother of mine knows you will win too. Let me ask this again, do you know you will win?"

Armed with pep talk and new knowledge, the team's energy took on new life. The players' shouts raised the hairs on JP's arms.

"OK then," said the head coach. "You guys are excused until I see you in the visitors' locker room on 2269 Dan Marino Boulevard in a few hours. Relax, focus,and reflect on these historic moments for our team."

As Coach Flash wrapped up his team's last practice of the season, he knew his twin brother's impromptu speech would bring confidence to the group. He hoped it would make one player in particular feel more at ease.

"So, do ya have a minute?" the high-school coach asked his former player as the group started to break.

"I don't know," JP joked. "My head coach, your own brother, told me not to listen to outside influences right now."

The player and his former coach shared a laugh.

"Seriously," the running back said with sudden gravity. "When I saw you walk on the field, I felt like I had taken my first deep breath since I've been in Florida. It's great to see you again, Coach."

"It goes without saying that everyone back at Jamesville-DeWitt High is *very* proud of you," Crash said. "That includes me, you know."

"Well, I owe all of my achievements to the strong line of coaches who got me where I am today," JP said. "There has always been some higher power looking over my shoulder to lead me to what everyone seems to think is my destiny."

"I don't know about that way of thinking, JP," Crash said.

The small running back looked at him with a raised brow.

"I'd argue that it's easy for people to say you're destined for greatness as an explanation for all of your ongoing achievements, especially when they look at you only from the outside and see your small size," Crash said. "You have undoubtedly had some great people in your life—your parents, my brother here."

"You," JP interjected.

Crash's stern face told JP the man was no longer joking around.

"Your own hard work and talent are what got you here today," Crash said. "Don't underestimate them."

The pair shook hands.

It was a concept that JP hadn't pondered. He felt frustrated over letting himself get caught up in a seesaw of emotions since taking up the starting position. But in these final hours before the game, with Crash's confidence in him, he finally felt relief.

"I'm going to give those undefeated Falcons a run for it!" he announced.

"That's it, man!" Crash said. "Don't overthink it. Just find a way to run and you'll pull this bowl off."

CHAPTER 33

ALL

C aroline and her fellow University of Boston cheerleaders lifted their maroon-and-gold pompoms and lined both sides of the Falcons' tunnel in anticipation of the favored team's sprint onto the field. The squad's cheers may have been perhaps their most boisterous ones of the season, yet they sounded mute within the sold-out Sun Life Stadium, an arena that frequently hosted the Miami Dolphins, Florida Marlins, and University of Miami teams. On this night, as two of the nation's best college football teams prepared to face off in the prestigious Orange Bowl, more than seventy-five thousand fans in the stadium had risen in anticipation of being in attendance at an exceptional matchup.

Caroline's cheer partner lifted her thin body into the air by pushing the soles of her spotless white sneakers upward with seemingly little effort. The motion made her red hair take flight with the white ribbon that dressed it. Her matching white uniform, trimmed with a maroon stripe on the skirt, showed off a toned frame. She lifted her pompoms with great energy, despite loathing the name pompom as well as the saccharine feeling she occasionally got when she waved them around.

On the tips of her partner's fingers more than seven feet in the air inside the rocking stadium, Caroline wondered whether she would catch Devin's eyes for the first time since their breakup. She wondered if her distant father had spotted her on the field from the sea of wild fans above. She no longer pondered if the thousands upon thousands of people surrounding her noticed on her pure white uniform a scarlet letter marking a troubled past. Caroline's short time in Father Santori's confessional booth had taken care of that worry at long last.

But still missing in the cheerleader's spiritual journey were the realizations that so many others were carrying around their own invisible letters that defined them—"good" or "bad"—and that the fans in the stadium that night would've served as the perfect sample for Father Santori's human corn husk experiment.

If Caroline could've peeled away the layers of each game goer, she would learn that the stadium held exactly 7,109 other people that night who also experienced abuse as children. She would learn that everyone in the packed stands carried around one burden or another. Precisely 2,249 of the fans in the stadium would go on to have a stay in prison at one point in their lives. More than 61,000 would experience the great joys and struggles of parenthood. An unsettling number of 23,954 would have a form of cancer at some point in their lives. Exactly 34,122 fans in the stadium would go on to stay married to their partners through life's good and bad times. More than 6,841 were currently facing the bump of unemployment in their careers.

The fans stood lonely together, anxious for a break from whatever weighed on their everyday lives. They stood lonely together even though strangers in close proximities shared some aspects of their layered lives in common.

And of the more than 75,000 fans in the stadium, 10,815 of them identified with being badly bullied in school. A sweet, shy boy named Henry was among them as his own bullies remained a safe 1,500 miles away in Brockton, Massachusetts.

>>>> <<<<

Henry's trip to the Orange Bowl had begun when his favorite Converse sneakers touched the sparkling floors of Boston's Logan Airport and his body took in the distinct excitement of airport air as passengers busily looked for their departure gates or taxis for the trip home.

"Does your stomach feel all right, Henry?" his mother asked as the boy had stared bravely through the Airbus window with pure fascination, taking breaks only to enjoy his complimentary soda and pretzels. "Do your ears hurt?"

Henry had shaken his head no as he realized that the plane ride was also his mother's first flight. His great appreciation for the trip made him do something he hadn't done in months. He had asked her if she was doing fine too.

"I'm fine, Henry," she said. "I'm just so excited to be here with you."

Upon reaching Miami Gardens Airport, the mother and son followed the signs to the baggage claim as if they had become professionals at air travel. Their first flight had also given them confidence in the taxi pickup line, where the easy-to-please boy felt thrilled to take his first cab ride.

"Holiday Inn Express in Fort Lauderdale, please," Misty said sweetly to their designated driver. "I brought directions if you need 'em."

The man behind the wheel thought Misty made a joke. He had already made that route four times that day.

"I guess he's all set," Misty whispered to Henry. "I guess there are no belts in this car. Should we ask to switch cabs?"

"No, Mom. It'll be fine." He didn't resist Misty's attempt to brace him in the seat like a human safety belt.

For Misty and Henry, their stay at the tidy Holiday Inn might as well have been the Four Seasons as they neatly placed their clothes in the matching dressers and enjoyed a respite on the firm mattresses and fluffy pillows. Lunch on their unfamiliar day of travel had featured a familiar outing—a salad and pizza picnic by the Atlantic Ocean. The comforting food and crashing waves provided a taste of home despite being a twenty-four-hour car ride away from their usual picnicking spot at Nantasket Beach in Hull, Massachusetts.

The pair spent the rest of the afternoon exploring Ft. Lauderdale, a city in which warm weather and palm trees made them feel like they were in a different, more exotic country.

They returned to the hotel too early, in Henry's opinion, to prepare for their dinner out with the man who made their trip possible. About thirty minutes into Misty's preparations inside what she thought was the fanciest bathroom she'd ever seen, the hotel phone rang, interrupting Henry from flipping through the numerous cable channels atop one of the hotel beds.

"Hello?"

"Henry! You made it, dude," Teach said. "How's Florida treating you? OK?"

"It's great," Henry said.

"Great, big guy. Hey, can I pick you and your chaperone up for dinner outside the lobby in half an hour?"

"Yeah."

"Oh, and Henry? Who is your chaperone, by the way? Did your mom end up coming with you?"

"Yup."

"Very well then, see you in thirty!"

As Henry internally debated whether Teach's voice sounded really happy at the end of their conversation, his mother marched out of the bathroom in a fluffy white towel and hair curlers.

"Who *was* that?" she asked, even though she knew Henry's one-of-a-kind grandmother wouldn't be checking in on them at the expense of a long-distance call. *The caller could only have been one person*, she thought.

"Teach," Henry mumbled, without taking his eyes off the television.

"And?"

"He asked if he could pick us up in half an hour."

"And what did you say?"

"I said it was fine."

"Oh, Henry."

Misty disappeared into the bathroom to kick her preparations up a notch. Her makeup application was rusty from serving only rare nights as a hostess at the restaurant and having even more rare dates out in Boston, but when she emerged from the bathroom in her purple wrap dress and a shiny, dark, and wavy hairdo, Henry couldn't resist tearing his eyes away from the television. His mother looked beautiful, even if she was wearing two different shoes.

"Which one?" Misty asked as she switched feet like a nervous flamingo with one sandal and one boot.

"I dunno," Henry said. "I know it's January, but isn't it too warm here for boots?"

Without a word, Misty changed into her other sandal and eyed her son's oversized, belted khakis and plaid, blue button-up.

"You look nice," she said. "Shall we?"

Henry clicked off the fancy television and escorted his beautiful mother to the lobby, where Teach was already waiting.

"Henry, my fine student, fancy meeting you here," Teach said with a fist bump. "And good evening to you, Mrs. Misty Miss."

The adults laughed as they recalled their earlier introduction fumbles.

"I don't know," Teach said. "I'm feeling a bit underdressed next to you two looking so sharp for our dinner."

Teach was having a hard time keeping his eyes off Misty. While the job of being a young mother gave Misty tremendous maturity, only one year separated Henry's mother from his teacher, and the teacher was surprisingly the more senior one of the two.

"Oh please," she said, thinking Teach looked perfectly handsome in an outfit that the man typically reserved for his summer wedding attendances. He had rolled up the sleeves and enjoyed the freedom on this night of unbuttoning a few buttons from his tie-less neckline.

Teach opened the door of his rental car for Henry before quickly jogging to the other side for the passenger who made his jaw line feel flushed.

"I barely recognized you without the earphones on, you know," Misty said, with hopes of keeping the mood light and avoiding an awkward evening.

Teach smiled, feeling relief over a date offering something funny to fill the dead air for once. He wondered if he was on a date. He thought it felt like one.

The car became silent yet comfortable as Teach focused on navigating through an unfamiliar city to a restaurant called Mangos on Ft. Lauderdale's East Las Olas Boulevard. Misty and Henry enjoyed every block of the city views.

Teach had selected the restaurant after an online surfing session made it appear fun and nice without being too fancy. To Henry, who had only ever visited his mother's restaurant and fast-food joints, it was the finest dining place he'd ever entered.

"Family of three?"

"Um yes, three please, but no," Teach said to the hostess with a deepening blush. "We are a teacher and a student and a mother. Our Henry here won a prestigious writing contest in my class to earn himself tickets to the Orange Bowl. Your finest table, if you please." Teach managed to wink at the hostess to relay his jest without appearing the least bit creepy or demanding.

"Well, of course," the hostess said toward Henry. As Henry took a seat, he looked around. While he didn't notice anything that made his table better than others, he still felt important.

As they returned their menus after ordering grilled pork chops, a sesame-crusted tuna salad, and a cheeseburger, Misty and Teach accidentally brushed arms. The touch shot unfamiliar electricity through Misty's right side and prompted her to excuse herself to the ladies' room to make sure her eyeliner hadn't spread up toward her brow.

The server returned to the table first.

"Young man, I forgot to ask how you'd like your cheeseburger done," the server said apologetically to Henry. The boy's face looked puzzled.

"How do you like it cooked, little dude?" Teach asked.

Henry's face turned from puzzled to red. It was a question that had never been asked by the cashiers whenever he ordered his burgers in Brockton's fast-food joints.

"I like mine with no red in the middle, so I usually ask for them well done or medium well," Teach whispered to his student.

"Well done, please," Henry said.

"Very well done, Henry," Teach said as the server left the table. "Spoken like a true pro."

Teach wanted to ask the shy boy about his mother's story, but he decided that would be inappropriate. When she returned, he mustered enough courage to offer her a drink.

"A glass of wine sounds perfect," Misty said, already looking forward to calming her nerves.

"Red or white?"

"White, please."

"Do you like sweet, dry with light body, or dry with medium body?"

Henry wondered if they were really talking about wine. He was just getting over the new terms regarding his burger.

"Dry with medium body sounds perfect."

Teach looked down the wine list to locate the most expensive one in that category, even though he sensed that for a woman like Misty, it wasn't expected or necessary. He flagged the server with a slight motion.

"A glass of the Ferrari Carrano chardonnay for the young lady, please, and a glass of Chianti for myself," Teach said. "And for the boy, a root beer?" Henry nodded in delight. His mother nudged him under the table.

"Yes, please," Henry added.

"As a restaurant employee myself, I'm fully impressed with your wine knowledge," Misty said.

"Oh, I had a cheat sheet," Teach admitted. "I know nothing about wine. There's a list here that spells out every glass in the category you like. Even I could follow the instructions."

Misty found his self-deprecating humor refreshing. She looked guiltily at Henry, who fortunately didn't seem to mind her conversation with his teacher.

As if on cue, live reggae music began to play, making the warm evening that much more magically fun. Misty felt as though she were in a movie.

"To the University of Boston Falcons," Teach said, lifting his glass of red.

"They just have to win," Henry agreed with a clink.

It was the most emotion Misty remembered seeing from Henry in months. She closed her eyes and hoped Devin Madison could pull off a win for her son.

Henry took a bite of his oversized burger and accidentally forced ketchup out the other side, onto his best shirt. The boy quickly tucked his napkin into the neck of his top to cover up the stain. Misty pretended not to notice. Teach quickly tucked his own napkin into his best shirt to match.

"I like your idea, little man," Teach said. "This is the only shirt I have that I can wear to warm weddings. We got to protect our styles, you know?"

Misty's heart felt as though it had jumped into her throat. She had never felt this way over a man before. She blushed over the fact that the man was none other than her son's teacher.

Later that evening, as she lay in the hotel bed attempting to sleep, she replayed the perfect dinner in her head while Henry also struggled to drift off in the bed next to her for an entirely different reason. For the shy boy with the challenging childhood, the game could not happen soon enough.

When the moment the mother and son were both anxiously anticipating finally came the following day, Teach entered the hotel lobby with quick steps. From his cap and jersey to his maroon corduroys that were sure to make him sweat, every garment he was wearing featured University of Boston colors. Misty couldn't help but smile.

"Sorry to keep you guys waiting. Traffic is so much worse than I expected. Shall we make our way to Miami Gardens for the Orange Bowl?"

Teach's words got more loud, dramatic, and comical with each syllable until it was Henry's turn to smile. Teach took a subtle risk in opening Misty's car door first this time, and as the rental meandered slowly through the traffic, Henry wondered whether they would miss a minute of pre-game activity. Misty wondered if they would get there in time to pick out a souvenir for her mother. Teach wanted to be there already.

The trio didn't fare much better in the parking garage, where they circled around and again and became convinced there were no more spots until they finally watched white lights appear on a car ready to reverse as though it were a miracle. Teach put on his blinker. A truck zoomed in opposite them for a face-off, even though Teach had been there first. The car reversed toward Teach, leaving him in a disadvantaged position for the take. The truck took their spot.

Teach rolled down his window. Henry rolled his down too. The sound made Teach remember that he wasn't with his college buddies.

"Hey Henry, dude, I'm not going to lose my cool," Teach said as calmly as he could manage. "I'm just going to ask where the next closest garage is."

"Well, I have a mind to give them a word or two," Misty said.

For the first time that day, the pair locked eyes and smiled. From her passenger seat, Misty felt the same electricity as the night before, only this time it traveled along the left side of her body.

Wasting only a few extra minutes to find another parking spot, the teacher, student, and parent excitedly made their way into Sun Life Stadium at long last.

"University of Boston has to win," Henry said for the fourth time that day as he wore his favorite Falcons shirt. "Devin Madison just has to pull it out."

Of the more than seventy-five thousand people in the stadium, exactly a dozen would eventually become professional athletes. Devin Madison, University of Boston's golden boy quarterback, was going to be one of them. As he led the Falcons out of the tunnel in a full sprint on the biggest night of his life, his guts felt the vibrations from Falcons fans' lively cheers. He passed Caroline quickly among the lineup of cheerleaders screaming his name. Devin had plotted against glancing her way, but he couldn't help himself. He wondered how it felt to be in her shoes, forced to cheer him on. He got satisfaction out of that thought. He turned and nodded his head instead toward the club seating where he knew his esteemed grandfather and father were watching before finally turning his focus to only the game.

Roughly a third of the fans in the stadium were dressed in maroon and gold. Another third were dressed in orange and navy. The remaining attendees were simply fans of the game, with the majority of them rooting for Craig Whistler, JP Hemmings, and the rest of the Syracuse College team because they were the determined underdogs.

The cheers for Devin's opposition as the Orange and Navy exited their tunnel sounded even more exuberant, even though moments earlier, that hadn't felt possible. Devin's anger grew along with the opposition's support. He vowed to take everything out on the field.

To his delight, University of Boston won the coin toss and chose offensive play first.

From the stands, Henry's eyes grew wide at the sight of Devin and the rest of Devin's team—Henry's team.

From the end zone, a wisp of an International Presswire photographer barely noticed the heaviest belt of equipment she had ever carried on assignment. Maxine clicked shot after shot, desperate to get accustomed to the lighting and the commotion before the game began. Her job hung on the line, yet she felt only excitement for the opportunity to cover an event like this. The thunderous noise rolling through the stadium made sure of that.

At the football field's center following the coin toss, Whistler offered Devin a pre-game handshake with a polite, genuine nod of his head. The golden boy accepted Whistler's giant hand, despite knowing the oversized defensive lineman nicknamed the Master, along with the rest of Syracuse's defensive unit, The Keys, would be after him all game.

The golden boy couldn't resist attempting to shake them all up.

"You guys are in way over your damn heads, but try to have some fun out there, huh?" Devin said.

Whistler simply pivoted in response and jogged to his Orange and Navy sideline, where he would be happy to use the star quarterback's comment for motivation. For the second time in minutes, a star player vowed to take everything out on the field.

From their unfamiliar, luxurious seats above, the professors came to life at the sight of their son's giant roommate.

"You can do it, Whistler!" screamed JP's mother, even though she had not always been the young man's greatest cheerleader when he was in her classroom.

Her husband began sputtering out letters. While the fans around him initially assumed he'd spell defense, JP's mother knew better. Her husband never went with the masses despite teaching about their rituals during his anthropology courses at Syracuse College.

"D-E-B-I-L-I-T-A-T-E!" he belted out.

"A little violent, don't you think?" his wife said as she shot him a look. "Our boy is going to be playing on that field soon enough."

Intensity spread from the teams' captains to the rest of the teams' sidelines as both sets of special teams took the field.

The referee whistled the start of the game.

Syracuse's place kicker booted the football solidly in the air with fine, soccer-like style as Whistler, JP, and their fellow Orange and Navy pounded their helmets in approval. The ball soared to reach eight yards from the distant end zone, yet it would soon be Devin and the rest of the University of Boston Falcons' turn to cheer.

The Falcons' kick returner eluded one Orange and Navy body after the next with a ninety-two-yard touchdown in his sights. While he fell short of that goal, he succeeded in running the ball an impressive seventy-one yards to the twenty-one-yard line.

As Devin stepped on the field to take over on offense, he passed his special teams players without a word or a pat of thanks, not even for the kick returner who had nearly put the first points on the board for Devin's Falcons. If there were going to be any superstars in the stadium on this night, Devin wanted himself to be the one and only.

Caroline's fellow cheerleaders joined the fans dressed in maroon and gold in screaming their delight over University of Boston's desirable field position. As Devin took the field, nearly everyone in the stadium, even the Syracuse fans, sensed an early University of Boston touchdown. Caroline thought of her father in the stands. She knew he was watching her with pride and maybe even screaming right along with them. It was her single motivator for cheering on the very young man she had grown to loathe so passionately.

"Let's go, Boston!" Caroline shouted genuinely with the others. "Let's go, Offense! Let's go, Devin!"

As Devin's fingers touched the leather and laces that had felt like a security blanket since his youth, he began his work with precision. The Hustler looked down on his son in the stadium with expectations that would appear unreachable for anyone but the golden boy. Devin managed to keep an eye on a charging, hungry Whistler while getting the football off just in time to his go-to player, a receiver who let the ball slip through his fingertips.

Whistler immediately worked to end his defensive charge, successfully stopping just before hitting his quarterback target. The competitors brushed shoulder pads with even less force than the motion in their handshake moments ago, but on the field, in the classroom, and in girls' hearts, Devin was used to getting whatever he wanted. He faked a late hit and crashed himself to the ground, looking desperately in false pain at the closest referee.

Orange and Navy fans booed for the first of what would be many times that game as the referee threw a flag and a personal foul against Whistler.

Devin may not have thrown a completion on his first play, but his acting won his University of Boston Falcons fifteen yards and a first down at the six-yard line.

Syracuse Coach Flash kept a calm demeanor and immediately signaled for a change in players to swap his small, fast defenders for ones shaped more like Whistler. Despite the warning from Flash's twin brother during the team's pep talk, the Eagle's offensive center succeeded in drawing the Orange and Navy offside by snapping the football quickly. The play gave the Orange and Navy their second penalty in as many minutes, earning the Falcons half the distance to the goal and another first down.

Heat traveled up Whistler's already sweaty body. The defensive lineman felt disappointed in himself and the rest of his Syracuse defense. He knew they were better than this. No one could've prevented Devin's acting performance, but they should've been ready for the center's quick snap following Crash's information. Boston's center had outsmarted them.

From the stands, an eleven-year-old boy, his teacher, and his mother rose to their feet as they watched Devin Madison throw a fast, short ball for a University of Boston Falcons touchdown. The three fans embraced in a single hug, and the mother wished she could bottle that moment for her shy boy whom she had never seen so happy.

>>>>— <<<<

Of the more than 75,000 people in the stadium, exactly 7,167 were physically unable to have children during what was supposed to be the fertile years of their lives. A pair of them looked down now on their adopted son with great pride. The parents wondered in silence how they had managed to get so lucky.

The professor adjusted her oversized glasses and felt surprised at feeling peace within her belly despite watching her small son take the field for the third time that night in one of the biggest college football games of the year.

She absorbed all the cheers for JP as complete strangers transformed their screams into a synchronized chorus. The sight of the orange T-shirts surrounding her made her feel like she was wrapped in a warm blanket. The air in the stadium smelled like a music concert and a ballpark as fans wore their perfumes and colognes worthy of a big event and snacked on hotdogs and beer. She reached for her husband's free hand, which felt like sandpaper. His other one was full of stadium candies.

"Jumpin' jellybeans!" the anthropology professor shouted. "Did you see that?"

JP finished running the ball with great heart as he attempted to create a path through a thick forest of bodies shaped like tree trunks. He had jumped over one of his own down men to advance five yards. His fans applauded his effort while reserving their more boisterous cheers for an overdue first down. JP came up just short.

"Jumpin' jellybeans!" the professor yelled again as he munched. "Hey, Mum, maybe that's why JP's biological mother named him JP in the womb."

His wife looked at him with puzzlement, as she often did.

"JP for J-U-M-P," the man explained. "Maybe that kid was really bouncing about in utero just as he does on this great earth."

His wife rolled her eyes, as she often did with him. His comment, though, made her think of the girl who had given them the greatest gift of their lives. She adjusted her glasses again as she felt both love and sadness for the mysterious young lady. She felt love for making JP's birth possible. She felt sadness for the girl's lack of opportunity to see who he'd become. The professor did the math and realized she was now a woman in her thirties. The professor hoped JP's biological mother was one of the ten million viewers watching the game on television. She also wished that the sound of JP's uncommon name from a sportscaster would make the woman who gave birth to him think it was possible for JP to be the baby she had given up so long ago.

Syracuse's quarterback threw an incomplete pass on the third down before its special teams emerged again to punt the ball away to University of Boston. JP's Orange and Navy remained scoreless into the second quarter, and it did not appear to be their night.

Devin moved his Falcons down the field with rhythmic, military precision before throwing his second touchdown of the evening. After a quick Orange and Navy turnover, he marched again and threw for his third. At the half, the Falcons posted twenty-one points to the Orange and Navy's zero. Syracuse fans' cheers faded into weak applause for the halftime performances.

JP's mother managed to stay upbeat despite the scoreless performance by her son's team. After all, JP had not made any mistakes, she thought. He was playing as solidly as anyone else. There were no boos rolling down on her son's overworked shoulders on this night. *Things could definitely be worse*, she thought.

On the other side of the stadium, a proud father named Kenny watched his daughter perform to the halftime music. He secretly couldn't wait to tell the guys at work of all that his daughter had managed to accomplish against odds that he wasn't even fully aware of. Kenny would have to dish out some rare boasting on coffee breaks as all these years later, the whizzing, drumming, and popping sounds of Harper's manufacturing floor still kept conversation to a minimum at his beloved workplace. Kenny knew his buddies were watching the game on this night from their television sets in Rhode Island. He wondered if they were trying to pick Caroline out of the lineup of University of Boston cheerleaders. He felt proud that the Falcons were on top thanks to a star quarterback who, unbeknownst to Kenny, had further broken his daughter's already fractured heart.

Kenny thought he felt the majority of the crowd's eyes on his captivating daughter. Caroline still reminded him of his late wife. He hoped Lindsay was looking down on their daughter with pride tonight. During his most recent trip to Mass at St. Matthew's Church last Sunday, he had prayed for it.

A few sections away, the shy boy named Henry was still trading high-fives with his mother and teacher in unusually grand, extroverted spirits.

"They're going to pull it off, Teach," Henry said. "I just know it. Devin's gonna do this, Mom."

A pop band that had been popular in the 80s took the field as Teach and Misty tried to come up with the group's name.

"It will come to me," Teach said. "Just hang on a second."

"I bet it will come to me first," flirted Misty.

The stadium lights made her dark hair shine. Teach believed that even if Henry hadn't been a student in his classroom, the woman would still be out of his reach. In different ways, he believed Misty was more beautiful than the dental student he had nearly taken as his date.

"I'll bet you a beer I can come up with it," she added.

Teach shook her delicate hand in agreement.

"I don't want to miss any of the game," the boy said excitedly. "I think I'm going to go to the bathroom, like right now."

Misty looked around at the crowds, instantly worried about her eleven-year-old son going off alone.

"I'll go with you, Henry," Teach said. "I could use a minute to freshen up."

Misty smiled at Teach's thoughtfulness and humor. Just like the actors in the romantic films, she thought he was too good to be true. She believed that even if Henry hadn't been in Teach's classroom, Teach would be out of her reach.

The unlikely pair made their way together through the crowds and stood in line in perhaps one of the only types of venues where the wait for the men's room is often longer than that of the ladies. When they met back up, Teach could hear the music of the 80s band still playing.

"Do you think we have time to get a couple beers and a soda, little man?" Teach asked.

Henry looked at his watch and studied the shortening line for refreshments. He flashed his favorite teacher in the world a smile and a nod.

Of the more than 75,000 people in the stadium, exactly 5,759 were adopted in their youth. The one among them with the shortest name carried on this night the greatest hope as he prepared to take the field in the third quarter.

JP strapped on his helmet and repeated in his head the simple advice his old high-school coach had given him earlier that day. *Don't overthink it. Just find a way to run and you'll pull this bowl off.*

The words grew to complement those of Crash's twin brother, SC Coach Flash, from minutes earlier in an uncomfortably still locker room.

"There are advantages to losing the coin toss," Coach Flash had said. "And we're about to prove it as we start fresh with the ball in the third quarter. We've all gone over each unit's halftime adjustments. We know what we need to do to win this game. We will win this game. Now believe in yourselves. Just. Start. Fresh."

The Falcons kicked off the football in the third quarter to a physically and mentally renewed team as the week of Orange Bowl festivities and the deafening stands of Sun Life Stadium finally felt less shocking to a scoreless, underdog Syracuse College.

The SC special teams blockers helped their returner advance to solid field position for JP and the rest of the offense. Whistler let out a deep growl of excitement from the sidelines. JP jumped with knees tucked momentarily into his armpits as he got himself ready for second-half play.

"There he goes again, Mum," JP's father said from the stands as the SC fans surrounding him found renewed energy themselves. "Jumpin' JP!"

In only the second game of his college career, the small running back would quickly make the sportscasters who had been predicting a University of Boston win at the half end any more of that talk.

JP's offensive blockers appeared more focused as the running back suddenly had more paths to choose from. JP picked one on the far left, running dangerously close to where Devin Madison was watching out of bounds, before doing what he knew best. His small frame slipped past a final row of defenders before sprinting a distance he'd practiced all week, all season, and all of his twelve-year football career. He ran forty yards to the end zone.

"Whatever," Devin said from the Falcons' sideline without making eye contact with anyone in particular. "We can give them one."

JP's run led to only seven points on the board against the Falcons' twenty-one, but it was enough to make the rest of JP's team believe they could help come up with the rest.

After an unusual interception on Devin's first throw of the second half under pressure by Whistler, it was quickly the Orange and Navy's turn to take over again on offense. JP's quarterback took advantage of a wide receiver's breakaway to put up another quick touchdown, bringing the Orange and Navy swiftly within seven.

The shift in the momentum at the Sun Life Stadium was palpable as the fans switched roles. It was suddenly Boston fans' turn to heckle and the Syracuse fans' opportunity to come to life.

From the sidelines, Devin's anger at his own misstep prompted him to release his fury on his defensive line as special teams took the field.

"What the hell are you jerk-offs doing out there?" Devin said as loudly as he could manage through clenched teeth as he attempted to avoid getting picked up by the national cameras. "These are rookies we're playing against here. Get your damn helmets out of your butts."

As the star quarterback passed by special teams to take the field on offense, he snapped at those players too.

"Oh great," he said. "I love starting my drive practically in the other team's end zone. Bravo, crapheads."

His talented offensive line worked hard at inching the team's way out of the danger zone to prevent a touchback, but Whistler's Keys were determined to prevent a Falcons first down.

The ref signaled third down.

Syracuse fans removed the keys from their pockets and, as if choreographed, began shaking them as though they were watching from the stands in their stadium at home. Whistler was determined not to let Crash's advice go to waste once again. He watched the golden boy twitch his right shoulder in the huddle.

"Chantilly!" Whistler yelled repeatedly toward his fastest defenders in the unit.

It was a play name the defensive line had created at the half to signal Devin's plan to throw deep. With great trust in their captain and zero hesitation, the Orange and Navy defenders sprinted as fast as they could following the Boston snap. They tightly covered a pair of Devin's receivers, who took off too and matched them stride for stride.

The star quarterback should've abandoned his plan and thrown short because his team was seven points ahead with another full quarter of play to go, but his pride got the best of him. To his coach's dismay, Devin stuck with his own plan and hoped for either a miracle or a pass interference call against the defenders.

But Whistler's Keys had been warned at the half about drawing a flag on their newfound Chantilly play. Their hands remained at their sides as they ran. Devin chose a receiver. The Orange defender leaped to intercept the ball and was successful. Devin called to the closest referee for pass interference, but this time his acting wouldn't be bought.

In the stands, Henry seemed to lose his new flow of words with each misstep by the Falcons. He sat on crossed fingers while his mother stole quick, worried glances at him and Teach, who no longer appeared in the mood to joke. The trio sadly watched JP run in a third touchdown for the Orange and Navy.

As Falcons fans yelled disappointedly at the risky turn of events, the Orange and Navy fans smelled a great comeback victory.

Henry silently uncrossed his fingers and folded his arms across a small, pounding chest.

Of the more than 75,000 people in the stadium, exactly 22,939 of them had never been married. Maxine was keenly aware of being in the single category from the friends and family members who would insist she was hitched to her job. But being alone was not the thought running through the photographer's head as she watched Syracuse's small running back prepare for work in the final minutes of the fourth quarter. Her camera was at the ready.

From the sidelines, the typically impartial journalist couldn't help but feel swayed by JP's strong work ethic. She thought of his youthful room in central New York where Most Improved Player certificates and other awards covered the plaid walls like a second, competing layer of wallpaper. Each certificate reminded Maxine of her own victories toward reaching this game too.

In a pause for a television timeout from Orange Bowl play, she thought of her trips a decade ago to three northern New York farms where she had established ties that would later bear fruitful images on the morning of the men's insurance reform testimony in Washington, DC. She thought about the exhausting time she spent in Syracuse College's stadium on her weekends off from the northern New York newspaper for only the sake of creating a portfolio of sports shots that she knew might or might not get her somewhere. She thought too about finally landing the sports job of her dreams at Syracuse's International Presswire Bureau, where she had recently managed to build a relationship with JP amidst tight protection by his coach and parents at the most critical time in her career. Each struggle had led her to a grander one until finally she reached a bowl game that the very best in her industry had hoped to cover. Along the way, each grumpy editor had appeared to follow another as she managed to exceed expectations to get to this moment.

Don't make us both regret me taking a chance on you.

With only a couple minutes remaining on the game clock, Maxine's opportunities to secure the shot of the game were dwindling. The warning from the wire's sports editor at their New York City lunch in preparation of this assignment rang a second time through her head.

Don't make us both regret me taking a chance on you.

Maxine had a number of solid action shots to file, but none captured the level of greatness she needed. The photographer knew that the full story of the game had yet to unfold. She refused to let herself panic. There was still a little time left. There was still hope.

As the commercial break of new beer, car, and insurance ads wrapped up on the sets of the more than ten million television viewers of the Orange Bowl, the players came to life on the field. Energized by the respite and the desire to avoid going into overtime, neither team appeared as though they'd already played fifty-three aggressive minutes. Both sides of the crowd amplified their energy too, as cheers for the offense and defense morphed into one unbearably loud noise.

Two University of Boston male cheerleaders tossed Caroline high into the air. Her legs shot up with force. Her father proudly joined the crowd's cheers from the stands as he uncharacteristically clapped and hollered with the rest.

"Come on, Boston!" he shouted even though he was the only one who could hear his words above everyone else's. "Defense, let's go now!"

Nearby, Henry clenched his hands in fists as he stomped and screamed as loud as he could. With all fans on their feet, Teach signaled for Henry to stand on the bleachers to better see the field. The boy looked to his mother silently for approval. Misty lifted him up there herself.

As the crowd heated up, the smell of hotdogs, pretzels, perfume, and cologne transformed into a warm stench of spilled beer and sweat. JP's father was nearly out of breath as he jumped and cheered with the sportiest of fans.

"Hey, Mum, that's my boy people are cheering for!" he screamed. "Did I mention that is my boy?"

At the referee's signal, the teams broke from their respective huddles and lined up for what each side believed would be a fight. JP's quarterback threw one incomplete pass followed by a second as Devin cheered his opposition's mistakes from his sideline. The Orange and Navy lost yardage and needed an improbable twelve yards on their third attempt to make a first down.

Coach Flash signaled a timeout from the sidelines, knowing he'd still have one left to hold in his pocket.

"Hurry up, guys," he yelled above the cheers as his Syracuse players were already sprinting to meet him. JP led the V-shaped pack like a captain of wild geese.

"We're going for the first down obviously, but we need at least five yards to get in field goal position. If we can just get ourselves a field goal, we'll be up a few points. From there, we can rely on Whistler and the rest of the defense to hold us there for the win."

Coach Crash turned to his quarterback and made succinct, clear orders.

"I need you to pump fake."

He turned to his fastest wide receiver.

"I need you to run out of the gate as though you are going to catch it."

He turned to his offensive linemen.

"I need you to exert every last bit of energy on this play to block for JP."

He turned to the young man who just a couple of weeks ago had served as the unlikeliest of players to end up with the ball.

"I need you to run. JP, I need you to run for at least five yards."

Whistler stood within earshot and screamed for his offense when they took back the field. He watched his team's center complete the snap. His wide receiver sprinted. His quarterback did a pump fake. His offensive line pushed. His roommate grasped the ball.

Maxine's heart raced as she squinted through her lens and realized that this might be the play of the game. JP's mother held onto her oversized glasses while her heart raced too.

JP saw no clear pathway. He darted left and then right as the amount of time that the pump fake bought him quickly ran out. The running back became every defender's target. He advanced two yards before being laid out by a duo of swift University of Boston Falcons.

JP knew it wasn't enough. Coach Crash was a wise man and wasn't going to risk attempting a field goal from out of reach only to give Devin Madison great field position in their final drive. They would still rely on Whistler to hold their score. They would hope now for overtime.

"It's not his fault," JP's mother said to herself amidst an instantly quiet crowd.

Some SC fans laced their fingers behind their heads. Some wore freshly made rally caps. Others wore complete disappointment on their faces.

"You're right, it is *not* his fault, Mum," her husband responded. "After all, it was I who served as his horrendous first instructor of football one fateful afternoon so long ago when my bum caught more air off the ground than the ball on my own attempt at a punt. It's my fault for getting the three of us in this most difficult of spots."

The man cleared his throat and raised his voice for the benefit of the disappointed people sitting around him.

"That is still my boy out there."

The professor hoisted himself to his feet to give JP a solo standing ovation as he watched his son slink off the field.

JP didn't blame his offensive line even though he could have. He was disappointed only in himself.

On the other side of the stadium, Devin threatened his own teammates despite finding himself suddenly in great spirits.

"If you buttheads don't block for me, I will personally destroy you," he said.

The quarterback knew he had the talent to pull off a win. With a challenging twenty seconds left on the game clock, he was the only one left on the field who didn't want the final bit of the game to be framed any other way. Devin believed it was his shot at making the play of the game. This was his chance to change his family bowl game history. For the second time that night, he looked up at the club seats and gave a nod toward the family who had pushed him harder and more harshly than any of the coaches ever had.

With the snap, Devin's wide receivers sprinted toward the edges of the sidelines as the quarterback threw one of the young men a ball that landed precisely between the jersey numbers for a first down. The receiver willingly stepped out of bounds to stop the clock.

Whistler growled in frustration, but it wouldn't help him any. In *deja vu* fashion, the golden boy repeated the same play. A second receiver dressed in maroon and gold stepped out of bounds with the ball for a second first down.

With the clock down to mere seconds, Devin knew it was time to make good on his failed Hail Mary attempt from earlier. He twitched his right shoulder before Whistler once again called a Chantilly play for his defenders.

Seeing no opportunities for a long throw for a touchdown, Devin wisely tossed the ball to his running back, who managed to accomplish what JP hadn't moments earlier—the Eagle ran his team into field goal position.

Maxine clicked away at the rapid turn of events.

Just behind her, Boston's newfound momentum made a smile reappear on Henry's face.

Kenny watched Caroline do a flip on the sideline, but it was the stomach of Caroline's cheerleading coach that did a flop.

"What the hell is wrong with you, Tommy?" the woman whispered as she recalled the morning back at University of Boston's practice field when Devin had harassed his kicker with those exact words. At the time, Tommy had clearly been anticipating this exact scenario.

Somewhere in the stands, the kicker's family members were feeling their own stomachs turn as well.

Coach Flash called his final timeout in an attempt to ice him. On the Orange and Navy sidelines, there was only one instruction left for Flash to give his own team.

"Let's hope for a miss," he said.

Some of his players knelt in prayer. JP stood tall with his chin up high. He refused to rest until the match was over.

Devin watched helplessly too from his own sideline, but he had reason to be much more hopeful. He knew that if Tommy missed the field goal, the story appearing in all of tomorrow's newspapers and replaying on sports channels would be about Tommy's miss that brought the teams into overtime. If the kicker made it—from an unspectacular distance of thirty-nine yards—the story would be about Devin's much more spectacular drive that got Tommy within range. Devin stood tall with his chin up high. He too refused to rest until the match was over.

Tommy's tireless practice paid off as the Falcons kicker booted the ball easily between the uprights. Devin Madison and his University of Boston Falcons won the Orange Bowl by three points.

A smile returned on Henry's face, along with a steady flow of his words.

Caroline cheered and searched for her father in the stands.

Devin's father and grandfather had already made their way onto the field, ready to celebrate their parts of the long-awaited bowl win for their family. As Devin moved toward them, flashing his star-like smile for the media, a dozen cameras surrounded them. Maxine watched the scene unfold, but didn't edge her way in. She thought of her new mentor's earlier words of advice regarding Devin's family history.

"That is an obvious angle," the veteran had warned.

Maxine chose instead a riskier route that would go on to win her placement on the front pages of major sports sections across the country. She jogged quickly and effortlessly toward JP. No one was surrounding him. She silently captured shot after shot of his pained yet tearless eyes. He was the complete picture of defeat.

He carried the look of coming up short after making it so far, but he was also the epitome of honor in loss.

Maxine would go on to win the prestigious "Best Photo of the Year" recognition by *Newswire* magazine for the shot, yet the far greater gift was delivered to her at the game's close. It came as quickly as a bullet to the heart.

Through staring at him through her camera's lens, Maxine had an epiphany over the boy's name. JP's skin was slightly darker than her pale brown skin, but it matched that of her first sweetheart. Together as kids themselves, the young lovers had made the heartbreaking decision to give the boy up for adoption. Maxine had named the baby JP from the other side of her womb after a hero of hers named James Presley Ball, an African-American pioneer of black photography in the 1800s whom Maxine had read about in school. Even as a young girl, she had dreamed of great things for herself. She had wanted her son to be destined for great things too.

The running back looked up, too drained to resist any shots from the lady he had already grown to admire. He would find out later that of the more than seventy-five thousand people in the stadium, exactly two were a lost mother and son.

"JP," Maxine said as though she were putting the letters together for the first time.

Weeks of distraction from frenzied assignments had prevented her from figuring it all out sooner. She had spent years trying to keep the name at the back of her mind. She had never dreamed, until now, that the adoptive parents would've honored her request as an immature girl.

Her neck strap caught the weight of the camera falling toward her belly.

PART 3

CHAPTER 34

ALL

What plates do you propose, Mom?" JP asked in advance of setting the splintered round table that still served as the family's most treasured possession.

"Well, let's get out only the finest ones, of course. There's much ado about everything tonight."

Over the noise of the professor's outdated, handheld mixer in the family's favorite cream cheese frosting, the mother and son each questioned whether they heard an additional buzz.

"Juh-ames Puh-resley," JP's father shouted through the window over a grill and a chuckle. "Mum! I think our guest is here. The doorbell is ringing, you two!"

It had been three and a half years since the Orange Bowl where Maxine had locked eyes with JP and realized who he was. It had taken her only a day to call the people who had raised the running back to reintroduce herself.

"Hello, Mrs. Hemmings," she had said. "It's Maxine, the photographer from the Syracuse Bureau of International Presswire."

"Oh, Max, we were just conversing about you," the professor had said. "Your fine photograph in today's papers of my boy after the game severed my heart and brought a smile to my face all at once. I do believe you managed to take his first picture as a man. He just looks so…grown up."

"Glad you approve, Mrs. H. I love the picture too, despite its sadness. Thankfully, my editors did as well."

"As does everyone in America. It's all over the national papers. If you're looking for the superstar, he's out to breakfast with Whistler. They're sick over the bowl outcome, of course, but I think they've found substantial relief in having accomplished so much. The city's response here at home has been quite welcoming since their return."

Maxine had grown accustomed to adrenaline rushes whenever she was on deadline for work, but the surges throughout her body were for unfamiliarly personal reasons now. The lonely photographer prepared to reveal to JP's adoptive mother that she could be his biological one.

"Well, it was actually you who I was hoping to catch."

"Maxine," the professor said. "We grew to trust you at even the most stressful of times for our family. It is now your time to trust me. Whatever is it, my new friend?"

"Where do I start? There are just too many coincidences. Please know that if you don't want anything to do with me after I say what I'm about to tell you, I will absolutely respect that."

Maxine had gone on to explain her painful decision to give up a baby nineteen years ago. She explained, too, that the baby's initials stood for the historic African-American man who had inspired her to become a photographer. She had even dared to disclose that she had recognized JP's sparkly, driven eyes as her own.

"You are JP's mother—period—professor," Maxine had continued. "If this is all more than a pile of coincidences and JP is in fact the one I gave birth to, please know I would never dream of overstepping any boundaries. You're clearly much better at this mom thing than I have ever dreamed. I'm calling, though, to see if any of you might want any part of me in your lives."

"How about coming over for Sunday dinner?" the professor had sputtered with great surprise and little hesitation. "Let me talk with my husband. Let me talk with JP. But let me also extend to you an invitation to come to our family's home this Sunday."

Three and a half years and nearly two hundred Sunday dinners later, Maxine stood at the Hemmings' familiar stoop.

"I thought I told you to just come on in, Maxine," the professor scolded with a wave of her frosting-covered beaters. "You're family, you know."

The comment, which tugged at Maxine's heart in a way that made it feel no longer lonely, was topped only by the warm hug and smile that followed from her biological son.

"Maxine," JP said. "I hear congratulations are in order."

"As do I."

"So where is he?" JP asked protectively. "Where's our final guest? You didn't come together, Max?"

Following Maxine's fateful reconnection with JP a few years earlier, the photographer had found one pesky, haunting cliché to ring true when it came to finding love: it comes when you're least expecting it. Her prize-winning photo from the Orange Bowl had prompted a call from a longtime admirer.

"Maxine here," she had said from her desk at the Syracuse bureau.

"Max. I don't know if you remember me, but this is Ed. We worked in northern New York together so many years ago at the paper? I cover politics? We once shared lobsters and beer on assignment in Washington, DC?"

"Ed, of course I remember you," Maxine had said, unable to contain a smile on the other end of the phone.

She thought of his humor. She thought of the chemistry they had shared over dinner. She avoided thinking of the bit of drool that had turned her off so many years ago as Ed had slept on their plane ride home to the bureau. Life had given her new perspective.

"It's so good to hear from you," she said, unaware that the comment had made the kind man on the other end of the line feel weak. "How are you? Where are you these days?"

"Oh, I'm still here, in northern New York, working at our same old paper. I'd ask how you're doing, but I can see from every major daily in America that you're not only living your dream, but becoming, like, one of the best sports photographers of all time. I just called to say congrats. If anyone deserves this success, it's you with all of your hard work. I'm thrilled for you."

Maxine had mustered enough courage to make an uncharacteristic and bold personal move.

"We're only an hour's drive apart," she had said. "Would you like to get together over dinner again sometime and catch up? No pressure, by the way."

"Um, I'll be there in an hour."

Maxine had hoped his comical eagerness meant he was still single.

"And I thought you only called to say congratulations, Ed."

"Seriously, Max, a girl like you with the looks of Halle Berry shouldn't get a guy like mine's hopes up. My palms are starting to sweat over the thought of a date with…another lobster."

"Well, there aren't many lobster joints here in the central part of the state, but would you settle for baby back ribs, BBQ sauce, and bikers?" she had asked.

The former colleagues had gone on to dine at Maxine's favorite Dinosaur BBQ, where their second, more formal date went just as well as their first impromptu one had more than a decade ago. Maxine had accepted and grown to love Ed's little imperfections—his five o-clock shadow, his pudgy waist, and the light snores that escaped his slightly asymmetrical nose in the middle of the night. Ed had immediately opened his bear-like arms to Maxine when she revealed her past to him.

A few years of effortless dating later, in the home of the family she had inadvertently helped piece together, Maxine giddily anticipated the dinner party's final guest.

"So, Max," JP persisted. "You avoided my question. Why isn't this new fiancé of yours chauffeuring you around already, huh?"

"Oh, JP, give the good guy a break, will you?" the professor interjected as she adjusted her oversized glasses. "Maxine, let me see the ring."

"The ring with the bling," the professor of anthropology added.

Maxine outstretched her newly decorated hand to the professors as she turned her beautiful eyes toward JP.

"He's coming straight from work," Maxine explained. "He's sneaking out before deadline just for us."

Ed had landed a job that spring as the political beat reporter for *The Syracuse Herald Journal*. He had celebrated the local offer with Maxine over his moving boxes in her apartment and a shiny engagement ring in hand.

A ring of the doorbell interrupted everyone.

"Please tell me I'm not late to my own engagement dinner," Ed said as he was shown in.

"Without further ado," the anthropology professor declared. "Let us celebrate."

With a heart that was finally full, Maxine looked admiringly at her unconventional family. She thought of the great loneliness that had been in her heart ever since she gave JP away. She knew deep in her bones that it was JP she had been missing all those years. Her mind and body finally felt at rest to have found true love in two unexpected places.

>>>- -<<<

Maxine and Ed's engagement was just one of the celebratory items on the family's agenda as each member found his or her place at the round table.

JP's graduation from Syracuse with a degree in exercise science was only a week away. While a NFL job had not been in the young man's future, Coach Flash had made certain that JP's football career would not end on his watch.

The coach had met his twin at the familiar gathering spot on the Jamesville-DeWitt High bleachers that had seen the brothers through four years of high-school play. Crash still coached there, but not for long. His twin's success at the Orange Bowl had inspired him to dream bigger, and he had accepted a coaching position with the nearby Ithaca College Bombers.

"So who's gonna help me find local high-school diamonds in the rough now for my SC walk-ons? You're leaving me without a secret resource," Flash had joked. "But, seriously, man, congratulations. I think it's great. I want to come out and see your team."

"I guess it's about time I graduated from this fine place," Crash had said. "It's still pretty damn hard to leave."

"Do you have a replacement?"

"Not yet, and I've been thinking about it a lot."

"Well, it just so happens I have an idea."

Flash had unveiled a book of SC stats, reminiscent of the other twin's plea for JP to walk on the collegiate team a few years ago. Crash had immediately gotten the message.

"Is he looking for a job?"

"I believe so," Flash had said as he tried to recall the exact words of his twin before JP joined the Orange and Navy's roster. "He's got the best attitude. He's the hardest worker. He plays each damn game as if it's his last, for some reason."

"For some reason, you don't have to convince me as hard as I needed to convince you," Crash had said. "But thanks for the information just the same. I'll be giving him a call and recommending the school make him an offer. He'll be a great addition to the Physical Ed department too, with that damn drive of his."

>>>- -<<<

Back at the Hemmings' table, JP's mother poured her son a glass of wine.

"I'm still not used to you being of age," she said. "Would you like to give the toast tonight, Coach JP?"

The young man looked at each of the loving faces around the table. He couldn't imagine a more perfect moment. His life's unusual turn of events made him struggle between his beliefs in predestination and free will through hard work, but he accepted either reality. He raised his glass and cleared his throat.

"To dreaming big, being surrounded by people you love, and embracing whatever the future may bring—or whatever we may bring to the future."

>>>- -<<<

More than 250 miles southeast of JP's family celebration, a gifted quarterback sat at his kitchen table in a clean, cool, and modern million-dollar home as he prepared to make a toast of his own.

Three and a half years after his final collegiate game at the Orange Bowl, Devin Madison still played football. He had earned the Heisman for his senior year performance with the University of Boston Orange Bowl Champions and an AFC East team draft pick to be a backup quarterback in the NFL.

Over sushi and sake in his grand mansion, Devin still surrounded himself with an entourage of buddies and one girlfriend or another. He held up a gaudy shot glass and spoke to everyone.

"To a never-ending summer that's light on the training and heavy on the good times."

The young man who had given up nearly every summer that he could remember still longed for a break. His heart wasn't into the game as much as he'd like, and he felt something was missing.

His girlfriend sat on the only piece of furniture that still remained from the old college days. The orange plaid couch still reminded Devin of the small amount of time in his life when Caroline had sat on it by his side. He had been unable to part with the eyesore despite its clash with the rest of his new home.

"Deal 'em up, boys," Devin said. "Who's in for a little Hold 'Em? We'll keep it fun. How about a $2 table? I bet even you could handle that, Rookie."

"I could handle that," replied one of the first-year players on Devin's team. "I can handle it like I did one of your many ex-girls last night."

The guys guffawed along with Devin over the joke that they knew to be the truth. Devin studied his girlfriend of the week. She had red hair, but to Devin's dismay, she had turned out to be nothing like the cheerleader who wouldn't have stuck around for the disrespect. This girl smiled at their laughter. She was clearly content with being part of the prestigious gang.

The only one who knew the secret of Devin's ongoing obsession with Caroline—and the humiliating night at the Gentlemen's Club that had ended it—was a psychologist who the quarterback quietly visited every other Monday to discuss topics ranging from the childhood that had been filled with adult-like expectations to the Monday morning quarterbacks yelling on sports radio during his drive to the appointments. When his guard was really down, he brought up Caroline.

"It must've been very difficult carrying such heavy expectations when all of your school buddies were out playing tag and hide-and-seek," his therapist had said during one of their earlier sessions. "How is your relationship with your family now?"

"Not great," Devin had admitted behind the safety of four walls containing no cameras, fans, teammates, or members of his entourage. "I'm bitter toward them, and they're disappointed in me for not making it to the starting quarterback position. I'm not sure that's even what I want anymore."

"What do you want, Devin?"

"I don't know, because football is the only love I've ever had," he said. "Well, just about the only love I've ever known."

"Have you ever been in love?"

"One time, I think, and I messed it up and let her slip away," he said. "She was perfect and imperfect all at once. She was perfect in that she was the one person who had the potential to put my attitude into place. Over time, she would've turned it around. I could see myself having a family with her, if you can believe that. She was imperfect because she was living a double life at her work, and I had been unaware of it. But she ended that double life when I uncovered it all."

"How did you leave things?"

"Weirdly. We had both lied. We both were at fault. But I can assure you, she had the better character of the two of us."

"Have you ever tried talking with her about how you both left things?"

"She's a few years younger, so whenever I visit the guys left on the team, I go to our usual bars and parties with hopes of running into her. I never have. She was probably at her dorm or apartment, behind a book or something on those nights."

"But have you ever thought about calling her?"

The conversation paused.

"Nah, you think I should? I'm not the type of guy to go running back with my tail between my legs. There are too many buddies of mine who would never let me hear the end of it."

"If it would make you happy to make amends with this girl—and I think I'm hearing from you that it could—then shouldn't your happiness make your friends happy too?"

Devin had avoided the question about his so-called friends.

"She's probably graduating right about now and heading out of Boston," he had said. "My chances of getting in touch with her are probably dunzo at this point."

>>>- -<<<

Back at the poker table, Devin dealt out the first hand of cards. He looked around at the guys, who were thirsty to take his poker money and who knew what else. Then he looked at the red-haired girl who he had hoped could fill the emptiness left three and a half years ago after the abrupt breakup with Caroline.

One of the guys leaned back on the couch to look at the redhead's cards.

"Let's just say if another heart comes up, we should probably fold," the guy reported back to the rest of the table.

"She's almost got the flush, huh?" asked another.

The young lady was unable to keep her poker face and blushed silently.

Age and therapy were slowly making Devin a hair more mature. If his girlfriend of the week didn't have the backbone to stick up for herself, he would stick up for her—even if she wasn't going to last one night longer in the girlfriend role.

"What's the matter with you losers?" Devin said. "Her money is as good as—if not better than—yours. Stop trying to get an easy win, you lowly jerk-offs."

The quarterback felt good about his defense of the girl, even though he knew his choice of words needed work. He accepted the fact that he was still a work in progress and wasn't the gifted golden boy he appeared to be. In Devin's opinion, he was a pretty insecure guy with a far from gifted childhood when it came to being loved.

He was also a guy trying to make sense of it all now in his young adulthood. As he thought of his tough father, who was still living in the family home in Chantilly, Virginia, Devin looked around at the guys doing their best to be cool around the poker table. He realized for the first time that they too were likely to have one hidden reason or another for lashing out.

Caroline was the last of her apartment roommates to remain in Boston before summer break officially began. A graduation gown was the sole garment hanging neatly in her closet. The only items that remained outside of tidily packed boxes were the beautiful peonies she had received that morning from her cheerleading coach and a small makeup bag that would fit in her clutch.

As she waited for her father to find a parking space in a reasonable vicinity of her building, the trill of her cell phone interrupted the stillness.

"Shoot," she said to herself. "I've got to remember to turn this darn thing off before commencement."

She glanced at an unfamiliar incoming number and answered the call anyway. "Hello?"

She listened intently but heard only the deep, bellowing horn of the T blare outside her open window.

"Hello?" she said again.

There was only quiet white noise on the other end. The potential conversation would never come to life as a knock on the door prompted Caroline to hang up first. She looked through the peephole and saw her kind father, who was bearing a modest bouquet of flowers. She quickly hid her coach's designer Winston's vase in the closet before letting him in to share the next phase of her life.

"Dad!"

"Congratulations, Caroline," Kenny said.

He was wearing his best Sunday pants and a navy necktie. It was the same tie he had worn as a younger man during his interview for a temp position at Harper Manufacturing, when Caroline was a little girl. They'd both come a long way, he had thought when he pulled the garment out of the closet this morning. His late wife had picked out the tie for him many years and struggles ago. On this day, though, Kenny was the one who clumsily tied it.

"Look at you, Dad," Caroline said. "You look really nice."

"It's a special occasion," he said. "And thanks, but I think all the looks in our small family of three came from the female side."

Caroline tugged on her locket as both of them silently wished Lindsay were there with them.

"I brought something for the graduate."

"They're beautiful, Dad. I'll dry the flowers and keep them forever."

"Oh those, yes, I almost forgot about those. I brought something else too."

Kenny carefully pulled a wrapped box from his travel bag. The father and daughter weren't experienced in giving gifts or celebrating holidays following Lindsay's death. Their favorite part about Christmas was attending midnight Mass together before walking home in peaceful silence over dark, snow-covered sidewalks.

"What's this?" Caroline asked.

"Please," Kenny said. "It's a very little something, but I think it's special."

Caroline fingered a frame under the paper and was slightly afraid to unwrap it. When she finally did, she found herself looking into the eyes of her mother and a much younger and more innocent version of herself. The trouble-free little girl in the photo was pulling the locket hanging around Lindsay's neck. Neither had been aware of Kenny's presence behind the camera in that happy moment.

"It's one of my favorites," Kenny said. "I found it in one of the old albums the other day. You look so much like her, Caroline. She must be looking down on you today with so much pride."

Caroline's eyes filled with tears. She knew she had made strides that would've made her mother proud, especially after emerging so strongly from a long tunnel of pain. Most recently, Caroline had been accepted into University of Boston's School of Medicine, where she planned to continue her studies in the fall toward becoming a psychiatrist. She hoped to stay in the city of Boston, moving only a few miles down Commonwealth Avenue.

"I love this picture so much," Caroline said. "This is the perfect gift for me on this day. Thanks, Dad. I'm going to hang it up prominently in my new place."

"Should we get going?" he asked awkwardly as he glanced at his watch and tried to keep back his own tears. "I'd hate for you to be late to your own graduation. It took me half an hour just to find a parking spot."

"Let's take the T and walk, Dad. I'm so glad you're here."

Caroline slipped her arm through her father's on their way to the ceremony, just as they used to do on their Sunday morning strolls to St. Matthew's when Caroline was a little girl.

"Do you remember that morning walking to church when you told me your promotion at Harper meant I could take my first dance class?"

"Of course."

"Well, that changed everything, Dad. Without dance, I wouldn't have received the scholarship here. I wouldn't be pursuing my dream to be a psychiatrist next."

Kenny straightened his back and walked a little taller.

"Just promise you won't change a bit when you have Dr. attached to your name," he said.

Caroline squeezed his arm with reassurance.

University of Boston's stadium felt more familiar to her than most of her fellow graduates as she walked behind a banner reading "Class of 2017" onto the field. Excited chatter rang through the facility instead of the usual cheers and chants. As Caroline took her seat on the field she thought of Devin and how he must've run over the exact spot where she was sitting at least a hundred times. She knew he made it to the NFL, but she hadn't watched any of his games, unlike so many of the University of Boston fans. She wondered for a moment how he was doing.

Caroline studied the banner that had predicted her year of graduation at her freshman convocation. Back then, the sign had given her so much doubt in a life so burdened that she was left questioning what the next day would bring, never mind the next four years.

As one impressive speaker after the next gave the graduating class their words of inspiration, her mind drifted and reflected on her transformation at the school.

Caroline watched a senior priest take the stage to proudly say the words of the Jesuit founder, Saint Ignatius of Loyola, just as he had at the class's freshman convocation four years ago.

"Set the world aflame!" he declared.

Caroline immediately recognized the priest—or, rather, his voice. It was the same voice she had heard in the confessional booth during her freshman year when she first learned about the corn husk experiment. He was the one who had helped her move away from her troubled past more than anyone else.

"Set the world aflame!" he repeated.

Caroline fixed her fiery hair under her graduation cap and confidently assured herself she would one day soon do just that.

As Caroline celebrated her new degree in her beautiful black dress and robes, the shy boy named Henry shifted uncomfortably in his first black suit just twenty-eight miles south at McCarthy's Funeral Home in Brockton, Massachusetts.

A lot had changed in the three and a half years since the Orange Bowl, a game that had marked a positive turning point in Henry's childhood. He was a teenager now, and over the course of the last few years he had experienced great happiness, pain, and, on this day, tremendous sorrow.

Henry sat shoulder-to-shoulder with his mother in the front row of seats in the family's designated room. Misty held Henry's hand and stared at the taupe-and-cream-colored wallpaper in an attempt to keep herself together as the casket holding her quirky mother, Henry's grandmother, lay before them.

His grandmother's random coughing fit that had prevented the bullied boy from spilling his classmates' positive reaction to a poem about her on the afternoon she had picked him up from school had become more persistent. When Henry and Misty returned home from the Orange Bowl with a plastic orange-shaped cup souvenir in hand for the elder woman, they were greeted at their apartment door by another violent coughing fit.

"Mom, did you come down with something while we were away?" Misty had asked.

"Oh, ya know, it's the time of year," the elder woman had replied. "Everything is goin' around. I'm constantly touchin' people's filthy money at the gas station. It happens to me every wintah."

In the weeks that had followed, the cough got even worse, and so did the older woman's stubbornness.

"Misty, no, I'm not goin' to the doctah!" she had said one morning over their regular cups of tea. "If I go theyah, I'll come home with somethin' else. You know how I feel about goin' to the doctah's office."

After an especially bad coughing spell later that night after returning home from her restaurant shift, Misty had enough. The family of three had piled into the family car and headed for the emergency room, where a handful of tests led to a doctor's office visit that revealed the elder woman's diagnosis of advanced lung cancer.

She had been a fighter until the end and never lost her outspoken attitude through it all. Insurance claims, chemotherapy treatments, and nurses' wide range of personalities had kept her busy creating more than one observation about life per day. She had battled bravely for more than three years—1,195 days, to be exact.

On the spring day of her burial, Alanis Morissette's "Ironic" played in the elder woman's honor in the funeral home. Even the guests who were unfamiliar with the 1996 alternative rock hit understood the reason for the selection once they listened to the lyrics.

The song that Henry's grandmother would've adored had been selected by the man sitting shoulder-to-shoulder with Misty on her other side. The man who was now Misty's boyfriend put his hand on her kneecap as the song played on. He wished he could protect her from the hurt.

Teach had waited until the last day of Henry's sixth grade to pull the boy aside and ask him an important question.

"Henry, can you hang back for a second?" he had asked as all the other kids ran from the classroom to their summer plans. "I guess I shouldn't take it personally, huh?"

"They're just excited school's out, Teach."

"Thanks, buddy. Hey, I want to ask you a question that I hope isn't out of line. I'm sure the principal will be thrilled with my latest shenanigans, but anyway, it's like way more important that I ask this. I want to get your permission to ask your mom out on a date. If you have any questions for me, I'm prepared, little man."

Henry's face had looked puzzled as he finally pieced together the reason why his mother and Teach always acted so funny whenever they crossed paths. Henry adored Teach. He loved his mother. He quickly made his decision.

"Uh, go for it," the boy had said with growing embarrassment. "Um, I'm going to head out now. My grandmother is waiting in the car."

Teach had felt a weight lift off his shoulders, similar to how a man would feel after asking his future father-in-law for his daughter's hand in marriage. After all, for the first time in his life, a ceremony like that was where Teach felt a relationship of his could be headed. He had reached inside his desk for his earphones and cranked up his music in private celebration.

>>> <<<

A few years later, Teach leaned forward in his funeral home chair to see how Henry was faring. He recalled how nervous the boy had been to read his poem in front of the class. Even though he knew Henry was about to do just that for a bigger audience of family members, gas station regulars, and colleagues from Misty's restaurant, Teach thought the boy looked as calm as he could be. Henry had matured so much under Teach's mentorship.

Henry felt a hand touch his shoulder gently. He turned to see the boy who was still his best friend and gave Oscar, Oscar's mother, and Oscar's mother's boyfriend each an appreciative nod for coming.

Life had turned around for Oscar too, especially following Teach's blind date setup for Oscar's mother and Teach's closest buddy at school, the comical nurse who had helped judge the students' poems. With the weight of the abusive, addict boyfriends out of his mother's life, Oscar slimmed down and led a healthier, happier way of life that was finally free of stress.

As Alanis's song about life's irony drew to a close, Henry pulled a piece of paper from his suit pocket and stepped up to the podium. Neither the distraction of the wallpaper nor Teach's protective hand on Misty's knee could help keep the woman's tears at bay now.

Henry took a deep breath and coughed through the thick, overwhelming smell of the room's daylilies. It didn't rattle him.

"I wrote this little poem in sixth grade, when my teacher asked us to write in couplets about something, anything, that mattered to us. For me, this was an easy topic. I wrote about my grandma."

Henry turned his back to the audience to look at the woman resting behind him and find the confidence to continue. He thought she looked cold and overly made up. She did, however, look pain-free and at peace.

"And please remember I was in sixth grade," Henry said as he turned back to the rows of seats. The comment helped ease the sadness in a room filled with people who were beginning to realize that Henry wasn't necessarily a shy boy after all.

"She greets me each morning with a smile on her face;
Despite her mind already stewing about the human race.
She touches my hand later and asks how was my day;
She knows not to push, for I'll retreat to my room and lay.
She covers me each night with an old blanket made with love;
I'll adore her into forever, when we'll be reunited again above."

ACKNOWLEDGMENTS

There are many people I want to acknowledge in the creation of *The Corn Husk Experiment*.

Dorothy, Melodie, Kelly, Barbara, and Charlotte were such giving mentors.

The management and staff of Fielding Manufacturing in Cranston, Rhode Island, opened their fine company doors to me so I could listen to the sounds and see the sights of their industry.

Thank you to my parents, as well as the

Cales

Binnicks

Asseos

Cunninghams

Mahoneys

Sosnowskis

Dellavias

Krebs

Craves

Stearns

Ashley, Emily, Jenni, MaryEllen, Nicky, Sarah, Sonja, and Sue-Ellen.

And finally, thank you most of all Marc, Harrison, and Graham. You are the inspiration for most everything I do.

ABOUT THE AUTHOR

Andrea Cale is a writer and a New York State Associated Press Award recipient for spot news reporting. Before writing her first novel, Cale also served in the press office of a top ten U.S. commercial bank holding company. She is a graduate of Syracuse University's S.I. Newhouse School of Public Communications and Boston University's College of Communication. Cale lives in central Massachusetts with her husband and sons.

Morgan James
Speakers Group

www.TheMorganJamesSpeakersGroup.com

We connect Morgan James published
authors with live and online events
and audiences who will benefit
from their expertise.

Morgan James makes all of our titles available
through the Library for All Charity Organization.

www.LibraryForAll.org